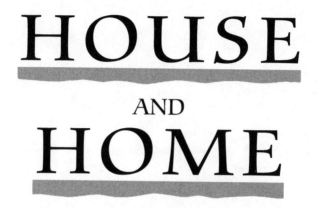

HOUSE

AND

HOME

HOUSE

AND

HOME

Steve Gunderson
and Rob Morris
with Bruce Bawer

A DUTTON BOOK

DUTTON
Published by the Penguin Group
Penguin Books USA Inc., 375 Hudson Street, New York, New York 10014, U.S.A.
Penguin Books Ltd, 27 Wrights Lane, London W8 5TZ, England
Penguin Books Australia Ltd, Ringwood, Victoria, Australia
Penguin Books Canada Ltd, 10 Alcorn Avenue, Toronto, Ontario, Canada M4V 3B2
Penguin Books (N.Z.) Ltd, 182–190 Wairau Road, Auckland 10, New Zealand

Penguin Books Ltd, Registered Offices:
Harmondsworth, Middlesex, England

First published by Dutton, an imprint of Dutton Signet, a division of
Penguin Books USA Inc.
Distributed in Canada by McClelland & Stewart Inc.

First Printing, September, 1996
10 9 8 7 6 5 4 3

Library of Congress Cataloging-in-Publication Data

Gunderson, Steve
     House and home / Steve Gunderson and Rob Morris with Bruce Bawer.
        p.   cm.
     ISBN 0-525-94197-5
     1. Gunderson, Steve.   2. Morris, Rob.   3. Legislators—
United States—Biography.   4. United States. Congress. House—
Biography.   5. Gay politicians—United States—Biography.   6. Gay
rights—United States.   7. Homosexuality—United States.
I. Morris, Rob.   II. Bawer, Bruce.   III. Title.
E840.8.G83A3   1996
328.73'092—dc20   96-19265
                                                              CIP

Printed in the United States of America
Set in Bitstream Carmina Medium
Designed by Stanley S. Drate/Folio Graphics Co. Inc.

*To the family that continues to ground and inspire us: our parents,
Art and Adeline Gunderson and Bob and Billye Morris, our ten
brothers and sisters, their families, and our family of friends.*

*To Tom, Glenn, Charles, and John, whose deaths
opened our eyes and filled our hearts.*

HOUSE

AND
HOME

1

When I went to work on March 24, 1994, I didn't expect that by the end of the day I would be outed on the floor of the House of Representatives and—thanks to C-SPAN—on live national television.

The business before the House that day concerned the reauthorization of the Elementary and Secondary Education Act. We had been debating the bill forever. It was an election year, and a lot of members had cooked up irrelevant amendments to the act as a way of demonstrating to their constituents their loyalty to right-wing positions on various social issues, from sex education to prayer in the schools. One after the other, every one of the amendments was proposed, defended, attacked, argued over, voted on. It was an endless, exhausting process, and as a member of the House Education Committee who'd helped put the bill together and who understood it as well as anyone, I was a key player in that process.

It was late afternoon when an amendment was offered by Congressman Mel Hancock, an old-line conservative from Missouri. Hancock didn't belong to the Education Committee, nor was he particularly knowledgeable about educational issues. But that didn't prevent him from trying to use the amendment to make political hay. Actually, it was the first amendment he had ever offered on the House floor.

Hancock's amendment was short and simple. It would prohibit any school receiving federal funds—which, in effect, meant every public school and almost every private school in the country—from instituting any program "that has either the purpose or effect of encouraging or supporting homosexuality as a positive lifestyle alternative." It would present problems to high school teachers who knew that the lives of some of their students depended on informing them about safe sex. And it would present problems to guidance counselors who, when confronted with troubled kids who were trying to come to grips with their sexual orientation, needed to be able to help them accept themselves.

The amendment didn't come as a surprise. My fellow Republicans were increasingly introducing such proposals to score points with their Religious Right supporters; in fact, the reference to "encouraging or supporting homosexuality as a positive lifestyle alternative" was classic Religious Right rhetoric, reflecting a notion of homosexuality that's completely at odds with reality. Far from being a "lifestyle alternative" that you can "encourage" or "promote," homosexuality is an innate, ineradicable orientation that you can either help a gay teenager to understand and to live with healthily and happily, or that you can condemn, thereby causing a gay teen confusion, torment, and alienation.

Ironically, though Hancock sought to attach his amendment to an education bill, the amendment wouldn't improve education but would exploit many Americans' *lack* of education about homosexuality. Instead of addressing that ignorance constructively, and thus helping to eradicate the fear and prejudice that flow from that ignorance, the amendment would perpetuate ignorance, fear, and prejudice.

In my view, the amendment posed a serious threat. Gay-teen suicide rates were sky-high; so was the teen AIDS-infection rate. Hancock's amendment, by barring responsible

AIDS education and supportive counseling for gay teens, could only make matters worse.

This was completely obvious to many of my fellow members of Congress, Democrat and Republican alike. But there's such a thing as political capital. Members of Congress can vote against their constituents only so often and still remain in office; they can defy their party only so often and still retain power. It's a simple fact of political reality that if you want to keep your seat in Congress, you have to be very careful in choosing the issues on which you're going to expend your political capital—the issues, that is, on which you're going to defy your constituents and your party and stand up for what you believe.

You have to be especially careful about this in an election year. Unfortunately, 1994 was an election year. Because homosexuality was a too-hot-to-handle issue for most members, very few were willing to expend their political capital on combatting the Hancock amendment. I knew that before the debate was over, I would have to weigh in against it.

The debate began with Hancock's defense of his amendment. "Pro-homosexual propaganda," he insisted, was "infiltrating our public schools. . . . Believe it or not, right now in community after community, our children are being exposed to the homosexual lifestyle as early as elementary school. That lifestyle is presented in an approving manner and as a legitimate alternative lifestyle." Schools, he charged, offer "secret counseling" in which "students must explore their sexual feelings."

> They are referred to gay and lesbian community centers to meet and interact with homosexual adults. Film strips, books, and other materials graphically portray homosexual acts. . . . Some even have a buddy system to help match up homosexual couples. . . . In New York City, even elementary schools are exposed to prohomosexual propaganda, including two books entitled *Heather's Two Mommies* [sic] and *Daddy's Roommate*. This is a clear effort to target our young people.

A clear effort? What was clear was that Hancock had been well trained in the Religious Right's elaborately distorted way of talking about homosexuality in general and, more particularly, about the approach that responsible high school teachers and trained school counselors take to issues of sexual orientation.

"Secret counseling," to begin with, was a repulsive term—a way of making a confidential discussion between a troubled student and a trained professional counselor seem somehow insidious. Likewise, Hancock's allegation that students in such counseling sessions "must explore their sexual feelings" was plainly a response to the fact that many school counselors do provide a supportive, nonjudgmental environment in which gay kids are allowed to be honest with themselves and with others about who they are and what they feel—and are thus helped to grow up into adults who are secure and emotionally integrated rather than tormented and self-hating.

Hancock's further comments implied a guileful—and sexual—purpose in everything that teachers and counselors did to help gay kids understand and accept themselves. Educational books about homosexuality were turned by Hancock into pornography designed to stimulate kids sexually; "safe places" for gay high school kids were envisioned by him as veritable brothels; and the matching up of "buddies" for purposes of moral support was characterized by him as a dating service. I knew very well—but how many Christian Coalition members did?—that the books *Heather Has Two Mommies* and *Daddy's Roommate* were not used in classrooms but were often recommended to gay parents so that their small children might be able to read about kids with family situations similar to their own and might thus feel less alone.

Hancock went on to quote from an article in Boston's *Gay Community News*. I wasn't even familiar with that publication at the time, but I've since come to know that it's one of the most radical of the hundreds of local gay publications around the United States. In the article, a gay activist named Michael Swift wrote:

We shall sodomize your sons[,] feeble emblems of your mascu-
linity. We shall seduce them in your schools, in your dormi-
tories, in your gymnasiums, in your locker rooms, in your
sports arenas, in your seminaries, in your youth groups, in
your army bunkhouses, wherever men are with men together.
Your sons shall become our minions and do our bidding. They
will be recast in our image.

It was a ludicrous quotation, one that the average gay
reader would dismiss as the ravings of a disturbed individual.
But Hancock presented it as representative of the views of ordinary, everyday gay people. "While this is just one activist,"
he said, "his mindset is highly instructive. I do not believe our
children should be recast in his image, especially with federal
dollars." Of course the whole purpose of responsible high-
school counseling of gay teens is to help them develop into
self-respecting, well-adjusted adults, *not* into angry, embit-
tered radicals. Make no mistake: homosexuals are born, not
made; but the rage and severe alienation of a Michael Swift is
very much the result of social conditioning—it's the product
of years of living in a society that tells you you're worthless,
despicable, immoral. Far from supporting Hancock's argument against responsible counseling, Michael Swift's article
underscored the desperate need to help young gay people to
like and respect themselves and to consider themselves an in-
tegral part of the society in which they live.

In closing, Hancock urged that before members cast their
votes on his amendment, they examine some pamphlets he
had brought with him and distributed to many of the members. He characterized them as being typical of materials used
in secondary-school AIDS education. Issued by Gay Men's
Health Crisis in New York City, they explained in sexually explicit terms how to avoid infection with the AIDS virus.

In fact, the pamphlets hadn't been intended for students at
all, but had apparently been placed by mistake on a table at a
high school conference in New York—an innocent error that
Hancock was exploiting to the hilt. Hancock apologized for

the "graphic and offensive" nature of the pamphlets, but claimed that it was important for members to examine them because such stuff was "being forced on our children."

Jolene Unsoeld, a Democrat from Washington State, rose to present an amendment. Her amendment, while allowing him to retain the meaningless language about "promotion of homosexuality" that would placate the Religious Right, proposed to add a provision that barred federal intrusion in curricular matters, thereby preventing Hancock's amendment from doing any real harm in the nation's schools.

"Education," Unsoeld said, "has always been a local matter. To change that now because of the gentleman from Missouri's, Mr. Hancock's, obsession or fear over pro-homosexual propaganda is not only misplaced, it would be illegal." She noted that outside the House chamber, material was being distributed coercing members to vote against her revision of Hancock's amendment and threatening that votes for it would be "scored in voters' guides as a vote to promote homosexuality." (One of the ways in which the Christian Coalition has made its power felt in recent years is by distributing "voter guides" in every congressional district; these guides, which purport to list the candidates' positions on a handful of issues, routinely lie or shade the truth about those positions in order to deliver votes to the Coalition's favored candidates.)

Hancock objected that Unsoeld's amendment amounted to a "gutting" of his amendment. "The Unsoeld amendment explicitly affirms the right of schools to use other public resources to bombard our children and grandchildren with pro-homosexual propaganda in the classroom."

A couple of other members rose to make brief comments. Henry Hyde, a highly respected Republican from Illinois, defended Hancock's amendment and perplexingly suggested that it would permit a counselor to help a gay student to accept himself even as it prohibited such a counselor from saying anything that would "encourage homosexuality." William Ford, a Democrat from Michigan who chaired the Education Committee, bluntly criticized Hancock, saying that he didn't "have guts enough to talk straight" about the subject of homosexuality.

Throughout this argument, I sat in my seat and listened quietly. Everybody, I reflected, was talking past one another; nobody was talking *with* one another. My colleagues were conducting a highly emotional debate about homosexuality in American society, and the rhetoric on both sides was familiar, but it wasn't directly relevant to the amendment and its implications, and certainly wasn't relevant to the real-life situations in American schools.

I knew that at some juncture I'd have to get involved—not because I wanted to, but because there were vital points that were not being made. My style in controversial debates is not to speak immediately, but rather to let the talking go on for a while, to allow people to work off their emotions, and then to jump in and bring the discussion around to the real point.

After Ford spoke, I asked for time and was recognized as a member of the Education Committee.

This was, of course, delicate territory for me. Hancock was a fellow Republican. During the debate on gays in the military I'd attacked homophobia and done everything short of coming out on the floor of the House. For me to take on Hancock's amendment now was, to say the least, politically unwise. It was an election year; the Christian Coalition would be ready to paper my district with voter guides telling them that I had supported the "gay agenda."

But there was no question in my mind: I had to take on Hancock.

I wanted to discuss Hancock's amendment with him, so I formally requested a "colloquy," as it's called. This was granted, and I proceeded. Exactly what, I wanted to know, did the amendment mean? "First and foremost," I asked, "what does the gentleman mean by program or activity?"

Hancock replied, "The program or activity is defined as an activity with the purpose or effect of encouraging or supporting homosexuality as a positive lifestyle. That, I think, is pretty explicit."

"Let me give the gentleman some examples," I said. "It is very important that we understand what we are or are not doing here. Will counseling in school between a certified school counselor and a student on that student's struggle for personal identity be considered a program or activity under the gentleman's amendment?"

Hancock said that it would.

After noting a 1989 finding by the Bush Administration's Department of Health and Human Services that gay teens were two times to seven times more likely than heterosexuals to attempt suicide, I asked Hancock, "What happens if a kid is found in a lunchroom or a rest room attempting suicide . . . and they take that to the high school counselor and the counselor says, 'Let's talk,' and the kid says, 'I think I am a homosexual'? Can that counselor respond in a way that encourages that person to accept themselves as a person, to accept themselves as a human being?"

Hancock insisted that counseling would be allowed, but questioned "whether we have very many people in public education who are qualified to counsel on this particular subject."

I then brought up AIDS education. Couldn't his amendment be construed as prohibiting it? Again, Hancock maintained this wasn't the case.

I wasn't convinced. In order to avoid any construction of the amendment that might impede responsible student counseling and AIDS education, I suggested that the words "or has the effect of" be deleted from his amendment. Hancock refused. I said, "I think my colleagues see the problem. . . . If we adopt the Hancock amendment by itself, it has the effect of prohibiting school counseling and guidance; it has the effect of prohibiting AIDS education."

I didn't stop there. "Now I put myself second to none," I continued, "in 'advocating Christian values' around here. . . . But I am going to plead with all my colleagues on this amendment to have the courage of their convictions." As of January of that year, I observed, 63,000 Americans between the ages of 20 to 29 had died of AIDS. "I ask my colleagues simply: How many kids do we have to kill before we have the courage to stand up and say it's time to educate them and to do what is right, not what is politically popular at that moment?"

The chairman of the Education Committee, Bill Ford, rose to thank me for my words. He added that Hancock's amendment was a product of sheer ignorance about education legislation. It didn't rise, he said, "to the intellectual level of scatological jokes exchanged by naughty little boys in the boys' room in a grade school."

It's fair to say that, at that point, we were clearly winning the debate on its merits. But then Bob Dornan, the leader of antigay forces in the House, came to the floor.

Dornan, who represents a district in southern California, is one of the most extreme far-right members of Congress. He's also unquestionably the most emotional. A former air force pilot, journalist, and TV talk-show host who often sits in as a replacement for Rush Limbaugh, Dornan doesn't hesitate to go for the jugular and to make personal attacks. In his 1980 reelection campaign, he called his opponent a "slick, pompous ass"; he referred to his 1984 adversary as a "sneaky little dirtbag." In 1985, he stood up on the floor of the House and called New York Congressman Tom Downey a "draft-dodging wimp," then grabbed Downey by the tie and threatened him with bodily harm; in 1991, he was kicked off a United Airlines flight for refusing to follow a flight attendant's instructions regarding seat backs and tray tables while taxiing prior to takeoff. Some people have described Dornan as crazy; his opponent in the 1994 election said he was "nearly a lunatic."

Now, apparently, it was my turn to feel Dornan's wrath. He began his remarks by mentioning that he'd been born in Manhattan and raised in Beverly Hills, two communities with "a particular penchant for poisoning little Dorothys in Kansas or Iowa or other parts of this country." Jerry Nadler, who represents a New York district, rose to protest Dornan's comment about Manhattan.

But Dornan wasn't through. Now he turned to me. He said,

''The gentleman from Wisconsin didn't tell you when he was debating this amendment that he has a revolving door on his closet. He's in, he's out, he's in. I guess you're out, because you went up and spoke to a huge homosexual dinner, Mr. Gunderson.''

At that, the House erupted in pandemonium.

Now, it's important to know here that the House of Representatives prides itself on being the greatest deliberative body in the world, and that it's been able to maintain that tradition throughout American history because of the strict formality of its procedures. You never refer to members on the House floor by their first names; you never question another member's motives; and you never make personal attacks. Watch the British House of Commons on C-SPAN, and then watch the House of Representatives, and you'll see the difference.

There are rigorous rules about decorum and respect. There's also a standard procedure whereby if a member brings disrepute in any way on the House and its proceedings, or impugns the actions or motives of any individual member, his words can be ''taken down.'' If he doesn't recant those words, he can be prohibited from speaking in the House for the remainder of the day. It's a very serious matter.

Dornan's attack on me went way over the established line. Of course I was incensed at him for descending to such a low level. But as I listened to him rant, I realized that it was vitally important for me to keep my cool, to rise above the situation. The last thing we needed on the House floor was an emotional gay congressman proving himself unable to take the heat! So as Dornan ranted on, I just sat there and shook my head in silent indignation.

I may have been the only one who did keep my cool, for everyone around me was furious at Dornan for resorting to such rhetoric. Most members disapprove in principle of the employment of personal attacks in House debate, and certainly they weren't happy to see such an attack launched against a member who is well liked and respected on both sides of the aisle, as I think it's fair to say I am. A number of my colleagues on the Education Committee, led by the chairman, Bill Ford, moved that Dornan's remarks be taken down. When you make such a request, proceedings stop immediately.

People connected to the Republican leadership took Dornan aside and tried to persuade him to retract his words. Now, Dornan is known as an emotional debater, and when he's in the midst of debate it's not easy for him to keep cool or to reflect responsibly on what he's saying. It took a while, but eventually he agreed to retract his words. He didn't apologize to me, but because he asked for unanimous consent that his words be stricken from the record, there was no longer a procedural justification for silencing him.

Unfortunately, after he asked for unanimous consent to strike the record, Dornan immediately left the House floor and went into the "speaker's lobby." This is a formal room just off the House floor—a wide hallway actually, with neoclassical embellishments, a tiled floor, and large portraits of former speakers. The only people who have access to it are members of Congress and the press corps. So Dornan went out into this room full of reporters and essentially reiterated what he had said on the House floor.

His rhetoric there was even more inflammatory. "We've got a homo in our midst in the Republican party," he told a reporter from one of my state's most influential newspapers, the Milwaukee *Sentinel*. "And they're destroying the country, to say nothing about the party, and we have a moral obligation to expose them and destroy them." Later, in a phone interview with the Eau Claire *Leader-Telegram*, one of the two largest newspapers published in my district, Dornan said that he'd "about had a stomach full" from listening to me "lecturing our party." How, Dornan demanded, could I call myself a Christian when all Christians denounce homosexuality? "Our moral standards in the Republican party are eroding, thanks to the shenanigans of Congressman Gunderson," Dornan said, and went on to describe me as "cocky, arrogant, and in our face about these cultural meltdown issues." I couldn't help reflecting that it was pretty weird to be called "cocky, arrogant, and in our face" by Bob Dornan, of all people!

While Dornan was ventilating in this fashion in the speaker's lobby, I was also involved elsewhere. Across Independence Avenue, the National Cattlemen's Association was holding a banquet in the Ways and Means Committee room of the Longworth Office Building. The banquet was a sort of tribute to two of our retiring colleagues, Congressman Bob Smith and Senator Malcolm Wallop, both of whom were big supporters of the cattlemen. As the ranking Republican on the Livestock and Dairy Subcommittee, I had been involved in arranging the dinner. In fact my lover, Rob, and I had agreed to help provide the entertainment. As it happens, one of our dearest friends is Phyllis Pastori, a terrific cabaret singer in New York. To our delight, Phyllis had agreed to perform at the dinner.

So while this heated debate about the Hancock amendment was taking place on the floor of the House, I was rushing back and forth between the two places, trying to keep up with the floor debate and still handle my duties at the dinner. It was a mad rush; though Rob was there, I didn't even find time during the evening to take him aside and tell him what Dornan had done.

Some gratifying things happened that night. Time and again, as I hurried from the Capitol to the banquet and back again, people whom I didn't even know would come up to me with tears in their eyes, giving me hugs and thanking me for my courage. Something else happened that I didn't learn about till later. While I was over at the banquet, introducing Phyllis and listening to her sing, Bill Goodling, the ranking Republican on the Education Committee, made his closing remarks, in which he alluded to Dornan's attack on me.

"There's not a member of Congress," Goodling said, "who cares more and works harder on educational issues than the gentleman from Wisconsin, and I hope we will never again see the kind of incident that we saw here today." I then received a standing ovation from my colleagues—and I wasn't even there to enjoy it! Which is probably good, because then I probably *would* have broken down.

In fact I had ample reason to break down, Congressional matters aside. The day before, my brother Kirk had called me from back home in Wisconsin to tell me that my father had suffered a heart attack. Fortunately Dad had survived it and was in the critical care unit of Luther Hospital in Eau Claire. Naturally the Dornan episode was picked up by the news media back home, where it received a good deal of attention. That night, my sister Kris happened to go into my father's hospital room when the story came on the local television news show. She held his hand as they watched together in silence. When it was over, my father turned to her and said, "Just because people are different doesn't mean they're bad."

You have to know what my folks are like in order to appreciate the significance of that remark. They're quiet, undemonstrative Norwegian-Americans who love me and Rob and accept him as a part of the family, but who don't really say "I love you" or talk about anything personal. So when my father does say something like this, it carries real emotional conviction, meaning, and power. What he said to Kris was the Gunderson equivalent of "I love my gay son."

ROB

It was a busy evening. When I first got to the dinner I saw Steve across a crowded room, talking to a bunch of people. I waved to him, smiled, and started chatting with friends of ours that I hadn't seen in a while. For the longest time he and I didn't even get a chance to speak to each other. Toward the end of the cocktail hour we finally spoke, and he mentioned, in his understated Norwegian way, that there had been an "altercation" on the House floor that day. He said it in such a casual way that I thought, "Big deal. Some Democrat got pissed at some Republican. This happens every day."

I didn't begin to find out the truth until later, at dinner, when Phyllis heard about it from somebody and came over to ask Steve what had happened. I was seated next to him, and as he filled her in, I listened. I was astounded that he hadn't pulled me aside to tell me about it the moment I'd gotten there.

But that's the way Steve is. He keeps this sort of stuff locked up inside and waits till the "appropriate time" to tell me about it. In fact, he waits till the "appropriate time" to come to terms with his own reaction, his own feelings. Steve's immediate response to any kind of altercation is to do "'damage control" on an interpersonal level. He never thinks about the extent to which he himself has been emotionally or psychologically hurt.

Later that night, in the calm of our bedroom, Steve told me every detail of the Dornan incident as I pulled the covers up on our four-poster bed. Meanwhile Steve was setting the alarm for 6:30 A.M. Listening to him, I felt a rush of protectiveness—and anger.

"Steve," I said, "what exactly can be done to let Dornan know this attack is not acceptable?"

He was quiet as he slipped into bed and pulled the covers up to his chest.

I went on. "I really do not think this is the time to sit back and let time heal. Dornan's attack wasn't just an attack on you. It was an attack on all gay people."

He rolled over on his side and thought a while longer. Finally he spoke. "The leadership," he said, "can do certain things officially. And Rob, they did not let his attack stand. His remarks were stricken."

I looked at him and rolled my eyes. "Steve," I said, "what difference does that make? Who is going to go back into the *Congressional Record* to read something that isn't there? It'll be in the paper tomorrow. It's public knowledge—and there should be a public apology. Aren't you pissed?"

As it turned out, several people in the leadership did reprimand Dornan publicly. Newt Gingrich, then the minority whip, and Bob Michel, the majority leader, even took the unusual step of writing Steve a letter, which they made public, declaring their respect for his leadership, professionalism, and courage, and explicitly stating that "intemperate, personal remarks have no place in the legislative process nor the Republican Party." Henry Hyde and Dick Armey wrote letters that were generally supportive of Steve, though they made no reference, explicit or otherwise, to the Dornan incident.

But Haley Barbour, who was the Republican party chairman, refused to do or say anything about Dornan's remarks. A lot of others took the same route. It all reflects that division within the party about what it's going to be when it grows up.

Steve's composure after Dornan's attack, and his unwillingness to press for a public apology, exasperated me. I wanted him to burst into Newt's office hollering with righteous indignation, demanding that Dornan be called on the carpet. But that's not Steve's style. He's a conciliator. Yes, he's an activist, but he's not the kind of activist that some gay people—and some Republicans—want him to be. He doesn't yell, he doesn't erupt in fury. He feels that if he did, he'd lose his power to effect any change at all. He takes an approach that he sincerely thinks will do the most good in the long run. He may be right. Or he may be wrong. Sometimes I'm the first one in line to criticize him for being so prudent and conciliatory.

Certainly prudence and conciliation don't seem to me the proper response to public figures like Hancock and Dornan, who don't hesitate to exploit, for their own cynical purposes, the average American's ignorance about and discomfort with gay people. Because most people don't know very much about homosexuals, they believe all too readily that we represent a threat to "family values," that we're godless, unpatriotic, and irresponsible, and that we're dangerous role models for young people.

That night, as Steve told me about the Hancock amendment, about the debate over it, and about what Bob Dornan had said, I thought back on our life together. It was ironic: by telling lies about guys like me and Steve, guys like Hancock and Dornan have become, in the eyes of millions of Americans, defenders of God, country, and family. Yet I knew that if only those millions of Americans really *knew* me and Steve—if they knew what our life together has been like, what challenges we've faced, and what values have guided us—they would find their ideas about gay people seriously challenged.

It was March of an election year. Steve was already in hot water with his party for his criticism of the antigay rhetoric at its 1992 convention and for his stand on gays in the military; Religious Right leaders back in Wisconsin, angered by his increasingly outspoken support for AIDS funding and for gay rights, had already made clear their determination to defeat him in the November election. Politically, the most foolish thing for Steve to do at this point was to be more open about his homosexuality. But the Dornan incident crystallized for both of us the need to be more open. In the days and weeks that followed that sorry episode, Steve and I talked about it a great deal, and our talks kept coming back to the same point: If Middle America was ever to see through the cynical rhetoric of the Mel Hancocks and Bob Dornans and recognize people like Steve and me as friends, not enemies, they needed to know who we *really* were. They needed to see the myths exploded. They needed to hear our stories.

The Dornan incident, in short, made Steve and me realize that, if we wanted to help heal the rift between gay and straight America that people like Hancock and Dornan had exploited for far too long, the most useful thing we could do was to put aside our intense desire for privacy and tell our story.

2

One thing that particularly angered me about Bob Dornan's attack on me was his implication that there's an essential contradiction between being homosexual and having something known as "family values." This is a key doctrine of the Religious Right—and it's an absolute lie.

I have lived my entire life according to the values on which my parents raised me in rural western Wisconsin. I was brought up in a very close, loving family with a strong Christian faith, patriotism, and work ethic.

The world of my childhood was one of gently rolling green hills and county fairs and dairy farms. It is often said that our part of the state had more cows than people. I grew up in the same congressional district that I've represented for sixteen years, and in the same house that my parents still live in, an old ochre and brown bungalow with an enclosed front porch and additions to the sides and rear. Our family's heritage is Norwegian, and our religion is Lutheran. Census statistics show that of all 435 congressional districts in the United States, mine has the lowest percentage of racial minorities. The largest ethnic group is German-American, and the largest religious group is Catholic, but Norwegian Lutherans, for

17

whatever reason, have put the strongest stamp on the region's character. I'm 100 percent ethnic Norwegian, and very proud of it.

I lived in a tiny unincorporated farm town called Pleasantville with a population of thirty-seven, counting the cats and dogs, and attended a two-room country school where there were from three to six children in each class. Everybody in Pleasantville, which is on the outskirts of the incorporated town of Osseo in Trempealeau County, knew everybody else. We all kept our doors unlocked and we all looked after one another. To a lot of big-city people nowadays, that world would doubtless seem pretty corny and unreal, like something out of a Norman Rockwell illustration. But for me it was very real indeed—and very precious.

My mother has always been our Rock of Gibraltar—the foundation of the family, the great performer in times of crisis. For years, and until very recently, she ran a general store that was the social center of the town. Men and women from the neighboring farms came in every day to have coffee and chat.

My father was less of a social animal. I'm much closer to him today than I used to be. When I was a boy, he was always consumed by his Chevrolet dealership—and he didn't have much time for family or personal matters.

But he and my mother did instill three things in me, as well as in my three sisters and four brothers. One was the survivor mentality. You can't grow up in a middle-class rural Wisconsin family with eight kids without developing that.

Second was a deep commitment to community and public service. I learned the meaning of service at a very young age. My parents were always involved in church projects, as well as in the Lions Club, the 4-H Club, and the school board. Their example inspired me. So it's no surprise that when some of my teachers' reports and my SAT scores suggested that I didn't have the most glorious future ahead of me, I naturally turned to the realm of public service to prove that I was more capable than some people might think.

The third, and most important, of the things my parents instilled in us was a deep religious faith. All my brothers and sisters are very strong in their beliefs. Unlike many of those in the evangelical movement, I haven't been born again—I've been a Christian ever since I was a child. I still belong to the church I grew up in, Grace Lutheran, a small country church with about eighty-five members. (Since I spend most of my time in Washington, I've also been an "associate member," for many years, of Redeemer Lutheran Church in McLean, Virginia.) When I was a boy it was unthinkable not to go to Sunday school and church. My dad always said, "You can go out Saturday night, and I don't care what time you come home, but you're going to church on Sunday morning!"

In the Lutheran church, confirmation is an important milestone, and in the Gunderson family it was impressed upon us children that we were expected, by the time of our confirmation, to have given serious thought to the question of what we believed. We all took this very seriously, with the result that by the time I was confirmed at age thirteen I had thought a lot about my faith and its place in my life. I know that I almost certainly would have become a pastor if I hadn't suspected from an early age, on a barely conscious level, that I was destined to spend many years struggling with my sexual identity, and that seeking ordination would only complicate that struggle. In retrospect I'm convinced that God's call to me was to do what I've been doing, not to serve in the church. But the church remains extremely important to me.

We had a series of pastors when I was growing up. For better or for worse, a small church tends to get its pastor fresh out of seminary; he or she stays on for a couple of years, gets the hang of the job, and then moves on to someplace bigger, only to be replaced by yet another recent graduate. I've been closer to some of the pastors at Grace Lutheran than I have to others, and was probably closer to them during my teenage years than at any other time. In high school, when my brother Scott and I worked as the church janitors, I was in that building all the time.

There used to be a lot of Gundersons in Grace Church, but now only my parents, my brother Matt, and I remain. That sort of change has taken place in a lot of those small-town country churches—the young people have grown up and moved away, leaving the churches less active and vibrant than they used to be. It's a shame. A unique thing about many Midwestern churches is that they were started generations ago by Scandinavian immigrant families or groups of families, some of which built their own churches even if someone else had already built one nearby. As a result, in the Pleasantville area, there are three small Lutheran churches within two miles of one another, attended by descendants of the settlers who founded them.

If the members of these three churches ever came together and formed one church, it would be a large, dynamic place. But that's not going to happen, unless through some freak accident all three churches are destroyed simultaneously by fire, tornado, or flood! You could get Newt Gingrich to join the Democratic party before you could get the members of any two of those Lutheran churches in the Pleasantville area to give up their identity and join the third. It's an understandable aspect of human nature, of course, but it's also something of a shame.

I was a very shy boy. I remember how terrified I was to go seven miles away to attend junior high school in a bigger town—Whitehall, Wisconsin—because I figured the "city kids" would pick on us "country kids." Sure enough, they did; but more often they just ignored us. When it came time to choose partners for science projects or other activities, the rural boys and girls were always the last chosen. We usually ended up pairing off with each other. It's no coincidence that my first two friends in junior high school were Mark Huff and Gary Tomter from Pigeon Falls, one of the other outlying rural school districts. By shunning us, the city kids forced us rural kids to seek each other out as friends.

When the time came to leave high school for college, I was scared of that, too. What made college seem especially daunting was the fact that those were the Vietnam War years, when campuses were being disrupted by antiwar protests. My parents would not let me attend any of the universities near home because they knew I would be running home all the time, and they wanted me to develop some independence. The closest place they would allow me to go was the University of Wisconsin in Madison, which was about one hundred and fifty miles from Pleasantville. So that's where I went.

I vividly remember the day I left home. Since my dad was a Chevy dealer, he was able to provide me with an old used car to take to school. I drove to Madison and was convinced that I would never find the dorm I was supposed to go to. Sure enough, I couldn't find it. I got lost.

Rob's experience was dramatically different from mine. While I spent my entire childhood in the same small community, Rob's father was highly motivated professionally and moved the family around a lot. By the time Rob was ten, he had lived in nine different houses. At about that time, his father cofounded an initially small business that soon became extremely successful on an international scale. The family moved to Columbus, Georgia, where Rob's father bought one of the grandest houses in town, a rambling 1920s Tudor. Even as putting down roots in Columbus fostered Rob's keen sense of the importance of community, living in that house nurtured a love of architecture that eventually led to his decision to major in that subject when he went to Auburn University in 1979.

The transition between high school and college was traumatic for me. I was an introverted, bashful small-town kid, and I didn't like the idea of leaving home and living around strangers. It was then that I realized the only constant in my whole life would be God. Everything else would change—my home, my friends, my career—but God would always be there, and would be my best and most constant friend. I figured I'd better get to know him when times were good, so that the rapport would be there when the times weren't so good. So college brought me even closer to God than I had been. In later years, when I was struggling with the challenges of my political career and with my sexual orientation, that closeness to God would make all the difference.

In retrospect, leaving Pleasantville was a very positive experience for me. In fact, probably the most important factor in my becoming a politician was my parents' insistence that I go away to college. Being at the university forced me to overcome my painful shyness and turned me into somebody who knew how to make friends and talk to strangers. Certainly, as the only freshman from my high school at a university of 38,000 students, I had to make friends with strangers in order to have any friends at all. In doing this, I worked up the courage to be much more extroverted than I had ever thought I was capable of being. I finally joined a fraternity, Beta Theta Pi, through which I met some of the politically active young people on campus and became interested in politics. Eventually I declared political science as my major. Meanwhile I was working part-time at Sears.

I was also working hard to avoid accepting my sexual orientation. I had been aware for some time that I was different from most other boys, and this difference posed a great problem for me. I spent most of college and several years thereafter tormented by it. Largely because I had been taught that an attraction to other men was at odds with my Christian faith, I wanted my feelings to be a temporary phase and not a permanent reality. In an attempt to deny those feelings, I dated a series of wonderful women, whom I know I put through some perplexing and emotionally difficult situations.

I think it's pretty common for gay men raised in Christian families in the Midwest to spend years avoiding the whole issue of being gay—and, indeed, to convince themselves that they *aren't* gay. It's easy to fool yourself and say, ''Well, I'm not having sex with women because of my moral principles; I'll do it when I fall in love and get married.'' If you happen to have one or two experiences with men, you can explain them to yourself as aberrant encounters that had no lasting significance and that took place because you'd had too much to drink. You tell yourself that these things happen because the heart of man is weak and sinful, and you apologize to God for them and go on with your life.

For my part, I managed to convince myself that I wasn't really gay. I told myself that the tension within me between a powerful attraction to men and a huge psychological resistance to it was typical of tensions within everybody. I told myself that if you weren't having sex with women, your hormones would tell you to have sex with someone, even a man, just for the sake of having sex. I didn't want to accept my homosexual impulses as amounting to anything more than that. Only over time did I begin to acknowledge what was staring me directly in the face. Only over time did it become clear to me that while I cared very much for many of the women I dated, I could never provide them with the kind of emotional and physical bond that a marriage ought to provide. I think that fear—the fear of marrying a woman and failing her emotionally and physically—haunted me even more than the fear of moving into what might be called "the gay arena."

And I did fear moving into that arena. I dreaded it. Even as I gradually came to acknowledge to myself that I was homosexual, I continued to find the gay arena socially unacceptable and professionally threatening. I also felt certain that it was spiritually destructive. And there's no question but that it involved some physical risk: even before AIDS, there was always the terrifying possibility of getting beaten up and robbed because you were gay, either by a marauding pack of teenage boys or by someone you had foolishly decided to smile at on the street or take home from a bar.

Through Beta Theta Pi I met a girl, Sue Shannon, whom I dated for a while. Her father was treasurer of the state Republican party, and they both encouraged my political ambitions. But after briefly entertaining thoughts of a political career, I decided instead that I would become a sports broadcaster. The reason was simple: I had always loved sports, but I wasn't a good enough athlete to be a successful participant. I didn't have the height or shooting skills for basketball, or the strength for wrestling. I had played football, thank God, at a small high school. When I told my University of Wisconsin fraternity brothers who were football players that I had been a nose guard on defense and a left tackle on offense, they looked at me—five-foot-eight and a hundred and thirty-five pounds—and laughed. But that's the beauty of going to a small school.

One sport that I hadn't been exposed to as a boy was hockey. For whatever reason, I didn't see a hockey game till I was at the university, and then I just fell in love with it. If I had grown up playing hockey, I think I would have developed into a decent college player, and I might even have taken a shot at a professional career. Of course, it was too late for that. But if I couldn't play hockey, I figured I could become a hockey broadcaster. So after graduating from the university, I enrolled in broadcasting school in Saint Paul, Minnesota. Fortunately, my sister, Kris, who lived in Saint Paul with her then husband, had an extra bedroom that they were willing to let me use.

It wasn't long, however, before politics entered my life again, thanks to Sue and her father. While I was in Saint Paul, I traveled to Madison on several occasions and joined them at a number of Badgers football games. One day, at one of those games, they urged me to run for the state legislature. I went home, and thought it over, and decided to go for it.

There were good reasons, it seemed to me, to run. First the personal ones. Even if I lost, I figured the campaign would give me an opportunity to practice my public speaking and make me a better sports broadcaster; the worst that could happen, I imagined, was that I'd make the incumbent, Eugene Oberle, pay more attention to the people back home.

Also I considered it important to make a serious run as a Republican. Over the years, many friends and acquaintances, especially gay ones, have asked me why I became a Republican and why I remain one. Well, like many Norwegian-Americans who grew up in the Midwest, I was raised with a strong belief in personal freedom and in personal thrift. My family had always been small-business Republicans in the moderate Midwestern tradition of Gerald Ford and George Romney, and as I developed a political awareness I came to realize how different my home town of Pleasantville was from Washington, D.C., where many decisions were made that strongly affected our everyday lives. Over and over, I saw that despite the best of intentions, what might sound like a good idea in the nation's capital doesn't necessarily work in rural Wisconsin. All this made it natural for me to run for elective office as a member of the party of Lincoln, for to me it is, above all else, the party of individual rights, of fiscal restraint, and of local control. Besides, in the wake of Watergate (this was 1974) I felt that the two-party system was at risk, and I thought I could make a small but positive contribution toward preserving that system.

To be sure, as the power of the Religious Right has increased in recent years, the GOP has increasingly been seen as the party of bigotry and exclusion. But that's not what it is to me. And the more vigorously others may try to turn the Republican party into that kind of institution, the more determined I'll be to stay within it and rescue it from them.

When I decided to run, I didn't tell anybody right away; I figured I'd turn in and do so in the morning. I went upstairs to my room in Kris's house and picked up my copy of that week's *Sports Illustrated*. It contained an article about Alvin Dark, who had just been hired by Charlie Finley as the new manager of the Oakland A's. The writer of the article described Dark's job as the most insecure position in professional baseball. He asked Dark how he could comfortably accept such an assignment. Dark responded that he operated by a verse in the Bible, Joshua 1:9: ''Be strong and of good courage, fear not nor be afraid: for the Lord thy God will not fail thee nor forsake thee.''

I thought it was ironic that, just moments after I had made the decision to go into politics, this comforting Biblical verse had popped up in, of all places, *Sports Illustrated*. (As it turned out, there was an additional irony in the fact that Dark, in 1979, would join Anita Bryant's group "Save Our Children" in opposing a Miami gay-rights ordinance, and, along with Bryant, would testify against it at committee hearings.) Later that summer, in the midst of the campaign, I told some family members about the verse from Joshua, and on election night my sister Naomi gave me a banner with those words on it. I still have that banner.

That verse from Joshua has continued to mean a great deal to me. Until pretty recently, I've referred to it sparingly in public speeches—although I did quote it at the Third District Republican convention in 1994, a week after the Dornan episode, to explain what drove me and sustained me amid such ugliness.

Anyway, here I was, a political candidate for the very first time. President Nixon had just resigned, the Republican party was in disgrace, the government was teetering on the brink of chaos, and here I was, a pale, skinny, baby-faced twenty-three-year-old who looked all of seventeen, running as a Republican against a middle-aged Democratic incumbent. There was no reason on earth why I should have won. But we put together the first of what would be many remarkable campaigns by the Gunderson clan. Everybody pitched in. And I won. And that was the beginning of a political career that I never intended to carry on with for so long.

My first officemate in the state legislature was a man named LaVerne Ausman. Like my people back in Pleasantville, LaVerne and his wife, Bev, were down-home folks. Bev, a plump woman who loved needlepoint, always seemed to be on her way to a meeting at church or to take a meal to some sick person. Years earlier, they had raised two kids on their Wisconsin dairy farm; as the kids had grown older, and as they had gradually turned the farm over to their son, John, LaVerne had turned to politics. His attitude toward his second career was reflected in the name of a book he gave me soon after we took our seats in the legislature. It was entitled *Politics as a Way of Helping People*. LaVerne and I hit it off largely because both of us saw government service as, above all, a way of doing good, of living out our Christian duty to love and serve our neighbors. It's funny how the relationship between religion and politics has changed in the past twenty years. For many politicians, religion used to be an impetus to do the right thing for other people, whatever their religion might be; now many politicians seek to use government as a vehicle for imposing their own religious views on everybody else.

Both LaVerne and Bev soon became good friends of mine—though back then I couldn't have begun to imagine how loving and loyal they would prove themselves to be in later years.

The 1978 election of our friend Lee Dreyfus as governor of Wisconsin brought career changes for both LaVerne and me. Dreyfus nominated LaVerne to the state's Industry, Labor, and Human Relations Board. But Dreyfus's victory put me in a difficult position—the sort of no-win situation that politicians with good friends in both the statehouse and the executive branch sometimes find themselves in. On the one hand, I couldn't stay in the legislature with Dreyfus as governor, since the people in his office, imagining that I could get my colleagues to do whatever I wanted, assumed that, as Dreyfus's friend, I would be far more useful to them in the legislature than I knew I could ever be. On the other hand, I couldn't leave the legislature to join Dreyfus's administration, because many members of the legislature would then think I could get Dreyfus to do whatever *they* wanted. It was not a comfortable position to be in.

So I left the legislature in 1989 and went to Washington to serve as the legislative director for Congressman Toby Roth. I found that position very eye-opening. From the beginning, I was overwhelmed by how much more complex the system was than the Wisconsin state legislature, and how much larger the issues were. Yet at the same time, sitting in my office day after day watching Congress on C-SPAN, I came to realize that the House of Representatives was not the intellectual bastion that I had imagined. *Heck*, I thought, *I can hold my own with these guys!* Meanwhile LaVerne and I and our friend Don Haldeman, then president of the Wisconsin Farm Bureau, were amiably trying to persuade one another to run for Congress. They kept saying no, so I finally said yes— provided they would agree to serve as my campaign co-chairs. They did.

It was easy, in 1980, to be motivated to run for Congress on the issues: double-digit inflation, double-digit interest rates, the energy crisis, and of course the Iran hostage issue. Our district had a very nice, very liberal, and very antidefense Congressman, Al Baldus. Certainly he should be challenged— the question was, should I be the one to do it?

The biggest personal reason I ran was simple. I said to myself, "Most people would give their eye teeth to be in this position. People want me to run. The worst that's going to happen is that I'm going to lose. So why shouldn't I run? If I don't run I'll spend my whole life looking back on it, wondering why I didn't do it when I had the chance." So I ran, and again we put together a terrific campaign. Our theme was "A New Direction for the 1980s," and as I went from town to town, I ended my speeches with the line: "With your help, we can make a difference. With God's help, I can make a difference. Together we can make all the difference in the world."

My aunt Shari, who was married to my father's brother Ray and who had three children, Kara, Trina, and my godson, Leif, worked full-time on the campaign. She came up with a great idea—she organized a group of high school students, including my younger brothers Matt and Kirk, into a swing choir called "Steve's Kids" that entertained at campaign stops. They were quite popular, and by the end of the year had actually gotten to be very good. Shari's work made a huge difference in the election effort, and nobody was more excited than she was when, after winning a tough four-way primary, we pulled off a major upset in November.

That victory felt wonderful. Our whole family had taken part in the campaign, and we all shared in the joy of election night. We felt as if we were sitting on top of the world. Then, on the Saturday two weeks after the election, the phone rang at my grandmother's house in Osseo, where I was staying at the time. At the moment it rang, I was raking leaves in the yard; my grandmother, my sister Naomi, and my friend and campaign manager Jim Harff (who would be my first chief of staff) were in the kitchen.

The phone call was from my father, and he wanted to speak to me. "Steve," he said in a low, solemn voice, "something's happened. Your mother and I are coming up to Osseo. Don't let anyone leave."

That was all he would say.

After hanging up, I told the others what Dad had said. Obviously something was terribly wrong. But what? Had Ray been hurt in a farm accident? We didn't have to speculate for long. A few minutes later, the phone rang again. I picked it up. It was Dad. "Steve," he said, "there's no use hiding this. Shari and Trina were just killed in a car accident outside of Osseo and Leif is hurt real bad."

I hung up the phone and took my grandmother and Naomi and Jim into the living room, where I sat them down and told them what had happened. My grandmother just sat there and cried. "Why couldn't it have been me?" she asked. "I've had a long, good life."

Meanwhile my parents had gone out to a farm where Ray was picking corn so that they could tell him what had happened. They brought him back to Osseo, and I went with him into his house so he could change clothes before visiting Leif in the hospital. Then my mother and I drove to the local hotel, the Alan House, where Shari's mother, Ethel, ran a small beauty salon. Shari was her only child, and she had moved to Osseo simply to be close to her. I remember how happy she was to see us when we got to the beauty salon. Then I sat her down and told her she had lost her only daughter and one of her grandchildren.

The deaths of Shari and Trina were tragic, of course, and also especially strange, since they happened after we had all been through a campaign together and had experienced the unbelievable high of winning an election. I can still remember the exuberance I felt during those two weeks at the prospect of becoming a congressman. But the victory that had seemed so momentous collapsed into perspective with Shari's and Trina's deaths. That tragedy taught me an unforgettable lesson about the unimportance of worldly position.

The next few hours were pure hell. Shari and Ray's only surviving daughter, Kara, was taking part in a musical competition in Iowa. We got word to the teacher chaperone that something was very wrong and asked her to bring Kara home. Then there were the preparations for the funeral, which took place on Tuesday. Governor Dreyfus came, because he had gotten to know Shari during his campaign in 1978. At the service Ray asked me to walk up with his and Shari's mothers—my grandmother on one side and Ethel on the other. I barely made it through the ceremony. I almost collapsed. When we left the church with the two coffins, we saw that Trina's classmates had formed lines on each side of the pathway. I can't describe how painful it was.

Some weeks after Shari's and Trina's deaths, I ran into a pastor from out of town who told me he had been scheduled to give the guest sermon that Sunday at the Congregational church in Osseo. He said, "You know, I drove into Osseo that morning and I knew something was very wrong. There was a pall over that community. You could just feel it."

That experience changed me permanently. I think it's largely because of it that I've never been consumed by a lust for political power and position.

Two days after the funeral came Thanksgiving. None of us was in any shape to put together a big meal, and fortunately none of us had to. Our neighbors in Pleasantville prepared a Thanksgiving dinner for all of us—the entire extended family. It was a beautiful gesture of love and neighborliness.

The Saturday after Thanksgiving I had to leave for Washington to begin the process of orientation and to start putting together a staff. I still remember that day as if it were yesterday. It was wrenching to leave my family so soon after Shari's and Trina's deaths.

I was sworn in as a member of Congress for the first time on January 5, 1981. Two busloads of my relatives and supporters drove out to Washington for the event. I was able to get four tickets to the gallery for the swearing-in, and I gave them to my parents, my grandmother, and Aunt Perk. My mother, as it happened, was given the seat where the first lady sits when the president addresses Congress.

I had bought a new suit back home for my swearing-in. It was shiny and blue, and I wore it with a red-and-blue–striped tie. Very patriotic. The only problem was, the suit was already extremely out of style, at least on the east coast. I didn't realize it until people started asking, "Where did you get *that*?" I don't think I ever wore the suit again.

The ceremony ran very long, and was followed by a hectic series of receptions. That night we had a big dinner for all my family, staff, and supporters at a restaurant overlooking the Potomac. There my campaign people presented me with a clock bearing a plaque that read: "Together we can make all the difference in the world." Then Steve's Kids gave their last performance, singing some of the same songs they had performed in the campaign. This was the first time they had performed since the accident—and it would be the last time too. The kids dedicated their performance to Shari, and they were great, and we were all terribly moved. In my memory that performance, and not my swearing-in, remains the highlight of that day.

3

When I first came to Washington as a member of Congress, two things surprised me most about the job. One, the immense number of constituents who want to talk to you and ask you for help. Two, the information overload: the supply of data is so great, and the issues are so big and complex, that no member can deal with everything he or she should deal with, can know everything he or she should know, or can be as adequately prepared as he or she should be. You're forced to specialize, to develop an expertise in a couple of areas and, when you have to make decisions about other areas, to depend enormously on the knowledge, judgment, and good faith of others.

The area in which I became an expert was dairy policy. Typically, a new member of Congress is given two committee assignments, or one major assignment. The interests of your district have a lot to do with which committee you end up on. If you represent western Wisconsin, where dairy farmers make up the bulk of your constituents, you simply have to be on the Agriculture Committee in order to represent them effectively. So I was on the Ag Committee from the start, and over the years I rose to a position of influence on it. Since our district contains more than its share of colleges, and since I consider federal commitment to education crucial to America's future, I also asked to be assigned to the Education Committee.

In Congress some committees are considerably more powerful than others and receive a lot more press coverage. The Ag Committee is not one of those that you hear much about in the national media. Agricultural issues don't dominate the Congress; the network news programs pay very little attention to them; C-SPAN rarely broadcasts Ag Committee hearings. I used to tell people, "You'll never see me on the *NBC Nightly News* or *Meet the Press*, because I'll never be chairman of the Budget or Appropriations or Tax or Health committee." The only real opportunity you have to make a mark as an Ag Committee member is to rise up through your party leadership, as Tom Foley did in the Democratic party and as I would later do in the GOP.

Perhaps the most glamorous moment in any Ag Committee hearing during my tenure was when Jane Fonda, Sissy Spacek, and Jessica Lange testified at a hearing on the 1985 Farm Bill. These actresses' only qualification as agricultural experts was that they had all played farm wives in movies. For once, the Ag Committee got plenty of media coverage. But the whole thing was a sideshow that had nothing to do with serious policy-making.

The Ag Committee, which usually has about forty-three to forty-seven members, tends to be broken down into subcommittees by commodity groupings: "general commodities," such as wheat, corn, and soybeans; Southern crops, such as tobacco, peanuts, and sugar; food and nutrition programs, such as school lunches and food stamps; foreign trade; and livestock and dairy. I've always served on the Livestock and Dairy Subcommittee, of which I've been the ranking Republican member since 1990 and the chairman since my party took control of Congress in 1995.

The Ag Committee is traditionally less partisan than almost any other committee, with members divided not along ideological lines but according to commodity and region. Dairy people, for example, will line up against tobacco people, or Midwestern dairy people against California dairy people. Until recently, there was very little ideological tension between Republicans and Democrats on the committee, a state of affairs that helped reinforce my own strong feelings about the need for both parties to work together in a collegial atmosphere.

As a new member of Congress, I felt that I had a lot to prove. In 1980, my opponent had been the incumbent, Al Baldus, who had been the chair of the Dairy Subcommittee. Al was a very nice sort, not too confrontational or controversial, but not highly motivated on issues, either. In the 1980 election, he received all the campaign contributions from the dairy industry, which made sense, because he chaired the subcommittee. In winning Al's seat, I inherited his obligations to the twenty-two thousand dairy farmers in my district without, of course, succeeding to the subcommittee chairmanship. I had my work cut out for me.

My most formidable challenge during that first term was the 1981 Farm Bill. I took a great interest in the crafting of the bill, did my homework, and became rather vocal in support of provisions that I felt would benefit the dairy farmers in my district. I soon established a reputation as the House's most knowledgeable member on dairy issues.

Meanwhile my personal life was almost nonexistent. I had few close friends, and hardly any gay friends. I was a workaholic. I've often thought about how much my district profited from my sublimation of my sexuality into my work! To be sure, there was a small group of gay men whom I met early on in the Washington bars and spent time with occasionally, but they weren't people that I felt very close to. Unlike many of them, moreover, I would never think of going into a bar during the week: the concept of "happy hour," of dropping in after work to have a couple of drinks and chat with friends, was absolutely foreign to me. On weeknights, after I had finished the day's work, I would go back home to my bland little apartment, watch some television, eat a TV dinner, and go to sleep.

I continued to agonize over what I saw as the contradiction between my homosexuality and my faith. I wanted very much to be in a permanent committed relationship, but at the same time the idea of such a relationship appalled me, because I had been taught to think that it would amount to living in sin. A one-night sexual encounter was different: I could have such an encounter, and then, in the morning, devastated by an overwhelming sense of guilt, I could pray for forgiveness, and by the time I got back to the office everything would be fine. It's absurd, but that's the way that a lot of our churches teach us to think about these things.

In any case, I had very few sexual encounters during those years, and most were extremely tame affairs that didn't even last through the night. The guy would leave, and I would say an anguished prayer, and fall asleep forgiven, and wake up in the morning feeling good about myself.

This was all very emotionally unhealthy, of course. But, as I later realized with a sense of grim irony, the powerful sense of guilt that kept me from being more sexually active in the late '70s and early '80s probably also saved my life. For during those years, sexual contact was spreading a then unknown and unnamed virus through the gay population. In 1980, while I was busy traveling around western Wisconsin campaigning for Congress, a few doctors in New York, San Francisco, and Los Angeles were beginning to be visited by gay patients whose immune systems were inexplicably crippled; suddenly, young men who had been models of health a few months earlier were dying of rare infectious disorders like *Pneumocystic carinii* pneumonia and Kaposi's sarcoma. In 1981, while I was busy laboring over the Farm Bill, reports of a puzzling "gay disease" began to appear in gay newspapers in New York and San Francisco; on July 5 of that year, news of this medical enigma appeared for the first time in the *New York Times*.

Little did I know at the time that the guilt which made it

difficult for me to experience intimacy with other gay men was also probably saving me from infection by a lethal virus.

Of course, I wasn't entirely friendless. I did have friends in Congress. Most of them were fellow moderate Republicans like Tom Tauke of Iowa and Rod Chandler of Washington state. But these were political friends whom I didn't really socialize with after work. I also continued to date women occasionally and to hope that I would develop a meaningful relationship with one of them. (Aside from the religious concerns, of course, this was the politically sensible thing to do.) As I had in the state legislature, I prayed to God night after night to free me from my homosexuality. Ironically, my parents' example of selfless service, and the habit I learned from them of just not talking or thinking about personal matters, made it easy for me, during my years in the Wisconsin legislature and my first few years in Washington, to let myself be consumed by public service and to suppress my personal needs and desires.

I went on like that until one night in 1982, when a remarkable thing happened. That evening started out in the same way as many others: I went on a date with a woman; it was, as always, friendly, civilized, and sexless; at a reasonable hour, I dropped her off at home and drove off alone through the streets of Washington, headed back to my empty apartment. That was when I suddenly heard a strong and compassionate voice speak to me. "Why are you so unaccepting of the person I made you to be?" the voice asked. "Why, if it's okay with me, isn't it okay with you?"

I remember that night, and that voice, as vividly as if it were yesterday. You could never convince someone steeped in a fundamentalist view of homosexuality that such an experience can happen, but it did. That was when I accepted myself—or, at least, began to.

From that night onward, I stopped dating women and began to think seriously about a committed relationship with another man. I knew I didn't want to live alone forever and grow into a lonely old man. I knew that for a lonely gay poli-

tician especially, the temptations that cross one's path can lead
to personal and professional disaster. I also knew that for me
to be happy as a gay man, I had to find a committed partner
who fit all the traditional notions of what I'd want in a wife
if I were straight. He would have to be someone I respected,
someone who truly loved and inspired me, someone who
made me feel safe and secure, someone whom I could trust
and be proud to introduce to people.

So I started seriously dating men with an eye to finding a
friend. I met some very nice men, most of whom were in politics, but nothing clicked. Then, with one of them, it did click.
Matt Fletcher was introduced to me by a mutual friend who
said that we had everything in common. We got together once
for dinner in 1983, and I found that our friend was right.
Slim, dark-haired, and twenty-seven, Matt was, like me, a
Midwestern boy from a Republican family. In fact, his dad,
like mine, was a Chevrolet dealer; as it later turned out, our
fathers actually knew each other. Matt had attended college
in Iowa and had then come to Washington to study for a master's degree at George Washington University with a special-
ization in foreign policy and defense. He had gotten his degree
a year or so earlier and had stayed on to find work in government. Unable to find the kind of position he had prepared for,
he had taken a low-level fund-raising job on the Senate Campaign Committee. Since he couldn't make enough money
doing that, he also waited tables at a restaurant on Capitol
Hill. I respected him enormously for his willingness to do
what was necessary to support himself. Indeed, his combination of intelligence, decency, quiet dedication, and unpreten-
tiousness—not to mention his passion for government and his
love of sports—drew me to him immediately.

I learned during that dinner, however, that Matt was unavailable. He was already in a committed relationship with a
twenty-four-year-old United Airlines flight attendant named
John Dent. I soon met John, and found him to be a very gentle, considerate, and sensitive young man with a ready smile
and a happy laugh. He was also spectacularly handsome, with

piercing dark eyes. He and Matt had been together for three years. As it turned out, instead of finding a lover in Matt, I ended up finding, in Matt and John, my first real gay friends.

Having Matt and John in my life made a big difference. But I was still lonely. In the fall of 1983, after working hard without a break for a long spell, I took a week off and drove to Chattanooga to visit a sports broadcaster whom I had gotten to know back home in Wisconsin. I thought he was a friend; I also had the impression that he might be interested in me romantically. Anyway, I arrived there on the Thursday after Labor Day weekend and found my way to a hotel. I called him a couple of times to schedule our get-together, but he kept asking me to call back. Eventually I realized that he had no intention of seeing me.

I was not happy. After spending a chaste night in Chattanooga, I got back into my car and made the eight-hour trip back to Washington.

By now it was Friday night, September 9, 1983. I got home at about eight o'clock, took a shower, had something to eat, and went out to Badlands, a gay bar on 22nd Street.

Rob was standing at the bar a few feet away from me when I first saw him. His intense, almost black eyes, blond hair, buoyant manner, and muscular build made me notice him immediately. He was dressed exactly the same way that I was, in blue jeans, a white polo shirt, and white tennis shoes. I indicated through eye contact that I was interested in him; he made it clear that the feeling was not mutual. Instead he was plainly interested in the person with whom I was talking, a handsome, broad-shouldered "Superman" type who was a friend of mine from Wisconsin. I knew this guy as a friend and only a friend, but Rob, observing us from several feet away and unable to make my friend with the movie-star looks pay attention to him, thought he saw something more going on between the two of us. That's when Rob decided, with an impish quality that is not uncharacteristic of him, that if he couldn't get the movie star, he was going to make sure that the movie star didn't get me!

So Rob started talking to me—and we talked, and we talked. For me it was love at first sight. He was twenty-three years old then, five-foot-ten, with an arresting combination of boyish high spirits and a mature man's self-possessed, commanding manner. A senior at Auburn University, he was finishing up his studies in architecture and was in Washington to look into the job market. Eventually the bartender announced last call. Rob was drinking scotch, and I said, "Well, I have scotch at my place, if you want to keep talking."

I've never been good at pick-up lines. Rob looked at me to see if I was serious. Knowing him as I now do, I suspect that he also looked to see if my friend from Wisconsin was still available. (A quick glance would have revealed that he had left some time ago.) In any case, Rob said, "Sure, why not?"

He really thought that we were going back to my place to drink scotch, nothing more. For my part, I thought and hoped that something far more than that would happen. What did happen was that we talked. Or, rather, he talked and I listened. At first there were some awkward moments of silence. But then he let loose. He told me a great deal about architecture, a subject about which I was almost totally ignorant. He also told me that the three things he didn't care to talk about were politics, sports, and religion—which happen to be the three things that are most important in my life. He also gave me the first of many lectures that I would hear from him over the years about the importance of home—and the importance of building new homes out of high-quality materials that will last.

When it became clear to me that Rob didn't want anything more that night than scotch, I finally told him, as we sat on my balcony, that he could stay and drink as long as he wanted to, or he could leave, but I was going to bed.

So he stayed there in my apartment, which he remembers now for its orange velvet sofa and "old-lady doilies," and finished his drink, and spent a quiet night in a guest bedroom with a big piano in it. And in the morning he left without ever having learned that I was a Congressman. I had just said, "I work on the Ag Committee,'' so he assumed I was a member of the committee staff.

We did exchange phone numbers. He was staying with a childhood friend, Billy Becker, and had plans to go to Rehoboth Beach, Delaware, that weekend. Coincidentally, I also planned to spend the weekend at Rehoboth. When I found myself taking long walks on the beach in hopes of running into him, I knew I was seriously captivated. I called Billy's number as soon as I got back to Washington.

It was September 13. Rob and Billy were sitting around Billy's apartment chatting about old times when the phone rang. Billy answered. ''Hello?'' he said.

''Is Rob Morris there?''

''It's for you, Rob,'' I heard Billy say.

Rob took the phone. ''Hello?''

''Hi,'' I said, ''it's Steve Gunderson. How are you?''

''Fine, how are you?''

''Great. Look, I was just wondering if you'd like to have dinner tonight.''

Rob told me months later that he'd been surprised by the invitation. ''You hadn't said very much at all during our night together, yet here you were asking me out.'' His first inclination was to turn me down cold and spend more time catching up with Billy. But when he excused himself for a moment, put his hand over the receiver, and told Billy what was up, Billy urged him to go. ''It could be fun!'' he said.

''Okay,'' Rob said to Billy, ''tell me the name of a good restaurant with great food and an interesting setting.''

''Dominique's,'' Billy replied instantly.

Rob got back on the phone and asked me, ''Do you know the restaurant Dominique's?''

''Yes,'' I said.

''Okay. How about eight? I'll meet you there.''

I showed up late at Dominique's. Rob was already seated. The hostess, Diana, showed me to the table, and when she said, ''I hope you enjoy your dinner, Congressman,'' Rob turned around to see who the congressman was. That's how he found out what I do for a living.

The sight of Rob at that table, dazzlingly handsome in an elegant coat and tie, confirmed for me that I was, indeed, smitten. Rob wasn't smitten yet. But he was intrigued. Having known countless gay men who were preoccupied with fashion and antiques and the like, he was shocked to find that I didn't know or care about such things. I couldn't tell a Sears suit from a Brooks Brothers suit, I had no interest in driving a fancy car when my dad could get me a good deal on a Chevy, and I was just as happy with a McDonald's burger as with a filet mignon. Rob found this aspect of me at once bizarre and oddly appealing.

But he was far less preoccupied with me, at that point, than with finishing his B.A. thesis. The point of the thesis was that if you design buildings, particularly homes, with respect for the human needs of the people who will use them, you can tap the good within those people, establish a stronger sense of community, and even make neighborhoods safer to live in than they would be otherwise. He realizes now that this was a bit idealistic. But he still believes fervently that architects, especially home builders, should be more sensitive to human needs and more respectful of the idea of community than they are.

Rob returned to Auburn several days after our dinner date, and during the next few weeks we kept in touch by phone. I realized that our conversations had inspired me to think about buying a home, and I soon began sending him photos of available houses and asking for his opinions. He gave them readily. I was impressed by his well-developed aesthetic sense, his keen eye for architectural strengths and deficiencies, his sensitivity to my own residential needs, and the bluntness and clarity of his judgments. Though he was still a college student, he was also well on his way to being a serious professional in his field.

On October 23, while I was experiencing the joy of new-found love, something happened thousands of miles away that resulted in the single hardest and most heartbreaking task I've ever faced as a member of Congress. On that day two hundred forty-one people were killed in a bombing of the U.S. Marine compound in Beirut. One of the victims was a constituent of mine. During the next few days, I spent much of my time making arrangements for the return of the body, for the military honor guard at the funeral, and so forth, and keeping the young man's family informed every step of the way. It was deeply painful to talk to those unfortunate people. They were very warm and gracious, and extremely grateful for every little thing I did for them.

I went to the funeral. Because I was the only "dignitary" there, and the sole representative of the U.S. government, I felt very strange. The county sheriff met me at the door of the gymnasium where the service was to take place and whisked me inside. The family, whom I had never met before, insisted that I sit with them in the front row. They even asked me to speak, though I declined, telling them that I felt it would be improper. I can't describe how challenging it is to be in that kind of a situation. What on earth can you possibly say to a family to justify the loss of their child in such circumstances? Nothing—absolutely nothing.

Not long after that, in November, having decided that a house I had seen on South Carolina Avenue was worth considering seriously, Rob flew up to inspect it.

ROB

We were gradually growing very close. Yet I was in the middle of a situation that's not unusual for many young gay men: I was living with a woman. Her name was Jamie, and we had decided that as soon as we graduated, we would marry, work together, and raise a family.

What was I doing in that relationship? Well, on the one hand, I had been comfortable with my homosexuality for a long time—or, at least, I thought I had. On the other hand, I had enjoyed successful sexual relationships with both a man and a woman, and I had figured that when I did find my way to a compatible long-term relationship, it might be with a person of either sex. I always felt that this would just *happen*—that I would meet somebody, male or female, who would determine for me which way my life would go. But I always suspected that it would be a man. Whether it was one or the other didn't trouble me as much as the crafting of the relationship itself.

Deep inside, I knew that I was rationalizing. I was gay and trying to run away from this fact, and I knew I wouldn't be able to fully acknowledge my sexuality until I actually fell in love with another man. Deep down, I knew that in part I wanted to marry Jamie because I sought to avoid all the conflicts that you take on when you acknowledge your homosexuality to yourself and others. I also wanted to do it because I longed to have a family.

Yet as my relationship with Jamie developed, it became clear to me that despite my desire for a family and a "place" in a community, the lie I would be committing in marrying her was deeply troubling to my soul. I knew that what I was planning, deep down, was to do what many gay married men do: I would have a family and then, whenever my wife went out of town, I would enjoy a fling with a man before hurrying back to "normal" life. In my heart I knew that what we had with each other was a great friendship, but not the stuff that long-term soulmates were made of.

That's when I began to understand what sexual orientation is about. It's not about being able to perform sexually with one gender and not the other. It's not even so much about sexual attraction. On the profounder level, it's about being able to forge the deepest kind of spiritual bond with members of one gender and not the other. Yes, Jamie could be my friend—but because I was gay, she could never be my soulmate. We could never have that deep-down spiritual bond. To be gay is to be made in such a way that you can have that kind of tie only with someone of the same sex. But this took me some time to understand and accept—and it would take Steve even longer.

STEVE

Anyway, I bought the South Carolina Avenue house and moved in. That December, after spending Christmas with his family, Rob came to Washington for a visit. We still didn't really know each other that well. We'd talked on the phone a lot and exchanged a couple of letters, but this was only his second trip to Washington since we'd met, the first being his visit to look over the house.

We still had no relationship to speak of, then, and I didn't really know a lot about his family. On New Year's Eve, when he and Billy were helping me paint the dining room, Billy asked Rob about his parents. Though Rob hadn't mentioned anything to me, I gathered from his reply that they had recently sold their house and moved from Columbus. "They're fine, I think," Rob said. "Dad's new business is going well. It's smaller and he has more control. I suppose that's good."

"What about your mom?" Billy asked. "She loved Columbus."

"Well, she's not particularly thrilled with her new setting, but she's acting strong."

After the paint job was done, I served up a steak and lobster dinner. Then we piled into my car and drove to Badlands to ring in the new year. Within the hour, Billy left, and shortly thereafter Rob grew strangely quiet. At his request, we headed back to South Carolina Avenue. As he stared out the frosty window at groups of exuberant young men on P Street, it was clear that something was on his mind.

"Rob," I asked, "is something the matter?"

He didn't speak. Finally he whispered something. Barely hearing him, I lowered the radio volume. "What did you say?"

"I—want—a—home," he said.

"You'll have a home, Rob," I said, "and my guess is that wherever it is, it will be a beautiful home."

"I don't want just a beautiful *house*," he said in a quiet tone. "I want a *home*. It's easy for someone who has never really *left* home to take the idea so lightly." He paused as we turned onto the rock Creek Parkway. "You still think of your parents' house as home. It's the home you and your brothers and sisters grew up in. You have the luxury of going back there whenever you want. I bet you can still find things in closets that you left there when you were ten." His eyes filled with tears. "Not me," he said. "My brothers and I got a month's notice to take our belongings from the attic before they were tossed out. I thought I could handle this. People move all the time. But this is killing me. I can't figure out why they would move."

He described the house to me. It sounded far grander than the little house in the country in which I'd grown up. "Rob," I finally said, as he stared out the window at the Lincoln Memorial across the frozen Potomac, "it sounds like an exceptional house. Maybe you were lucky to live in it for as long as you did. And you have your entire life ahead of you to create a place like it for yourself."

Suddenly he jerked away from the window. "Right, Steve," he said with surprising hostility. "I'm going to have a family and a home and a 'place' in a small town as a goddamn faggot. What planet are you from? Do you think I can go back to my hometown with a goddamn boyfriend, adopt a couple of kids and run to the monthly P.T.A. meetings without raising an eyebrow? Oh, yeah, I can see the invitation now. 'The Junior League requests the honor of your and your silly-ass boyfriend's presence at the spring cotillion.' Which of us wears the dress, Steve? I don't think so!"

He turned back toward the window. "I'm sorry, Steve. Your constituents may have voted you into office, but they haven't rolled out the red carpet for you at the Lions Club. Have they? Face it, we're both destined to be gay ghetto rats."

Having no ready response to this, I drove on as he stared out the window. This wasn't the New Year's that either of us had intended. Yet Rob had addressed an essential aspect of being gay with which both of us had secretly and painfully grappled. How could we embrace the totality of who we were without spurning many of the things that had *made* us who we were? How could we accept our sexuality and be fully open and honest about it, on the one hand, and still, on the other hand, have a home, a family, and a sense of membership in a community of the sort I had known in Pleasantville and he had known in Columbus?

Rob's strong desire for a traditional home and family was one reason for his hesitation to commit to a relationship with me. Another reason was his lingering uncertainty about me. Aside from being a member of Congress (which he considered a liability, not an asset), who was I? How did I feel about him? How, for that matter, did I feel about myself, and about being gay?

These were important questions for Rob, and he still wasn't sure of the answers. In a sense, he felt he didn't know me at all. That was entirely reasonable, and entirely my fault. As a rule, Norwegian-Americans don't talk much about their feelings, and I'm even more closemouthed about them than most. As a result I was, in many important respects, a question mark to Rob. There were many things he needed to know about me before he would commit his life to me.

Over the course of 1984, we gradually became closer. In June, he was graduated from Auburn, broke up with Jamie, and moved in with me on South Carolina Avenue. Meanwhile, I spent much of the year wrapped up in my reelection campaign, which kept me from spending much time with Rob. Finally, after the 1984 elections were over, Rob insisted that I take off a few days and go with him to New York. There, in Greenwich Village, we went into a coffee shop and he just *forced* me to talk.

I talked more about myself that day than I had ever done in my whole life. Rob started, quite simply, by asking me, ''How are you sure you're gay?'' It was a hard question, and in 1984 I was still struggling with it. I knew for sure that I was not able to carry out physical or emotional relationships with women to the degree that would be necessary for a successful long-term relationship. The question was whether I could have a long-term relationship with a man. At the time I frankly didn't know the answer to that.

What I did know, beyond a shadow of a doubt, was that I wanted to be with Rob. I was deeply in love with him. At the same time, my imagination was so limited that I couldn't picture us as anything more than glorified roommates. It astonishes me now to think that I would have been comfortable with him as a mere roommate and sex partner, with no explicit ties beyond that for the rest of my life. Or, rather, that's what I was willing to settle for: the sex, the companionship. How hollow that would have been compared to what we have now. I thank God that Rob forced me to deal with the realities of a genuine relationship—forced me to see that caring for someone, for yourself, and for the two of you as a couple involves much more than I had ever realized. I learned all that from him.

Why hadn't I learned it from my parents' marriage? Mainly because I couldn't yet conceive of a gay relationship as functioning in the same way as a marriage between a man and a woman. And partly because Norwegian-American parents don't make a point of displaying their affections for each other.

In any event, during that visit to New York, Rob bombarded me with questions and pressed for answers. His point was not to harass me or corner me or embarrass me, but to make me think and talk about myself in a way I had never done before—to force me to see things from a perspective I had never considered.

That discussion, I should add, took place against a backdrop whose tragic dimensions Rob and I had not yet begun to recognize. While the two of us were taking steps toward making a life together, many other young gay men, less fortunate but no less deserving than we, were dying agonizing deaths. Rob and I didn't happen to be close to any of those young men, though, and while the Reagan administration's inadequate funding of AIDS education and research outraged Rob, as it did many gay men, AIDS didn't occupy a key place in our consciousness. The announcement in late July of Rock Hudson's diagnosis with AIDS had stunned America and awakened it to the seriousness of the epidemic. But AIDS remained a back-burner issue for Rob and me. It is striking now to realize that though we talked about a lot of things during that visit to New York, AIDS wasn't one of them. So distant was it from the center of our minds that we didn't even consider the possible consequences of our own sexual intimacy. Like most Americans, we still thought of AIDS as something that happened to extremely promiscuous gay men—and neither of us, we knew, fell into that category.

November 1984 saw the beginning of Rob's and my favorite household tradition. After three years of fighting snowstorms and unbelievable air traffic in order to get back to Wisconsin for Thanksgiving, Rob and I decided to stay in Washington and host a dinner for friends in town with no place to go. John Frank, a brilliant lawyer from Eau Claire who had helped in my first campaign for Congress, was my legislative director; over the years to come, he would serve in turn as my chief of staff, as my district director, and as counsel and dairy policy director for the Ag Committee. The idea appealed to me especially because it offered an opportunity to spend the holiday with Rob. The 1984 dinner was a success, and on every Thanksgiving since then Rob and I have continued the custom.

In the weeks and months that followed our talk in New York, Rob and I moved gradually closer to a fully committed relationship. I spent as much time with him as I could, though my congressional duties continued to weigh heavily upon me. Nineteen eighty-five was a particularly busy and intense legislative year. I played key roles in putting together the 1985 Farm Bill and the Higher Education Act, and worked hard to find common ground in the highly polarized debate that began that year over National Endowment for the Arts funding. The House as a whole was kept busy debating the 1986 Tax Reform Act and arguing about whether we should continue to fund the Nicaraguan Contras. When the August break came, I was ready for the vacation that Rob and I had planned.

But I didn't realize how transforming that vacation would be. Our trip took us to Florence, Rome, Athens, and the most beautiful place on earth—the Greek island of Mykonos. It was there that Rob and I talked not about our past or present, as we had in New York, but about our future; it was there that the two of us started dreaming as one, started learning to see ourselves not as two separate individuals but as a single entity, heading together into the future.

The trip was entirely Rob's doing. He wanted to take me to all the places he had loved the most as a student of architecture, wanted to share with me the things that meant the most to him. It was kind of a Cliff's Notes version of an art and architecture tour: Michelangelo's *David*, the *Pietà*, Saint Peter's, the Parthenon. It was my first visit to Europe.

In Mykonos we booked rooms at the Hotel Lido, where Rob had stayed during an earlier trip. The hotel is absolutely beautiful. It's perched high on the hillside, and affords a sweeping view of the city and the sea beyond. All the rooms have terraces. The access to the hotel is through a garden filled with fragrant flowers that has the feeling of an Eden.

From the moment Rob and I arrived at the Lido, the staff treated us very deferentially. They bowed and scraped. I felt like royalty. "My God," I told Rob once we were alone in our room, "these people are really going out of their way to take care of us!"

"Wellllll," he said, "you don't know the whole story."

"What story?" I asked.

He confessed that when he had first called the hotel some weeks earlier to make reservations, he had been told that it was booked solid. So he had phoned the Greek embassy, told them that he was calling on behalf of Congressman Gunderson, and asked them to intervene with the Hotel Lido in Mykonos to make a room available for me, because it was very important that I stay there. So the hotel had booted somebody—and had obviously alerted its staff that Rob and I were VIPs!

"I should have known!" I said. I was annoyed at Rob for taking advantage of our relationship in this way. He apologized, and said that he felt guilty about it, and has never done anything like it again. He was only twenty-five at the time, and making that call to the embassy seemed to him like a reasonable thing to do. Besides, he had loved the experience of staying at the Lido, and he wanted desperately for me to have that experience too—wanted me to step out of my mundane, stuffed-shirt, upright, buttoned-down Midwestern Congressman persona and, for once in my life, to get a taste of life.

And I did. The trip marked, for me, nothing less than the discovery of my inner self. It also represented an absolute reversal of roles. I was totally dependent on Rob. He had put the schedule together; he knew where to go and what to do. I was just going along, being led as a little child is led, being taken around from place to place to experience the cultures of Greece and Italy. We had set aside two weeks in which we could be totally consumed by ourselves and each other and these cultures, and suddenly I felt a desire to experience life at a level that I hadn't realized was possible. That trip opened up the whole personal side of life for me in the richest and most beautiful way.

Everything on that trip seemed to be touched by magic, by an almost excruciating tenderness. Every night, whether we were sitting at a table in a square in Florence or at Harry's Bar in Venice or on a terrace in Mykonos, we had a glorious dinner at which we stared into each other's eyes and planned our life together. Every morning we had coffee and pastries, usually at an outdoor café. And the rest of the time we explored a culture that was utterly exotic to me, from the Sistine Chapel to the Acropolis to the canals of Venice.

To have all these experiences within a two-week period is almost more than the mind and body—at least *my* mind and body—can handle. For me it was just a revelation. In many ways I felt that I had finally arrived at an understanding—at once physical, intellectual, emotional, and spiritual—of what life could be and was meant to be. I was a world away from the dairy farms of Wisconsin and from Washington's day-to-day grind. For the first time in my life, I relaxed and simply enjoyed myself. Until then it had never entered my mind that I should take care of myself—not just in terms of bodily pleasure, but in terms of emotional and spiritual sustenance. Until then, indeed, it had hardly occurred to me to think of myself as having real, honest needs that were deserving of attention. In Mykonos, by beginning to learn to think about *us*, I began to learn to think of myself. That vacation drove home to me in a powerful way what I had been missing during my entire adulthood—and its name was life, and love, and family. And Rob.

ROB

That trip established the foundation upon which the two of us have communicated ever since. It was the first time I had ever seen Steve outside of his stuffed-shirted context. I saw what was beneath his veneer and I was very much able to relate to it, as opposed to the congressman. I don't relate to the congressman very well. Congressmen aren't really people; they're offices. You might say that in Mykonos, I saw the child in Steve. And when you see the child in an adult, you understand who that person really is.

There is a bar named Castro's at the western edge of Mykonos where they play nothing but classical music. People, mostly gay men, come every afternoon to listen to that music and to celebrate the setting of the sun over the windmills and the mountains and the Aegean Sea. It sounds rather insignificant, perhaps, but it's not. It's extraordinary. The music in that place at that hour, with the red sun sinking into the wine-dark sea, is a ritual in Mykonos. It reminds you that the day is over and that the night will soon be upon you. And Mykonos is ultimately about night.

Steve and I had wonderful conversations sitting at that bar. We talked about his Midwestern conditioning, which made it so difficult for him to express emotion, and about my Southern cultural imprinting, which had made me feel doomed by my homosexuality to a life outside of the world in which I had grown up. We talked about the changes we had been through, about what we wanted out of our relationship, and about how to deal with our families. We talked about what to do if Steve died. That was an important question for me, because if Steve died the government and his family would come in like birds flying down on a dead squirrel in the summertime, and I would be pushed aside. I was very worried about that. The official government funeral for a member of Congress was not something I was prepared for, or would participate in. Or be invited to.

In fact what we were really talking about, quite simply, was the rest of our lives together as a couple—a family.

4

Unfortunately, Mykonos didn't change everything overnight. My life continued to be focused on Congress, while Rob's life centered on creating a home for us, pursuing his fledgling career in Washington as an architectural apprentice, and having fun with his friends. At twenty-five, he was independent, energetic, and spontaneous, and certainly not the type to sit at home waiting for me. I learned early on that I would constantly be trying to catch up with him.

One of the first friendships Rob developed in Washington was with someone he had known in Atlanta. Raised on a southern Virginia dairy farm, Glenn Perrow had been a brash, precocious youth whose parents, encouraged by his promise, had lavished upon him the best education they could afford—and the best material possessions, too. When Rob had known him in Atlanta, Glenn had worked as a bookkeeper at a major bank. Since then, however, he had experienced some dramatic changes. Having suppressed awareness of his homosexuality until his early twenties, Glenn, after recognizing that he was gay, had found his way to Atlanta's gay bar scene. Like many gay men who have put off self-knowledge for too long, Glenn was so excited by his new sense of wholeness and self-discovery, and by the feeling of acceptance that he found in the gay community, that he overreacted somewhat and made the gay bar scene the center of his life. When he fell in love with an older man, he put his career on the back burner. But the older man already had a lover, and though Glenn hung in there for a while, thinking that the man would leave the lover for him, that never happened.

Later that year, Glenn developed an attraction for a young man with whom he thought he might enjoy a meaningful relationship. When the young man moved to Provincetown, Massachusetts, Glenn promptly quit his job with the bank and followed. For reasons that Glenn never discussed, that relationship fizzled. Finding himself alone and unemployed, Glenn took a job as a flight attendant. That job brought him to Washington, where he ran into Rob at a party thrown by mutual friends.

It didn't take long for Glenn to get to know Washington's gay community inside out. Whenever we went out with him to the Dupont Circle bars, he seemed to know *everybody*. He had a unique knack of making people think, after fifteen minutes of conversation, that they had known him for years. His bright, outgoing manner and his physical attractiveness drew all sorts of people to him.

It was through Glenn that Rob met another young Southerner. Raised in Durham, North Carolina, Charles Ross worked at a headhunting agency in Tysons Corner, Virginia, where he placed psychologists with corporations. He was then twenty-eight, but he had the energy, ebullience, and mischievousness of a sixteen-year-old. Rob first introduced him to me over drinks at J.R.'s. That night Charles was especially cheeky, perhaps because he knew that I was a Congressman, was a bit intimidated by that, and was overcompensating. In any case, when Rob went to the bar to order a round of drinks for us, Charles pulled me aside and, pointing to his absolutely hideous pastel madras tie, explained that he had stopped by his house after work in order to change ties. He had put on his newest tie just for me! What did I think of it?

I was at a loss for words. I stammered out an insincere compliment. Of course, Charles knew that the tie was horrible and was just putting me on, but I didn't realize it at the time. That was Charles.

Charles was gay, but as long as we knew him he never had a serious relationship. Any time a friendship seemed in danger of turning intimate, Charles would destroy it. At first we couldn't understand why. Perhaps it was that he enjoyed the social whirl too much to allow himself to be tied down to one person. Or perhaps it had something to do with his severely limited attention span. Or perhaps he was just constitutionally incapable of maintaining a long-term relationship; maybe the very idea exceeded his psychological and/or emotional grasp.

In fact, as far as we knew, Charles didn't sleep with anyone. He certainly didn't talk about it. We all assumed that he never had sex. As best we could tell, the only thing he ever took to bed was a glass of vodka. We came to joke about the fact that by day Charles was far too serious to return personal phone calls or to have lunch away from his desk, but that by night he couldn't shut up or quit drinking.

The dark side of Charles was that he was always uncomfortable about being gay. Outside his small circle of close friends, he was basically closeted. This discomfort, I think, was one reason he drank. And perhaps it was also yet another reason why he never had a committed relationship—for if he did have such a relationship, he would be forced to be more open.

Instead, Charles lived through our relationship—Rob's and mine. During his nine-to-five workday life, he acted the part of a heterosexual; but in the evenings, on weekends, and on the vacation trips we took together, Charles lived out his gay identity—which is to say that he essentially he lived out *himself*—through us.

Charles's attachment to Rob and me was flattering, but it

was also odd and occasionally frustrating. Charles was such an attractive and loving person that Rob and I couldn't see any reason for him *not* to find somebody, fall in love, and build a life together. His underlying guilt about being gay made it impossible. That sort of thing was just too open, too *real*, for him.

If the people Rob brought into our life in the early years were gregarious, animated free spirits, the people I brought into it were serious, cautious professionals. Rob insisted that the only real difference was that his friends were Southern and mine were typically Midwestern. Two members of my staff were also close social friends. One was John Frank. The other was Kris Deininger, whom I first came to know as the beautiful, dark-haired woman who worked with my sister Naomi on Governor Dreyfus's staff and who always seemed to be wearing an elegant red dress. Kris, who is exactly my age, was Dreyfus's personal secretary from 1979 to 1983; when he left office, she went to work for the state Department of Transportation. It wasn't a very fulfilling job, so when I was looking for a new person to handle my scheduling, Naomi immediately suggested Kris. I invited her to Washington, talked to her, and offered her the position. She didn't jump at it. Her hesitancy surprised me. She wanted the job, she explained, but she wasn't sure she wanted to come to Washington.

What I learned from Naomi, and what I came to know from my own experience with Kris in the years that followed, was that she always second-guessed herself. Like me, Kris was brought up never to let the personal overwhelm the professional, and consequently developed into a very dedicated worker with virtually no personal life. Severely timid and self-conscious, she found it hard to break away from the Midwest, and in particular from her family in the small town of Darlington, Wisconsin, and to live on her own.

Her insecurity was particularly unfortunate because it was absolutely unfounded. Kris was, in fact, extremely capable. I very much wanted her to work for me, so I struggled to convince her that she would be happy in Washington. Eventually she agreed to come, and did a terrific job. When John Frank left the job of chief of staff in 1988 to return to Wisconsin and teach, Kris took up most of the slack. But when I asked her to assume his place officially she again hesitated, unsure that she was up to the job. I said it was absurd not to give it a try. So she agreed to. And she was great. She worked long hours, was highly disciplined, and handled the staff very efficiently. She also felt it was her professional responsibility to carry on her shoulders every problem, every worry, that cropped up in the office. She did all kinds of work herself instead of delegating it to others; if I had let her, she would have lived at the office night and day.

Kris started working for me shortly after I met Rob. It didn't take them long to form a close personal bond. But they also developed, almost immediately, a fiercely competitive love-hate relationship. They were always working against each other.

This was inevitable: Kris was running my professional life, while Rob was trying to establish a home for him and me. Though they had great affection for each other, and though she became an intimate part of our circle of friends, she and Rob fought tooth and nail. Part of it was over scheduling: Kris would routinely commit me to dinner dates with politicians and lobbyists on nights when Rob had already committed us to dinners with friends. And part of it was over larger issues: Rob always pushed me to do what was best for my conscience; Kris always pushed me to do whatever would minimalize practical difficulties for me. She wanted me to remain in office and to do so without scars, while Rob wanted me to leave office with my integrity intact. Those are very different goals. And so they fought. Some of their fights were amazingly intense. But they were both motivated by love for me, and from the start they recognized and respected that in each other.

Matt Fletcher and John Dent remained good friends of mine, and became friends of Rob's as well. Matt also became, for a time, a member of my staff. When a job opened up in my office in 1985 for a foreign policy and defense expert, I immediately offered it to Matt and he took it. He was excellent at the job and soon moved up to become my legislative director. Shortly after the 1986 elections, he accepted a staff job with the House subcommittee on Government Operations.

In Glenn, Charles, Kris, Matt, John Dent, and John Frank, Rob and I had the beginnings of a family of friends that would become very important to us over the years. But those first couple of years after he and I moved in together were difficult ones for both of us. He was still learning my language, still coming to terms with the fact that it was different from his, still struggling not to come to false conclusions as to how I felt about him and about our life together. And I was, as he would learn, not yet as comfortable with my homosexuality and with the idea of a gay relationship as I let on.

Largely as a way to avoid dealing with that lingering discomfort, I continued to immerse myself in work. In the fall of 1985, I was especially busy with the 1985 Farm Bill. Until then, the dairy industry had been one of the most highly subsidized of agricultural industries. Dairy farmers had come to rely on government subsidies and to take them for granted. Rather than being based on supply and demand, prices for dairy products were fixed by government fiat at artificially high levels. In the minds of people in the dairy industry, this was just the way things worked. I wanted to change that.

Knowing that the reduction of subsidies would not only save money for the government but would, in the long run, also bring about greater efficiency in the industry and generate larger revenues for dairy farmers, we sought in the Farm Bill of 1985 to establish something called a whole-herd buyout program. The idea was that, rather than eliminate dairy price supports outright, we would give the industry a chance to put supply and demand into balance while gradually lowering the level of supports.

That bill was the first significant event in what was proven to be a very good working relationship with Bob Dole. He was on the Senate Ag Committee then and had just become the

Senate majority leader. (This was during the two-year period in Reagan's second term when the Republicans had a majority in the Senate.) It was my second farm bill, and as a result of my work on the 1981 bill, I was well respected in the Congress as an expert on dairy policy. With my encouragement and that of others, the House had voted for the whole-herd buyout program.

The Senate, meanwhile, had passed a bill that, in accordance with the Reagan Administration's desire to make significant cuts in the dairy program, would have dramatically reduced the price supports without instituting any other program reforms. When the House and Senate pass different versions of a bill, you have to go into conference to work out a compromise. Well, we got down to the final days before the Christmas recess and the entire Farm Bill had been ironed out, with the sole exception of the dairy provisions. It was literally the last issue remaining on the table, and it was the only thing keeping Congress from closing up shop and heading home for the holidays. It was also the only thing keeping me from heading home to the Christmas party that Rob and I had planned. All of Congress was on hold: both houses were staying in session in order to see what kind of compromise the House and Senate dairy subcommittees would come up with and to vote on it.

One afternoon days later, Bob Dole finally sent word that he wanted to see me in his office. I went and found him with John Block, Reagan's Secretary of Agriculture. Dole said, "Whether we can get this Farm Bill done or not is dependent on whether we can come to some agreement on dairy." I agreed. Dole said he would let Block and me plead our cases, and then decide what to do about the Senate bill. Block, who supported the Senate bill in the form in which it had been passed, made the case for simply cutting price supports and letting the free market do its work. I made the case for whole-herd buyout. Dole listened to both our cases. Finally he said to Block, "I'm going to side with Steve." And he said to me, "I think you're being fair and reasonable."

That was a major victory for me, one for which I've been eternally grateful to Bob Dole.

It took some doing to get that bill signed. President Reagan sat on it for a few days. He was getting a lot of pressure from certain people in the White House to veto the bill, which they felt didn't move far enough from the farm-subsidies structure toward the free-market approach. Finally one day, just before Christmas, the president called me and some other members to the Oval Office and tried to talk us into voting for the 1986 Tax Act.

As someone who has never been a fan of tax increases, I was hesitant to support that bill, even though my party leadership was behind it. Noting the opportunity to strike a deal, I said, "Mr. President, the 1986 Tax Act is important to you, but it's equally important to us that the 1985 Farm Bill be signed."

"Well, all right, Steve," he said genially, "I promise I'll go back and take a look at the Farm Bill."

"Thank you, Mr. President," I said.

A few days later, just before Christmas, President Reagan signed the 1985 Farm Bill. It was one of those times when the president calls you into the woodshed, so to speak, and if you're prepared to take the offensive you can use the situation to your advantage.

In Congress, I was building important alliances and gaining my colleagues' respect. But things at home were bumpy. Communication between Rob and me remained a problem. Like many Southerners, he's physically affectionate and likes to talk; like many Midwesterners, I remain distant and am not predisposed to idle chatter. I don't express myself by throwing my arms around people and getting gushy. Nor do I talk about my private life. Rob loves talking about personal things.

And I hate confrontation. John Frank told Rob early on that if he tried to force me into an argument about something he felt we should discuss, I would shut up and concede almost anything just to avoid conflict. It was, John explained to Rob, "a Norwegian thing." Rob soon realized that this was absolutely true. For me, the pain of the personal showdown almost invariably outweighed the importance of the issue at hand, whatever it might be. So I would say, in effect, "I'm not going to talk about it, I'm not going to deal with it, I'm closing down." Rob's reaction was, "You can't close down, damn you, this argument isn't over."

But it *was* over! As Rob soon realized, there's no way to fight by yourself. On numerous occasions in our first three years together, he tried and failed to force a confrontation and resolution. Eventually he realized that things had to resolve themselves more slowly. Clearly if he hadn't gradually learned my language, the relationship would never have lasted.

For a long while, in fact, it seemed destined to fail. Partly because of my innately uncommunicative nature, but also partly because I remained uncomfortable, deep down, about my homosexuality and about the idea of a committed gay relationship, I maintained what you might call a spiritual independence from Rob during our first years together.

Rob has told me that he remembers with special vividness one Friday night early that October when we had dined in Georgetown and gone out for drinks in Dupont Circle. Rob had assumed that we would both sleep in the next morning and had planned some things for us to do around the house. But as we were getting into bed, he noticed that I was setting the alarm for 5:45. He asked what was going on. I explained that I was going to Wisconsin for the weekend. Rob blew up, left the room with a slam of the door, went downstairs and waited for me to follow. Instead, I fell asleep. After about an hour, he gave up and came back upstairs. I was sleeping. It outraged him that I could fall asleep under such circumstances. He walked over to the clock that I had set, picked it up, and tossed it out the large bay window onto the front lawn. He crawled into bed feeling somewhat better.

The next morning, he awoke to the bright sun pouring in through the south-facing window. It was around ten A.M. I was gone: the bedside clock hadn't been there to wake me, but my biological clock had.

Rob spent the better part of that fall in turmoil over my

unwillingness to commit more time to the relationship and my inability to open up about what I was thinking and feeling. Rob finally gave up in mid-November. Tom Keller, a college friend of his, had been sharing a flat in Rosslyn, across the Potomac from D.C., with a man named Michel. When Rob learned that Tom was vacating his room, he decided to take it. So one week before Thanksgiving, while I was at work, Rob packed his clothes, furniture, pictures, and record albums and cleared out. The only large object remaining in the place was my piano. When I got home that evening, I found a note on top of the piano reading, ''I give up. Sleep with the farm bill instead.''

I was deeply upset, but, as always, kept my feelings in check. The next day I called Rob at his office and calmly asked him to join me for dinner, suggesting that we could discuss everything then. Rob agreed. That evening, I was still calm. Rob was irked at this: plainly he had hoped I would be angry, or hurt, or at least annoyed. After all, Thanksgiving was only a week away and I had invited a couple of guests—Shari's mother, Ethel, and my then chief of staff, John Frank—for a holiday dinner. And Rob had taken all his furniture.

Yet I behaved as if I were unperturbed. If we couldn't make our relationship work, I told Rob, we could still be friends. Perhaps, I said, we had rushed into a commitment; if we put some distance between us for a while, things might be easier and might work out in the end. Rob took all this reasonably well, and when I drove him back to Rosslyn that night, he invited me up to meet Michel and see the apartment. As it turned out, Michel wasn't there, and I didn't leave until sunrise.

Over the next few days, Rob and I talked occasionally but we did not see each other. On Thanksgiving, Rob came by as promised and told me he was amazed to see how well I had pulled the dinner and the place together. Having expected metal folding chairs and turkey TV dinners, Rob was impressed that, while carrying on my professional duties, I had also managed to find time to look through cookbooks, put together a dinner menu, shop for ingredients, cook, and even buy a couch and chairs for my guests.

In spite of our separation, Rob and I both enjoyed the occasion. Afterwards we cleaned up and avoided discussing our relationship problems. Neither of us wanted to know what the other was doing outside of work.

That weekend we drove up into the Blue Ridge Mountains to look at a house on which Rob was working. Outside the pressure cooker of Washington, we found that we were remarkably compatible. At once we hit on an idea—we should buy a piece of land, start a little "gentlemen's farm," and force ourselves to spend time with each other away from D.C. Over the next three months, we spent weekends combing the countryside for a suitable site. Finally we found it.

5

Rob has a knack for recognizing the unique potential in things that seem, well, underwhelming to me. Wanting to please him, I feigned enthusiasm for a ninety-eight-acre lot that was located forty-five minutes from D.C. As we scrambled through a hole in a barbed-wire fence, scurried through a patch of thorny vines, and climbed up a hill that seemed to rise forever, I saw his childlike excitement growing. I was out of breath as we reached the hilltop and advanced into a clearing. He laughed and said, "Look, you can see Georgia!"

Well, you couldn't really. But the view of rolling hills and pastures was unlike anything I had seen east of Pleasantville, Wisconsin. Rob was already planning where he would situate the house and where the front entrance, courtyard, and driveway would be located. We made an offer that afternoon. A week before settlement was to take place, Rob phoned me at my office and said that the lot was much smaller than we had been told. The seller claimed to have forgotten that in 1954 she had sold her bottom tract to a friend.

"So what?" I said. "We never needed ninety-eight acres anyway. Let's renegotiate the price."

But the seller refused. In fact, she tried to force us to settle at the agreed-upon amount. John Frank scotched that quickly with an effective letter detailing her legal responsibilities. In the end, she canceled the contract and returned our deposit.

While Rob and I continued to seek a rural homesite, I spent a lot of time at his Rosslyn apartment. Though Michel was always pleasant, I knew he had never bargained on two roommates. Nor had I, at thirty-five, anticipated living in a dorm. As for Rob, he couldn't bring himself to move back to South Carolina Avenue: he said it would be bad karma. I had listed the place for sale, but was trapped there until it sold. Rob, meanwhile, left Michel and rented a three-bedroom Georgetown rowhouse with Brad Smith, an Atlanta friend. When my house finally sold, I joined them there. Brad took the large front bedroom, while Rob and I occupied the rear bedrooms, one of which we slept in and the other of which we used for guests.

It soon became clear that Brad and I didn't share the same domestic priorities. We were Felix and Oscar: I cleaned obsessively, while Brad washed dishes and clothes once a week. He even hung laundry out the window to dry! As a result, the place often looked more like an eyesore than an elegant Georgetown residence. Often, when I was home on a free night hoping for some peace and quiet, Brad would invite ten or twelve people over for dinner. The friction between us grew. I found more things to do around the office. Rob and I increasingly had dinner at restaurants.

Yet despite the household tensions, we had happy, harmonious times that summer. We went to Rehoboth Beach frequently with Matt and John. And as Rob grew more interested in my career, we talked increasingly about politics. Though we rarely agreed, our discussions gave each of us insight into the other's values, experiences, and thought processes.

That fall we spent several weekends driving around the foothills of the Blue Ridge Mountains. On those excursions, we talked at length about the possibility of buying a home in the country. These conversations excited us and made us feel a taste of the closeness and harmony that we sought, but nothing came of them: when Monday rolled around, we would inevitably go our separate ways, only to reunite on Friday.

Yet as the fall wore on, the joys of those weekend escapes were outweighed increasingly by my dread of the situation at home. Although I didn't complain about it, the Felix and Oscar situation was steadily wearing me down. Brad got on my nerves—and the fact that he didn't get on Rob's nerves *also* got on my nerves.

Deep down, I now realize, I was filled with hostility toward Rob for getting me into a situation that I felt was beneath my dignity. And Rob knew something was up: as the autumn progressed, he found that more and more often, when he phoned me at my office or on the House floor, I seemed distracted, distant.

Rob had looked forward that year to preparing a big Thanksgiving dinner for several friends. In fact, he got so involved in planning the meal, the guest list, and the place settings that he didn't stop to notice whether I was enthusiastic at all about the holiday preparations. I wasn't. I love our Thanksgivings with our friends, but for me that particular Thanksgiving was missing the kind of pleasant, relaxed interaction that I cherish. Frankly, I was just too agitated by our whole domestic situation to enjoy myself.

The day came. Rob set the table for twelve and arranged the flowers that fanned out over the table like a spreading oak tree. Our guests arrived, and after a convivial cocktail hour he served the meal. It was, by all indications, a great success. Afterwards he cleared the dishes, which I washed while he set up for the twenty or so additional guests who had been invited for dessert and after-dinner drinks.

It was twelve-thirty or so when Rob and I finally said good night to our friends. He had had a wonderful time. But when he turned to discuss it with me, I wasn't there. He found me in the kitchen, on the phone with my brother Scott, with whose family I had arranged to spend the weekend. While I laughed with Scott, Rob gathered glasses from the dining room, emptied ashtrays, and took down the bar. "It suddenly occurred to me," he later observed, "that this was the first time all day that I'd heard the sound of your laughter."

The next morning I was packing for my trip when he woke up and looked at me with a look of befuddlement.

"Steve," he asked, "what on earth are you doing?"

"I'm packing for my trip to California."

"Your *what* to *where?*"

"My trip to California. I told you about it, Rob."

"You did not."

"Yes, I did," I said in a level voice. "I guess you forgot about it. I'm spending the weekend with Scott's family and I'm also speaking at the National Milk Producers' Convention."

"Well, this is the first *I've* heard of it."

"It's been planned for a long time," I replied as I slammed the suitcase shut, "and I know I told you."

The expression on Rob's face vividly communicated his anger, confusion, and dismay.

I returned from California on Tuesday evening having done a lot of thinking. Our domestic situation, I had decided, was unbearable. I had to make a change—and I needed to share my decision with Rob as soon as possible.

Yet when I got home I found the house dark and quiet. Rob, I guessed (correctly, as it turned out), had met Glenn and Charles for happy hour and had then gone on with them to dinner. *All right*, I told myself, *I'll talk to him soon enough.* While I waited, I carefully unpacked my bags, then put on my pajamas, took some legislative papers out of my briefcase, and started reading them in bed.

Rob finally came home at about ten. Entering the bedroom, he looked at me with surprise. Not because I was home, but because I wasn't usually in bed so early.

Well, the moment had come. It was not an easy one, and I had no idea how he would react. "Rob," I said in a flat, matter-of-fact voice as he approached the bed, "I think we should start sleeping in separate beds."

Rob looked astonished. Clearly, he couldn't believe what he was hearing. He looked into my eyes as if he were looking into the eyes of a hostile stranger—someone who was hostile to him for reasons he simply couldn't fathom.

"Why?" he asked in a voice that was measured, yet edged with anxiety.

I shook my head. "Not now," I said with a practiced calm. "I'm tired. I'd rather discuss it later. Maybe over dinner Friday, if I'm in town."

I put down my papers, rolled over, and went to sleep. And Rob moved into the guest room.

That week passed without incident. Every night I came home late and went straight to bed. Rob, I know, felt threatened and hurt, but didn't want to confront me. Every night, instead of sitting home alone, he joined Glenn and Charles for a movie or dinner and drinks. He didn't tell them about his problem with me. Every night he would drive back home at about eleven with a knot in his stomach, worried that I wouldn't be there, and every night he would breathe a sigh of relief when he saw my black Chevy Blazer parked at the curb. When he got inside, we didn't say hello to each other, didn't even make eye contact. Eventually I would go upstairs to my bedroom—the room that had been *our* bedroom—and read a book in bed. After a while he would join me, and sit silently at the foot of the bed until I looked up from my book. "What's up?" I would finally ask, trying to be as matter-of-fact as possible. And we would have a superficial exchange about the day's events.

Rob couldn't figure out what on earth was wrong. He had been over the possibilities in his head a hundred times. Had I met someone else? Had something bad happened at the office? Was some family member sick? Or, God forbid, was I sick? One evening at the foot of my bed, when his patience had reached its limit and his imagination had run out of control, he said, "Will you please tell me what's going on?"

I didn't answer. I felt awful for subjecting him to this silent treatment, but I genuinely couldn't help it. In all my life up till then, I had never learned the words for what I was feeling. What could I say to him to make him understand a complex, murky set of feelings that I couldn't really understand myself?

Part of what I was feeling, I can say with certainty, was sheer anger at our domestic situation: after having worked long and hard to build a career that I was proud of, I absolutely hated living in this sloppy excuse for a freshman dorm. But there was something more. These past few years with Rob had been my first and only experience of living in a relationship with another man—and over that time I had come to realize, with increasing clarity, that if *this* was what the "gay lifestyle" was all about, I wanted no part of it!

What did I want? That was easy: I wanted a *home*. I wanted a place that I could be proud of, a place where I could feel safe and secure, a place to which I could come home at night after a hard day's work and relax in the company of my loved ones. What I didn't want was this chaotic house, with its piles of dirty laundry and stacks of unwashed dishes and hordes of unexpected raucous guests showing up at all hours. I hated it, and I resented Rob for getting me into it. He had talked to me about how he wanted a home, too; yet he seemed perfectly content with this zoo we were living in.

At the same time I felt guilty for resenting him. For all he was doing, after all, was living the way he'd lived at college. He was in his early twenties and full of energy, able to put in a crushing day of work and then spend the evening painting the town red. That was fine for him; it wasn't what I wanted at all.

Yet I couldn't bring myself to say any of this to him. I couldn't. Every Norwegian bone in me rebelled against it. And so, when he asked me to tell him what was going on, I rolled over in bed, turned out the lamp, and settled in to fall asleep.

That's when Rob went berserk. He still doesn't remember it. He says—I have no reason not to believe him—that his memory of the next five or six minutes was blocked out immediately afterwards and has never been fully recovered. Suffice it to say that he became physically violent and that I raced from the house in genuine fear. Afterward, when his rage had abated and he paced numbly through the debris in my bedroom, he noticed that the mattress was half on the bed and half against the wall.

He waited up for me. I came back hours later, still deeply upset. He apologized for what he had done.

"Leave me alone," I said firmly. "If you touch me again, I'll go."

Weeks passed. Soon the Christmas season was upon us. There were many reasons for us to be happy, and to some of our friends and colleagues it may have looked as if we were. Both our jobs were going well. Several light dustings of snow had left Georgetown looking absolutely beautiful. It was very pleasant to walk to the market in the cold, crisp air, and then return home and sit in the cozy living room with its fireplace and antique pine floor.

But we weren't happy. We were still not speaking. Knowing that he could only make matters worse by pushing me for answers, Rob concentrated on decorating the house for the holidays. I, meanwhile, concentrated on my work and, in dread of causing conflict, kept my frustration and torment to myself.

Rob and I didn't really celebrate Christmas that year, but we did attend several friends' parties. Rob was struck by my behavior at them. However distant I was from him at home, at these parties I was invariably polite and gracious. I guess it was the first time he realized quite how self-disciplined I had learned to be during my years in politics; you can't stay in Congress for long, after all, if you're unable to keep the whole world from knowing when you've been having a bad day. Milling among our friends, Rob and I would exchange smiles and jokes; on the way home, we would even drop into a bar and laugh over a nightcap. Rob later told me, "It was as if you were doing an imitation of your former self."

He loved the easy, friendly way we related to each other during those party and barroom interludes. Yet once we returned home, my distance always snapped right back into place. Long after I went to sleep, on those December nights, he would lie alone in his bed and stare for hours at the shadows on the ceiling, wondering what to do about me. I knew that he was wondering and worrying, and in addition to being irritated at our domestic arrangements and unhappy with the "gay lifestyle" as manifested itself in our life together, I was tormented by guilt over everything I was putting Rob through.

It was during one of those pleasant post-party interludes that a young guy came over to us in Badlands and introduced himself as Franklin Maphis. Rob was wearing a tight blue Puma tank top, and Franklin, who would soon become one of our best friends, began to ask deliberately provocative questions like, "Does that Puma shirt come with biceps? If I put that shirt on, would my chest look like that, too?"

This black-haired kid with penetrating black eyes made no secret of his attraction to Rob. There was no reason why he should have: since Rob and I weren't wearing rings at the time, Franklin had no way of knowing we were a couple (and at the time, frankly, Rob wasn't too sure that we still *were* one). When we told him we were together, Franklin laughed and accused me of being Rob's father. The accusation wasn't as outrageous as it sounds: I was already prematurely gray and very serious in my demeanor, whereas Rob was an unusually lively twenty-six.

As for Franklin, he was obviously even younger than Rob. I was immediately uncomfortable with that. "He's a really nice guy," I said to Rob at one point, "but what's he doing in a bar?" Franklin, as it turned out, was only eighteen and still in high school.

We soon learned that Franklin, a vegetarian, had a great interest in animals and a passionate devotion to animal-rights activism—which made him a pretty unusual friend for me, the ranking Republican on the Dairy and Livestock Committee, whose job it was to get people to eat meat, and lots of it! Franklin's devotion to his cause was strong and serious, though his expression of it could take unusual, even amusing forms. One Friday night not long after we met, Franklin phoned Rob and asked if they could get together. I was in Wisconsin, so Rob agreed to meet Franklin for dinner and drinks. After a meal in a Dupont Circle restaurant, Rob asked Franklin which bar he wanted to go to. Rob mentioned a place around the corner called the Frat House. Franklin hemmed and hawed and made excuses, then said he wasn't interested in going there. When Rob asked why, Franklin hesitantly admitted that, well, he *couldn't* go there.

Some weeks earlier, he explained, he had gone to the Frat House and had been incensed at the sight of deer trophies mounted on the wall over the dance floor. He had somehow managed to pull the trophies off the wall, one by one. Eventually most of the deer heads were off the wall and on the dance floor, being swung around animatedly by inebriated dancers. It took quite a while for the management to figure out what was going on. They finally caught Franklin red-handed as he hung in midair from the largest of the trophies, trying in vain to pry it from the wall. He was asked to leave and never come back. That story was vintage Franklin—at once outrageous and well meaning.

On the Saturday before Christmas, I flew out to Wisconsin to spend the holidays with my family. That night Washington was ablaze with glamorous parties. Rob, who had been invited to two or three of them, didn't go to any: he didn't feel terribly festive. Instead, as I later learned, he tidied up the house, which really did look beautiful when everything was in order, and invited friends over to exchange gifts—a woman from his office named Pam; Glenn, who brought with him a funny, aggressive guy named Randy Latimer, whom he was dating; and Charles, who had already been to one party that evening and had another lined up for later. Rob later told me that after the guys left at eleven-thirty, he and Pam sat by the fire on an old camelback sofa, sipping port, and she listened sympathetically as he told her about the difficulties he was going through with me. She was lonely, too, and eventually she curled up against him and they sat there for hours, in the glow of the Christmas tree, in a silence that was broken only by the occasional sound of carolers in the street, the chime of the university bell tower, and the crackle of a burning ember on the fire. Together they dozed off to sleep in the toasty warmth of the yellow room.

Rob spent Christmas and New Year's in Pensacola with his family, never calling me but constantly checking for phone messages from me. There were none. It's not that I wasn't thinking about him: on the contrary, during those days in Wisconsin I thought long and hard about my life with Rob and came to the conclusion that I had let a sorry situation drag on long enough. I decided that I absolutely had to make a radical change in my life. And it was clear what that change had to be. Having settled on this decision, I didn't hesitate to implement it. No sooner had Rob and I sat down to our first dinner together after returning to Washington than I broached the subject of the uncomfortable distance between us that had existed for months.

My words were clear and unapologetic. "I've concluded," I said, "that neither of us is happy. You're unhappy with my inability to involve myself personally in this relationship. I can never do enough to please you in that regard. For my part, I'm unhappy with the whole gay thing. I feel I've given it a fair shake. While I want to remain friends with you, I've decided to pursue a more conventional relationship with a woman."

Rob was flabbergasted.

"Rob," I went on, "the reason I've been distant from you during the last few months is that I can't stand living here. I can't stand the tension in this house, and the tension it creates inside me. It's unbearable. I'm not living like a third-term member of Congress, I'm living like a junior in college. This is not a home, it's a poor excuse for a fraternity house.

"My parents taught me that your home is your castle. Well, I would be embarrassed to have my parents walk into this place. The kitchen is so dirty it should be condemned by the health authorities. There are clothes hanging out the front windows. There's no home life. Instead of coming back here after work to cook a nice meal and relax, we avoid this place like the plague. Yes, personal relationships are important to me. But domestic tranquillity is, too.

"I've taken many risks in my political career. And I'm willing to risk my whole career for a personal and home life that has meaning. And this life we're living just has no meaning. *I don't like it.* Maybe I can't find total happiness with a woman. But I haven't found it here, either. I do know that with the right woman I can have a comfortable public social life. I do know that a woman would enhance, not endanger, my political career, though that's far from the most important consideration for me. And I know that a woman can give me a home I want to go to at night.

"Now I acknowledge," I went on, "that I may not be able to carry out all aspects of a heterosexual relationship as satisfactorily as a straight guy might. But I do think there are millions of women out there who would respect the kind of love that I would be able to give. What's more, I want to be a father. I want to have a family like the family I grew up in, and raise them in a house like the one I grew up in. It seems to me now that to be able to do that would bring much more meaning to my life than any gay relationship could."

Plainly, Rob was stunned by my words. He had thought my attempts to "go straight" were a thing of the past. Struggling to gather his thoughts and to restrain his emotions, he talked to me in a dispassionate tone about the moral implications of what I was suggesting. Wouldn't it be dishonest, he asked, for me to pretend to be straight and marry some poor woman? It was a good question—but my only response was to reiterate that I was frustrated with our relationship.

Then I went to bed.

Rob could hardly stick around after that. He left in March. His ex-roommate Michel had moved from Virginia to a rowhouse a couple of blocks from us in Georgetown. Rob had arranged for Glenn to take Michel's second bedroom, but since

Glenn had just decided to move in with Charles, Rob snapped up Michel's second bedroom for himself.

On the day Rob moved, Franklin called him at his office to see if he was free for dinner. Franklin had no idea that Rob and I were having problems, and when he called about dinner Rob didn't tell him that we were separating, only that he couldn't go out because he was moving and had to finish packing.

That night, Franklin dropped by unexpectedly to offer his help. He was in his usual upbeat mood when Rob, somber and preoccupied with the unhappy task ahead, answered the door; I was upstairs, reading in bed. Accepting Franklin's offer, Rob explained which boxes had to be filled and what went where, and returned to the kitchen.

When he had finished packing a box or two, Franklin skipped upstairs to use the bathroom. On the way, he popped his head into my room to say hello. He saw me reading in bed. The room was neat. No boxes. No newsprint stacked for wrapping. "Hi," he chirped. I didn't respond; I was in no mood for this kid's high sprits. Franklin persevered. "Ya know," he said, "from the looks of things you'd best get your little fanny out of that bed before Rob catches you reading. He's got most of the downstairs packed. You have a long way to go!"

I seethed at this buoyant, happy chatter, but said nothing.

"You want me to help you?" Franklin asked me. "I'm at your service!"

At that point, summoning all the self-control I could muster, I looked up from my book and said evenly, "I'm not going anywhere, Franklin. But thanks for all the help."

Franklin stumbled. "But Rob is down—I mean he told me that—you mean you're *staying*?"

"The relationship's not working," I said calmly. "I'll be moving out in May when the lease expires."

Thrown by this news, Franklin backed away and stalked back into the kitchen. "Well, I sure made a fool of myself!" he told Rob, who apologized for not having told him that we were breaking up. Franklin expressed his condolences and resumed helping; a minute or two later he was once again chipper and chatty.

ROB

Later that night, Randy Latimer dropped by to help me transport a few boxes in his huge late-model Delta 88. Randy, the abrasive, outrageous guy whom Glenn had brought with him to dinner at Christmastime while Steve was in Wisconsin, was no longer dating Glenn, though they had remained good friends. He had also become a good friend of mine.

I spent the rest of that night alone, listening over and over to Elton John's "Sorry Is the Hardest Word" as I unpacked my things in the new house. One line still lingers in my head as if it were yesterday: "What've I got to do to make you love me?"

What indeed? It was one thing to lose one's love to another guy. But I felt I had lost Steve to an even more formidable opponent: his social conditioning. I had been bested by a persistent little voice inside him saying that our love was wrong and that a relationship between two men could never be equal to a marriage between man and a woman.

To this day, Steve continues to maintain that his discomfort with our life in Georgetown was based on the mess Brad was making. Not true. The house, which had recently been renovated, was quite exquisite, and Brad's mess was pretty much limited to his own room.

For the next two months Steve and I remained out of touch and tried not to think about each other. By day each of us distracted himself with work and fought off the temptation to phone the other; by night Steve would continue to work, while I read or drew or got together with Charles or Glenn and Randy. Every night, on my way home, I drove by our old house in which Steve was still living. Occasionally, instead of going to my new place, I would park near the dark house where Steve was sleeping, take out my old key, let myself in, and walk quietly up the creaky stairs to Steve's bedroom. There, unbeknownst to him, I would sit motionless at the foot of his bed, watching him sleep in the blue glow of the digital alarm clock. Some nights I stayed till dawn, when I crept out, bleary-eyed, without his knowing that I'd ever been there.

At one point during our estrangement Matt and John invited me to dinner. It would, they said, just be the three of us. I casually told them that I wanted to introduce them to a new friend, and asked if I could bring Randy. They said yes. They hadn't met Randy and were not prepared for his strident, off-the-wall sense of humor or for the closeness that had developed between him and me. So close were the two of us, indeed, that Matt and John came to the conclusion that we were dating. I later learned that friends all over town had whispered: "Rob is seeing this guy Randy. Very obnoxious!" I also learned that Matt and John had been appalled that I would bring my "new boyfriend" to dinner at their house so soon after breaking up with Steve. They were, after all, among Steve's closest friends. Randy, for his part, was thrilled with the controversy.

And then it was spring. On Mother's Day, which that year fell on Steve's thirty-sixth birthday, I had brunch with some friends. Afterwards, unable to shake off thoughts of Steve, I felt the need to touch base. I wanted to know what was going on in his life. Impulsively, I drove to Steve's house, walked up to his door, and knocked.

He came to the door, and beamed joyfully at the sight of me. I smiled back and, on the spur of the moment, made up a lame pretext for being there. "Um, I just came by to see if there's any mail for me," I said.

"None," he said, his voice quavering.

"Uh," I offered tentatively, "happy birthday."

"Thank you. Do you want to come in?"

"Sure. Thanks."

We chatted, navigating our way around the danger zones.

"Well," I finally asked, "what are you doing for your birthday?"

I wasn't sure I wanted to know the answer. I half feared that Steve was so alone now that he hadn't made plans at all. But I also half feared that he *wasn't* alone, and that he had filled his schedule for the day.

Tears began to roll down his cheeks. "I'm not doing anything," he choked out.

"Do you mean to tell me," I demanded incredulously, "that you haven't planned anything—no brunch, no dinner, no nothing?"

"No."

"Nobody," I said, "is throwing you a party?"

"No."

"I can't believe this!" I said. To me, a birthday without a party is like a day without sunshine. "It's your birthday, and you haven't even called anybody to do something!"

He shrugged. "If somebody wants to call me to do something, that's fine. If not, that's fine too."

I looked at him, my lingering anger mixed with a pang of compassion. "Can you be ready for dinner at six o'clock?" I asked. He nodded. "Okay," I said. "I'll make reservations."

I left. Both of us spent the afternoon in a state of both enthusiasm and trepidation.

I made reservations at Le Lion d'Or, which had been a favorite meeting place of ours and seemed the perfect setting for this unexpected reunion. Over dinner that night, I tried not to push Steve too far. But by the same token I was determined not to leave the place without a better understanding of where he was now, psychologically, and of the mental processes that had led him there. If there was any chance of working things out between us, I wanted to do it. And so, I realized, did Steve.

Over dinner, Steve acknowledged that he was still having a difficult time coming to terms with being gay. He also acknowledged that he had missed me immensely. "I don't actually mind being gay," he said. "What I mind is not being straight. Which is to say, I'm still unwilling to accept that I'll never have children."

Steve and I had already had that argument. He felt strongly that until the notion of gay parents became more accepted by society, it wasn't a good idea for gay people to raise children, because it was the kids who would suffer most from society's prejudice. I disagreed, arguing that the idea of gay parents wouldn't become more accepted by society *until* more and more gay people raised children.

"But that's not the whole problem," he said. "I'm also concerned about my place in the Republican party. How far can I go in making a whole and honest life for myself without destroying my political career?'' Not until he and I had moved in together, he explained, had he come to realize how much he was giving up, how much he was taking on, and how great a distance he would have to travel every day between the world he lived in with me and the one he inhabited as a Republican member of Congress for rural Wisconsin. It had never once entered my mind to think about all this.

Steve hastened to point out, however, that these difficulties were secondary. For him, the bottom line was that he wanted a home and family—and deep down he still couldn't believe that he would be able to have anything worthy of being described by those words in a gay relationship.

When you come right down to it, the struggles we went through in those first years were about my attempt to get Steve to recognize that two men or two women who love each other could be much more to each other than bedmates—that they could be, in every sense of the word, family, and could create something that was very much a home.

So Rob and I moved back in together. Because I longed to live in a clean place that we wouldn't have to share with anybody, I bought a small, characterless new condominium in Rosslyn, Virginia, that Rob sarcastically called the "walk-out basement." The bedrooms were at street level; on the floor below, opening onto the backyard, were the living room, dining room, and kitchen. In later years, as I've watched Rob design and build one graceful, people-friendly home after another, I laugh at the thought of his living in that antiseptic, vinyl-ridden place. Then again, it was, I think, the unpleasantness of that condo that impelled Rob to create a *real* home for us.

Two months later, in August, a realtor mentioned a quarter-acre lot on Hitt Avenue in McLean, Virginia, that was priced considerably lower than any lot Rob had looked at. Rob drove over to inspect it.

Some people have always assumed that with our combined incomes, housing shouldn't pose a financial problem for Rob and me. But it's very expensive to live in the Washington area, where an undeveloped suburban lot can easily cost as much as a medium-sized home in, say, small-town Wisconsin. That is why Rob considered the lot in McLean such a find, even though it was flat and covered with vines. Yes, there was a dilapidated house next door; yes, the back of the lot bordered Old Dominion Drive, a major artery. But Rob saw promise in it, and was already beginning to picture the house he would build on it.

When he showed the site to me a couple of days later, I was not impressed. Nonetheless, deferring to his judgment and enthusiasm, I agreed that we should make an offer. We did so the following day, and it was accepted on the spot. Our gay friends couldn't believe that we would leave the "comfort zone" of Washington for McLean. "McLean!" they would exclaim. "Land of big tract houses and fag bashers!" Rob countered that the gay ghetto of D.C. was nothing but a big closet in which gay men and lesbians huddled together, excluding themselves from the rest of society. He was more than willing to risk the venture into the suburbs in order to find, as he put it, a "place."

We celebrated Thanksgiving that year in the condo. Franklin, who dropped by the night before with a friend, Gabriel Nossoviych, laughed about the long makeshift table that we had squeezed into the room, covered with a tablecloth, and set with flowers, china, and candles. "It's fabulous, guys," he said, "now you've *really* made this room look like a basement." Gabriel agreed. It was clear that the two of them had struck up quite a friendship, and that Franklin had something of a crush on Gabriel. And why not? In his early twenties, Gabriel had come to Washington from his native Argentina to study at Georgetown. He was bright and poised, and had a charming hint of an accent.

The following day Glenn brought two gay men with him to dinner. One was a pastor, the other a schoolteacher. Both kept their private lives secret in the small town they lived in. The pastor was married with two children; the teacher, thirty-eight years old, still lived with his mother and bragged about their matching Cadillacs. Both men had arranged their lives in such a way that they could live in the town in which they had grown up; yet they had done so, as countless gay men and lesbians do, at an immense price. Both had sacrificed truth, wholeness, integrity—and this sacrifice had clearly taken its toll. For Rob and me, the marks of pain and loneliness that they could not wipe from their faces were haunting reminders of what small-town America still tends to demand of gay people who wish to live as a part of it.

Aside from the memory of those two men, that Thanksgiving exists in memory as a series of happy snapshots of our friends. Glenn made corn pudding and bread pudding from his mother's recipes and was thrilled at his success. Randy made a splash with a tasteless tartan plaid jacket that made him look as if he was on his way to play golf, and that Glenn and Charles made merciless fun of. Kris Deininger, dressed to the nines, met Gabriel for the first time that evening and they hit it off marvelously, spending most of the evening chatting cozily with each other.

The dinner, in short, was a success, in spite of the cramped, unpalatable venue. When the last guest had left at one-thirty, Rob closed the door and asked me, "Better than last Thanksgiving?" I paused and reflected on the previous year of emotional upheaval and hugged him. I said, "Let's go to sleep. I promise I'm not going anywhere this weekend."

Finally everything seemed to be moving along smoothly and happily for Rob and me. Then we stepped into a nightmare.

That year Randy decided to throw a Christmas party. This was an unusual thing for him to do; in fact, he's never thrown one since. He invited his parents, his siblings, and an assortment of friends, both straight and gay. When we arrived at his house in Annandale, Virginia, we meandered through the crowd of his friends, most of them strangers to us, and went to his bedroom, where Rob figured we would find Glenn and Charles.

In fact we found several of our friends in the bedroom, though Glenn and Charles were nowhere to be seen. Noting that the bathroom door was slightly open and that the light was on, Rob assumed that they might be in there, fussing in front of the mirror. So he knocked on the door, opened it, and saw a cluster of familiar faces. While I chatted in the master bedroom with friends of Glenn's, Rob squeezed into the tiny bathroom, prepared for the usual jokes and laughter and general silliness that invariably surrounded Glenn and Charles.

It wasn't until we were in the car on our way home that Rob, weeping, told me what had happened. The tone in the bathroom, he said, had been deadly serious. Walking in, he had seen Glenn at the mirror, looking at himself, grim-faced. Charles was beside him. He and several others were focused on Glenn's face, which was covered with large red splotches of the sort that you sometimes see on old alcoholics. Glenn had apparently been trying unsuccessfully to cover them with various substances that he had found in Randy's medicine cabinet.

Rob was immediately concerned. Turning, Glenn saw him and gauged his expression. Backing away from the mirror, Glenn motioned Rob over to the small niche where the toilet was located. Glenn had tears in his eyes as he stood inches from Rob's face and told him that he had just gotten back the results of an AIDS test. He was HIV-positive.

In fact, as Rob didn't learn until several years later, Glenn lied to him that night. He had actually been tested over a year earlier, when he had been dating Randy. He had told Randy of his diagnosis immediately, out of consideration for him as a sex partner, but had not told Rob because he worried that Rob would think less of him for it. Only now, with his face covered in blotches, did Glenn feel he could no longer hide the truth.

When faced with difficult emotional situations, I'm like my mother: I project firmness, serenity, a sense of control. Not Rob. When Glenn revealed his diagnosis, Rob responded with a display of self-defensive emotion that apparently looked to Glenn like anger. "I'm sorry," Glenn said, his expression scared and helpless. (At the time, this remark was inexplicable; not until years later did Rob realize that Glenn had been apologizing for keeping his diagnosis secret for so long.) Rob hugged Glenn tightly and struggled to conceal his own anguish and pull himself together.

Like me, Rob knew very little about AIDS at the time, but he did know that an HIV-positive diagnosis didn't necessarily mean that death was imminent. On the contrary, he figured naively that since the epidemic was in its eighth year, a cure must surely be around the corner. There must be some equivalent of insulin in the wings, a handy cure-all waiting to be stumbled upon at any moment by the armies of brilliant researchers who were working day and night on the problem.

As he pulled away from Glenn and wiped his eyes with the heel of his hand, Rob felt his protective instincts kicking in. Forcing a grin, he filed away the bigger issue for the time being and focused on doing something at once about Glenn's scaly, raw blemishes. "Stay calm," he told Glenn. "I saw Katherine out there when I was coming in."

Katherine, a woman who occasionally dated one of Randy's roommates, always wore several layers of base makeup, which produced something of a Kabuki-mask effect. In any event, Rob just knew that she would have enough base makeup on her to conceal Glenn's blemishes. Rob told Glenn that he would grab a vodka tonic for Glenn and a scotch for himself, borrow Katherine's makeup, and return to the bathroom with a sure-fire remedy—a cosmetics first-aid kit, as it were.

Sure enough, Katherine turned out to have a good supply of makeup in her purse, and was more than happy to let Rob have some. Rob and Glenn spent the next thirty minutes in the bathroom, downing two stiff drinks apiece and applying the stuff to his face, plus a "bronzer" from the medicine cabinet to make him look tanned. By the time they joined me and the others, they were tipsy enough to be distracted from the horror of Glenn's diagnosis and to carry on with their usual high spirits. Rob made it through that party, in fact, without displaying his true emotions at all.

When he tearfully blurted out the truth in the car, however, I was shocked. During the long ride back home on the Beltway, Rob talked the situation out, trying to come up with a logical course of action. Glenn was not good at caring for himself, and Rob's first instinct was to take over. First, he decided, we would learn the names of the best AIDS specialists in D.C. We would find out what were the best medications for him and would look into his insurance situation. Rob also vowed to me that he would assume the responsibility of getting Glenn to lay off the alcohol.

That winter Glenn's T-cell count dropped to a dangerous low. So did his weight. His doctor placed him on AZT. Glenn soon discovered the drug's awful side effects, mainly nausea and diarrhea. By March he had grown accustomed to both. He also stabilized, regaining some of the weight he had lost.

In the meantime, Rob and I went to settlement on the Hitt Avenue lot, and we started to build our first home. It wasn't a large place: three bedrooms, three baths, living room, dining room, and kitchen. Because the rooms were large and open, however, the shingle-style house promised to be great for entertaining. As Rob pointed out, the plan was entirely modern and yet the windows, the trim, the antique pine floors, and other details helped create the impression that it was quite old.

On a chilly afternoon in February 1988, we were surveying the freshly excavated site when a couple from across the street walked over and introduced themselves. Gloria Freund was short and wore an oversized sweatshirt that made her look plump; Gary Aztalos was tall and handsome, with a quiet demeanor. They had just finished renovating their 1920s Queen Anne house, and invited us to come over and take a look when we were finished inspecting our own property. They added that they'd like to hear all about the plans for our house. After they left, Rob rolled his eyes, grumbled about nosy neighbors making trouble during construction, and insisted that I say as little as possible to them.

To our surprise, when we went over to Gloria and Gary's house, we found ourselves warming up to them quickly. They told us about their backgrounds: she was Jewish and had grown up—believe it or not—on a dairy farm in Connecticut;

he was Catholic and had been raised in Philadelphia. They had met years ago in the navy, and had been married for eight or nine years. She was now a Mideast expert at the Defense Intelligence Agency; he worked for a defense engineering contractor (yet, curiously enough, griped about the high defense budget that paid his handsome salary). They gave us a tour of their house, which was clean and tidy, except for two things. First, there was a vacuum cleaner sitting in the exact center of the family room. Gloria laughed and explained that it was new, they had paid over a hundred dollars for it, and she thought it deserved to be on display until the newness wore off. Second, we found in their bright pink master suite a pile of clothes, obviously Gloria's, stacked at least four feet high. Gary apologized. Gloria explained that she enjoyed looking at her clothes. "They don't enjoy being in a closet," she said with a grin.

We left well after dark. As we passed the large black-and-white plywood cows in their front yard, Rob said, "She is a *kook*." I agreed. But we were both fascinated by her.

During the seven months that it took us to finish the house, Gary and Gloria became great friends, and in the ensuing years we became inseparable. We had meals together, vacationed together, and took long walks together through the neighborhood. Every spring and summer, the four of us would tend the garden belonging to Bill Waugh, the old man who lived in the dilapidated house next door. I didn't always enjoy tilling, weeding, and planting vegetables on humid, gnat-infested summer mornings, but I always took part. Thrilled by our efforts, the frail but stylish Mr. Waugh would come striding out of the house in polyester checked slacks, a striped shirt, and a blazer, his fingers clutching a filterless Camel, and point out areas of the garden that needed particular attention.

By March, the house was well underway. At the same time, the residential design firm for which Rob had been working as a manager decided abruptly to close his division. He was relatively calm about this turn of events and looked upon it as an opportunity to work firsthand on the house we were building. He also kidded around about opening his own construction firm. For the balance of the summer, he spent his time at the site with carpenters, plumbers, and electricians. We became the painters and, ultimately, the landscapers as well.

That year also saw my involvement in the 1988 presidential election campaign. Bob Dole had decided to run for president, and my work with him on the Farm Bill of 1985 and the Americans with Disabilities Act had produced a mutual trust and respect that made it easy for me to decide to support him. I had no doubt that Dole, of all the Republican candidates, would make the best president; his extraordinary knowledge of agriculture would certainly make him the best chief executive for western Wisconsin.

Since most of my colleagues supported George Bush in the primaries, my support for Dole meant that I had a chance to be a much bigger player in the campaign that I would have had otherwise. Dole asked me to be one of the two co-chairs of his group of congressional supporters, as well as the honorary co-chair of his campaign in Wisconsin. During the winter I traveled around the country and gave many speeches in support of Dole. But as it turned out, the Dole campaign didn't last long. The New Hampshire primary results in March were disappointing, and Dole and his people had to decide whether to continue the campaign or throw in the towel.

The weekend after that primary we brought Dole out to western Wisconsin. I put together a whirlwind schedule: a breakfast speech on agriculture in Amery, an appearance at a technical college in Eau Claire, and finally an address at a large auditorium in La Crosse. It was a great day for Dole, with big and enthusiastic crowds. I remember that when we walked into the hall in La Crosse to the roar of hundreds of people, one of the Dole campaign directors looked at me and said, "You guys are unbelievable. It's amazing that in a week, in a rural area, you can put together three events like this and bring out so many supporters!"

When we came back to Washington, Dole had a meeting with his major donors, who were nervous because of the New Hampshire results. Dole asked that I come and speak to them. "Steve wants to talk to you," he said to the group, "about what we experienced yesterday in Wisconsin."

I talked at length about the enthusiasm that we had seen in Wisconsin. I said that if they wanted to go forward with the campaign, there was no question in my mind but that it was still extremely viable. Owing to cash problems, however, Dole's people decided not to go forward. George Bush wrapped up the nomination soon afterward.

In August, Rob and I flew to New Orleans with Kris Deininger and John Frank to see Bush nominated for the presidency. We were there when he gave his acceptance speech, in which he promised a "kinder, gentler" America and "no new taxes" and coined the phrase "a thousand points of light" as a metaphor for neighbor helping neighbor through volunteer organizations. The speech did a good job of setting Bush before us as a solid, experienced, and quietly decent public servant who, while lacking Ronald Reagan's extraordinary charisma, might well serve as a welcome agent of healing and reconciliation if elected president.

Because I was a congressman, I had been chosen as a Bush delegate. The Bush people, however, continued to be wary of me and of others who had backed Dole earlier in the year. I understood their feelings, and did my best to alleviate their suspicions and reassure them of my genuine enthusiasm for Bush's candidacy. Yet I must admit that this enthusiasm was rather challenged when he announced his choice of Senator Dan Quayle of Indiana as his running mate.

I wasn't entirely without respect for Quayle. During his time in the Senate, he had created the widely esteemed Job Training Partnership Act, which effected dramatic changes in domestic training policy. As someone who had been involved in crafting similar legislation in the House (in the course of which I actually worked with Quayle on a limited basis), I honestly felt that he never got the credit he deserved for that program.

Yet, like virtually everyone else in the Republican party and the federal government, I still found Quayle's selection as Bush's running mate very hard to fathom. Though he was older than I, Quayle still seemed young and untested. His rather giddy response to being chosen as the vice-presidential nominee didn't enhance my confidence in him, either. He lacked *gravitas*. I told my friends, "I can't wait to read Bush's memoirs on this one. There must be something to it that I just don't understand." Trying to put the best possible spin on it, I told the members of the state press gathered in the Wisconsin hospitality suite at the hotel, "This is wonderful. It once again proves that anyone can grow up to be vice-president of the United States."

Well, that it did. But even as I said this to the reporters, I was feeling sorry for Richard Lugar, the senior senator from Indiana. I knew Lugar better than I did Quayle, and I wondered why, if Bush had wanted a Midwesterner on the ticket, he hadn't chosen Lugar, who seemed to me infinitely more presidential than Quayle.

The Quayle nomination dealt Bush a devastating blow in the media. Reporters asked: If this was an example of Bush's decision-making, did America want him running the country?

A month after the convention, on Labor Day, Rob and I moved into the house on Hitt Avenue. I hadn't realized what an extraordinary feeling it would be to take occupancy of a home that we had built ourselves. I had owned two houses before, but now, for the first time, I felt that Rob and I finally owned a home.

As we settled in, we found that the neighbors were very curious about us. That fall I was often away campaigning, but Rob was around, and he noticed that each morning at around seven-thirty a beautiful blonde would walk by, heading south, pushing an infant in a stroller and flanked by two small boys. Twenty minutes later she would pass heading in the other direction without the two older children. On occasion, standing at one of our large front windows, Rob saw her pausing to peer curiously into the house. Late that autumn, he happened to be in the front yard when the woman came along pushing the stroller. She stopped to introduce herself and her child. Her name was Linda Kosovych, her one-year-old son was Andre, and they lived two blocks away with her husband, Ostap. She was fascinated by our house, she said, and wanted a tour.

She wasn't the only person in the neighborhood who was fascinated by the house. During construction, it had drawn a good deal of enthusiastic attention. At about the time that we moved into it, Rob opened his own firm in partnership with another architect, and the Hitt Avenue house proved the perfect advertisement for his services.

In the weeks that followed their first encounter, Linda and Rob got into the habit of chatting at the curb before he left for work and after she had dropped off the two older boys, Stephan, then eight, and Danylo, five, at the nearby Catholic school. Linda was both an artist and homemaker, and spent her days juggling domestic chores and covering canvases with paint; Rob enjoyed her unconventional way of thinking, her creativity, and her independence. He guessed that she was about twenty-five. I was surprised to learn that she was in her late thirties.

As the election drew closer that fall, Rob agreed to come to Wisconsin for a taste of political campaigning. He did this very grudgingly, after I had pleaded with him for some time to at least give it a try. So he spent a day traveling with me from town to town. He took part in four different parades. In each town, while I shook hands, Rob helped my staffers hand out four-by-eight cards that had my name on one side and a recipe on the other side. One man started to hand his card back to Rob. "I never vote Republican!" he barked. "I don't either," Rob drawled. "Use the recipe on the back."

He's not exactly a born politician.

Rob later told me that he didn't know which he would hate more: walking up and down streets begging for votes or peddling his flesh. The members of my district staff weren't thrilled with his involvement, either. They didn't dare to say anything directly to me, but certain people did ask my sister Naomi to do all she could to discourage me from involving Rob any further in the local campaign. This was not an issue: Rob had had his taste of campaigning, and had no interest in repeating the experience.

A few weeks later, while I was campaigning in Wisconsin, Rob had an adventure that was more up his alley and that underscored the difference between his interests and mine. It was a happy time for him and his friends: Glenn, after his first bout with AIDS symptoms, had stabilized physically and was dating a landscaper named Justin. On the Saturday night before Halloween, just for kicks, Rob, Glenn, Charles, and Randy met at Charles's place with several other guys, had a professional makeup artist work them over, and got dressed up in full drag. None of them made particularly attractive women, but that didn't matter: they had fun getting dressed up, and even more fun poking fun at one another. When they had poked fun at one another long enough, they decided to harass the people at the drive-through window at the Burger King down the street. So they piled into Glenn's station wagon, which he had named Connie, and pulled up to the drive-in speaker. Glenn ordered for them in an unnaturally deep voice: "Yeah, we'll have eight cheeseburgers with extra pickle, large fries, and eight cups of ice."

"No tomato," Randy interrupted.

"Extra mayo!" Charles bellowed.

Then they drove around to pick up their food. When the large black woman at the window, who expected a car full of Southern boys, saw instead eight drag queens in dresses and pearls and Kabuki makeup, her eyes opened wide. For the longest time, she stared at them in utter silence. "My God almighty!" she finally breathed before gathering her composure and processing the order.

"What's the matter, honey," Glenn asked her in his Virginia twang, "ain't you ever seen a drag queen?" He told her he could pay in three-dollar bills, but she didn't get it. Neither did Charles.

I must admit that when Rob told me about that little adventure, I winced. I have no problem with drag, but I don't have any interest in it, either. But for Rob and his friends, that adventure was a happy, exuberant experience. And now, many years and tears later, when I picture them in that car at Burger King, I grin at the innocence of it all and the love that they had for one another. I know that for Rob, that memory is a glorious emblem of happier, more carefree times.

For Rob, these adventures with his friends were part of a transition. Not too long ago, he had been an undergraduate at Auburn who had partied as hard as he had studied. As he moved into his late twenties, and into the sober world of business, bills, and greater responsibility, Glenn, Randy, and Charles provided a link to his college days, answering his lingering need for youthful adventure. I knew that he was heading gradually toward a way of life more like mine—a life of long work hours and relatively sedate amusements. I knew that one night he would be too tired to stay out long after midnight, and that one morning he would wake up with a hangover. I also recognized, with gratitude, that these friends with whom I occasionally felt like a fifth wheel kept him out of trouble when I was tied up late in meetings on the Hill or spending the weekend back in the district. Thanks to them, Rob didn't have much time to meet someone else who might have been more attentive to him (though no more loyal).

In retrospect, I realize that when we moved to McLean, our lifestyle underwent a major shift. We found ourselves going to bars less often and having dinner with friends more frequently. We attended school plays and neighborhood meetings. Rob says we "mainstreamed"; I merely believe we settled down.

In any case, we became good friends with Linda and Ostap and their children. A physicist who worked on the Star Wars program, the gruff, serious, and very Catholic Ostap, a second-generation Ukrainian-American who had grown up in

New York, formed a dramatic contrast to his wife. Indeed, from the time we first met Ostap it struck us as odd that he could be so committed a Catholic and yet be married to Linda, who insisted on understanding God on her own unconventional terms. Yet the marriage seemed to work, and, as I pointed out to Rob, the contrast between Linda and Ostap didn't seem any more formidable than that between us.

At first, Ostap was suspicious of the two men down the street. While it seemed obvious to him that Rob and I were gay, his growing anxiety over Linda's friendship with us, and especially with Rob, caused him to worry that we might not really be gay—or that Rob might possibly be bisexual enough to fancy a fling with his wife. Despite these initial and unjustified concerns, Ostap accepted our friendship with Linda early on. On one rare occasion he even took part in one of our escapades. One night, after we had celebrated Linda's birthday with cake and coffee, several of us decided to go to a club called Ziegfeld's to see a drag show by Jimmy James, who does impersonations of people like Liza Minnelli and Bette Davis. At first we assumed that Ostap would beg off on the show, but to our surprise and delight he came along and enjoyed himself immensely.

Stephan, Danylo, and Andre also came to be a key part of our lives. That fall they spent weekends with us in our pool. A few days before Halloween they came to our house to carve jack-o'-lanterns with us and ten or so of our friends. We finished just before sundown, and I still remember the way little Andre's face lit up as he watched the faces on the pumpkins come to life under the darkening sky.

A few days after Halloween came Election Day. I was running for reelection, and Bush was battling Dukakis for the presidency. While I went back to Wisconsin for election night, Rob had dinner in McLean with Glenn and Justin and Charles, then sat up with them watching election returns. At three in the morning, he called me in Osseo and learned that I had been reelected.

When I returned from Wisconsin, we dove into our plans

for Thanksgiving. That year we had thirty friends over, including Glenn, Charles, Randy, and Gabriel, Gary and Gloria, several members of my staff, and old Mr. Waugh. As usual, Rob set the table, I carved the turkeys, and Randy played bartender. Before dinner, friends gathered around the piano and our friend Callista, who had come from Whitehall, Wisconsin, for an internship in my office and had stayed on as a staff member, played everything from Chopin to the Shirelles.

At one point, with the pre-dinner festivities going full blast, Randy and Gabriel were standing at the piano, competing to recall lyrics to Diana Ross tunes and being generally outrageous, when Karen, a friend of Callista's who was doing graduate work in music at the University of Maryland, stepped up to the piano, as planned, to sing Malotte's setting of ''The Lord's Prayer.'' I tapped my glass for silence. Caught up in their silliness, Randy and Gabriel kept on singing ''Stop! In the Name of Love'' over the first few notes of Karen's song. Rob was tickled by the contrast. What he didn't notice was that I was growing furious. Finally I blurted out, ''Goddammit, Randy, will you please shut up! She's singing 'The Lord's Prayer'!''

My rebuke left the room bare of sound. Rob, afraid that he might burst into laughter, escaped into the kitchen. Karen began the song again. When she finished, the room again fell into silence—which was immediately broken by Randy hollering back, ''Hey, Steve, Gabriel was singing too, you know!''

Randy didn't interrupt my toast, which was about the meaning of family and home and the importance of taking time to honor friends. I offered our new house to everyone present as a place of security and refuge to which the door was always open. What I didn't know was that Rob had already given copies of our house keys to most of them.

Yet our joy in that house was short-lived. The very next day, as we were reflecting on our fifth Thanksgiving together and on how beautifully the house was working out, Rob mentioned that we had to address a few things about the house that he hadn't expected. Because he was now self-employed, the bank had turned us down for a refinancing loan. The construction loan would expire in a couple of months and we had experienced several large cost overruns. After weeks of negotiating with various banks, we were forced to recognize a tough reality: that we had secured the original loan based on both our salaries; now that I was the only one of us with a stable income, no bank would approve the loan we needed. We had lived there for only four months when the ''For Sale'' sign went up on the front lawn.

A contract for the house came through in January. We packed and moved in the dead of February to a rented ranch house down the street.

7

As the Reagan era entered its final days, Republicans in Washington had every reason to expect an era of political stability. In the 1988 elections, the Democrats had once again retained control of Congress. President-elect George Bush promised an era of "kinder, gentler" stewardship. And at the helm of the House Republican conference were two competent but noncombative men—Bob Michel, the minority leader, and Dick Cheney, the minority whip—who seemed sure, in the foreseeable future, to lead the party down a quiet, predictable path.

Newt Gingrich was unhappy with that prospect. Seeking to consolidate the party's activist wing, he held an informal planning session in early January 1989. "Republicanism with a human touch" was the theme. George Bush did want to soften the hard edge of the Reagan years, though he clearly sought to do it in a conservative way; Newt took it as his job to formulate a coherent domestic agenda for the party that would accomplish just that. Bush's relative lack of passion about domestic issues created an unusual opportunity for Newt to influence White House policy in this area.

Newt had been laying the groundwork for these developments for years. During the early 1980s, it had become clear that the House Republican conference contained three basic elements. First there was the Old Guard—the more traditional, go-along, get-along governing Republicans, such as Bob Michel. Increasingly clear, even in the '80s, was the emergence of a New Right conservative element which (though they would never admit it) believed in larger government, as do the Democrats, although their focus was not on legislating economic parity but on legislating morality. I always thought it odd that people who didn't trust the federal bureaucracy to handle Americans' education or health care felt comfortable asking that same bureaucracy to help mold its children's values.

Finally, there were the rest of us. We weren't members of the Old Guard, comfortable with the status quo; nor were we the New Right. We were a small but growing group of militant moderates. We believed in changing and reforming the government, not eliminating it. We were economic conservatives who had great suspicions about government playing God. But our approach to government, if not as accommodating as that of some members of the Old Guard, was basically an establishment approach; we believed in working with the opposition to craft necessary reforms. We certainly didn't practice the guerrilla tactics that were soon to mark House Republicans.

Many people, alarmed by the party's growing divisions, believed it was only a matter of time before they resulted in serious confrontation that would tear the party wide open. Some of us, however, felt that the party, if properly managed, could be a strong, unified, and effective force. Newt Gingrich was one of the first to acknowledge and address the ideological differences within the GOP. He was convinced that activism within the party could unify it, not divide it. He also realized that, for all the ideological differences between him and me, the two of us shared a commitment to the kind of activism that produced real change.

In the early 1980s Newt had brought conservative activists together in something called the Conservative Opportunity

Society. Shortly afterward, Republican moderates began to organize as well. With the support of right-wing Southern Democrats, who were known as Boll Weevils, the Reagan White House had sought to dismantle a number of progressive programs that were important to the "rust belt" states of the Northeast and Midwest; in response to this powerful bipartisan coalition, Carl Pursel of Michigan, Stu McKinney of Connecticut, and others formed a moderate GOP group called the Gypsy Moths (whose name wittily suggested our attitude toward the Boll Weevils).

By the mid-1980s, I had become increasingly identified as an activist member of this moderate faction. Then one day in 1985 Newt came up to me on the House floor and said, "I think we ought to try to bring together a group composed of some of us from each side. I think there's a lot more uniting us than dividing us. I think we should focus on the things that unite us."

I agreed. And so I, along with three other moderates, Tom Tauke of Iowa, Olympia Snowe of Maine, and Nancy Johnson of Connecticut, began to meet regularly with Newt and three other conservatives, Bob Walker of Pennsylvania, Vin Weber of Minnesota, and Jon Kyl of Arizona.

Before putting together that group, House Republican conservatives and moderates had already come together on an important issue. For years, House Democrats, led by the Black Caucus, had attempted to impose economic sanctions on South Africa. House Republicans had resisted this attempt. The members of our party's Old Guard weren't inclined to use government to help advance black America, let alone blacks halfway around the world. They argued that apartheid was a domestic issue for South Africa, and none of our business; in their minds, we should do whatever best served the interests of American business at home and abroad, period. Sanctions would most assuredly *not* serve those interests.

But the new young conservatives saw the issue differently. Since they claimed to be passionately committed to the economic empowerment of individuals—to economic self-dependency, that is, as opposed to the crippling government dependency that they felt had been encouraged by Great Society social programs—these conservatives felt obliged to address the condition of the black majority in South Africa, whose empowerment was made absolutely impossible by government oppression. An important fact here was that these conservatives were especially concerned with preaching empowerment to black Americans, many of whom saw their message as a cynical attempt to unload the urban underclass from welfare rolls. These new young conservatives figured that they couldn't preach empowerment convincingly to black Americans unless they sent it a strong signal of good faith. And how better could they send such a signal than by supporting sanctions against South Africa?

For moderate Republicans, the issue was simpler. Shaped by the politics of Lincoln, we saw sanctions against South Africa as a simple matter of social justice.

While Old Guard Republicans and President Reagan continued to resist sanctions, then, moderate and New Right Republicans came together with Democrats to develop a veto-proof majority in favor of sanctions. In doing so, we made it clear that we had begun to redefine the Republican party and to create a new Republican philosophy. In this case, the real political heroes were not the moderates—after all, people *expected* us to vote for sanctions—but Newt, Vin Weber, and Bob Walker, who took a lot of heat from traditional conservatives for their support of sanctions.

Discussions between conservative and moderate Republicans became more involved as we moved toward the 1988 convention. Newt became increasingly visible, and we all supported him in that. In 1989, shortly after the Bush administration took office and John Tower was turned down by the Senate as Secretary of Defense, Bush nominated Dick Cheney, then the Republican House whip, to that position. This opened up the job of Republican whip, the second highest position in the House Republican leadership. The whip's job is to count votes—to keep track, that is, of how many House Republicans say they will vote this way or that on a given bill—and to win and retain as many party-line votes as possible on major bills. When Newt heard about Cheney's appointment, the first person he called was Vin Weber, whom he asked to run his campaign for minority whip. The second person he called was me. He asked if I would support him. I said I would.

Why? For one thing, despite our ideological differences, Newt and I shared that commitment to activism. In the early 1980s the congressional Republicans, as a group, were too often lax, unenthused, and disorganized. Newt was a dynamo, a visionary, a breath of fresh air, a fountainhead of ideas about how we could best prepare America for the post–Cold War world of cyberspace and open markets. I didn't agree with all his proposals, but I was impressed and inspired by his intellectual curiosity, his openness to new educational and economic concepts, the air of can-do enthusiasm that he brought to every task before him. I saw in Newt someone who could energize and organize the party and help us win a Republican majority in Congress. And that, of course, is exactly what ended up happening.

The kind of activism that Newt stood for, in my eyes and those of other Republicans of various ideological stripes, was most assuredly *not* the kind of rigidity over social issues that now threatens to take over the Republican party and that Newt is routinely identified with. Rather, we saw him as embodying a kind of activism that, setting the social issues aside, concentrated instead on an agenda that promised to unite Republicans across ideological lines—and that, indeed, might well manage to unit Americans as a whole across party lines.

As someone who deeply admired Newt's gifts for political strategy and creative solutions, I had often sought him out to ask his advice on building coalitions and crafting imaginative legislative answers to thorny problems. Newt appreciated my interest and always responded thoughtfully to my queries; plainly, many of the questions that preoccupied me were also a subject of reflection for him. For his part, Newt admired the fact that I was willing, as he put it, to "go outside the box" in

search of solutions. (In 1995, for instance, rather than allow
the D.C. schools program to become bogged down in predictable conflicts over school vouchers or local control, I raised the
whole issue to a new level by seeking to create, in the nation's
capital, a world-class schools initiative.)

Our talks would often go on for some time. Newt kept telling me that I could have a great future in Congress, if only I
would pursue it. When I would demur, suggesting that I was
unlikely ever to move up in the leadership for "various reasons" (he knew very well that I meant my homosexuality),
Newt would shake his head vigorously. "Steve," he would
say, "this town recognizes competence. You are a very competent person. Use it!" What was most important to me in this
were the words that remained unsaid: "Steve, as far as I'm
concerned, your being gay needn't keep you from going as far
as you can go in politics."

Friends of mine have been astonished to hear me say this,
but Newt was instrumental in my coming to terms with my
homosexuality. During the early 1980s, when I was still uncomfortable about being gay, Newt made it clear to me that
my sexual orientation was not an issue for him. He was one
of the few Republicans who plainly saw no contradiction between my being gay and my being a Republican. Though my
homosexuality was widely known in official Washington, and
though Newt knew very well that many of his most vocal and
powerful supporters despised homosexuals, he made it clear
to everyone that he trusted me, enjoyed my company, respected my judgment, and considered me a friend.

Many of my nonpolitical gay friends wonder why I am so
committed to a man whom they think of as public enemy
number one. All I can tell them is that the Newt I know is not
the Newt they read about in much of the press. The Newt I
know is a man with whom I share a strong but unspoken
bond, a bond that other people might not notice or fathom,
and that causes each of us to protect the other in an almost
reflexive way. I don't think it's an overstatement to describe

that bond as fraternal: Newt is, as I've often told my friends, the closest thing I have in politics to an older brother.

So when Newt told me he was running for minority whip, I immediately got to work campaigning for him. I spent that first afternoon, a Friday, phoning every moderate member that I was close to and asking them not to commit to anybody else until they had at least had a chance to listen to Newt and to hear why he was running. From the start, it was a very intense, aggressive campaign.

And it was, especially for me, a ticklish one. Part of what made it so was that Newt's opponent turned out to be Ed Madigan, who was at that time the ranking Republican on the Ag Committee. Ed, who would later become President Bush's Secretary of Agriculture, was a member of the Republican Old Guard and had always been a friend and ally of mine. Along with Newt and Bill Goodling, who was then the ranking Republican on the Education Committee (and is now its chairman), Ed Madigan was one of the three people in Congress to whom I owed the most.

In supporting Newt over Ed, I was probably taking the biggest political risk of any of my Republican colleagues in the House. In fact I was putting myself in what some would consider a no-win position, because if Ed won the leadership race, he would presumably be hostile to me for having supported Newt, and if he lost the race, he would remain the ranking member of the Ag Committee and would presumably make it very difficult for me to have any kind of input there. As it turned out, I was the only Republican on the Ag Committee who didn't support Ed. Yet I explained to him that I had promised to back his opponent before he had decided to run, and he, to his credit, respected me for my commitment, conviction, and candor, and our relationship continued to be good. I think Newt also respected me for having the courage to make what was probably the most difficult choice of anybody in Congress in terms of the potential price I would have to pay.

In the end almost every moderate Republican supported Newt, even though Ed was considered the far more moderate candidate. Why? Because most of the moderates shared by commitment to activism in the party—and Newt represented activism.

One Republican who wasn't supporting Newt was Bob Michel, the House Republican leader. Bob and his lieutenants exerted a lot of pressure on Members to vote for Ed. It was awful, very tense. House Republicans were like a family at war. There was horrible infighting among people who had always been friends and allies. It got uglier and uglier. Finally, on March 16, when we were holding a meeting of Newt's campaign steering committee, Newt strode into the room, obviously very upset. His emotional state was understandable. He had been campaigning for weeks, and was under immense stress. He had taken too many meetings and gotten too little sleep.

"I don't get it," he said to the group at large, throwing his hands up. "I just don't get it. I've done everything possible. I've worked the vineyards in this party. I've been across the country speaking for candidates. I've raised money. I've articulated the issues. I've put together the campaign. I've played by the rules. And yet if I lose this election it'll be because Bob Michel and the Republican leaders are using the power of their leadership to pressure people to support Ed Madigan."

At that point, Newt actually broke down crying.

I was stunned. This display made it clear to me that Bob Michel had to be confronted on the issue. Of course Bob had the right to support whomever he wanted. But he had to know that if he used his position as party leader to force an outcome, he ran the risk of dividing the Republican conference to a degree that was beyond repair. Those of us who were Newt's most loyal supporters spoke about the situation and decided to go over to Bob's office and confront him directly.

"You're the moderate here, Steve," Bob Livingston of Louisiana said to me. "It would be best if you were the one to speak for us."

"Yeah, right," I joked. "With friends like you guys . . . !" But I agreed to do it.

So all fifteen of us, including Bob Dornan, made our way directly over to Bob Michel's office.

Now, I have to say that even as I supported Newt's activism, I also admired Bob Michel. He's not the headline grabber Newt is, but he has always been a decent man and a selfless public servant, and when he has spoken impromptu and from his heart, he has given some of the best speeches I have ever heard. More than once I told members of Bob's staff that when he was preoccupied and had to read from a prepared text he wasn't very effective, but when he spoke sincerely and extemporaneously, he was extremely convincing. That his underlings were making threats in order to corral votes for Ed Madigan couldn't necessarily be blamed on him or, for that matter, on Ed; it was quite possible that he was unaware of much that was being said and done in his name.

Anyway, when we reached the reception desk at Bob's office I told a member of his staff that we had to see him right away and wouldn't leave until he spoke to us. "He's tied up in a meeting," the staff member told us, "but I'll try to reach him and tell him you're here."

They reached him. Needless to say, when fifteen members walk into the Republican leader's office and say they're not leaving till he speaks to them, the staff locates the leader and gets him back to the office pretty fast.

"What's up?" said Bob when he came into the office. His demeanor made it clear that he was as stressed out as Newt by the tension surrounding the whip campaign.

"Bob," I said in an even but firm voice, "frankly we've got a problem. And it's this. You have every right to support whomever you want for the whip position. But if it's true, as we believe indications are beginning to suggest, that you're using your position to influence members and force an outcome of the election, you need to know that you may win that battle and yet lose the war. Because this party will be eternally fractured if that's the means by which we see victory achieved."

Bob listened carefully. Then, to my astonishment, *he* broke down in tears. "You have to know," he said, "that my goal is not to destroy the party. My goal is to support my friend. If what I'm doing is being interpreted as going beyond that and forcing an outcome, I'm sorry. I'll try to refrain from doing that. I'll try to make it clear that people have the right to support whomever they want, and that, however they vote, their position here won't be jeopardized by me."

In their March 22 *Washington Post* column about our confrontation with Bob, Rowland Evans and Robert Novak made some percipient points about the larger meaning of the conflict. Michel's "genuine dismay" over our complaint, they observed,

> displayed the very personality trait that impelled backbench Republican congressmen to revolt against Old Bull leadership.
>
> Michel, 66, the prototypical Old Bull starting his thirty-third year in the House, is a hail-fellow-well-met from Peoria, Illinois, who likes to be liked. Consequently, he was shattered to find Republican colleagues unhappy with him. They informed him that they did not appreciate hard-nosed tactics by him and his lieutenants against their candidate for minority whip, Representative Newt Gingrich.
>
> Michel replied that he did not condone high pressure tactics and would instruct overzealous surrogates to cool it. That confirmed the basis for the revolt. Michel does not like to offend anybody, including Democrats. . . . The minority leader's collegiality with Tip O'Neill and Jim Wright in fact created the Gingrich candidacy.

I'll never forget that day. Here I was, in 1989, eight years into my membership in Congress, and I really thought I had seen everything. Yet within a two-hour period I had seen something that I'd never imagined seeing in a hundred years—I had seen the two most powerful Republicans in the House of Representatives break down and cry.

This is such a difficult business, I remember thinking as I watched tears stream down Bob Michel's face. *Such a mean business*.

I have a good friend back home in Pleasantville, Debbie Dahl. She plays the organ at our church and is a couple of years younger than I am; her husband, Warren, is the high school basketball coach. One day in 1994, the three of us, along with my youngest brother, Matt, were talking at my mother's general store about how mean politics is. Debbie said, "I'll bet if Steve had to do it over again he wouldn't do it."

Without hesitation, I said, "You're absolutely right." When I went into politics, I had no idea how horrible it can be—the ambition and lies, the tension and treachery, the hunger for power. So if I had known at twenty-three what I know today, would I have gone into politics? No. But that said, do I regret having done it? Not at all. I'm convinced that I was chosen by God to carry out the work I've taken on. That isn't an egomaniacal statement: I think God calls on each of us to do his work. It's up to us whether we listen for his call and act on it. I have no doubt that God gave me, and gave those I love, the ability to do what good we've done and the strength to endure the bad we've had to endure. And God knows we've had a lot to endure.

Newt won the whip race by two votes—votes that made possible the notoriety that he would gain in years to come and ultimately, of course, his speakership. The *Washington Post* ran the news of Newt's election as its lead story on March 23.

> House Republicans yesterday narrowly elected Rep. Newt Gingrich of Georgia to their No. 2 leadership position, effectively voting to turn their party toward a more activist and controversial style of leadership in the House.
>
> Gingrich defeated Rep. Edward R. Madigan (Ill.), a quiet and skillful legislator who was backed by Minority Leader Robert H. Michel (Ill.), 87 to 85, in a secret ballot election for House minority whip. Gingrich's election was a victory for a younger and more activist generation of House Republicans who have chafed under what they consider the Democrat-accommodating old-guard leadership of Michel, Madigan and others.

The *Post* suggested that Newt's election would result in "a more polarized House."

There was no question in anyone's mind that the moderates, myself included, had made a critical difference in Newt's election. I have often reflected on the irony that, as a gay man and a leader of moderate Republicans, I was instrumental in securing the ascendancy to power of the most conservative Republican leader in a generation, and one who is widely considered, fairly or unfairly, a vicious homophobe. Yet for me the contest between Newt and Ed Madigan was not a contest between conservative and moderate ideology, but between active and passive leadership.

Many members speculated that I would be given some kind of reward for my efforts on Newt's behalf. I shrugged the speculation off: I had only done what I had thought was right for the party. Nonetheless, shortly after his election Newt called me at my office and surprised me by asking out of the blue if I would become one of two chief deputy whips. One of the deputy whips would aid in the traditional whip job of counting votes; the other deputy whip—me—would take charge of formulating party strategy. The idea of a "strategy whip" was original with Newt; before him, there had never been such a position in the House.

My appointment as strategy whip was a momentous event, not only for me but for my state. Never before had a Republican congressman from Wisconsin belonged to his party's official leadership. Some, such as Melvin Laird, had served as committee chairs and had exercised great influence in the party; but I was the first member from Wisconsin ever to rise above that level. The appointment received a tremendous amount of press back home. It also provided me with a great professional and political opportunity—one that I took on at considerable personal expense, because the workload was huge.

The position was problematic in other ways, too. Though Newt had had some justification for creating the job of strategy whip—you can't count votes, after all, if you don't have a strategy to *get* votes—his doing so created a real tension between him, in the whip office, and Bob Michel, in the leader's office. Michel felt that formulating strategy was the prerogative of the leader; Newt didn't agree. To put it plainly, Michel's staff saw me as a threat, an instrument that Newt was using in a power struggle with Michel, and Newt, in a response that was not entirely uncharacteristic of him, kept avoiding opportunities to sit down with Michel and resolve the matter.

The deputy whip job obliged me to meet weekly in my office with Newt and two other members—Nancy Johnson and Jon Kyl—to talk strategy. We met on Wednesday mornings at seven; given our crowded schedules, this was the only time in the whole week when we could all get together for an hour.

When I became involved in the whip organization, and in doing so became much more active in issues of national concern, Rob began to pay more attention to those issues and to the Republican rhetoric about them. He also paid more attention to Newt. While he acknowledged that his own personal encounters with Newt had been pleasant enough, Rob didn't entirely trust Newt's motives where I was concerned. Rob worried, too, that my loyalty to Newt would cause me to drift away from my moderate positions and allow myself to become Newt's tool.

I tried repeatedly to convince Rob that Newt was not the big enemy of the gay and lesbian community that he was purported to be. But Rob didn't change his mind. Several times, when I was on one of my frequent weekend visits to my district in Wisconsin, the phone would ring late at night at my parents' house in Pleasantville and it would be Rob. Either he had been out with friends who had told him about the latest antigay proposal by some Republican member of Congress, or he had picked up a copy of the *Washington Blade* (the city's weekly gay newspaper) and had read about some such proposal himself.

Invariably, these calls were highly confrontational and angry. Rob would demand explanations that I was unable to provide. On rare occasions the press would have misrepresented the truth. But all too often, I found myself embarrassed by the issues that Rob raised and at a loss for a satisfactory answer.

I remember one night when my mother woke me up, her voice sleepy, and said there was a call for me. I looked at the clock: it was about two A.M. I picked up the phone. Rob was on the other end, livid. He had read an item in the *Blade* saying that Newt had compared homosexuality to alcoholism. In his most snide tone, Rob said, "I just wanted you to know that I'm both drunk *and* queer—and I'm *pissed.*"

ROB

After Steve returned home from Wisconsin that weekend, I copied the article in which Newt had made that analogy between homosexuality and alcoholism and placed a copy of it on Steve's plate instead of dinner.

When other articles were published, citing similar remarks by Newt, I would clip them out and, as Steve was putting his things together before driving to work in the morning, I would wave them in front of his eyes and slip them into his briefcase accompanied by a sarcastic smile.

Long before Newt became a household word, he was a nightly preoccupation in *our* household. I've known him for all my life, it seems. Coincidentally, my college roommate, Clay, worked in Newt's district office in the early '80s. He got to know Marianne very well—in fact, he got so close to Marianne that Newt worried that Clay had his eyes on her. Steve and I spent some time with Newt at the Republican convention in New Orleans in 1988, and I've talked to him at various fund-raisers.

When Steve first started working for Newt in the whip organization (Steve insists that he worked *with* Newt, but nobody really works *with* Newt), I had enormous reservations. One, because it was additional work with no additional pay. In the private sector, theoretically, if you work harder, you get paid more.

But the money wasn't the real problem. (Frankly, neither of us had ever been very motivated by money.) More important were my problems with Newt's agenda. Not only was I forfeiting my dinner companion to late nights at the office, I was forfeiting him to a bad cause. If Steve had said, "I'm going to be working late at the Whitman-Walker clinic," I would have said, "Well, maybe I'll join you, we could do some good and have some fun." But that was not what was going on.

Within the first few months of Steve's growing involvement with Newt, it became clear to me that Steve trusted him implicitly, regardless of their occasional ideological differences. Steve contends that it was Newt who gave him the nerve to come out of the closet. Maybe he's right. But that implicit trust unsettled me. As soon as Newt offered him the strategy whip job, Steve knew I would have problems with it—which is why he scheduled a dinner with me that night in a romantic restaurant, Two Quail, to break the news.

I didn't disguise my irritation. I knew it would mean additional work that would take him away from me and our friends. Also, I knew Steve's time would be spent scheming with more conservative Republicans to advance the party's agenda, which for me was far from an attractive proposition. I had always vowed that so long as his work was on behalf of his constituents in Wisconsin, who deserved his time and attention, I wouldn't kick up a fuss about his unpredictable schedule and long hours; but the whip effort had little to do with the immediate interests of the dairy farmers of western Wisconsin. Finally, I knew that because of the personal rapport between Newt and Steve, Newt might well be able to motivate Steve to persuade Republican moderates to vote with him against their better judgment. This sort of thing is an ugly political reality—but most politicians are so used to it that they don't perceive it as ugly.

That night at dinner I conceded that I didn't dislike Newt personally. I had listened to him onstage, I had observed him behind the scenes, and I had talked to him on the phone, and I could see why Steve was compelled by his presence. But I didn't trust him.

The dinner ended in an uneasy truce. "Do what you want to," I finally said out of frustration. "I don't care. But do not lobby *me* on behalf of your cause."

8

As if the tensions that my whip job caused at home weren't bad enough, the promotion added yet another stress factor to our lives. For it suddenly placed me at the center of the radar screens of many gay activists. They knew I was gay—and now they also perceived me as a leading ally of Newt and of the other conservative Republicans whom they considered their deadly enemies. These connections made me, in their eyes, the very personification of closetedness and hypocrisy.

The subtitle of Michelangelo Signorile's controversial 1993 book *Queer in America* refers to "the closets of power," meaning the closets inhabited by gay businessmen in New York, gay show-business figures in Hollywood, and gay politicians in Washington who, while occupying powerful positions in the American system, do nothing to stop it from oppressing their fellow homosexuals. To many far-left gay activists, my role in the House Republican leadership made me America's number one inhabitant of the "closets of power." I was no longer just Steve Gunderson, a public man with a private life; I was the symbol of everything they saw as being wrong with Congress, the Republican party, and the American system generally. In 1989, then, I became a regular preoccupation—and target—of a host of radical gay activists who regarded me as a despicable reactionary.

At the same time, Glenn was experiencing some dramatic ups and downs. Early in 1989 he left the two-bedroom Alexandria condo that he had shared with Charles and moved with his boyfriend Justin into a flat near Dupont Circle in Washington's gay neighborhood. He and Justin and Rob and I had rung in the New Year together; the four of us met occasionally for dinner and to celebrate birthdays, and we continued to meet whenever possible for drinks after work.

With Justin, for a brief period, Glenn enjoyed not only good health but a more stable and fulfilling domestic life than he'd had in all the time Rob or I had known him: he got home at regular times, made dinner, and spent quiet evenings at home with Justin. Rob and I were pleased to see them settle down.

Then, in the fall of 1989, Glenn's health took a dramatic turn downward. He had thrush and diarrhea, and experienced a huge weight loss. His doctors were at a loss to explain what he was suffering from. They offered up a wide range of diagnostic hunches and prescribed various pills. They even took him off AZT for a while to see if the problem lay with his medication. Glenn lost hope. His relationship with Justin became turbulent, even violent. Unable to deal with his sudden bad health, Glenn took it out viciously on Justin. Justin, not understanding why Glenn was turning on him, became deeply upset.

Then one day, Rob called me at work in a panic. "I just got off the phone with Glenn," he said. "He told me he wants to bail out of his relationship with Justin and move South to a warmer climate." It was as if Glenn thought he could escape AIDS by leaving town. The very next day he did move—just like that. Leaving behind his photo albums, birth certificate, and college diploma, he relocated to Hollywood, Florida, where he found a job as an errand boy for the Disney Corporation. He figured he would die there. Justin was so distraught that he phoned Rob and said, "I want this stuff out of here tomorrow!'' So Rob called a friend who owned a truck, hauled Glenn's stuff away, and stored it in our basement. A year and a half later we gave Glenn's clothing to Goodwill; we still have his memorabilia.

While upset by Glenn and Justin's break-up—and by that of Gloria and Gary, too, who also separated that fall—Rob and I took heart from the endurance of Matt and John's relationship. In November, they commemorated their tenth year together. Given that no committed relationship ever has a completely smooth path, and given that gay unions can be particularly fragile on account of other people's attitudes, Rob and I admired Matt and John for staying together. Wanting their tenth anniversary to be something all of us could celebrate, we asked to give them a party, and they agreed. Since John was from Maryland, where they both had many friends, and since our house wasn't big enough for the kind of party we envisioned, Rob called Kurt Decker, a friend who lived in a wonderful old Baltimore rowhouse, and asked him if we could use his place. Kurt agreed enthusiastically. The party was a blast. At Matt and John's suggestion, we indicated on the invitation that donations in their names could be made to an AIDS education project. For many of our friends—such as Gloria and Kris, who helped Rob create the elaborate handmade invitations—that party was the first of many "gay events."

A couple of weeks later came Thanksgiving. Again, Rob needed to find a suitable venue; the house we had rented wasn't the right place for a Thanksgiving crowd. Rob and I had become friends with Walter and Brenda Day, the couple who had purchased our house on Hitt Avenue. Since Brenda loved to cook and had met most of our friends, she agreed to Rob's idea that we have a joint Thanksgiving dinner at her house. In the weeks preceding the holiday, Rob and Brenda planned the meal, mailed the invitations, and coordinated the china, flowers, linens, and chairs. Rob and Walt built two plywood tables to accommodate twenty-four people.

That year, for the first time, Rob's parents and his brother Dana came from Florida for Thanksgiving. The five of us went over to Walter and Brenda's early that afternoon to pitch in with the final preparations, and as our car pulled up we saw Charles walking toward the front door, dressed in a starched white shirt and a red and green tartan plaid tie. He was carrying four pies. Even before he said hello, he announced proudly that the pies were pumpkin praline pies and that he had made them himself. He insisted that we taste them and explained that he had worked on them for days and hadn't been so excited about anything in months. He claimed that he had followed an old family recipe, though Rob knew he had found it on a Graham Cracker box. All this happened even before we got into the house.

"Does he always talk so much?" Rob's father later asked incredulously.

At dinner I offered my annual toast, in which I thanked Brenda and Walter for their friendship, welcomed Rob's family, and spoke about the family of friends gathered at the table. Charles took pictures of everybody. After dinner Callista played "up" tunes on the piano and Randy, Gabriel, and Steve sang hymns. Charles drank and talked about his praline pies. By ten-thirty, having exceeded his limit of vodka, he said good night.

The following morning at eight, Brenda and Walter were still in bed when they heard a knock at their front door. Walter went down to answer it. He opened the door to see Charles standing there, smiling broadly. He had obviously had a good night's sleep and risen early. Charles started prattling immediately, telling Walter that he had greatly enjoyed the party and couldn't wait to get his pictures back. He was going to order duplicates, he said, and give them to Walter and Brenda.

Walter looked at Charles with openmouthed disbelief. Eight o'clock in the morning on a day off! Resisting the temptation to slam the door, he thanked Charles for the offer.

"Did you have any of the pumpkin praline pie?" Charles asked.

"Yes I did," Walter said. "I'm glad you made it."

"Is there any left over?" Charles asked. He explained that he had forgotten to have a piece himself.

Walter invited Charles in and handed him two and a half pumpkin praline pies.

"Have you made any coffee yet?" Charles asked.

"We're out of coffee," Walt said. "And I have to get some more sleep." As graciously as he could, Walter ushered Charles out of the house and went back to bed.

When Brenda called later that day to tell Rob the story, he couldn't help but laugh. It was clear that Charles had woken up hungry for the kind of warmth he had experienced the night before. On some level, I think he had hoped that when he got to Walter and Brenda's that morning, the party would still be going strong, with all the music and drinking, the friendly conversation and familiar laughter.

No one could understand better than Rob and I Charles's wish to prolong the joy of that evening. I don't know exactly when I had come to realize that we had gathered around us a circle of friends who were, in a very real way, our family. I know that on that Thanksgiving evening, I felt very grateful for that family and for the gift of friendship that we'd been given. I looked forward to years of closeness with them— years of love and sacrifice, laughter and tears. Despite Glenn's medical situation, I didn't realize at the time how much sacrifice and how many tears were in store for us, and how soon they would come. It didn't occur to me that before too many more Thanksgivings were over, there would be empty seats at the table and I would be tormented by my conscience over my lack of involvement in gay-rights and AIDS issues. Like Charles, I think that Rob and I, on some level, believed that the party would keep on going strong, year after year, with the same happy faces around us. It was, indeed, that naive assumption that kept me from getting more politically involved in AIDS issues in the 1980s.

Nineteen eighty-nine was Bush's first year in office and the Republicans in Congress were consumed with trying to get his initial agenda through. We were able to pull off some rather

dramatic legislative successes. The 1989 tax-code change re-
pealing Section 89 (which was a paperwork nightmare) had a
dramatic impact on the business community. People said that
we wouldn't be able to repeal it because Dan Rostenkowski
was against repeal. But we organized, through my part of the
whip organization, a strategy that managed to get the repeal
passed. It was, for me, a great personal victory.

But the congressional euphoria over the Bush administration dissipated with stunning rapidity in 1990. As the economy began to falter, the debate over a bipartisan budget
agreement grew more and more passionate. That debate led to
the Budget Act of 1990, in which George Bush, who had won
the 1988 election with a vow of no new taxes, capitulated to
the Democrats' proposed tax increase.

President Bush was a great leader on international issues
but not always on domestic ones. I enjoyed dealing with him:
he was always on top of things, smart, well-informed, and
affable. But he made a terrible mistake when, for the sake of
governing, he allowed his advisors to talk him into a tax-hike
package that not only violated his pledge to the electorate
about "no new taxes" but was also highly damaging to the
economy, which was then very weak, and to the GOP, because
it split us wide open. That agreement created the most intense
polarization within the party that I've ever seen on an economic issue.

That tax hike was the first test of intraparty divisions during Newt's tenure as Republican whip. Newt led the faction
against the budget agreement, while Bob Michel, who grudgingly supported the tax hike out of loyalty to Bush, led the
contingent in favor of it. Some of my best friends in Congress,
moderate Republicans such as Nancy Johnson, Fred Grandy,
and Amo Houghton, joined ranks behind Michel. They did so
mainly, I think, because they felt that their dedication to governing obliged them to do so. For my part, I felt strongly that
taxes should not be raised in a recession. The year 1990 had
seen a bad economic downturn, and so, devoted as I was to
the idea of working together in the interest of governing, I

thought that the tax hike was absolutely the wrong move at that time.

Because President Bush had agreed to a tax hike, then, we had a big split right down the middle of the Republican party. The tension between the two sides was so huge that you could have sliced it and boxed it up. During that period I would run into Nancy Johnson or Fred Grandy on the floor and we wouldn't even speak to each other. They had decided that the true Newt had been revealed and that he was an egotist who was dividing the Republican party out of pure self-interest. That impasse lasted for the entire fall of 1990. It was just awful.

At a time when most of the Republican moderates in the House had turned away from Newt, I think it mattered greatly to him that I shared his views and was willing not only to say so but to preach the gospel, as we understood it, to such interest groups as the retailers and the restaurateurs in Washington and elsewhere. I spent a lot of time talking to these groups, for when Newt was unavailable to give a speech, his office would routinely ask me to go in his place to explain what we sought to accomplish.

The budget conflict dragged on. But something else soon overshadowed it. In August 1990, Iraqi dictator Saddam Hussein invaded and devoured Kuwait. President Bush responded with a troop buildup in neighboring Saudi Arabia. House and Senate debates on the question of war were scheduled to take place in January, immediately after the swearing in of the 102nd Congress.

In the meantime, I learned all I could about the situation in the Gulf, so that I might cast as well informed a vote as possible. A room on the first floor of the Capitol was given over to CIA and Defense Intelligence Agency experts who were made available to brief House and Senate members on all relevant intelligence information. I went down to speak to them and asked every question I could think of.

Gloria, who was a Mideast expert at the DIA, was also helpful during that time. Under ordinary circumstances she would hesitate to discuss such matters with me, but in this case personal exchanges of opinion proved enlightening. I especially wanted to know about Saddam Hussein. And the more I heard and read about him, the more clear it became to me that I had no choice but to vote for the use of military force to stop him.

For Saddam was plainly a man who understood and responded to nothing but power. Unless we forced him out of Kuwait, Saudi Arabia would be next—and then what? At some point we would have to draw a line in the sand. The question was whether to do it now or to wait until Saddam had amassed more territory. It seemed wise to do it as soon as possible. My decision, then, was to vote for the military operation. But I kept that decision private for some time, ready to change my vote if it seemed unjustified by later events.

Before voting, I had to discuss the issue with my constituents. In early January of almost every year since I first entered Congress, I've held a series of town meetings throughout my district. In 1990, those meetings happened to be scheduled for the week before the House vote on the Gulf War resolution. Consequently the meetings took on far greater interest than usual. They were, in fact, the best attended, most emotional, and most confrontational town meetings I'd ever had. Feelings on both sides of the issue ran sky-high. Like most Americans at that point, most of my constituents were extremely isolationist. Constituents would stand up, their voices trembling, and would tell me: "If you vote for this war, we will hold you accountable in the next election!"

The first time that happened, I was dumbfounded. "Who cares?" I replied. "The very last thing on my mind is whether I get reelected in 1992. I'm talking about doing what's right for this country and what I believe is necessary. Whether I vote for or against war, I'm going to do it because I think it's the right decision, not because I think it's going to help me politically. And I know very well that if I do vote to go to war, I'm going to have to call up the parents of slain servicemen and women and explain the vote that I cast to send their children to their death."

Rob and I argued vehemently about the war. He felt, as many people did, that all the talk about defending the freedom of Kuwait and other American allies in the region was merely a cover, and that President Bush's real motive in calling for war was to safeguard our oil supply and to protect the assets of American oil companies. He demanded to know why I was willing to defy my constituents in the matter of declaring war on Saddam—an act that might lose American lives—but was not willing to defy them by publicly speaking up for increased AIDS funding, which might *save* American lives.

Yet in due time Rob stopped arguing with me about the war. As is occasionally the case, he respected my independence and recognized my determination to follow my own mind.

He doesn't argue with me any more, for example, about abortion or the National Rifle Association, subjects on which we differ strongly. On abortion, he's strictly pro-choice. I used to be considered pro-life, and routinely received endorsements from pro-life groups. Over the years, however, the pro-life movement has become increasingly extreme and in the last two congressional elections my support of fetal tissue research, of equal abortion rights for military women, and of government funding for abortions in cases of rape or incest or to save the life of the mother has resulted in my being denied pro-life endorsements.

As for the NRA, no issue better reflected the difference between Rob's upbringing and mine than that of gun ownership. To Rob, the necessity of something like the Brady Bill goes without question. But he didn't grow up in rural Wisconsin, where guns aren't an instrument of terror but simply a way of life. When I was a teenager, my friends would show up at school with their guns in their pickups, so that they could go hunting afterward. For us, guns were a weapon of sport, not of crime. In my district, then, gun laws really do punish the law-abiding citizen, not the criminal. Rob used to argue with me endlessly about this issue—for a long time he couldn't believe that I really felt as I did about it, and insisted that I was just voting as I did to please my constituents and the gun lobby—but finally he gave up and agreed to disagree.

After a certain point, then, he concentrated his energy not on arguing with me about the Gulf War but on lending me moral support. He knew how difficult a time I might have before the war was over. He had been there when that young constituent of mine had died in the Beirut barracks in 1983, and he knew how painful that experience had been for me. He and I both knew that American military involvement in the Gulf might well result in many such deaths, and many more grieving parents and draining funerals and flag-covered coffins, and he knew how deeply I dreaded them.

The debate on the Gulf War resolution, which took place on the first Friday and Saturday of January, was long, emotional, and very high in quality. People on both sides did the Congress proud. The vote was completed on Saturday afternoon, and the next morning, while I was singing a hymn in my pew at the Church of the Redeemer in McLean, tears began to pour down my face. That kind of emotional display was very much out of character for me—but I was under such tension and in such pain. What had I done? What would come of the decision I had helped to make? I felt I had voted the right way, but only time would tell for sure. Never before had the rightness or wrongness of a vote seemed of such immediate and weighty consequence.

One evening in January, I was at my office, watching the *ABC Evening News* and getting ready to go and meet Rob at J.R.'s, when the ABC correspondent in Baghdad announced that he had heard shots. The allied bombing had begun. Instead of joining Rob, I spent the next five hours answering phone calls from the press in Wisconsin and elsewhere. My staff stayed late, too—as did virtually every staff on the Hill. Somewhere around the second hour, Rob called from a pay phone at J.R.'s, where he was drinking with Charles. "What's happening?" he asked.

"Rob," I said, "we've gone to war."

"I know," he said, and explained that the music videos on

the TV screens at J.R.'s had been interrupted by news bulletins.

"What are you gonna do about food?" he asked.

I told him that none of us in the office had eaten. He hadn't either; he and Charles had expected to have dinner with me. I explained that I would be tied up for hours. "All right, then," he said, "I'll leave Charles and come over. What's your office number again?"

Rob never comes to my office, but that evening he drove over immediately. When he arrived at about eight-thirty, the four staffers who were there with me were either glued to the television or on the telephone, trying to find out as much as they could about the situation in the Gulf. I was on the phone, talking with reporters in Wisconsin. Rob was extremely hungry, and rather piqued by the war's interruption of his evening plans. Unable to get a pizza delivered—everybody in Washington was apparently working late and ordering pizzas—he went out and picked up six orders of sauerbraten. The six of us were there till midnight or so, polishing off the sauerbraten, trying to get a handle on what was going on in the Gulf, and also seeking to satisfy the demands of the western Wisconsin press for information.

Like many other Americans, Rob and I were preoccupied with the war. Nor were we untouched by the dread of terrorist activities that the conflict had generated on Capitol Hill. Since the Capitol is the most visible of American buildings, and the Congress the most visible of American institutions, it was no surprise that we had received many threats of terrorist attack. At private briefings with State Department officials shortly after the commencement of bombing in the Gulf, members of Congress were advised that there was a very real danger of terrorist activity against us and were told to be exceedingly cautious. We were discouraged, for example, from walking on the streets around the Capitol; instead, they suggested that when we had to travel back and forth between the Capitol and the outlying House and Senate office buildings, we always take the underground tunnel. They also suggested that we remove our names from our mailboxes at home and insisted that those of us, like me and Rob, who didn't garage our cars at home lock them every night.

So it was that in addition to the threatening letters and calls that my office was now routinely receiving from radical gay activists, my position as chief deputy Republican whip made me feel especially vulnerable to possible Mideast terrorism.

I made the unfortunate mistake of telling Rob about the State Department's cautionary advice. Initially he brushed the advice off. But his concerns were intensified as he thought about our house, which was conspicuous and located on a major thoroughfare, and about my whip job, which Rob figured would place me high up on any list of possible targets.

One morning shortly after the bombing of Iraq commenced, Rob and I happened to use each other's cars. I left home that morning before he did, and heard later from him that he had discovered that I had inadvertently left my car unlocked all night. Suddenly my words about the potential for bombings came back to him. He didn't want to overreact, but he didn't want to be careless either. I had talked about terrorist attacks; the State Department had talked about terrorist attacks; even Gloria had expressed concerns. Who was he to doubt experts? So he opened the car door very cautiously. He threw his briefcase on the front seat, just in case the seat had been wired to explode when someone sat in it. Once that proved not to be the case, the next possible danger was that when he turned the key to the ignition, the car would explode. He had seen cars explode on *Mission: Impossible.* So he leaned in, stuck the key halfway into the ignition, and darted away from the car. Nothing. He walked back to the car, got in, and started it. No problem.

So far, so good. His next thought was that the car might have been rigged to blow up when it was put into reverse, but he dismissed that possibility as unlikely, given that the car was a stick shift. By that time he was late for work, anyway. So he shifted into reverse and drove off. But he was careful not to exceed thirty miles an hour, since he thought that maybe it had been rigged to explode when it hit thirty.

When he told me this story that evening, I laughed hysterically. So, we later learned, had some of our neighbors who, unbeknownst to him, had watched the entire spectacle that morning as they sat behind their wheels in stalled rush-hour traffic in front of our house.

I spend a lot of weekends back home in the district, and on the first such weekend after the bombing began, Rob came home from work and decided that terrorists might attack our house in the middle of the night. What could he do? He knew that our bedroom, on the second level, would be difficult to escape from, so he decided that he shouldn't sleep there. Nor would it be a good idea to sleep on the main floor, with its numerous French doors and windows on all four sides. That left the basement. Logically, he figured that intruders approaching the dark house in the middle of the night would assume that we were sleeping upstairs. The clatter of the numerous pots and kettles that he had piled up on chairs in front of the glass French doors would announce their entry, and while they were searching upstairs he would have time to scramble out through the basement window. So he slept in the basement.

When we told the story to Gloria, she cackled and said, "Good grief, guys, terrorists wouldn't take the time to wire a car or break into your house. They'd just blow the whole place to smithereens. You wouldn't stand a snowball's chance in hell of surviving."

Over the course of 1990, our circle of friends underwent some major changes. In February, Randy's employers transferred him to Pittsburgh. Of the four musketeers, only Charles now remained in Washington with Rob. That spring Gabriel began dating a young man named Brad, whom he introduced to us at a Fourth of July picnic on the banks of the Potomac. A mechanical engineer who worked for a large computer company, Brad was as laid-back as Gabriel was aggressive, and clearly felt comfortable in the background while Gabriel held the stage. Like many of our friends, Brad was a Southerner. He and Gabriel soon moved in together.

Nineteen-ninety wore on without a word from Glenn, who didn't return our calls or reply to our letters.

Then one night in the spring of 1991, Rob went to Brad and Gabriel's house for dinner. He knew that Charles would be there, too, and looked forward not only to catching up with him but to knowing whether Charles had talked with Glenn. He told me later that when he arrived at their condo, he saw Charles, Gabriel, and several other friends smoking on the balcony. Grabbing a drink at the bar, he went outside to join them. It was immediately clear that Charles and Gabriel were arguing, and that Charles had incited the argument by being ornery and cantankerous, though it wasn't immediately clear what he was being cantankerous about. "Hi, hon," Rob said, embracing him. Charles was surprisingly distant, even hostile—as different as possible from his usual jovial self. Rob gathered immediately that Charles was tipsy. This was not an unusual condition for Charles, though it *was* rather unusual for him to be quite so tipsy this early in the evening. It was also unusual for him to be so angry; Charles was a happy drunk.

Listening to Charles rant on, Rob learned that Glenn wasn't the only friend of ours who had abruptly grown tired of living in the Washington area. No sooner had Rob said hello than Charles announced he was frustrated with the D.C. crowd and that he planned to move back to his native North Carolina as soon as possible. He stumbled drunkenly through various insults directed at Rob and Gabriel, saying that they had become "Washington insiders" and that there was so much more to life than the petty, insular concerns of people who lived in D.C.

It didn't take long for Rob to decide that he had had enough of this. "Don't argue with him," he told Gabriel, right in front of Charles. (Rob had no hesitation about discussing Charles, in his presence, in the third person.) "I'm sure something's up. I'll nose around later and find out what it is. Come on, let's go find happy people." And Rob and Gabriel went back in the house.

Charles slipped out early that night without saying good-bye to anyone. Though Rob left several messages for him over the following days, he never phoned back. This was completely out of character for him. During the next two weeks we kept receiving reports from friends who had spotted Charles drinking alone at various bars. Without exception, each of these friends voiced concerns about his drinking.

Rob called Charles's neighbors Cathy and Marie to find out what they knew. They generally saw Charles every day. They had only one bathroom in their apartment, so every morning while Cathy was showering, Marie would go next door to Charles's apartment, use his bathroom, and have coffee. To her, this offered an opportunity to keep an eye on Charles, which she felt he needed; Charles, for his part, humored her, feeling that he didn't need anybody to keep an eye on him. Anyway, when Rob reached Marie, she told him that Charles had been away for several days and that when he had come back a day or so earlier, he had looked terrible, as if he hadn't slept in days. Alarmed, Rob decided to drop by Charles's office unannounced.

ROB

Charles was on the phone when I walked into his office just before lunch. I was shocked to see how he looked. Charles was usually meticulous about his appearance: his monogrammed white shirts were invariably starched, and his hair, albeit long and curly, was always in place. Not today. He was disheveled, unshaven; his eyes were puffy and bloodshot. He looked up from the phone, smiled wanly, and motioned for me to take a chair.

After Charles finished his phone call, we went down to the office building's high-ceilinged lobby. There, among the potted ficus trees and beside a marble fountain, we had sandwiches. Without any sign of his recent hostility, Charles explained his recent behavior and his decision to move. He said that he felt he was spinning his wheels in Washington financially and had decided to start his own business in Durham, where the cost of living was lower and where he could purchase a wonderful old house for what it cost to buy a dreary condo in Washington. He had already looked into listing his condo for sale, and planned to be out of town by the end of summer. I was surprised by the apparent seriousness of Charles's intentions and by the practical steps he had actually taken toward making a move. This wasn't at all like Charles.

Despite the reasons Charles laid out so smoothly, I knew that there must be something he wasn't telling me—that there were deeper reasons for his move that he didn't want to disclose. I pressed him to tell me the whole truth, though I was careful in doing so, for I knew I could push Charles only so far before he would clam up entirely. When I asked how he could make such a decision without consulting his friends, Charles shot back, "Cut the judgmental shit, Rob! You *always* do what's best for you regardless of its effect on anyone else. I intend to do the same!" He snapped his fingers and grinned to cover his underlying anger. The lunch ended on amiable but uneasy terms.

Before leaving Charles, I told him that we hadn't heard from Glenn. Charles said he hadn't either.

STEVE

Shortly thereafter, the war ended. Allied forces had suffered losses, as of course had Iraq. Thankfully, not one soldier from my district had died.

In the first week of June, there was a terrific parade in Washington to welcome home the troops. A section of the viewing stands across from the presidential box was reserved for Members of Congress and their families. I sat next to Rob, and directly behind us were our neighbors Dave McCurdy, then a Congressman from Oklahoma, and his wife, Pam. Dave, a moderate Democrat, had come to Congress the same year that I did, and we had quickly become friends. When Rob and I had built the house on Hitt Avenue, near the McCurdys, Dave and I grew even closer. Like me, the McCurdys attended the Church of the Redeemer in McLean. Both Dave and I loved to jog, and we soon fell into the habit of meeting for runs around McLean.

At the parade Rob and I were lucky to sit in front of Dave, because as a member of the Armed Services Committee who could identify every last tank and gun and knew where each of the military units was from, he made the perfect play-by-play commentator.

As I sat there in the stands, listening to Dave's play-by-play, I was aware of what an incongruous situation I was in. As a member of Congress, I had been awarded a place of honor in the viewing stands. All the other members seated around us knew that Rob and I were a couple; we had never hidden from anyone the nature of our relationship, and nobody seemed terribly scandalized by it. Yet if I had been one of those brave men and women marching down Constitution Avenue, and if a fellow member of my unit had discovered that I was gay, I would have been hounded ignominiously out of the armed services. The irony was strange, uneasy, and bitter. Little did I realize that within a few months the debate over gays in the military would be a front-page issue, that I would play a key role in the controversy—and that it, in turn, would play a key role in changing my life.

The joy that day was also mixed for other reasons. That very morning we had gotten word from Minnesota that my aunt Perk, who had attended my swearing-in years before with my parents, had just died of cancer. As it happened, my parents were visiting me and Rob at the time. I had needed a new car and had always wanted a convertible; my parents had picked one up through my father's Chevrolet dealership lot and had delivered it personally. My oldest sister, Melinda, played chauffeur. They arrived in mid-afternoon, after the parade but before the big fireworks display that evening. We had a picnic in their honor at the Iwo Jima Memorial in Arlington.

There, with a picturesque view of Washington across the Potomac, we set up a blanket and chairs and waited for the friends we had invited to join us.

The first to arrive was Charles. My parents had never met him before—and they would never forget him. How could you forget someone who talks at you constantly for six hours? Charles loved to talk. He loved to hear himself talk even more when he was drinking his beloved vodka. And so that afternoon he talked nonstop.

We thought the Charles we saw that day was classic Charles, happy-go-lucky and fun-loving. We were wrong. It was, rather, the beginning of a summer of unusually heavy drinking for him.

Soon it was clear: something had to be done. But what? None of us believed for a moment that Charles would respond favorably to an attempt on anyone's part to bring up the subject directly. So Randy suggested a different tack. ''Let's try and cut down the drinking,'' he said. ''I know Charles well enough to be able to say that if we're not drinking or smoking, he won't either. Rob, Charles worships the ground you walk on. Let's see if he follows your lead.''

Alas, he didn't. By Thanksgiving, Charles's drinking would be a serious problem.

Washington wasn't the only place to see celebrations of the Gulf War victory. President Bush had asked members of Congress to organize ''welcome-home-the-troops'' events in our respective districts on or around the fourth of July. So I asked Pat Zielke, the mayor of La Crosse, the largest municipality in my district, to host one such event in his city on the Fourth of July. We had a parade and then a ceremony with speeches. I went from there to Pleasantville, which every year celebrates the fourth of July with a softball tournament, dances, and other festivities. I had told the Lions Club in town, ''You know, you should consider whether you want to hold a county-wide 'welcome-home' event as part of your Fourth of July celebration. If you do, I'll organize it for you.''

They did hold such an event, and I did organize it. The day

was a tremendous success. We recognized everyone in Trempeleau County who had served in the war. We rented a large video screen and showed a "welcome-home-the-troops" video. The Pleasantville Community Choir sang "The Nation's Creed"; the Osseo High School band played; all the local legislators gave speeches; there were professional fireworks. It was all quite big-time for such a small town.

Unfortunately, those celebrations of the end of the Gulf War coincided with the first major salvo in another war.

9

On June 30, 1991, the Sunday night before the Fourth of July recess and the "welcome-home-the-troops" event in La Crosse, Rob and I met friends for drinks and dinner at a small establishment in Old Town, the historic district of Alexandria, Virginia, the name of which was the same as its address: 808 King Street. On the first level of this Old New Orleans–style building was a very good restaurant; on its second level was a gay bar. Rob and I had been there several times and had gotten to know some members of the staff. When we arrived that night at around nine o'clock expecting to eat, the maître d' explained that they had already closed the main dining room for the evening and suggested that we grab hamburgers or light fare upstairs. We thanked him and climbed the steps to the bar, which was crowded. While we waited for a free table, I stepped away from our group to order a round of drinks at the bar.

It's not uncommon in Washington for people to introduce themselves at public places to chat for a while about pending legislation, so I wasn't surprised when someone tapped me on the shoulder and introduced himself. Initially the short, swarthy young man who was standing there with a drink in his hand seemed friendly. With a broad smile, he said, "You must be Congressman Gunderson."

I extended my hand and smiled. Rob was a few feet away talking with our friends, and I tried to get his attention so that I could introduce him. "I'm Peter Carmichael," the stranger said, taking my hand, "and I want to know when you're going to come out." (Peter Carmichael is a fictitious name that we have chosen to use here; the person in question gave his real name.)

By this time, Rob had caught my glance and walked toward us. I said to Carmichael, "I *am* out. I'm in this bar, aren't I?"

Carmichael's expression turned dark. He screamed, *"People are dying and you are in the closet!"*

Well, to my way of thinking I wasn't in the closet. I maintained a private life as best I could, but I didn't make concerted efforts to avoid being seen in gay settings, nor did I hide my homosexuality from my friends, family and coworkers.

I knew that Rob was not going to be thrilled with this confrontation. As he neared us, able to gauge the immensity of Carmichael's rage by his tone, Rob interrupted and said, "Steve, our table is ready." I noticed that our group was moving toward the front of the establishment to a vacant table. Carmichael got even louder. *"When are you going to come out!"* By now the bar had grown quiet, except for the sound of a music video playing in the background; the eyes of all sixty or so of the patrons were on me and Carmichael. As Rob gestured for me to walk away from him, Carmichael screamed again: *"When are you going to come out!"* I followed Rob's lead to the table. Carmichael followed. The room remained quiet except for the solitary voice of Carmichael screaming the same words over and over again. As we neared the table and Rob sat down, Carmichael tossed his drink on me. The glass had been full, and the drink splattered most of the people at our table. The room was silent. Two members of the restaurant staff raced forward and physically removed Carmichael from the bar. As he kicked and fought with them, he screamed, *"We'll get you,*

Gunderson! I'll have a hundred queers here in five minutes! You'll come out! You'll come out!''

As we sat in silence, the owner of the restaurant came over and apologized. He had no idea who Carmichael was, but he feared that he might be serious and asked if we would rather leave.

I looked at him, and then at Rob. I didn't say anything. I was numb. And wet. And embarrassed. But Rob was furious. He looked at me and shouted, ''You can put a gun to my head and pull the trigger before I'll let anyone bully me!''

Not cherishing the idea of another altercation, I asked the owner if he thought a group would join Carmichael. He said he didn't know, but promised that they wouldn't be allowed in.

Rob wasn't about to be intimidated. ''I'll have a Dewars and soda and a hamburger, please,'' he told the owner in a loud voice. ''Steve will have a gin-and-tonic.''

Clearly, we were not going anywhere. The dinner that followed was one of mixed emotions and fragmented conversations. But no group of protesters materialized.

In retrospect I realize that this encounter wasn't Carmichael's first gesture in my direction. The previous February, I had received at my office a blizzard of Valentine's Day cards, most of them postmarked in the Washington area. On the faces of the cards were the usual Valentine's Day images: hearts and flowers, Snoopy or Bugs Bunny blowing kisses. But the sentiments scrawled inside were something else again: ''Come out and be mine.'' ''Break the silence and be my Valentine.'' ''Your silence is deafening.'' ''Stand up for your community and we'll stand up for you.'' ''Be my Valentine and make me proud! Come out today!'' ''Love the gay community and we'll love you back. Break the silence.'' ''Stand up to homophobes like Newt Gingrich. We homosexuals have to stick together.'' ''Roses are red, violets are blue, come out of the closet and we'll love you.''

The cards were mostly signed with first names, which in

some cases were followed by the words "ACT UP." One of the cards, however, bore the signature of Peter Carmichael.

I was struck by the cards' messages, which reflected a naive understanding of how politics works and how someone in political office makes a real difference. I was far more interested in working for gay rights from within the system than I was in making myself a Republican poster boy for the gay community. In election after election, my Democratic opponents had routinely been more conservative on gay issues than I was. It seemed to me that the gay community was far better served by me, a member who was sensitive to gay issues, even if I felt obliged to remain quiet about my sexual orientation to preserve my electability, than it would be by an antigay Democrat who might succeed in winning the district if I publicized my homosexuality. By and large, gay activists disagreed with me. For them, aggressive confrontation was the paramount goal. But I knew Congress well enough to realize that aggressive confrontation over gay issues was not a winning strategy. Since most members are conditioned not to think for themselves but to serve the opinions and prejudices of their constituencies, trying to educate or to awaken the consciences of members about gay issues could only have limited effectiveness.

Many of the messages on the cards also reflected a basic ignorance of my political record. "Stop bashing your gay friends," one of the cards read. "Support the civil rights bill. We know all about you. Hypocrasy [sic] is not pretty. There is power in truth. Come out now." In fact I had never been a hypocrite in my voting. "It has come to my attention," wrote someone else, "that you, while enjoying the privileges of a gay lifestyle, are still in the closet and have a terrible voting record on issues of gay/lesbian rights and issues concerning AIDS. Aren't you ashamed of yourself for lying and abusing your position of power? If you came out of your closet and stood up to the vicious homophobes of Congress, such as William Dannemeyer, you could achieve great victories for some 25 million Americans."

Again, though I had not done anywhere near as much as I should have done to press for AIDS funding and to stand up to bigotry, my actual voting record on gay, lesbian, and AIDS issues was far from "terrible." I had not been as courageous as I now wish I had been, but neither had I voted directly against my conscience as a gay man. On the contrary, I've always stood up against prejudice of any kind—and that's a record I'm proud of.

Though the Valentine's Day cards were obviously part of a coordinated effort, the tone of their messages varied widely. A few of the senders wrote thoughtful, respectful notes and signed their names; some, by contrast, were hostile, sarcastic, vulgar, even threatening. "Every gay man in the closet helps to isolate me and make my life more difficult and dangerous. Every gay man in the closet is my enemy. Come out, and be my Valentine instead." That one was signed by a prominent ACT UP member in New York City who has since died of AIDS. Other were unsigned: "ACT UP/DC is watching *you*. Come out. Support your community now." "ACT UP is watching!" "We're watching where you work and play!"

Well, fine. ACT UP members were perfectly free to watch me at "play." Rob and I patronized gay bars in and around Washington, where I was always up-front about my identity. Everybody who knew us personally was aware that I was gay. Yet because I didn't stand up in Congress and announce my homosexuality, ACT UP saw me as a hypocritical closet case.

In retrospect I can see that it would have saved me a lot of grief if I had just issued a press release saying, in effect, "I'm gay. Let's get on with the job." Every fiber of my being, however, resisted the idea of issuing such a statement. Republicans don't issue press releases about their personal lives. I certainly wasn't about to let a handful of terrorists dictate my actions as a representative of the 540,000 residents of the Third District of Wisconsin.

What made reading these cards even more difficult was that I understood what motivated their senders. I understood that for a long time, gay people who had made the decision to be true to themselves by acknowledging their homosexuality did so knowing that they would thereby invite much of the mainstream public's opprobrium. Because of the public's attitude toward homosexuality, "coming out" was not just a matter of publicly admitting that you were gay—it was also essentially a matter of agreeing to become part of a subculture that automatically operated on the quite accurate assumption that most mainstream institutions were its enemies. The recognition that society as a whole had, in effect, declared war on gay people created in their minds a siege mentality. Feeling alienated from society and its institutions, many openly gay people were naturally disposed to think of themselves as radical and to pursue a politics of confrontation. I understood that.

At the same time, I believed in the good of working within the system—and in the wrongness of outing. Then as now, I believed very strongly that gay individuals should have the right to decide when and how they come out. Such decisions depend on a variety of social, professional, and emotional factors, which differ from individual to individual.

To be sure, a gay person does forfeit a right of privacy when he or she is a hypocrite. Certainly that's the view that the national press corps took of the matter. Reporters told me, "As long as you are not a hypocrite, the press will not identify you as being gay. But if you stand up on the House floor and demagogue the gay and lesbian community, if you seize opportunities to legislate against them, if you appear to be the voice of the pro-family movement as defined by the far right, then you're a hypocrite and the press will go after you." The same standard holds for straight politicians: the senator who spouts moralisms on the floor of the Senate and then goes to massage parlors isn't going to last long with the national press.

That Fourth of July weekend I was scheduled to fly home to Wisconsin. Aside from planning to attend the "welcome-home-the-troops" events in La Crosse and Pleasantville, I had work to do, town meetings to attend, and mobile office hours.

I had neglected, however, to schedule time to deal with further unpleasantness from the persistent Mr. Carmichael, who, in the moments after his attack on me in the 808 King Street Bar, had taken steps to ensure that I would have a lively weekend. Immediately after our encounter, he had gone out, written a press release about how he'd splashed a drink on me in a gay bar, and distributed it to the media. A Minneapolis cohort of his whom I'll call Carl Bell had announced to the press that they would confront me personally and demonstrate against me at the "welcome-home" event in La Crosse. Alerted to these developments, reporters had been calling my offices in both Washington and Osseo. I headed home with a great sense of trepidation, and, from the moment I landed, was bombarded with questions from the press about my personal life and about Carmichael.

All this happened on a day when a particularly gratifying event was to take place. My district's National Guard unit had served in the Gulf War. They were proud to have taken part in the war, but once it was over, they found themselves sitting around in the desert with nothing to do. This made no sense to them. Their leaders had spoken to highly placed people at both the federal and state levels to ask whether the unit might be sent back home, but nothing happened. They felt they were getting a deaf ear.

Finally they turned to me. I talked to someone at the Pentagon about them, and the return had been arranged and set to take place on July 3. I was to meet the plane and welcome the Guard home personally. So on the afternoon of July 3, I found myself standing at the airfield at Camp Douglas in Juneau County waiting for this plane and knowing that I was going to be demonstrated against the next day. It should have been one of the greatest moments of my congressional career, but instead it was a time of real unease.

When the plane pulled in, I walked out onto the landing strip with the Guard members' families and friends, stood at the foot of the stairs on the tarmac, and greeted the Guard members as they came off the plane. The first person to welcome them home was Governor Tommy Thompson, the second was the commander of the Wisconsin Guard, the third was Steve Gunderson. I had been told that the Guard members felt I was the only person who had been kind and helpful to them, and indeed, as they came off the plane, each of them thanked me profusely for bringing them home. They knew I'd done it, and they were grateful.

Did any of them know I was gay? I wonder. Did they care? I doubt it.

After the Guard got off the plane, we had a rally in one of the buildings. Just as I was preparing to get up and deliver some welcoming remarks, the Milwaukee *Journal*'s Washington reporter, Patrick Jasperse, came over and started firing questions at me about my personal life. I couldn't believe how infatuated the media were with this nonstory, even at a time when there was a very real, human drama taking place on that airfield.

But I hadn't seen anything yet.

On the next day, July 4, I went to La Crosse for the parade. The gay group that had promised to show up turned out to consist of Carl Bell himself, who, before the parade began, walked along the parade route on Main Street handing out pink flyers announcing my homosexuality and calling on me to come out. A policeman arrested him for littering and hauled him off to jail, although he was released in time to return to Main Street for the parade. When my car passed by him, he stepped into the street and handed me one of his flyers. I looked down at it. The flyer entreated me to "come out now for gay rights" and to "join the sponsors of the gay and lesbian rights bill in Congress." It added: "No votie! No nookie!" (One of the assumptions that seemed to underlie a lot of the gay-left propaganda about me was that I was out at the bars every night picking up guys.) It was, to say the least, an unpleasant thing to experience while I was trying to carry out my professional duties.

I found it amazing that all somebody had to do in order to create a firestorm of media attention (or, at least, the western

Wisconsin version of a firestorm) was to throw a drink at a public figure and issue a press release. Instead of ignoring the whole thing, or treating me as a victim of an unprovoked personal attack, the press cast me in the role of a villain—simply, I think, because I'd been in a gay bar.

One curious footnote to this whole episode was that when Carmichael "outed" me, he also outed a certain senator, who flatly denied that he was gay. The press never touched that story; they never breathed a word in print about the senator, who many reporters knew very well was lying. They did run stories about me, however, because I had enough integrity not to flatly deny who and what I am.

Not that I deserved any awards for full disclosure. While I didn't want to lie about my homosexuality, I wasn't yet prepared to talk about it publicly. In a quixotic attempt to be honest about my private life while at the same time keeping it private, I said some things to reporters that Rob still complains about—and that still make me wince. On July 22, 1991, for example, an AP story in the Eau Claire *Leader-Telegram* quoted me as saying the following in response to reports that I was gay: "I have been accused of being a womanizer by some, abstinent by others. I can't prove any of them." The AP reporter asked if I was gay. "I can't answer that," I replied, "because I can't prove it to you." What kind of personal life did I have, then? "I'm married to my job. I don't really have a personal life. That's it. I'm here at seven o'clock [in the morning] and here late at night. For better or worse, I've committed my life to public office. The rest is pretty boring."

In retrospect, those remarks were not models of clarity or honesty. Nor were they fair to Rob. All I can say is that I was motivated at the time by my very strong natural inclination to separate myself as an individual with personal needs and desires from Steve Gunderson, the professional public servant. It would take a few more years for me to realize that I couldn't make that separation, however much I wanted to. Though I fought it energetically, I would eventually be confronted with the fact that my responsibility to myself, to Rob, to my district, to the gay community, and to my country all demanded that I explicitly come out.

A lot of people wouldn't have an easy time believing this, but the first person who called me after the Carmichael incident to ask how I was doing was Newt. He phoned me at home in Wisconsin that very weekend. "I'm calling," he said, "because I want to know how you're doing. I'm aware of what happened and I'm concerned about how it's affecting you." Not politically concerned, he explained, *personally* concerned. I remember vividly that he made that distinction, and I appreciated it more than I can say.

Another person who was very sensitive in his treatment of me after the Carmichael incident was Dave McCurdy. The next Saturday, while Rob and I were working on our front yard, Dave drove by in his Blazer, saw us and pulled into the driveway.

"How are you?" he asked with real concern.

"Fine, how are you?" I said jauntily, avoiding the issue.

Though he didn't bring up the outing, it was clear that there was only one reason why he'd stopped by—to give us moral support. Rob and I invited him inside, and the three of us drank iced tea and talked about everything but the Carmichael incident.

And then he left. It was a seemingly small incident, but both Rob and I experienced it as a beautiful gesture of friendship and affirmation that went beyond the call of collegial duty.

I had never talked to Newt directly about my sexuality, although of course he knew about me and Rob, whom he had met socially on several occasions. That long-postponed discussion finally took place one evening that summer, between the July and August breaks. It was a Wednesday night. The whip organization had been holding a long-range planning meeting. We had been in the habit of getting together for these sessions on Wednesday nights over pizza. When the meeting was over and the other members had filed out of the room, Newt and I sat there alone in the room, surrounded by empty pizza boxes.

"So how are you doing?" Newt asked me. "Personally, I mean?"

I could tell that he really wanted to know the answer. This isn't always the case with Newt. In his now-famous twenty-hour lecture course on American civilization at Reinhardt College, he says, "Anytime I run into somebody and I say, 'How are you doing?' and they start by telling me how they feel, I worry." He's bothered by what he sees as excessive self-absorption or self-pity; he prefers to see people who are out-ward-directed, involved in worthwhile projects. That's proba-bly one reason why we get along so well, because I'm not the sort of person to open up about my feelings at the drop of a hat, not even with the people closest to me.

So instead of telling him how I felt, I changed the subject from me to the larger issue at stake—the ignorance of conser-vative Republicans about the real lives of gay people in America.

"Newt," I said, "you've got to understand that someplace between the radical gay left on the one hand, and Bill Danne-meyer and the radical right on the other hand, is truth and justice on this issue. Dannemeyer and the far right are just plain wrong when they say that being gay is a choice. You've got to know that I spent years desperately trying to change my orientation. I don't know a single person who would *choose* to go through the hell of being a gay person in a society that despises you. You've got to understand that. And you've got to know that the radical gay community does not speak for all gay people. There are literally hundreds of gay people right here on Capitol Hill, within the Republican party, whom you and I both know, who are respected, competent profes-sionals but who are also gay."

There was silence.

"As you know," I went on, "I'm totally aware of the politi-cal environment we're dealing with. If you feel that I've be-come more of a liability than you can handle and you want me to leave the whip organization, I'm willing to do that."

Newt shook his head in a pensive way. Softly but forcefully, he said, "I would never ask you to resign over that nonsense."

The Carmichael and Bell incidents drove home for me the downside of my position in the Republican leadership. Rob had warned me that the whip job would result in such personal ordeals. But I was willing to endure them for the sake of serving my constituents—and I knew that by accepting the whip job, I had done something very good for my district, even as I had done something disastrous for my own sense of freedom, privacy, and security.

By joining the leadership, I had provided a ready target for every gay person with a grudge against my party or against President Bush. If any Republican anywhere did anything they didn't like, certain gay people would attack me for it. Yes, there were many closeted gay men in both the House and the Senate. But I was the only one in the Republican leadership—and that made me a sitting duck for Queer Nation and ACT UP.

Matt took a special interest in my travails with Carmichael and Bell. He and John had long since become involved in AIDS activism. They had both participated in AIDS Walks and attended HRCF fund-raising dinners; they had delivered food to people with AIDS and tended to ailing friends; their tenth anniversary party in 1989 had been an AIDS benefit. Shortly after my initial encounters with Carmichael and Bell, I was talking to Matt on the phone when he said, "Steve, you know that John and I will support you in whatever you do. But have you ever thought of just plain coming out? I think maybe it's time you did." This was the very first time that any of our friends ever suggested I come out publicly.

"Matt," I replied, "I know what you're saying but I'm not sure this is the right time and the right way." I was not about to let radical gays dictate the terms on which I would come out.

In the wake of my encounter with Carl Bell at the parade in La Crosse, Bell began to issue charges about me that were almost entirely false. He said that I had "voted for motions that would have required mandatory [HIV] testing for beauticians, food service personnel, and health care workers." This was a reference to the Chapman amendment to the Americans with Disabilities Act, an amendment I had twice opposed. He said I had "voted for antigay restrictions on AIDS education money, requiring that no material can be produced which treats homosexuality as normal." False: the limitation on funding had prohibited any material that "promoted or encouraged" any given lifestyle; it was not a provision to reduce or limit AIDS education funding.

Bell further charged that I "was one of the people involved in the Mapplethorpe controversy" and had "voted against Mapplethrope and Serrano"—a reference to two controversial NEA-supported artists whose work right-wingers had cited again and again as reasons to dismantle the agency. In fact, on a procedural ballot I had voted to cut $45,000 from the NEA allocation rather than let stand a cut of $1.4 million. As a major Republican supporter of the NEA, and of the arts generally, I played a key role in developing the compromise with the far right that made the NEA's reauthorization possible; I had also voted against an amendment that would have placed restrictions on NEA funding.

Bell charged that I had "voted for an amendment that would have allowed Catholic colleges in the Washington, D.C., area to discriminate on employment." Wrong: I had been the only member of the Wisconsin delegation, and one of only twenty Republicans in the entire House, who had voted against this amendment (proposed by Bill Dannemeyer) to the 1990 D.C. appropriations bill.

While failing to note that I had voted for the Hate Crimes Act, which passed overwhelmingly in 1989, Bell claimed that I had voted to criminalize sodomy in Washington, D.C. No such vote had ever been taken in the House. He said that I had opposed the establishment of the National AIDS Commission, when in fact I had voted in favor of an omnibus AIDS package that, among other things, had established the National AIDS Commission in 1988.

He also maintained that I had failed to sponsor the Gay and Lesbian Civil Rights Act of 1991. In that case he was right. I had opposed that measure because it had implied a need for quotas, which I don't support. Aside from that, there was the matter of priorities. To my mind, the gay issues that the 102nd Congress should focus on were gays in the military and AIDS funding. The Civil Rights Act was a nice idea in theory, but I didn't consider it particularly beneficial in practical terms. Its point was to define equal justice as a basic right. I have no quarrel with that as a goal. But I've experienced great frustration in dealing with people who believe that if you pass bills that define equal justice as a basic right, then somehow equal justice will suddenly materialize out of nowhere throughout society. Life doesn't work that way; democratic government just isn't that powerful.

I should know, for I happen to have served all my career on the subcommittee that oversees the Equal Employment Opportunity Commission. The last time I looked, that commission had a backlog of over 100,000 cases—a three-year turnaround. Now, if the Gay and Lesbian Civil Rights Act had been passed, the enforcement of the job provisions would have fallen under the jurisdiction of the EEOC. What practical good would that have done the average gay man or lesbian? Most people who are fired because of their sexual orientation can't afford to wait three years for a government decision.

Ideally, we do need such protections. But it seemed to me that those who were preoccupied with getting the Civil Rights Act passed were focusing their energies on trying to pass a bill that, first of all, didn't stand a chance of passing anyway, and second, wouldn't accomplish all that much if it did pass, and third, contained provisions that were extremely controversial and ultimately, in my view, counterproductive. In 1994, the Human Rights Campaign Fund came back with a revised version of the Gay and Lesbian Civil Rights Bill in which ninety percent of the provisions that I had a problem with were eliminated, and that time I did agree to cosponsor it.

My office responded to Bell's bogus accusations with a statement. "Queer Nation has embarked on a campaign to humiliate and blackmail a United States congressman into voting one hundred percent for their agenda. *No* group can use character assassination, lies and actual threats to intimidate Gunderson into voting their agenda. Such an approach is both morally and principally wrong—these McCarthy-like tactics are repugnant and, in fact, the ultimate in hypocrisy."

Indeed. But those tactics were nonetheless very effective. Thanks to Carmichael and Bell, many people in the gay community believed that I was a hypocrite, spending my nights picking up guys at Dupont Circle bars and spending my days casting vicious votes against gay rights and AIDS funding. Rob found it interesting that my slanderers, for all their supposed research into my life and record, never managed to uncovered a simple little fact that every other gay guy in Washington seemed aware of—namely, that he and I had been together for years. In the months to come, the gay press would be full of articles based on Carmichael's and Bell's false charges.

Meanwhile, life moved on. For a long time, Rob had wanted to have a dog. I always nixed the idea without explaining why. He thought I didn't like dogs. Not so. As a boy, I had had a small, furry dog named Queenie. We were inseparable. Then one day I crossed the street in front of our house in Pleasantville, and Queenie followed me, and walked right into the path of an oncoming milk truck. I turned to see the truck run over my dog and spit her crumpled body out into the street. Queenie was much bigger than I was, but, in horror, I picked up her mangled body and carried her home to my parents. She was dead, of course. After that, I didn't have another dog, and didn't want one. I didn't want to relive that nightmare.

ROB

Then, on a Sunday afternoon in September 1991, I took the bull by the horns. Instead of asking Steve if we could have a dog, I *told* him we were going to have one. "I've found a breeder who has a six-week-old litter of boxers," I announced abruptly. "Linda's boys are going with me to pick one out. Join us, it'll be fun."

Steve capitulated. With Andre and Danylo in the backseat, we drove to the breeder's house. We played with the pups and all agreed on the friendliest one, who had a big pink nose. I named her Della.

That first night I established rules about where the puppy could be in the house and what she would be allowed to do. I was firm with her—*and* with Steve. When we set her down in her sleeping place beside our bed, she started to whimper. Steve wanted to let her get in bed with us. "No," I said. "The dog cannot get in the bed. Rule number six."

That firmness didn't last too long. The whimpering continued, and I ended up spending that night, and several nights to come, on the floor with the puppy. My behavior, I'm afraid, set the precedent for how we would both end up handling Della, who soon came to realize that she could go anywhere she wanted in the house and do just about anything she cared to.

Later that month, on a sunny, pleasant Saturday, Steve and I and several other friends gathered at Charles's place to help him load the large U-Haul truck he had rented to move himself to North Carolina. We separated things that were to be put in the truck from things that were to be left behind. We swept and scrubbed the condo and argued about what to do with the things we hadn't packed in the truck. Finally we all had a late lunch with Charles at a nearby restaurant. True to form, Charles thought it was only right that we buy his meal for him—and this, after we had all broken our backs moving his stuff! That was vintage Charles.

After lunch, Charles climbed into his U-Haul, turned the ignition, and drove off. That was that: he was gone. It all happened faster than we had expected. Not till we saw that truck disappearing into the distance did Steve and I fully realize that the life we'd enjoyed with Charles—the lighthearted nightly get-togethers, the warm camaraderie at the dinner table—was over forever. With Glenn in Florida, Randy in Pennsylvania, and Charles in North Carolina, the dispersion of the group that Steve had thought of as "the four musketeers" was complete.

In October, I finally managed to reach Glenn and learned that his condition had deteriorated. It was also in that month that Charles came north for a few days' visit, planning to stay first with his ex-roommate Buck on Capitol Hill and then with us. Our first news that Charles was actually in town came in a phone call on Tuesday from Gabriel, who told me that he'd run into Charles at J.R.'s the night before, and had a couple of drinks with him.

Later that night, I received a call from Buck. At first, Buck's tone was rather lighthearted. He told me that Charles had arrived in Washington on the previous Friday, had been staying with him, and had planned to move to our place on Wednesday. "I'm surprised to see how much weight Charles has lost," Buck said tentatively. He continued to talk about Charles, filling me in on what had been happening with him. His tone grew darker and more somber with every sentence. It was clear that Buck was gradually leading up to something, that he was trying to break some very bad news as gently as possible. Finally, unable to take it anymore, I interrupted him. "Buck," I demanded, "where is Charles?"

"Rob," Buck said, "don't get alarmed. We had to rush him this morning to the emergency room at George Washington Hospital. He's still there, undergoing tests." Buck paused and took a breath. Then he said paternally, "Our friend is very sick, buddy."

"What is it?"

Buck explained: Charles had been diagnosed with pneumonia. He was in the intensive care unit. The prognosis wasn't good. One lung had collapsed. The doctors suspected that if they could arrest the pneumonia, they could stabilize him. But that they had no idea if that was possible. If he didn't respond to the medication, he might not make it through the night.

Steve and I left the house shortly afterwards and drove to the hospital. There we found Charles's neighbors, Cathy and Marie, in the waiting room. Before we went into his room, they warned us that he had lost an incredible amount of weight and was only partially conscious. Marie told us not to act surprised when we saw him. Then she said that he had been diagnosed with AIDS. He was in the advanced stages.

We were shocked. This was the first time any of us had thought of AIDS in connection with Charles. In all the years we had known him, he had never so much as hinted at having had a sexual encounter; we had never seen him picked up in a bar or seen him pick somebody else up. He came off as virtually asexual.

Cathy and Marie told us that Charles had known for quite some time that he was sick but had hidden the symptoms from most of us. His move to Durham had been motivated not by any sudden loathing for the Washington scene or a longing to live more cheaply, but exclusively by a desire to keep his illness a secret from his friends.

Suddenly things that had previously not made any sense came together. We couldn't believe that Charles had felt the need to conceal the truth from people who loved him and to carry the burden of a potentially terminal illness alone.

We hugged Cathy and Marie and went in to see Charles. He looked even worse than we had expected. He was hooked up to a respirator. His face was gaunt and colorless and his facial expression was tortured. And his weight loss was amazing. He was asleep, and he remained asleep for the five or ten minutes that Steve and I stood there in silence by the side of his bed. Nothing about the man in that bed resembled the animated character whose possessions we had packed into a U-Haul just three months earlier.

10

Throughout most of the 1980s, Rob and I had a pretty tenuous relationship with AIDS. We had followed its course with concern, and had participated in various AIDS fund-raisers. But that was about it. Now things had begun to change. The pain of the Carmichael incident was nothing compared to the pain of watching beloved friends suffer with AIDS.

Before they became ill, Glenn and Charles had not been as close to me as they had been to Rob. AIDS altered that. Part of the reason is that our friends come to Rob and me for different things. They come to Rob to learn how to live. They come to me to learn how to die. They see me as a pillar of religious strength. Even those who aren't churchgoers know that I'm one; even those who don't pray know that I do. With Charles, in times to come, I would have deeply personal conversations in which he sought assurance and confidence. I was able to give these things to him in a very different way than Rob could. Partly it's because of the age difference: in a way I serve as an older brother to our friends, because most of them are closer to Rob's age than to mine.

He would start a phone conversation by telling me that he

was depressed and that he considered himself a personal and a professional failure. On the personal level, he had never sustained a romantic relationship. On the professional level, he worked as a headhunter in a headhunting agency. That's quite respectable work, but in Washington, which is centered on government, a job like that just didn't carry any prestige. I said to him, "How can you say you're a personal failure? Look at your sister and her kids, how much they love you. Look at all your friends." And I would start naming his friends. "Look how important you are to them, look at how much they've done for you. Why do you think they've done it? Not because they hate you, but because they love you."

AIDS had brought him face to face with his mortality, and he worried about what would happen to him after he died. He knew I was a Christian, and he asked me about God and death and salvation. The most important thing that I can say to someone who happens to be gay who has lived in American society in the 1980s and 1990s is that my God is not a God of judgment but a God of love. If you consider yourself a Christian and know anything about the New Testament, you know that the mission of our faith is a mission of love for *everybody*. That was the message I tried to communicate to Charles. I never tried to be complicated about it, never got into theological niceties. I just told him things that he desperately needed to hear.

He wasn't alone in that regard. I would find that same need over the years in our other gay friends. Certain people who call themselves Christians have been so relentless in insisting that gay people are bad and that AIDS is God's vengeance that when some of us are suffering with AIDS, we can't help wondering whether they're right.

Charles made it through Tuesday night and got perceptibly better on Wednesday. On Thursday, he was disconnected from the respirator and moved into a private room. His improvement continued, and several days later he was released and returned immediately to Durham. Tests later revealed that his

T-cell count had dropped to 50. (Most healthy people have T-cell counts between 500 and 1,000.)

Charles didn't make it to our Thanksgiving dinner that year. But he was unquestionably present. He was the main topic of conversation. In my toast, I welcomed the new friends who were joining us that day and lamented Charles's absence from our table.

Over the next few weeks Charles and Rob had innumerable conversations about Charles's health. Charles said that he had suspected he was suffering from AIDS for a long time. Instead of seeing a doctor or telling his friends, however, he had done a very Charles thing—he had fled Washington in an attempt to run from reality and from potential embarrassment. Just as he couldn't deal with the idea of his straight friends, relatives, and coworkers knowing he was gay, he couldn't bear to let his gay friends know he had AIDS.

He also shared with us his concerns about insurance. That May, his employer had distributed a memo stating that preexisting conditions would not be honored by the terms of the company's health plan. Charles knew then that he was out on a limb. He also knew that in the commonwealth of Virginia, the results of any AIDS test conducted by his primary-care physician would not be confidential. He couldn't bring himself to go to a clinic. What did that leave? He thought that if he could get back to North Carolina, things would be different. He would be able to get tested and get insurance. Yet it hadn't worked out that way. His insurance companies in both Virginia and North Carolina had refused to pay his hospital bills, and attorneys for both insurance companies had begun to bear down upon him mercilessly.

The next day, having been told that Charles was out of the woods for the time being, we took a few hours to do laundry and catch up with other household work. Matt and John, who had heard about Charles's hospitalization through mutual friends, phoned to ask about him, and Rob raced through a narrative of everything that had happened. He kept repeating that he couldn't believe how much Charles had changed—that he simply didn't look like himself. As he spoke, his fury welled up inside him and his exhaustion began to manifest itself in his tone of voice. (We hadn't had much sleep the night before.)

Matt listened patiently, allowing Rob to get some of his anger out of his system. Then he said quietly, "Rob, John and I have buried so many of our friends, so I know what you're feeling and I wish I could help. But you must come to realize, Rob, that you and Steve have been extremely lucky so far to have escaped the losses that many of us have long since gotten used to."

At that moment, stressed out by the events of the previous day and preoccupied with thoughts of Charles, Rob read Matt's remarks as an attempt at consolation. But then Matt went on to say something that Rob didn't understand at all until later. "Rob," he said, "you know many people who are sick. You just don't know that they are."

That night Rob was lying in bed while I was across the room folding clothes and watching the eleven o'clock news. Suddenly Matt's comment came back to Rob, and hit him like a ton of bricks. *"You know many people who are sick."* Suddenly Rob realized that Matt had been telling him in his own way that he and John were also sick. Tears began to roll down Rob's cheeks. He told me what Matt had said and what he knew it had meant. I stopped folding clothes, stopped looking at the news, and sank quietly onto the bed, numbed by the suddenness of it all.

As I watched our friends, one by one, fall under the shadow of AIDS, and as I saw my Republican colleagues rant viciously about "family values," I knew that Matt had been right when he had suggested that I come out; I knew that I should stand up and speak out for respect and understanding. But I didn't. I resisted the impulse with all my might. I can't stress enough how alien such a move would have been to me, with my strong sense of privacy and my disinclination to draw attention to myself.

Now, just a few years later, ACT UP and Queer Nation are both pretty much history. They were too hot not to cool down. These groups were less about making a reasonable attempt to effect political change than they were about releasing rage. The rage was understandable, but the politics were often counterproductive. Many of their members have died or moved on, either leaving activism entirely or realizing that if they really want to get things done, they have to take a more pragmatic, inside-the-system approach.

But they were right: I had not done enough for people with AIDS. The illnesses of my friends, and of the hundreds of thousands of other AIDS sufferers around the world whom I didn't know, challenged me at the depths of my soul and conscience. My friends and fellow gay men were dying, and here I was, a leader of the party of Jesse Helms and Strom Thurmond, doing too little to combat their antigay rhetoric. And the rhetoric was getting worse.

One ominous sign of things to come was brought to my attention by Rob during one of our late-night arguments in April 1992. Opening that week's issue of the *Washington Blade*, he showed me a reprint of a letter that had been sent a couple of months earlier to President Bush. The letter criticized Bush's commerce secretary and campaign director, Robert Mosbacher, for meeting with officials of the National Gay and Lesbian Task Force. ''The invitation and meeting,'' the letter charged, ''was a slap in the face to every voter who affirms the traditional family.''

The letter was signed by eight of the more right-wing House Republicans. Among them was Newt. As was often the case in such circumstances, I couldn't provide a defense against Rob's charge that Republicans are heartless. Instead I fired off a private letter to Newt. It was perhaps the most personal letter I had ever written to a colleague; unlike the letter that I would write three years later to Bob Dole challenging his return of a contribution to a gay Republican group, the missive to Newt wasn't released to the press. In it, I informed Newt that I was deeply disturbed to see his name among the signatories of the Mosbacher letter. Within the month of December, I said, I had learned that three close friends were dying of AIDS.

"They are good decent people," I wrote. "One is a high-ranking Republican staff member on one of our House committees. As I watch them get progressively weaker and grow increasingly thinner, I hurt for them and my pending loss. When I know that they know of our working relationship and see the kind of banality this letter represents, I am sickened." About the Mosbacher letter's reference to "family values," I wrote:

> I think I share the values you espoused. Here in Washington we are a key part of our neighborhood. We care for our neighbors' children and their pets. We attend the functions at their separate churches and synagogues. In many ways, I think, we represent a foundation for friends, straight and gay, through good times and bad. At home I am the godfather for a cousin, a nephew, and a niece. I serve as "Uncle Steve" to sixteen nieces and nephews. During my family's recent financial hardship I took additional time to care for my parents and their far-ranging needs.
>
> In short, I recognize and embrace family values. I am Republican. I happen to be gay. If your definition of family values is actually a euphemism for the continued oppression of minorities, please accept this as my resignation as deputy whip. If I have misunderstood some nuance about this letter, then please explain yourself to me as well as others who are unclear about the discrepancy that your signature on this letter suggests. You must understand that I, for my friends' sake and my own integrity, cannot sit back and be a party to further discrimination, hypocrisy, and insensitivity on this issue.

After receiving my letter, Newt phoned.
"We need to talk," he said.
"Yes, we do," I replied.
"Look," he said, "I'm sorry I signed that letter. The problem is that I get asked to sign so many things that I don't pay attention to what I'm being asked to sign. If it's a letter from a Republican colleague I try to be nice, so I sign the letter. I've got to quit doing that, because I'm obviously getting myself

in too much trouble, as I did in this case. I just didn't look closely enough at that letter and shouldn't have signed it and I'm sorry about it."

Cynics would say that Newt had the best of both worlds there: he was able to win approval from his right-wing allies for signing the letter, and able to placate me personally by making that phone call. That may or may not be true. I just don't know. Time will tell.

But I will say this. Given how incautious Newt can be in his public statements on controversial issues, he would seem to have been extremely careful not to declare war on the gay community. He has said that he doesn't support "promotion" of homosexuality, whatever that means, but he has also made it clear that, despite the pressures on him in recent years, he is not about to engage in the kind of active demonization of gay people that Pat Buchanan, for example, practices. And I think that's the best we can hope for from a leader who has as conservative a political base as Newt has.

People ask me a lot about Newt's attitude toward gay men and lesbians. I think that Newt, like most members of Congress, has had to become educated slowly and gradually about gay issues. He certainly isn't all the way there yet. His comparison of homosexuality to alcoholism indicates a profound misunderstanding. Some of his comments I've simply had to put in perspective, recognizing his relative lack of interaction with openly gay people and his relative lack of understanding of the reality of gay people's lives.

Rob disagrees with me about all this. He feels that Newt's problem is not ignorance about homosexuality but a cynical readiness to bash gay people for his own political purposes—even as he's willing to be a friend and ally of a gay man, also for political purposes. I simply don't want to believe that's true.

My distress and guilt over my party's assault on gay people unexpectedly surfaced on a beautiful day in the spring of 1992, when I attended my niece Kaija Hanson's high school graduation in Decorah, Iowa. That Sunday, before the graduation ceremony, I went with several family members to a worship service at Decorah's main Lutheran church. The church was crowded, the pews packed with young graduates, their parents, brothers, and sisters, as well as a number of relatives, like me, who had come from out of town for the big day.

The service went along as usual until the time came for the sermon by the young assistant pastor. Rather than speak from the pulpit, which is the usual practice in the Lutheran Church, the pastor took a microphone and stood in the middle aisle, near most of the high school kids, among whom, I had been told, he was very popular. As he began to speak, I found myself overcome with emotion at the story he had to tell.

He told about a man he had known many years ago. The man was named Mr. Moore and he had been the preacher's high school teacher, wrestling coach, and all-around life model. Shortly after the pastor had graduated and gone on to college, it had become widely known in the community that Mr. Moore was gay. Subsequently Mr. Moore was driven out of the school system and out of town. The pastor lost track of Mr. Moore after that, and had no contact with him for a number of years.

Only recently, the pastor had heard that Mr. Moore was dying of AIDS. He had obtained Mr. Moore's address and had written him a letter of support. The message of his sermon was plain and simple: Mr. Moore had been a good man and a good teacher, and the people at the high school all those years ago had been un-Christian in their treatment of him. The pastor exhorted the students in the congregation not to be that way as they went on to assume positions of responsibility in the world, but rather to stand up against inhumanity and act with Christian love.

I was deeply moved and impressed by the power of the pastor's preaching. So, it was clear, was everyone else in the church. As the sermon reached its conclusion, you could have heard a pin drop. Soon after I returned to Washington, I wrote the pastor a letter thanking him for the sermon and also revealing my own inner turmoil.

In the letter, I informed the pastor that I was Kaija's uncle, and added that I was also a congressman, a Lutheran, and a homosexual. I was comfortable with my homosexuality, I said, and lived in a rewarding committed relationship that I expected to last the rest of my life. But that happiness hadn't come easily. "I prayed literally every day for eight years," I wrote, "asking God to lift this from me."

I went on to explain why his sermon had hit home for me. "Last fall, within a two-month period, we received word that three of our very closest and best friends were HIV-positive. One now has advanced AIDS."

I told the pastor that I wanted to help my friends and that I knew my identity as a Christian compelled me to help them. But I was weak. I was scared. I couldn't yet bring myself to do what I knew I had to do. The sermon that he had given that morning, and that I would never have heard if I had not been in Decorah for Kaija's graduation, had helped me to move in the right direction. His courage, I wrote, had motivated me "to stand up for those hurting among us, and the discrimination they feel."

Some weeks later, the pastor wrote back to thank me for my letter and to give me more encouragement. "I am sure you know," he wrote,

> that as you allow your concern and compassion for people with AIDS to become more public you risk people finding out more about you and your background and private life. It is my prayer that God will protect you from slander and the harsh judgment(s) that our society is so adept at serving up. It is also my prayer that a man of your strength, sexual orientation, and position of influence will, at least on some front, be (someday, soon) a voice of reason, a voice of love, a voice of call to action, and a voice for God.

On June 9, Dan Quayle gave a brief preview of the Republican national convention when he addressed the Southern Baptist convention. In that speech, which contained Quayle's first notorious jab at the "cultural elite," he said of liberal intellectuals who looked down on him, "I wear their scorn as my badge of honor."

After watching Quayle's speech on C-SPAN, Rob said, "That's one of the dumbest speeches I ever heard." Along with his friend Dwight McNeill, an architect who works for him at Morris-Day, and Dwight's lover, Brian Noyes, a professional graphics designer, Rob designed and printed a few dozen T-shirts with the words "cultural elite" and Quayle's "badge of honor" line printed on them. Later that month, they sold those T-shirts at the Gay Pride Day festivities for fifteen dollars apiece. The shirts went like hot cakes.

That spring, Glenn moved for the summer to Provincetown, Massachusetts, where he got a job waiting tables at a restaurant called the Lobster Pot. He explained to us that he had moved to Provincetown after noticing that many of his sick friends lived there during the summer. They all worked as waiters, and helped one another out: if one was too sick to stand, another would take his work shift until he got better. They also shared work whites when time didn't allow for a trip to the laundromat to clean diarrhea-stained clothes.

Since we hadn't seen Glenn in several months, Rob decided to spend a long weekend with him. It was the weekend of the Fourth of July 1992. I had to be in my district to attend the usual parades on Saturday, but arranged to fly on to Massachusetts afterwards.

Rob later told me that when he arrived at the Provincetown airport on Thursday evening, Glenn met him, looking surprisingly well. Though he was thinner than when we had last seen him, his energy level was high and he still had the boyish charm that always made him stand out in a crowd. He wanted to go out for dinner, so he and Rob went to a restaurant and talked at length about his health, his doctors, and his medical bills. Rob was happy to see him so robust and buoyant.

The following morning, however, Rob woke up to find Glenn curled up and shivering on the daybed. He was experiencing cramps and chills and an excruciating migraine headache, and the neuropathy in his feet made walking unbearable. He remained in bed all day and Rob did what he could to help. That night, a friend waited Glenn's tables at the Lobster Pot.

I arrived on Saturday night, and Rob and I checked into a guest house that Glenn had reserved for us. (His one-room efficiency was large enough for two but not for three.) Though Rob and I dropped by Glenn's place several times that weekend and made repeated efforts to do things for Glenn—to get his meals and medication, to wash his clothes and run errands—Glenn, as always when he was at his sickest, wanted to be left alone. When we did drop by, we usually found him asleep; and when we left late that Sunday, he was barely able to force himself out of bed for a quick hug.

Glenn called from Provincetown in late August to tell us that his health had deteriorated further, that he hadn't worked since we'd seen him in July, and that he had decided to move back to his family's dairy farm in the Blue Ridge Mountains. His parents hadn't seen him in quite a while, and though he had tried his best to prepare them for his condition, he was concerned about how they would react when they saw how gaunt and frail he looked. He had arranged, he said, to travel with a friend to New York City, where he would stay with other friends until his older brother could find time to drive to New York and take him home.

Rob took the train up to New York that weekend and stayed with Glenn at his friends' apartment on the Upper West Side. Glenn could barely walk. His legs were weak and the pain from the neuropathy made movement unbearable. He wore a hat most of the time to cover his hair loss. He would sleep most of the day, saving his stored-up energy for a lively dinner. He would then go back to sleep, only to awaken in pain in the wee hours of the morning. Rob left Glenn on Sunday night, and made plans to get together again once he had settled in at his parents' farm.

That August was also the month of the Republican convention in Houston. For months, as the House Republicans' deputy whip for strategy, I had been privy to the planning of the convention and of the campaign generally. Early in the campaign, Newt had suggested that we bring some people from the executive branch into our whip group discussions, so that we might more closely and effectively tie our activities in Congress to President Bush's reelection campaign. So Gayle Wolinsky of the White House Domestic Affairs Office came and met regularly with the group. Jim Pinkerton, a young policy specialist who had been in the White House and who was now with the Bush Campaign, joined us as well.

Every Wednesday morning, I had a standing appointment to meet at my office with Newt, Nancy, John, Gayle, and Jim. As the weeks wore on, Newt expanded the group to include other people as well. It soon became clear to me that the strategy being developed in those meetings was so nasty that it would drive wedges in the American body politic. I knew we would risk losing the presidential election, because I knew Americans would reject such hateful rhetoric. I was not alone in these sentiments: Nancy and Jim, among others, shared my views. "This isn't going to work," we kept telling Newt.

I realized early on, then, that Houston would not be the party's finest hour. With the economy in bad shape and the deficit out of control, party leaders had determined that Bush could not be reelected on an economic agenda, and had accordingly decided to embrace the radical right's social agenda. In 1988, the so-called Willie Horton commercials, which tapped into the racism and racial fears of many voters, had worked effectively against Michael Dukakis; now, convinced that the only way to get Bush reelected was to paint the Democrats as radicals and thus get the electorate to vote Republican out of fear, GOP leaders cynically hoped that demonizing gay people would prove equally potent.

As I watched this happening—and as I saw myself, in the role of deputy whip for strategy, expected to further this despicable agenda—I felt increasingly alienated and frustrated. Knowing that the convention would be a riot of ultraconservative social rhetoric, I stayed home. In a pre-convention interview with Bob Franken of CNN, I predicted that the rhetoric

at the convention would be intolerant and that it would back-
fire.

It didn't take long to see this prediction confirmed. On the
convention's first night, Pat Buchanan rose and delivered a
speech that shocked longtime party members, news reporters,
and the general public alike with its belligerence. "Like many
of you last month," Buchanan said, referring to the Democratic convention in July, "I watched that giant masquerade
ball at Madison Square Garden where twenty thousand radicals and liberals came dressed up as moderates and cen-
trists—in the greatest single exhibition of cross-dressing in
American political history. . . ."

While identifying himself with the idea of a Christian
America, Buchanan exhibited a thoroughly un-Christian
mean-spiritedness, especially toward gay and black Americans. "There is a religious war going on for the soul of
America," he declared in a bullying tone. "It is a cultural war,
as critical to the kind of nation we will one day be as was the
cold war itself." He made it clear that the supposedly Christian
culture he sought to defend was one that had little Christian
compassion for gay or black Americans.

While I was in Wisconsin watching this horror show on TV,
Rob was back in Washington. I had taken Della with me, and
Rob missed us both. One day during the convention, Franklin
called him and said that the Humane Society, for which he
worked, had picked up a boxer that had been left tied to a tree
in northeast Washington. Franklin had named the dog Rex. He
asked Rob for help in finding Rex a home. "Your clients all live
in big houses and have large yards," Franklin said. "Surely
one of them wants a dog. They all seem to love that spoiled
excuse of a dog that *you* have."

That night Rob was going to La Fonda, a restaurant in Dupont Circle, to celebrate Dwight's birthday with several
friends. He told Franklin to bring the dog there at eight
o'clock. "I'll take the dog home," he said, "and figure something out."

So Franklin took Rex to La Fonda. When Rob saw that little

dog, his heart went out to him. He was skinny, had a terrible cough, smelled bad, slobbered profusely, and was trembling with fear. He also had the largest eyes of any dog Rob had ever seen. Rob decided immediately to keep him.

Meanwhile, unaware of these developments, I continued to follow the convention, hoping that the intolerant sentiments of Buchanan's speech might be countered by the speakers who followed him. But Pat Robertson, Dan Quayle, and others enthusiastically echoed Buchanan's mean-spirited remarks. While a few, such as Barbara Bush, sought to strike a somewhat more inclusive note, no one in the party officially repudiated Buchanan's remarks. The phrase "family values," a code term for antigay sentiments, was ubiquitous; even Mrs. Bush did not neglect to invoke it.

So manifest was the gathering's antigay tone that, on the convention's closing day, August 20, the *New York Times* ran a front-page story on the subject. "Homosexual issues," wrote Jeffrey Schmalz, "have flared into the open at the party's national convention. . . . Beginning with a speech by Patrick J. Buchanan on Monday night and continuing with remarks by other Republicans over the last two days, the party made it clear that it would make its opposition to homosexual rights a major issue in the campaign."

As Jackie Calmes wrote in a *Wall Street Journal* article after the convention, "religious Republicans have succeeded in pushing the national party platform to its most hard-line conservative position in years on issues such as abortion and homosexuality. . . . Increasingly, the fight is against gays."

Given that the Democratic convention had sounded a very positive, inclusive note, and had sent an unprecedented message of acceptance to gay Americans, the ugliness of Houston seemed especially pronounced. The shining exception to this ugliness was provided not by a political figure but by Mary Fisher, a former aide to Gerald Ford and the daughter of a longtime Republican benefactor, who delivered an impassioned plea on behalf of people living with AIDS. After Buchanan had vilified gay, poor, and black Americans, the HIV-positive Fisher's loving words about AIDS sufferers who belonged to these groups were especially poignant. She was, she declared in a memorable phrase, "one with the lonely gay man sheltering a flickering candle from the cold wind of his family's rejection."

America cheered Mary Fisher, and rejected the hatefulness of Buchanan, Robertson, and company. Yet some party leaders were slow to get the message that their cynical attempt to exploit antigay prejudice would not work. In the *Wall Street Journal*'s lead article on August 21, James M. Perry and David Shribman wrote that "Some Republicans, such as Rep. Newt Gingrich of Georgia, are arguing in the private councils of the Bush campaign for a 'decapitation' of the Democrats by an attack on Mr. Clinton's character and a new 'gay-bashing' offensive."

As it turned out, the party leaders had miscalculated disastrously. Not only had they set themselves on the road to election loss in November; they had awakened a sleeping giant.

That giant was the huge majority of gay and lesbian Americans, most of whom didn't fit Pat Buchanan's—or anybody's—stereotypes. Far from being irresponsible, sex-obsessed radicals who sought to tear down the nation and institutional religion, these gay men and lesbians were patriotic men and women who cared for their families, held down responsible positions, and played valuable roles in their communities and (in many cases) their churches. They were doctors and lawyers, police officers and businesspeople, teachers and ministers—people who lived respectable mainstream lives, often in the face of immense societal prejudice. Few of them had any involvement at all in gay activism; many were staunch Republicans.

Yet instead of being honored by the GOP as loyal, hardworking members of the American family, these solid citizens saw themselves demonized by a party desperate to win votes. They were infuriated—not only at the Republican party, but at themselves. For they realized that the ultimate blame for their demonization lay with them. America's ignorance and fear of gay people, they realized, was mainly the fault of gay people like themselves, who had kept a low profile and refused to stand up to the lies and distortions that kept ignorance, fear, and prejudice alive. Listening to the ugly words of Buchanan and Quayle and Robertson, these gay and lesbian Americans were determined to do everything they could to keep such a spectacle of hate from happening again.

The Houston convention, in short, turned out to be the best recruitment poster for gay activism in history. It brought countless formerly complacent gay people out of the closet and onto the barricades. Yet these were activists with a difference. Unlike many gay activists of the 1960s and '70s, they weren't marginal figures who sought to tear down the system; rather, they were pillars of American society who happened to be gay—and who demanded to be recognized and accepted as such. In the companies for which they worked, in the universities where they studied or taught, and in the churches where they preached or prayed, those gay Americans soon began to come out, to assert their equal rights, and to demand equal respect.

I was one of those gay Americans. Watching the convention on TV back home in Wisconsin, I found myself compelled by the obscene spectacle to do something meaningful. Yet though I spoke out once or twice against the intolerance of Pat Buchanan and others in the days after the convention, protesting that it was not only offensive but strategically foolish, I soon decided that perhaps the best thing to do was to put out of my mind what was happening on the national level and focus on my own reelection campaign.

Part of the reason why I made this decision was that I had my own problems. The '92 campaign was the first to be dominated by the anti-incumbent sentiment that has colored American politics ever since. For House members, the sudden rise in this hostility toward incumbents had a lot to do with the House bank and post-office scandals. Almost every member of Congress had drawn a few checks on the House bank that had bounced; some had racked up hundreds of bounced checks. It didn't make us look good as an institution. While I had bounced a few checks, anybody who looked at my record in an objective way would have said that the bank had not recorded my deposits in a timely way, that it was just bad accounting, and that I hadn't done anything irresponsible or devious.

This didn't matter, however, to people who were anti-Congress and anti-Washington. The hostility toward incumbents was fierce. And here I was, an incumbent, fighting against the tide to get reelected. I had my hands full with that task, and so I ignored the national campaign as much as possible.

I ignored it, that is, until one day in October when I was touring the Black River Falls Memorial Hospital in my district with a group of federal health-care officials. As we walked through a ward, shaking hands and exchanging pleasantries with doctors, nurses, and patients, a nurse asked if she could speak to me for a moment about the election campaign. I said that of course she could. What she said shouldn't have come as a shock to me, but it did.

"I'm not surprised by Pat Buchanan's remarks," the woman said pointedly. "I didn't expect any better from him. But I'm shocked by the silence from the rest of you."

Her rebuke struck at my conscience. It made me realize that I had an obligation to speak up for what was right and to challenge Pat Buchanan and his ilk. Thanks to them, the Republican party—the party of Abraham Lincoln, the party that had been built on the premise of basic equality of opportunity for every American—was quickly becoming the party of preferences and prejudice. And too few of my fellow Republicans were actively and openly resisting this change. As the Bush campaign moved into the fall, and the hate rhetoric continued, it occurred to me that I was one of the few people in Congress who could make a dramatic point about the offensiveness of it all simply by standing up and taking a walk.

Soon after Bush lost the presidential election, I wrote Newt a memo explaining that I had come to two conclusions: there should no longer be a chief deputy whip for strategy, and if he chose to continue the position, I should not occupy it.

I went on to explain that while the White House had to take the brunt of the blame for losing the election, House and Senate Republicans were not without culpability. Our party's image was at its lowest point since Watergate; we were seen as being out of touch with real people's problems and values. We were also seen as dangerous.

"The next two to four years," I wrote, "will be marked by intense civil war within the Republican party, and an image of total obstruction and negativism legislatively." The Republican leadership in the House, I added, "will become increasingly conservative, intolerant, and negative." I noted that the uncontested selection of the national right-to-life leader, Henry Hyde of Illinois, as chair of the House Republican Policy Committee was a bad sign of the GOP's drift away from the center. Henry, I felt, belonged in the leadership, but putting the spokesman for the right-to-life movement in charge of policy development sent the wrong signal.

The memo closed with some strong accusations:

1. Your ability to lead House Republicans or the national party to majority status is increasingly impossible due to the continued development of your reputation as a hard-right Republican. You seem willing to risk your entire career to take on Democrats, but not willing to risk even a small public step in challenging the religious and hard right.

2. You believe that "listening" to moderates is sufficient. Frankly, it is clear to me that from day one, you have seen Nancy Johnson and me as moderates who would provide for you the limits of our tolerance, and nothing more.

3. You have never been willing to make the "Strategy Whip" process work. Despite repeated requests to you and Dan Meyer, there has never been a resolution between you and Bob Michel on what role we legitimately have. Without legitimization, we are nothing more than your sounding board. . . . I have been told by many, "Newt has just used you." I am afraid they are right.

4. Thus, today we don't have:
   - A commitment to a broad-based Republican party.
   - A legitimate role recognized by the leader and the conference for a strategy whip.
   - A structure and authority to develop and execute any strategy on a regular basis.

But the memo fell on deaf ears. In the December elections for the new congressional leadership, every one of the moderate candidates—including those, such as Nancy Johnson of Connecticut and Bill Gradison of Ohio, who were clearly more qualified than their conservative opponents—went down to defeat. Clearly, not even the election of Bill Clinton had helped conservative Republicans in the House to understand how turned off America was by their exclusionary politics. They still hadn't gotten the message that we had to be a diverse party.

I wasn't the only member of the Republican leadership who was disturbed by the party's rightward drift. My friend Fred Upton of Michigan made it clear that he shared my concerns. A protégé of David Stockman, Upton had come to Washington as a member of Stockman's congressional staff, had followed Stockman to the White House Budget Office, and had gone on to win his own House seat in 1984. We had been close friends ever since. Shaped, as I was, by the moderate tradition of midwestern Republicanism that had produced such people as Gerald Ford, George Romney, and Melvin Laird, Fred shared with me, among other things, a love of sports and a lack of self-importance. He also shared my alarm over the rise of the radical right.

Intraparty tensions weren't the only tensions I was suffering in those days. In addition, there were the tensions between my professional obligation as strategy whip to cleave to the general party line, whatever my personal convictions, and Rob's and my passion for a nation that cared about justice for all, regardless of party line. Ever since I had taken the job as strategy whip, my occasional willingness to subordinate personal principle to party unity did more damage to my domestic tranquility than I had bargained for. Unifying the Republican party in Congress was one thing; unifying it in a way that met the legitimate concerns that Rob persistently raised was quite another.

At least once a week during my tenure in the whip organization, Rob and I had intense discussions bordering on arguments over what my party was doing in Congress. He understood and supported many of the fiscally conservative measures. But he did not understand our priorities. Why was the repeal of the Section 89 tax code more important than making our schools work? Why was funding the B-2 bomber more important than cancer and AIDS research? Why did we allow the premise of "local control" to justify our indifference to urban blight? And if the Republicans truly believed in "local control," why did they reverse D.C. domestic partnership legislation? Rob felt strongly that our nation must stand for some essential values, regardless of party. He also felt even more strongly about protecting what he saw as my basic sense of compassion from the impulse, born of an entire adulthood spent in government service, to make coldly pragmatic political decisions.

Ronald and Nancy Reagan don't have a corner on "pillow talks." I suspect there are few members of Congress that have spent more time discussing and, yes, debating issues with their significant others than I have. These discussions tested our relationship more than anything ever had, underscoring, as they did, the depth of our philosophical disagreement and differences in temperament.

First, I could seldom convince Rob of the positive value of political pragmatism. Pragmatism, I would argue, makes it possible to work out compromises that preserve party unity. Rob countered by questioning the supreme value of party unity.

Second, I tried to use cold, hard facts to win a debate in which the issue of compassion figured importantly—foolishly forgetting that you can never win a debate about compassion by using cold, hard facts.

Third, I was often tired, as these discussions would begin at around ten in the evening and would often come at the end of a long day of wearying political debate. Tiredness makes for a poor thought process; and my tiredness resulted, most nights, in a victory by Rob and a neat clicking into place of my strong Norwegian defense mechanisms. As Rob says, when Steve becomes defensive with you in a discussion, you might as well stop talking, because no more progress can be made on the issue at hand.

So the tensions at home were, in and of themselves, a good reason for me to leave the Republican leadership. Another good reason was my growing frustration with the way the whip organization was working. The tension between the Republican leadership and the whip office over my role as strategy whip had never been resolved. I spent more time meeting with Billy Pitts, Michel's political aide, in an attempt to resolve differences, than I did getting things done. I'm not one who has a lot of patience for not getting things done. Newt could have made more of an attempt to sit down with Michel to resolve the conflict over my mission and authority. But he didn't. (It's not uncharacteristic of him to avoid facing practical details of this kind, preferring instead to focus on the formulation and articulation of a general vision.)

The most compelling reason to quit the whip job, however, was my recognition, in the wake of the hateful rhetoric at the Houston convention, that the party desperately needed some voices from the political center. While I was not the only moderate in a position to leave, I was clearly the most visible.

I was also one of the few House Republicans whose personal experiences were making it increasingly difficult for me to stay silent. In December, after Glenn had settled at his family's Virginia farm, Rob and I drove out for a visit. Glenn's mother had insisted that we stay with them. He was, we knew, spending most of his time in a rented hospital bed in his parents' living room, hooked up to mobile monitoring devices and IV's, and could only get around in a wheelchair. Yet when we arrived in mid-afternoon at his family's rambling white farmhouse, Glenn wasn't home: a friend of his from Boston had arrived earlier in the day and had taken him into the nearby town of Bedford for the Christmas parade. We awaited their return.

When we saw Glenn he looked feebler than ever. His weight had dropped from 130 to 90 pounds on a five-foot-ten frame. Yet his spirit hadn't been broken. He was excited to see us and, after weeks of lying in bed, was eager to go out with us that evening.

It was a cold, crisp afternoon as Rob and I drove Glenn and his friend through the mountains to a country inn where the four of us had a wonderful dinner. Glenn ate only small portions of each course, but insisted on having a glass of vodka. By nine o'clock, he was exhausted. We drove back to his parents' farm and put him to bed; he fell asleep at once.

Shortly afterward, his mother came into the living room and sat down in an old rocking chair next to the bed. She was a frail woman with a bright smile that suggested an inner strength and energy. When I asked quietly how she was managing, she glanced at her sleeping son and looked solemnly at the three of us. Glenn's condition, she explained, had turned her life upside down. Her neighbors had all heard about it. Though they never mentioned his illness to her directly, she knew that they talked about it among themselves. Since Glenn had moved back home, the neighbors dropped in less often; some of them phoned occasionally, but what they communicated was less sympathy than fear and curiosity. Most devastatingly, the woman who had taken care of Glenn's mother when she was a little girl, who had tended to Glenn and his brother when they were children, and who had been the mother's closest friend and greatest source of strength, had quit abruptly at her first sight of Glenn, fearing that his disease was contagious. We could only imagine how her departure had affected Glenn, who had talked about this woman over the years with intense affection; he had used her recipes all the time, and her pet phrases were a part of his vocabulary.

Glenn's mother knew he was gay, and knew that we were, too. She admitted she didn't really understand what that meant. Having been exposed to religious-right propaganda about homosexuals, she voiced her curiosity as to whether Glenn and Rob and I were all part of "that community." I don't think she expected or wanted answers from us; she merely mentioned her concern. She had a difficult time with her husband, who refused to accept Glenn's homosexuality and couldn't deal with his illness. She had always served as the mediator between her husband and Glenn, and now, it was clear, she was mediating as well between her husband and Glenn's dying. She admitted that she often got tired, but then she blinked back a tear and, in the most polite "Old South" way, said slowly, "No, I *cannot* get tired. He is my baby until his last breath."

With that, she rose from the rocking chair. "Can I get you anything before I go upstairs for the night?" she asked. We thanked her and said no. It was around ten-thirty. She turned to climb the elaborate old stairs and thanked us again for coming.

I found it deeply ironic that Charles and Glenn, who had been roommates in an urban area, now found themselves both disabled by AIDS and back at home in their rural places of origin. In many ways they represented the changing face of AIDS in the early '90s. No longer outcasts left to die alone in some large urban center, more and more gay men were going home to their families' love—though not always, it must be said, to unequivocal acceptance and understanding.

That night, Rob and I shared a guest room upstairs in Glenn's family's farmhouse. Together we snuggled under a patchwork quilt and fell asleep to the sound of the cold November winds whistling outside.

On the following Saturday, Rob held a Christmas party for his company's subcontractors and clients, many of whom had also become our friends. Among the guests was Dwight, the architect who works for Rob. I had never met Dwight, but I liked him immediately. He was telling me about his lover, Brian, when the phone rang.

It was Charles's former neighbor, Marie, calling to tell us that Charles, who was in Washington for Christmas, had been rushed to the emergency room at George Washington University Hospital. Randy, who was spending the weekend with us, left for the hospital immediately. By eleven, when most of the guests had headed home, Rob and I left the party and drove to the hospital.

In the waiting room we found Randy, Cathy and Marie, and Charles's mother and her niece. Charles, they told us, was in rough shape. He had been diagnosed with pneumonia and tuberculosis. His left lung had collapsed. The doctors were treating him. There was nothing to do but wait and see.

For several hours, we all sat there in shock. Every now and then, one of us would say something in an attempt to fill the silence. At two A.M. Charles was moved to intensive care; the doctors told us he would pull through, though they couldn't say how long the recovery would take. Rob and I left in low spirits. In the parking lot he said, "I fear we are going to become all too familiar with hospital visits. And I don't think I like it at all."

The next day, Sunday, we returned to the hospital to find that Charles, though still in critical condition, had stabilized. Before entering his room, we were given masks to wear; the nurse explained that Charles's immune system was severely depressed, which rendered him extremely susceptible to infections. We spoke with him briefly about his health. He was weak and clearly too tired to sustain a lengthy conversation. But it was also clear that he did not want to discuss AIDS.

On Monday Charles seemed more rested. The doctors had told him that he would have to remain hospitalized through Christmas. His sister, Carol, and her family had arrived that morning from North Carolina. Originally they had planned to spend Christmas in Durham with Charles and his parents; as it turned out, they spent Christmas in Washington and celebrated with him in his hospital room. No one talked about AIDS.

Charles spent not only Christmas but New Year's in the hospital. On New Year's Eve Rob and I stopped by in tuxedoes, on our way to an AIDS Action Benefit dinner. Charles was thrilled to see us, yet at the same time our festive attire reminded him of all he was missing. Weak, afraid, and melancholy, he was an emotional wreck, laughing one minute and crying the next. When we were about to leave, I hugged him, and he broke down. "Please hold me for just a second," he said. "I feel so alone." As my arms encircled his light, bony frame, we both cried. "I love you both," he said, "more than I can say."

11

Three days later, on January 3, 1993, the opening day of the 103rd Congress, I announced my decision to quit the Republican leadership.

Opening day is always chaos. Members are allowed to bring their children onto the House floor for the swearing-in. All 435 members are present to take their oaths of office, and usually attention is scattered in 435 different directions. But on that day, I was the center of attention, the lightning rod. When I walked into chambers, colleagues besieged me with comments and questions. The actions I had taken were among the first visible signs that someone in the Republican party thought the party had gone too far.

The decision had become inevitable. Many House Republicans had embraced a right-wing agenda that neither I nor Fred Upton (who had quit the leadership a few days earlier) could feel comfortable standing behind. Rob had been adamant in his insistence that I not allow myself to be perceived as acquiescing in the politics of prejudice and intolerance.

Fred's and my announcements created a firestorm inside the Beltway. It didn't hurt that the news of my resignation broke on the first day of the congressional session, which is usually a slow news day in Washington. My press release was just the kind of thing the media would love amidst the tedious, familiar procedures of opening day.

"There is no question," I declared in my press release,

> that the House Republican leadership is becoming increasingly hard right. I do not believe our present leadership represents mainstream Republicans in this country or even in the Congress. I suspect that much of their agenda will be rigid confrontation and opposition, a strategy that simply does not suit my style of political cooperation. I was critical of the Democrats for doing this to President Bush, and I can't strategize to do the same thing to President-elect Clinton.

In succeeding days I would point out to reporters that the new GOP leadership was all-white and all-male, and had abandoned the unifying themes of the Reagan era for a narrow social agenda that was turning off young people, moderates, and minorities. "There is no question," I said, "that the Religious Right wants as big a government on the right as they despise on the left."

I had known that my announcement would cause a media frenzy. I had also known that it would automatically be interpreted by both the press and the political community as a sign of a major falling-out between me and Newt.

Newt, of course, had been completely aware of my growing frustration with the party and the party line. From the moment he had received my memo in November, he had known that I wanted to leave the whip position—and why. But he ignored my complaints instead of taking action to deal with them. I don't think he realized how seriously disturbed I was about the widespread perception that the GOP was a party of extreme ideology and prejudice; rather, he believed, or wanted to believe, that my desire to quit the whip job was a sign of exhaustion over procedural matters as much as it was an expression of moral outrage. Until the last minute, in any case, I think Newt clung to the notion that my objections could be resolved with a pep talk. (Newt is very big on pep talks.)

My announcement unnerved the newly elected, very conservative members of the party leadership. It wasn't as if they had been unaware of the anger and exasperation that the shrill right-wing rhetoric on social issues had caused among Republican moderates. But they simply hadn't expected that any of us would do anything about it. That was hardly an unreasonable expectation: moderates are not known for dramatic gestures.

As I approached Newt that day in the back of the House chamber, his eyes were full of anxiety. While he understood—and, I think, subconsciously approved of—my gutsy move, the question of how to define our relationship in this very public moment was difficult. I cut the ice quickly. "You can't be surprised by the press release," I said to him. "I told you weeks ago that I would have to do this."

"I understand," he said, "but my staff doesn't. They read what you have done as a direct political slap at me, the one guy trying to hold this party together. And they are pretty mad at you. I would advise you to find Dan, Tony, or Lynn and talk to them." Dan was Dan Meyer, Newt's chief of staff; Tony was Tony Blankley, his press secretary; and Lynn was Lynn Swineheart, his floor assistant.

Newt's staff had reacted as any staff would. They were offended and angry, because they read my resignation as an attack on Newt. They were also worried that it would result in the defection of moderates from his camp. When I eventually did find Dan later in the day, he said that he wished I had let Newt make the announcement of my departure from the job. This remark made it clear that Dan totally misunderstood what I was doing. This was not one of those cases in which Newt could save face by announcing, for example, that I could no longer find the time to do this job and was accordingly going to be replaced. The whole idea was *not* to gloss over the intraparty divisions and keep everybody happy. The idea was precisely to shake up the party and to say to its leaders, "Do you know what your people are doing to this country and to this party?"

Before I could get to any of Newt's staff, however, a reporter beckoned me off the floor into the Speaker's gallery for yet another of the umpteen interviews I would give that day. As I approached the exit door, Henry Hyde walked in. Large, white-haired, and highly respected for his wit, intelligence, and articulateness, Henry was the House Republicans' new policy chairman.

He had his own special reason to be angry at me. In my press release I had complained that the new House Republican leadership not only contained no moderates; in addition, it was more male, more white, and more conservative than the party in Congress, and certainly in the nation. I had used Henry as an example. "Why," I had written, "after the results of the last election, would we choose the voice of pro-life to lead our party's policy development?" Did the Republican party really want America to perceive it as inflexibly against a woman's right to choose abortion? I had made it clear that I felt there was a place in the leadership for a man of Henry's intelligence and reputation; I just questioned the role he had been given.

This clearly had not gone down well with Henry, who looked at me and quickly blurted out the words, "Steve, I'm sorry you did it. And I'm sorry you felt you had to do it." He seemed caught between a justifiable feeling of offense and a desire to sit down and counsel me.

Not prepared for this face-to-face meeting, I could only respond, "Henry, sometime I would like to sit down and discuss this. It is not in any way personal. If it came off that way, I am deeply sorry."

The frictions that day offered only a taste of what was to come. Over the weeks and months that followed, it became clear that conservative Republican activists in Washington and elsewhere viewed me as a villain. This surprised me, though it shouldn't have. It is one thing to vote independently of the party line; it is quite another to be a vocal critic of that party line and a cause of tension within the party. While I didn't expect a warm round of applause in response to my resignation from the party leadership, I didn't fully realize at the time that I had set myself up as the prime symbol of moderate resistance to the right's takeover of the party, and thus as my opposition's chief target. Nor did I realize that I was laying the groundwork for what would be the first primary-election challenge of my Congressional career.

Both the Washington and the Wisconsin press gave my announcement much stronger play than I had ever expected. Since I was the first member from our state ever to serve so high in the party leadership, local reporters viewed my resignation as an event of major importance and ran it on front pages across the state. "In resigning his leadership post in the House," the Milwaukee *Journal* editorialized, "Wisconsin Congressman Steve Gunderson is doing some needed conscience-rattling. His Republican party ought to pay attention, lest it be reduced to a noisy but ineffectual fringe group. . . . It's a gutsy, responsible move. . . . Three cheers to Steve Gunderson for trying to nudge his own troops back to the center."

As a result of my resignation, then, I went through a brief period when I was a hero to some and a villain to others. Everybody in political Washington seemed to put me in one category or the other—everybody, that is, except Newt and Marianne. On the very day that I announced my departure from the whip job, Marianne Gingrich took me to lunch at La Colline, a Capitol Hill restaurant. Marianne and I have a good rapport. A native Ohioan, she has a Midwestern sensibility that's very similar to mine; she also has an admirable self-assurance, a no-nonsense manner, and a lack of affectation that distinguishes her from the typical Washington insider.

Marianne was confused by my action, and as Newt's closest advisor she wanted to get to the bottom of it; so she grilled me like a reporter. "I need to understand," she said, "what you're trying to say by doing this."

"Part of what I'm trying to say," I replied, "is that unless this party changes, Newt can be leader, but he'll be unable to lead. And a leader without a constituency is of no value. Congressional Republicans seek to win the confidence of the

American people. But as long as the party leadership is perceived as narrowly and rigidly conservative, the American
people will not give it their confidence.''

Marianne listened respectfully, and we remained friends. So
while everybody tried to paint my departure from the whip
job as a personal falling-out, it wasn't anything of the kind.
While there was no way that Newt or Marianne or I could get
up and say to everybody, ''You've got it all wrong,'' the fact
was that people *had* got it all wrong. Despite my quitting the
whip job, there remained a deep personal affection between
me and the Gingriches.

In 1995, after Newt became speaker, I said to him, ''You
know that nobody, other than yourself, has paid a bigger price
than I have in order for you to get to where you are today. I
gave up my seat at the table, I gave up my membership in the
inside circle, I was willing to endure the alienation and the
criticism of many within my party, because I thought it was
important that we send to America the message that we're a
broad-based party, and that we force this party to find what
unites us and to focus on that, rather than on what divides
us.''

Because I had taken myself out of the inner circle, I wasn't
one of those who put together the so-called Contract with
America in 1995. But when you look at the Contract, you
can see the lasting effects of my resignation as strategy whip.
There's no question that by quitting our positions, Fred and I
mobilized the moderates and created among the conservatives
a sensitivity to moderate views. As a result, we moderates
were able to go to the conservatives as they were putting together the Contract and say to them, ''This and this are unacceptable,'' and be listened to. They realized that in order to get
our support, they had to be attentive to our concerns. And
that's why the Contract focused on economic and regulatory
matters and not on the so-called wedge social issues. Thanks
to us, the Contract made no mention of school prayer, abortion, guns, or gay issues; in return, we agreed to vote for a
blanket tax credit of $500 per child, which otherwise few of

us would support. (Why should a stockbroker earning half a million dollars a year get a tax credit for having children?)

Newt is fond of saying to me, whenever the going gets rough, that "with leadership comes controversy." Since the going has been rough pretty often in the last few years, I've heard those words from him a lot. Newt knew that I always wanted to get along with everyone, that I'm conciliatory to a fault—and he respected the impulse behind that. But he also knew that unless I was willing to take tough stands and face the consequences, I would not be the leader he thought I could be.

While in his heart, then, I think Newt probably knew where my conscience would take me in response to our party's rightward movement and its increasingly strident antigay rhetoric, and while he suspected that my future actions would bring unprecedented stress to bear on the close working relationship he and I had enjoyed over the years, I think he also knew that I was one of the few members of Congress who were in a position to provide some healthy tension for our party from the political center.

While some of the costs of that action were unanticipated, moreover, Newt truly did believe that the party needed to be perceived by the American public as broad and welcoming, not as narrow and exclusionary. That's why he went out of his way to make clear that he wanted his leadership team to include women and moderates—and that if House Republicans did not elect women and moderates to the leadership, he would appoint them. (A prime example of Newt's determination to put women in visible positions is Robin Carlyle, a woman who, appointed by Newt after his ascendancy to the speakership, is the first female to serve as clerk of the House.)

As we plunged into 1993, of course, the paramount symbol of the cost of being a narrow and exclusionary party was the upcoming inauguration of Bill Clinton as president after twelve years of a Republican White House. Charles, who had taken an upswing after his Christmas bout with pneumonia, had loved the Bush inauguration four years earlier and wanted very much to attend Clinton's inauguration on January 20.

As far as Rob and I could see, Charles didn't have any politics to speak of or any party affiliation, but he did enjoy the stirring and splashy national spectacle that is a presidential inauguration. Since, as a Republican, I had fewer demands on me for tickets than I'd had for the Bush inaugural, and since I had fewer professional commitments related to the inaugural than I would have if the new president were a member of my party, I was in a position not only to provide Charles with an excellent seat but to show him a good time as well. So Rob and I told him to come on up to Washington.

ROB

Twice a day for two weeks before the inauguration, Charles would phone me at work and proceed to gush excitedly about the plans for his Washington trip. He made lists of things at various shops that he absolutely had to buy and planned dinners with people whom he absolutely had to see. He read me recipes that he had come across for winter meals and he asked which of these feasts I would prefer to prepare. It was clear from the amount of time Charles spent on the phone with me discussing such things that he had nothing at all to do in Durham.

When Charles arrived, the consequences of his earlier bout with pneumonia were apparent. His once cherubic face was thin and sallow, with pronounced cheekbones. His eyes looked more recessed than usual; his hairline had receded. But he insisted he was getting stronger by the day. He had started taking walks in Durham and had even thought about exercising—though, he said with a weak laugh as he lit a cigarette, he hadn't quite gotten around to it yet.

That week Charles slept in our guest room, and our two big boxer dogs did too. Every morning Steve and I would leave for work while Charles snored on with Rex and Della playing guard dog at the foot of his bed. When I returned at lunchtime, Charles would have roused himself and worked up enough energy to eat something, walk around, and take some of his medication, which made him violently sick to his stomach. After lunch I would go back to work, leaving Charles with the dogs and with copies of *Architectural Digest, Gourmet,* and *Southern Living* to thumb through. At around three, I would phone to see if Charles had been able to take a shower. By six or so, Charles would usually have enough energy to get dressed and socialize. Every evening, a different small group of friends came over for a festive dinner; Charles enjoyed the attention as well as the opportunity to chat with people he hadn't seen in a while.

On the morning of the inauguration, three days into the trip, Charles was uncharacteristically energetic, racing to get ready. He gathered together his camera and several rolls of film and rode to the Capitol with Steve. Walking down the halls of the Rayburn House Office Building, where Steve's office is located, Charles was as excited as a little boy. At Steve's office they had coffee and doughnuts with a group of people from Wisconsin, mostly Democrats, to whom Steve had distributed most of his inauguration tickets. Charles snapped pictures of them all.

Later that morning, Linda and I took the Metro into town and joined Steve and Charles, and the four of us walked across Independence Avenue to the Capitol grounds for the ceremony. Charles took pictures of the crowd. Spotting Jack Lemmon, he introduced himself and handed a stranger his camera so he could get a picture with the movie star. John Kennedy, Jr., sat several rows ahead of Charles that morning, and Charles snapped about twenty photographs of the back of his head. He later sent us copies with the words "John-John" circled and a line drawn to the tiny head in the foreground.

Whichever party you belong to, the inauguration of a new president is a thrilling event that speaks at once of continuity and of new beginnings. To be there with Charles was an especially poignant experience. The poignancy was underlined by some of the words of Clinton's inaugural address.

"Today," our new president told us, "a generation raised in the shadows of the cold war assumes new responsibilities in a world warmed by the sunshine of freedom but threatened still by ancient hatreds and new plagues." Unlike Ronald Reagan, who was notorious for not having mentioned AIDS for many months during his time in the White House, Bill Clinton referred to it by name in the first moments of his presidency. He went on to say, "We need each other. And we must care for one another."

Clinton's message was echoed by the poet Maya Angelou, who after the inaugural address stepped up to the lectern and, with great dignity and feeling, read her poem "On the Pulse of Morning," which she had composed especially for the occasion. We were moved by her beautiful words about the wisdom of peace, and especially pleased, during her litany of different types of people—"the Catholic, the Muslim, the French, the Greek, / The Irish, the Rabbi, the Priest, the Sheikh"—to hear the word "Gay": certainly this had to be the first time that gay people had been referred to, as such, from a lectern at a presidential inauguration. We were glad that Charles was there to hear her.

12

If the public announcement of my departure from the whip organization was the root of my troubles with the far right, then my actions over the following months were the fertilizer that made the opposition grow.

For my part, I had no wish to infuriate certain elements within the party or the country. Quite the contrary. I believed then, as I do now, that reasonable people can differ. I also know that in politics, how the issue is framed can be much more important than the issue itself. What I wasn't prepared for was the reality that my opponents were about to frame the issues against me. As the new administration got underway, I thought that my character, my conscience, and my twenty-year history of trying to do what was right would serve me well in Congress, even with Bill Clinton in the White House. But I was being naive.

During my first twelve years in Congress, my belief in working in harmony with the executive branch had not been controversial, since the White House had been occupied by Republicans. Yet after Bill Clinton became president, when I sought to work harmoniously with the him in the interest of serving my country's needs, I soon came into conflict with people whose goal was to destroy the Clinton agenda, period. These people were mostly not my colleagues within the party (though some of those colleagues *were* angry at me), but were mostly members of single-issue interest groups.

While my efforts at working with a Democratic president, then, were making things difficult for me in Washington, back home in Wisconsin other developments were taking place that would result in the most challenging campaign of my career.

Playing a considerable role in these developments was WWIB, the dominant religious radio station in western Wisconsin. The people at WWIB would probably never believe that my father, who is often on the road in his truck with his radio playing, is one of their most ardent listeners. Combine the familiar Christian hymns with around-the-clock sermons and inspirational talks and you have designed my father's ideal radio station.

Yet as the conservative community increasingly targeted the homosexual community, and as Christian radio stations like WWIB were consequently fed more and more antigay programming, the gay issue, for WWIB, soon found its focus in me. This was only to be expected, as my sexual orientation, as well as my willingness to speak up for gay and lesbian civil rights, were becoming more and more widely known in the region.

Mark Halverson hosted WWIB's afternoon talk show, on which I was a frequent guest. By all indications Mark sought desperately to play the nonbiased host, and he often asked if I thought he was treating me fairly. The problem was not his questions, per se—any questions ought to be fair game for a public official. Rather, the problem was his station's preoccupation with my homosexuality. Over the course of 1993 and 1994, every time I would speak on a gay-rights issue in Congress, every time I addressed a primarily gay audience, every time some radical gay activist threw a drink at me, it initiated a whole new wave of discussions on WWIB. If the station had paid the same attention to my work on agriculture, education, or rural health care, I would have had a stellar reputation throughout my district. But because WWIB was preoccupied with my sexuality and issues related to it, an otherwise uninformed listener might well legitimately conclude that I spent all my time in Congress talking about gay rights.

Because I believed stubbornly in the inherent goodness and fairness of people, and thus naively thought that I could overcome the propaganda against me, I went on the station a number of times to be interviewed by Halverson and to debate preachers. I sought to educate listeners about my record, my views, and my work in Congress. I tried to explain the importance of maintaining the separation between church and state—between religious institutions, which have the right to teach whatever beliefs and encourage whatever prejudices they wish, and individual citizens, who have the right to equality before the law regardless of what other people's religions may say about them. I even thought that I might be able to help WWIB's listeners to attain a somewhat more sophisticated understanding of Christian theology, an understanding that might help them to grow beyond the false and obscene identification of their fears, superstitions, and stereotypes about gay people with the teachings of Jesus.

Rob thought I was nuts to try to educate WWIB's judgmental listeners in this way. More than once he said to me, "You're not going to win a debate with preachers on a religious radio station. No politician has the credibility to do that. And you know you can't talk sense to idiots. So why waste your time?" In any event, I failed in my attempt to correct the listeners' false impressions and to overcome their prejudices.

Meanwhile, a movement that had succeeded in swallowing up the Minnesota Republican party was migrating across the Mississippi River into my western Wisconsin district like a swarm of killer bees. Shortly after the 1992 election, we had been told by local Democratic activists that the Republican party in Eau Claire County, my district's second most populous county, was about to be taken over by a very conservative group. And they were right. In February 1993, a whole new wave of people who had never been seen before at party meetings showed up for the annual caucus at the Eau Claire Civic Center, the purpose of which was to elect party officers for the next two years.

Those people were all very conservative social activists. And they had in their corner a local party old-timer, Winnie Close. Winnie would fit everybody's image of a perfect grandmother. But her all-consuming love was Republican politics—and her goal was to be chair of the Eau Claire County party. Having been passed over for that position two years earlier when she had thought it was her turn, she was ready to do anything to get elected. Having served as a Bush delegate at the 1992 convention, moreover, she would presumably be acceptable to Republican moderates. Thus she made the perfect tool for the new arrivals who were eager to take over the party in Eau Claire. And that's what happened. Winnie became chairman, and Harlan Reinders, one of the leaders of the takeover, became vice-chair.

No sooner had they taken up the reins of the local party then they started trying to destroy me. First they tried to convince my constituents that I no longer could be regarded as meeting the criteria for a Republican congressman. Letters and flyers were sent around my district to active Republicans, maintaining that the only way to save Third District Republicans from division in the next election was to persuade me to retire at the end of the 103rd Congress.

Second, they raised the question of term limits, an issue popular with the strong Perot contingent in the area. When I had first taken office back in 1981, I had supported the concept of term limits. Though I had always said that the limits should be set at somewhere between twelve and twenty years, Reinders and his allies tried to hold me to the twelve-year position. Since I was now serving my thirteenth year in Congress, they argued that I was duty-bound to retire.

One afternoon in April, while on a weekend trip to Wisconsin, I phoned Rob at work to check in and tell him about Reinders and company's latest shenanigans. Rob had just walked into his office when I called, and as we talked he looked through the messages that had been left on his desk. I was telling him about Reinders's hijinks when he interrupted me. "Well, shit," he said.

I knew by his tone, and by the ensuing silence, that something was wrong.

"There's a message here from Glenn's mother," he finally said. He read the note to me in a soft, halting voice. *Glenn passed away early this morning in his sleep. The funeral is tomorrow and for family only."*

Rob was quiet. I could hear him breathing heavily, trying not to cry.

"Rob," I said, "I'm sorry. He's out of his pain."

"Oh, Steve," Rob replied flatly. "He's just gone. He's really gone."

Rob called Randy, Gabriel, and Linda to tell them the news, and to tell them that the family had asked that none of us attend the funeral. We knew that in their rural community, additional men at the service would have made Glenn's family uncomfortable around their neighbors. Instead of attending, we sent flowers and made a donation in Glenn's name to a local AIDS facility.

Many Americans, especially in places like western Wisconsin, still think of AIDS as something that happens to people who are different from themselves and very far away—people in places like San Francisco and New York, Los Angeles and Washington. Certainly I had become convinced, without really articulating the thought to myself, that AIDS would pass me by. In any event, I simply hadn't imagined that we would lose any of our friends to AIDS. Somewhere people would die—but they would not be people I loved. Yes I would feel an abstract compassion for them—but their suffering would not touch my life in any profound way.

My constituents accept that I take a special interest in the AIDS funding issue, but they don't necessarily feel that it's something I'm doing for *them.* Many of them look upon it as a special gay thing, and they accept it as such, so long as it doesn't seem to be taking too much time away from my work on dairy issues. Yet it's ironic to me that the first friend that we lost to AIDS was Glenn, the son of a dairy farmer very much like my typical constituent in Wisconsin.

In the following months I helped put together an organization to bring together, on a regular basis, House Republicans who resisted the takeover of the party by confrontational conservatives who sought to exclude us. The organization still exists. We call it the "Tuesday lunch bunch" or the "Tuesday group," because it really has no official name—and, for that matter, no elected leadership, no public agenda, no spokesperson. We're all equals. We wanted to avoid anything that might bring in people's egos or might result in people claiming to speak on behalf of other members.

We have about forty members. I insist on calling us "governing Republicans." It's the term I like to use, rather than "moderate Republicans," because I think ideological labels are increasingly difficult to define and, I think, increasingly irrelevant in American politics. What, after all, is a conservative Republican today? Is it a libertarian, such as Governor William Weld of Massachusetts? Is it an economic conservative like George Bush? Or is it a member of the big-government social right, as exemplified by the leaders of the Christian Coalition? People in all three categories would call themselves conservative Republicans, but politically they're dramatically different from one another. For my part, I prefer to set aside the words "conservative" and "liberal" altogether whenever possible.

That's why I've increasingly felt comfortable in defining us as governing Republicans, because we want to work through government to get something accomplished. We're not driven by some narrow ideology; we're not willing, as some are, to throw political hand grenades in order to make an ideological point. We're pragmatic Republicans who are there to get the job done. Yes, we do have a preference as to who's elected president. But when the election is over, it shouldn't matter to us whether the person in the White House is George Bush or Bill Clinton or Bob Dole. We should put party labels on the shelf and sit down and govern in a bipartisan way, working together constructively, not destructively.

We governing Republicans tend to be moderates, though not all of us are. Many in the Old Guard, those who believe in the institution of Congress and believe in two parties working together to fulfill the obligations of a governing Congress, are also comfortable with our group and its goals. Somebody like Pat Roberts, who's the chairman of the Agriculture Committee, is hardly a moderate Republican, but he's very clearly a governing Republican who believes that you've got to get things done.

Contrast him with somebody like Congressman Tom DeLay or Dick Armey, the current House Republican leader, who believe that unless you're in the majority, you have no role in government except to try to bring down the other party. When the Democrats were in control, Armey saw it as his sole purpose in Congress to secure a Republican majority. He thought there was no productive way you could govern as long as Democrats were in control. We governing Republicans don't agree.

Our Tuesday lunches are very casual, but the attendance is strictly limited. Only members of the lunch bunch are invited, and any given member's staff people are welcome only if that member is present. Lobbyists, guests, and reporters are not allowed. We do ask various people to come in and speak to us—party leaders, cabinet officers, journalists, and fellow members of Congress.

But mainly we talk policy, hashing out our agenda for the week. Part of the group's purpose is to get out the message that the Republican party as a whole is not driven by a narrow ideology and that our party and its membership must be as big and diverse as the nation it seeks to represent. It was three members of our group—Fred Upton, Chris Shays, and me—who led Republican support for President Clinton's proposed National Service program. I had talked for years with Dave McCurdy about putting together such a program. While I hadn't supported Dave's original version of it, he knew that I was intrigued by the idea. So out of loyalty to Dave, as well as out of respect for the chief executive, I agreed to become the lead Republican cosponsor of President Clinton's National Service Bill.

As it happened, Dave's and my friendship and mutual loyalty would cost each of us in the 1994 election. Dave, who ran for the Senate that year and deserved to win, lost the election largely because conservatives were irked by his strong support for the gays-in-the-military compromise, a position I suspect he took largely out of loyalty to me. (Though the compromise, which emerged from a debate in which I would play a major role, proved in practice to be little better than the old ban, it seemed at the time to be the lesser of two evils and at least a symbolic step forward. Under the circumstances, it was the best possible outcome to an ugly situation.) In the same way, my willingness to take the lead in my party on a Democratic president's National Service plan convinced some members on my side of the aisle that I wasn't a true Republican.

I was proud to be a sponsor of the bill, because I felt it represented the best of both parties: it reflected the highest ideals and goals of the Democratic party, but it sought to accomplish those goals through the Republican ideal of no big bureaucracy, local control, and local initiative. I was sorry to see it become a political football when it could have become a perfect example of a bipartisan effort to do more for less.

After the '92 elections, we governing Republicans made a real gesture of outreach to the Clinton White House. We said to the administration, in essence, "Look, we're not your biggest fan club. We don't claim to be responsible for your getting elected. But if you want a bipartisan government, as you say you do, we're the ones you're going to have to talk to and deal with. We're here to let you know that we're more than willing to give you the benefit of the doubt."

Unfortunately, some people in the Clinton White House were so shortsighted that they missed that message totally. As somebody who dealt with Hillary Clinton on health care, I know that if the White House had been willing to work out a

truly bipartisan health-care agenda with us Republican moderates—and we were willing to go quite a long way to meet
them—things could have turned out very differently than
they did.

The health-care debacle was a classic example of what's
wrong with excessive partisanship. The Democrats saw
health-care reform as a way of winning public esteem—and
votes—for their party for years to come, in the way that Social
Security had done decades ago. For this reason, no Republicans
could be intimately involved. The more that Republicans were
perceived to have a part in crafting health-care reform, the
less it would be seen as a Democratic party achievement.

Since I represent a district in desperate need of health-care
reform, and since I sit on one of the three committees with
jurisdiction over health care, I jumped into the debate energetically. No one, I argued, paid higher premiums for less coverage than farmers. No element of the delivery system was
under greater stress than rural health care: doctors didn't
want to serve in rural areas; reimbursement formulas penal-
ized people who lived outside cities and suburbs. Even in the
1990s, constituents of mine sometimes died because they
could not reach a medical facility in time.

For these reasons, I fervently welcomed the idea of health-
care reform. Yet I had serious problems with the Democratic
proposals. For example, they included provisions designed to
reduce overhead that would, I felt, ultimately result in the
closing of rural hospitals. This notion scared me. I also felt
that, generally speaking, the reform plan should stipulate less
government control and more private-sector involvement. In
a less polarized atmosphere, I think the two parties could have
worked out a reform plan that would have pleased the great
majority of Americans. Partisanship killed that hope. Though
I tried my best to work something out with Hillary and her
people, in the end they simply wouldn't budge.

That I continued nonetheless to believe in bipartisan governing is testified to by the fact that Tuesday lunches became
a major part of my life. They also helped make me a visible

symbol of Republican moderation in a time of right-wing siege. As the '93–'94 session wore on, various incidents drove home to me the urgency of that situation and the importance of my role as a leader of moderate GOP forces, as an advocate for the "party of Lincoln," and as an opponent of discrimination—including antigay bigotry.

The greatest challenge I faced in that role was the controversy surrounding the ban on gays in the military. During the 1992 election campaign Bill Clinton had promised to lift the ban, and in the early months of 1993 the issue spawned an intense national debate. For me the issue began to take on human form that spring when a friend of my barber came to my office and told me his story.

He was an all-American young man from rural Pennsylvania. He was, or had been, an air force officer—a nuclear missile combat-crew commander with top security clearance and a perfect record. Recently, he had been communicating by e-mail with a fellow military man who, it turned out, was being investigated for child pornography. The air force had learned about their e-mail correspondence and had asked this officer for permission to search his private barracks for evidence relating to the case. Since he had never had anything to do with child pornography, and figured he had nothing to hide, the officer consented.

During a seven-hour search, the investigators found nothing related to their inquiry—but they did discover some gay magazines. They then asked the officer's permission to search his quarters for homosexual materials; he refused. They promptly returned with a search warrant and confiscated the magazines. The officer later discovered that the warrant hadn't been signed by air force authorities until after the search, which should have invalidated the whole procedure. But it didn't. In March 1993, the officer was ejected from the service simply because he was gay.

This officer was only the first of many ex-servicepeople who came to my office that spring and summer to tell their stories. The injustice of their experiences haunted me. How could such things happen in the United States in 1993? But they did, on a daily basis. That officer's story drove home to me the unfairness of it all—and it impressed upon me my responsibilities toward gay men and lesbians. Not simply because they, like me, were gay, but because we were all Americans entitled to equal treatment. Coming so soon after Glenn's death from AIDS, the officer's experience made me feel increasingly compelled to challenge the rising tide of bigotry in the nation and in my party.

That May, Rob and his mother planned an extended Memorial Day get-together for us and several friends in Panama City Beach, Florida, where Rob's parents have a summer place. Rob and I rented a beach house near theirs. Joining us were Kris Deininger, who flew down from Washington; Randy, who flew from Pittsburgh; and Linda and her three boys, who with Rob and me and the dogs drove down in a two-car caravan. (Ostap remained in McLean; he and Linda had been having marital problems and she wanted time away.) Charles had originally planned to go, too, but canceled at the last minute because he felt too weak.

On the drive back to Washington from Panama City, we stopped off in Durham to visit Charles, whom we hadn't seen since Rob's birthday in March. We didn't know quite what to expect. Since Glenn's death, telephone conversations with Charles had grown extremely unpredictable. One day he would be excited about moving to his own house; the next he would be depressed. On the bad days he would complain about the emptiness of his days. He just didn't have anything to do—and was often too sick to do anything anyway.

It was a sunny afternoon in Durham when we arrived at Charles's parents' house and piled out of the cars. When we went inside, we found that Charles's younger sister, Carol, and her son and daughter were visiting from Texas. We had spent a great deal of time with Carol and her husband during Charles's hospitalizations, and we were pleased to see them. Rob and I had also known Charles's mother for several years; Rob had spent time in her company during previous trips to

Durham, and during several of her visits to Charles in Washington, Rob had joined them for dinner. Now she and her husband welcomed us with a North Carolina–style day-long barbecue that was also attended by some relatives and neighbors.

Rob had braced himself for the sight of Charles, but if the goal was to conceal his pain at Charles's appearance, he failed. When we entered, Charles was resting in a lawn chair on his parents' screened porch with a tall glass of iced tea in one hand and a cigarette in another. He was wearing a pair of sweatpants that Rob and I had bought him for his birthday in May. Knowing that he had lost weight, we had been careful to select a small size, but the pants still hung like draperies around his now-tiny waist.

Charles rose shakily and reached out to Rob. Rob hugged Charles's frail body and bit back tears. Charles whispered that he was glad we had come. He said that he wasn't feeling very well at all. With Linda, the three of us sat around a small table and chatted about her children and our dogs. Charles had actually acquired a dog and spoke of his desire to move into a place of his own. We didn't want to discourage this ambition, but it was clear from Carol's expression that the move was, to say the least, not imminent.

It was not only hard to see Charles. It was hard, too, to visit with his parents. We reached out as best we could, to show our care and concern for them. But they were running low on optimism and had grown tired of the barrage of attorneys, lawsuits, and legal papers. His mother was virtually numbed by it all. His father broke down as we talked on the patio away from Charles. He couldn't bear to see his son waste away.

Later, in the backyard, Carol took Rob aside and told him something surprising. Charles, she said, had told their parents that he had probably contracted AIDS in the early 1980s when he had attended a number of elaborate Washington orgies. At these orgies, he claimed, men and women had taken drugs and had wild anonymous sex, both heterosexual and homosexual. Rob suggested to Carol that Charles had invented that story, and said that to the best of his knowledge Charles had never been to an orgy in his life. Carol shared Rob's doubts, and suspected that Charles had concocted the story on the assumption that his parents would be able to deal with the idea of impersonal orgies more easily than they could deal with his homosexuality, because at least the made-up story put the sex in a partially heterosexual context. Reckless and sordid, yes, but heterosexual. The awful part is that he was probably right: his parents seemed to accept that story, and were probably less troubled by it, than they would have been had Charles simply said, "I'm gay."

One thing is certain, and that is that *Charles* felt more comfortable handing his parents that absurd story than he would have felt telling the truth. Rob never could understand why Charles harbored such feelings of guilt about his homosexuality. Nor was Rob very pleased by Charles's lie. "Charles," Rob said many months later, "I don't understand why you think that random sex and drug-taking with anonymous male and female partners is less morally corrupt than having sex with a man."

Charles had nothing to say to that—he had no answer. What's ridiculous about all of this is that Charles's parents, who had known Rob and me for years and to whom it was no secret that we were a couple, knew very well that Charles was gay. There was no question in their minds about that. Carol and her husband had spoken with us about that fact during Charles's first hospitalization. But Charles couldn't bring himself to talk to his parents about his homosexuality, and they didn't want to bring it up either. It may sound ridiculous, and horribly counterproductive, but as Rob says, it's one of those typical and tragic Southern situations: it's okay for a son to be gay, and it's okay for a family to know about it, but it's *not* okay to talk about it. Because if you talk about it, you make it real.

We spent much of that afternoon with Charles talking about our friends in Washington. Charles wanted to know about Brad and Gabriel, Franklin, and Kris. To our surprise, we learned that he had actually memorized the poem that Maya Angelou had read at Clinton's inauguration. We discussed the possibility of getting together during the summer, either in Washington or elsewhere, though it was clear to both Rob and me that Charles wouldn't be able to drive anywhere on his own. Rob and I mentioned that we were planning another trip to Mykonos; perhaps Charles might be able to come with us? He was very enthusiastic about that suggestion.

As the evening progressed, we moved on to grimmer matters. Rob and I asked about the details of Charles's health and his medical care. He was being cared for by doctors at Duke University whose expertise he trusted. But he was still having legal problems with his insurance companies, both of which had continued to deny him coverage. The attorneys and credit agencies phoned regularly. Charles's mother said that they she and her husband spent three hours a day on the telephone, trying in vain to sort out the mess.

Because of the insurance situation, Charles was very concerned about his savings, which essentially consisted of the money he'd earned from selling his house in Virginia. Rob had attended the settlement in his place, so we had a pretty good idea of how much money Charles had—and we knew as well that this sum was almost surely dwarfed by the amount he owed in hospital bills. Charles told us that he wanted to divest and declare bankruptcy, although he was horrified, he said, at the thought of becoming a ward of the state. Rob and I both found it disgusting that after Charles had paid premiums to an insurance company for over ten years, the company had now abandoned him. Nonetheless I naively encouraged Charles and his family to pursue an accommodating path with both insurance companies and their attorneys. Rob disagreed, saying that it would be absolutely crazy for Charles to assume the debt.

Charles raised one subject with Rob in private: his desire to make a living will. He said vehemently that he did not ever want to be "propped up." And he gave Rob a special charge. "You're forceful enough to be able to bulldoze my family if necessary and keep them from putting me on life support. When it's time, it's time. I don't want to linger." Rob promised to do everything he could to prevent that from happening.

By late afternoon, when it was clear that Charles had grown tired and that Linda's children were getting restless, we rose to begin the five-hour final leg of our drive back to Washington. Before we pulled away, Charles's mother snapped a group picture. Charles, who had not lost all of his vanity, put on a cap to hide his now nearly bald pate and climbed into a bulky robe to cover his thin frame. He attempted a big smile—but we could tell that smiling wasn't easy for him anymore.

When we returned to Washington, Rob and I vowed to get more involved in the fight against AIDS. On the professional front, I sought to help by involving myself more fully in health-care issues. On a personal level, both Rob and I decided to establish a public presence by, among other things, participating more aggressively in the AIDS Walk, which takes place every fall. We had walked in previous years and had raised sizable sums, but this year we decided to dedicate more time to the event by volunteering as team captains. The first planning session took place early that summer in a large reception room in the Corcoran Gallery of Art. Just when the official program was about to begin, someone tapped me on the shoulder and said, "So when are you going to come out?" Rob had already noticed Peter Carmichael walking toward me in the crowd, and had moved closer in an attempt to prevent an altercation. "*People are dying,*" Carmichael screamed, more loudly, "*and you won't come out!*" I started to explain to him that I *was* out. As I then saw it, I was: though I hadn't issued a press release announcing my homosexuality, everyone in my life knew I was gay. Now that I am publicly out, I have a better understanding than I did then of the degrees of being "out" and of the moral importance and psychological benefit of explicitly declaring one's homosexuality. Interrupting me, Carmichael raised his voice and repeated himself. "*When are you going to come out?*"

Instead of helping, the affluent-looking gay men around me scattered or pretended to ignore the situation, which got worse by the second. When Rob stepped between us, Carmichael raced around him to get in my face once again. *"Come on, Steve!"* he screamed. *"Come out!"*

Rob looked at him squarely and said, "Go home, Peter." Then he pointed at me and asked me to go grab a couple of drinks. Carmichael began to follow me, but he was stopped by a couple of staff members who asked him to leave. When he refused, they carried him out. He continued screaming all the way to the door. Rob looked at me and said, "Should I throw a drink on you just to keep the tradition alive?"

That summer we shared a beach house in Rehoboth with Gloria, John Frank, and Linda's family. By then it was clear that Linda and Ostap were harboring deep and irreparable resentments toward each other. The breaking point came one night in June when we had planned to have supper at the Blue Moon, a large, predominantly gay restaurant and bar in Rehoboth. After a day on the beach, Rob and I returned to the house and could tell from their manner that Ostap and Linda had had words. Nonetheless we put the kids to bed and went out. No sooner had we arrived at the Blue Moon than Linda excused herself and walked back to the house.

Instead of following her back, Ostap and Rob and I stood on the Blue Moon's front terrace and discussed Ostap's marriage to Linda. They had always had very different ideas about what her role should be. She wanted adventure, independence, creative fulfillment; he wanted a conventional housewife who would stay at home and keep the rooms clean. Despite months of marriage counseling, tensions between them had escalated as Ostap had angrily voiced his resentment of her busy social calendar. He told us that Linda had asked for a divorce that evening, the third time she had done so, and he had said yes.

Rob and I were not only stunned by the news but also felt strangely threatened by it, as if their marital problems might in some weird way be contagious. The fact was that Linda and Ostap were so close to us, so much a part of our family, that a breakup between them was, for Rob and me, very much a family tragedy. I suggested to Ostap that they hold off on a divorce and try to let time heal their wounds.

That night Ostap talked affectionately, and with uncharacteristic openness, about our friendship with his family over the past few years. I had worried that he might harbor an unspoken resentment over our involvement with Linda, and especially over the part we had played in introducing her to the many other gay men who had become friends of hers over the years. On the contrary, Ostap thanked us both for having opened his eyes to the love that can exist between two men, and for having exploded his stereotypical notions about what it meant to be gay. When he bummed a cigarette from Rob but didn't smoke it, I realized that he was probably intoxicated and might later regret having spoken so openly. In any event, he went on to say that he felt it was important that we understand his profound feelings for us. He said that he believed his Church was out of touch with the truth about homosexuality and he hoped that we would remain his friends if he and Linda separated.

While things with Linda and Ostap were going downhill, Charles was on the upswing. Throughout that summer, he and Rob kept in touch daily by phone. They talked again about our plans to meet in Mykonos. Charles's health was still shaky but improving under a new medication, and his doctors were confident that it would continue to do so. If nothing else, the brochures Rob sent him about Mykonos and the stories Rob told him about the paradise that awaited us on those white Aegean beaches distracted him from the pain and boredom of life in Durham and gave him something to look forward to.

He called one night in July to report enthusiastically that he was feeling better and better. He had found a small house that he wanted to buy. He was exicted about these positive changes in his life and looked forward to joining us in Mykonos in August. Rob booked his reservations the next day.

13

On June 30, 1993, for the second time in two years, the House of Representatives debated a particularly heartless piece of legislation. Two years earlier, residents of the District of Columbia had approved a domestic-partnership law, a measure that would offer committed gay couples at least a semblance of equal treatment under the law. That was too much for the Congress, which exercises ultimate control over the affairs of the District. Under pressure from the Religious Right, the House had voted a year earlier to prohibit the District of Columbia from implementing the domestic-partnership law. Now, once again, we were examining the question of whether to allow the District to implement the law.

I was still struggling with the pain and frustration of not having come out of the closet and taken on Republican homophobia head-on. The full House debate on the D.C. domestic-partnership law provided a great opportunity to challenge homophobia in a conspicuous way—but, because of the way that House rules function, I didn't have that opportunity. My own party, led by Religious Right legislators, was spearheading the assault on the D.C. law, arguing that domestic partnership was a mockery of the ''traditional family'' and ''Judeo-Christian values.''

The Democrats were defending the law. But I was frustrated by the way they handled the issue. I felt that they might manage to swing some votes if they took a strategic approach, arguing that the Republican enthusiasm for local control demanded that the District, if it wished, be permitted to pass and implement a domestic-partnership law. Instead, the Democrats took a predictable—and losing—route: the openly gay Massachusetts Congressman Barney Frank personalized the debate, talking about his lover, Herb Moses. I shared Barney's passion and admired his courage, but how his emotional speech could be expected to change any votes on the Republican side of the aisle was beyond me.

I wanted desperately to speak in favor of the law. But in order to do this, I would have had to ask the Democratic side to grant me a few minutes of their allotted quarter hour. As the debate got under way, then, I looked over at the Democratic side in an attempt to detect whether I might be able to get some time from them. But it was clear from the beginning that their time had all been allocated. Much of it went to those members with large and visible gay constituencies. Then Barney was given six and a half minutes to finish. With time so tight, I would be lucky to get a minute to speak. And I had a lot more inside me than could be articulated in a one-minute statement.

That day, as expected, the House once again voted to prohibit the District from implementing domestic partnership. As I walked back to my office afterward, the words that I had wanted to say were ringing in my mind and I had to get them off my chest. Not having been able to speak them on the floor of the House, I did the next best thing: I sat down and wrote myself a memo. At the top of the page I wrote: ''If I could have been heard on this issue, this is what I would have said.'' The memo read as follows:

> My colleagues, please. What hatred and intolerance will we pursue in the name of God!

When will we learn that one can promote the traditional family without attacking the gay and lesbian community in our nation?

Earlier today, we spent hours of debate and emotion on the issue of abortion. To my conservative pro-life colleagues, will you also understand that this vote will determine whether a lot of people will live?

Over 180,000 Americans have died from AIDS. We will double that number in the next two years. And yet tonight, we again deny communities from taking the very steps they choose to reduce those numbers. And so in our own perverse way, we say that promiscuity in the gay community is OK, but we will not encourage a monogamous relationship between two people who happen to be gay.

One does not have to promote a gay lifestyle—to promote measures which reduce the infectious disease called AIDS.

One does not have to promote gay relationships—to promote local government to accept those lifestyles they choose within their own community.

Or to promote ways to assist individuals in obtaining health-care coverage.

Or to accept domestic arrangements that save us billions in health-care expenditures later, should they be overcome with AIDS.

I wish everyone here tonight knew someone with AIDS. Not because it would be pleasant, but because then you would understand that these are real people too!

Two of my friends who used to live in this town contracted AIDS. One died about a month ago at his parents' Virginia dairy farm. The other is fighting the disease today at his parents' home in Durham, North Carolina. I wish they had had domestic partners ten years ago.

I wish I could have spoken in the House on that issue. I never was able to. I could have turned my memo into a press release, but there would have been no practical point: the media wouldn't have paid attention, and nothing would have been accomplished.

Early that summer I had interesting news from my brother Matt. For months he had repeatedly urged me to run for the Senate against Wisconsin's senior senator, Herb Kohl, in 1994. Matt, who had thrown himself with gusto into every one of my campaigns, offered to be my campaign manager. I had repeatedly said no: I had no interest in giving up my House seniority to join the Senate, with its lack of rules, its less orderly debate, and its even later hours. Now, assured of my determination to stay in the House, Matt told me that he had decided to run for the Senate himself.

I was both proud and scared. I considered Matt brave to take on Herb Kohl, a respected elder statesman with a big bankroll. But I worried that, given Matt's youth (he was in his early thirties and looked even younger) and inexperience, his candidacy could look like an act of colossal political stupidity, and could ultimately prove a dismal embarrassment to all of us. Yet I gave him my blessing, and told myself that if he *did* win, it would be the political story of the year.

The improvement in Charles's health didn't last long. He called us in early August to say that the results of some of his most recent tests hadn't been promising and that the doctor had ordered him not to go to Mykonos. The orders made sense: there was no health care on Mykonos to speak of, and it takes about an hour to get from there to Athens, which isn't the best place in the world for medical treatment either.

On the weekend before we were scheduled to attend my brother Kirk's wedding in Wisconsin, Carol called to say that Charles's condition had worsened. Carol was plainly shaken. While the doctors had not come to any conclusions about his prognosis, they knew he was in serious trouble. I told her that Rob and I had been preparing to leave for Wisconsin and asked if she thought we should come to Durham instead. She insisted that we go to the wedding and call occasionally.

Rob's first reaction was strangely flippant: "No big deal! Charles will bounce back." Charles had been brought low by illnesses and infections before, only to rebound each time. Rob expressed full confidence that Charles could do it again. Besides, as Rob said to me and Randy, Charles talked so much that God didn't want him anyway. "Charles isn't going to die," Rob kept insisting. "Charles isn't going anywhere."

I suspected that this was all major-league denial. The thought of losing Charles was so unbearable for Rob that he wouldn't let himself consider the possibility. We went to the wedding and called Charles's family regularly. No change. When we returned to Washington, we talked with Carol again. He had stabilized. We considered canceling the trip to Mykonos but Carol urged us not to. The doctors had told her that Charles's condition was not worsening. He could linger for weeks in his semicomatose state.

Though we didn't cancel the trip, then, Rob took precautions. During one of his many visits to Washington the previous year, Charles had asked Rob to take care of his funeral if he should die. Rob had agreed. Charles had joked to me, "Steve, you know Rob can do flowers better than anybody in Durham, North Carolina. I'd rather die than be surrounded by a batch of carnations. And he can coordinate a program better than my parents can. I want lots of yellow roses. And I want you to read Maya Angelou's poem from the inauguration."

In the few days before we left for Mykonos, Rob talked to Charles's mother daily. He also talked to Carol, who was more realistic than her parents, and to the nurse. Through these conversations it became clearer and clearer to him that Charles wasn't going to bounce back from this downturn as quickly as he had from the earlier ones. Rob decided that the recovery would simply take longer; he still wouldn't consider the possibility that Charles might die.

By the night of Monday, August 16, Charles had been moved to intensive care. His condition had again worsened. Carol said that his doctors didn't expect him to make it through the night. That night, while I sat opposite Rob at our long pine kitchen table, he spoke to Charles over the phone while Carol held the receiver to her brother's ear. Charles couldn't talk, but he could hear Rob's words. Carol told Rob to say good-bye.

Rob was shattered. He couldn't believe this was happening. Charles had to bounce back. He couldn't leave.

Rob knew Charles must be terrified. He also knew that amid all his terror, Charles was also crushed at the thought that back in Washington, people were sidling up to bars and swilling vodka tonics. They were partying on without him, and without even noticing his absence. I heard Rob say to Charles, "It's okay to quit fighting, Charles. I'm sure that Glenn is having a big party with free vodka and you're going to find it. Just let go and relax. I'll come as soon as I can get away." He was silent as his eyes filled with tears. "I love you, Charles, and I'll see you soon."

Rob handed the receiver to me. Within seconds, Carol came back on the line. She told me that Charles had just moved for the first time in several days. He had tried to wave his hand— and he was crying.

Carol handed the phone over to her mother and we spoke about his condition. From my half of the ensuing dialogue, Rob gathered that Charles's parents had decided to do everything possible to save him. He didn't like this at all. Interrupting me, he pointed out that Charles had made a living will. I motioned for Rob to keep quiet as I listened to Charles's mother. Rob grabbed a piece of paper and scrawled a note in large letters. *I PROMISED CHARLES THAT WE WOULD NOT LET HIM BE PROPPED UP.* He shoved it in front of me. Calmly, I asked Charles's mother, "Does Charles have a living will?"

"No," she said firmly.

Rob watched my expression as I listened to the answer. I shook my head no, and proceeded as diplomatically as possible to convey Charles's request to his mother. My words fell on deaf ears. By the time the conversation had come to an end, it was clear that Charles would remain on artificial life support.

Rob called the hospital repeatedly over the next few days. Charles remained unconscious. We considered driving down to Durham, but Carol dissuaded us, saying that Charles wouldn't know we were there. We looked into the possibility of canceling or delaying our trip to Greece, but by this time there was no way to change the arrangements.

The doctors said that in his present state, with life support, Charles might hang on for weeks. That was a problem. It was a problem because Rob felt as if he had violated the last promise he had made to Charles. Then again, Rob wasn't Charles's mother and Charles wasn't his son. Rob asked his own mother, who comes in handy when dealing with truly emotional issues, what he should do. She reminded him that he couldn't know what Charles's mother was feeling and told him to tread lightly. Finally he called Carol and asked her to put her mother on the phone. Rob tried to talk to her.

Without insisting directly that she should take Charles off life support, Rob talked to her in a sensitive, calm way about the request that Charles had made. Charles's mother grew very angry. In a hostile tone she said to him, ''It's obvious you'll never have children, but I'll tell you one thing, Rob Morris, if ever you do have a child and you can let them go, then tell me I'm wrong. But until then *don't—ever—say— anything—about—this—to—me—again. This—is—my—boy— child.''*

Rob didn't know how to reply to that. He wanted to say, ''Yes, and your only child wanted to go in peace, and all you're doing is denying his last request.'' But he couldn't bring himself to say that. Instead he handed the phone to me. I'm always more calm than he is about these things. I talked some more with Charles's mother, though I didn't bring up the matter of life support. There would have been no purpose to it—she plainly wasn't going to budge.

So Charles lingered. On Thursday, August 19, he lost consciousness completely. Rob and I were at a loss about what to do. We were scheduled to leave for Mykonos that Saturday. Charles might hang on for weeks. Should we go or stay? Rob and I discussed our options with each other, and with various friends, all of whom urged us to go ahead and take the trip. So we decided to go, all the while feeling an immense guilt about it. Meanwhile, in the event that Charles should die while we were gone, Rob made notes of his plans for Charles's funeral and gave them to Linda so that she and Randy could carry them out. Rob also made arrangements to fly down to Durham immediately upon our return from Mykonos.

And so Rob and I flew to Mykonos, as scheduled, on Saturday, August 21.

On our first full day in Mykonos, Monday, August 23, we returned from the grocery store to find a note on the door of the hilltop house we were renting. It was from the house's owner and it said we should see him immediately to pick up an urgent message. Rob went to his flat at the end of the property fully prepared for the news. In a regretful tone, the man told Rob that Linda had called. "Your friend," he said in broken English, "has passed away."

Numb, Rob returned to the house, took a shower, made drinks, and came out on the terrace where I was sitting. I had already showered and was waiting for the sunset, which promised to be a beautiful sight from this hilltop spot. As the sun set over the rocky terrain and the deep blue Aegean, Rob quietly said, "Charles died."

I didn't say anything, and neither did Rob. And then, at that moment, as the sun dipped below the horizon, Rob had a curious experience. He felt a breeze that was strangely unlike a breeze, or a cold shiver; it was just something that went through him. And as it went through him, before he even had a moment to think about it, he felt himself gripped by a powerful, deep-seated sensation that Charles had just gone by him.

In retrospect Rob doesn't know whether he created that sensation of a breeze subconsciously in order to make himself feel better, or whether it really happened. All he knows is that something dreadful was inside of him before he felt the breeze, and then the breeze took it away and left him at peace. He looked at me and smiled.

"What are you doing?" I asked, shocked by his smile.

Rob said, "He made it! Charles made it." Tears rolled down

his cheeks as he continued. "He was here. He's gone. He's okay." Rob believed that with all his heart.

That night, in the same restaurant along the Aegean at which we had eaten during our first trip to Mykonos many years earlier, Rob and I buried Charles, metaphorically speaking. We sifted through happy memories. We talked about what Charles had meant to both of us. We had lost a true friend, who had never been comfortable enough to admit his sexual orientation, to a disease that he had been too embarrassed to mention. After supper, Rob and I went from bar to bar, having a drink here, a drink there. At each bar we would talk about Charles, and our memories of him, and eventually we'd both break into tears. We'd cry for a while, then pull ourselves together, pick ourselves up, and go on to the next place, where we would talk some more and cry again. That's how we spent that evening in Mykonos—talking and crying, talking and crying. Amid all the laughter of Mykonos that night, Rob and I were the only ones in tears.

One of our last stops that night was at a place called The Piano Bar. It was a lively spot crowded with animated tourists and an incredible American singer whose beautiful voice and obvious passion brought us calm. We knew that of all the things we had experienced in Mykonos, Charles would have enjoyed hearing her most of all. As we later learned, the singer, Phyllis Pastori, lived in New York, where she sang regularly at a couple of well-known cabarets; every summer, she had a two-week engagement in Mykonos. As she began another song, Rob ordered a drink and lit a cigarette and said to me, "This one's for Charles." When Phyllis took a break between sets, we introduced ourselves to her, and ended up making a new friend. It's curious how life can work sometimes: on a night when we had lost one of our best friends, we met someone who would also become a good friend.

Rob phoned Linda the next morning. Everything, she said, was under control. She had arranged to take a group of people to Durham for the funeral; Randy had already flown there from Pittsburgh. The service ended up being pretty much what Charles had wanted. He had asked me to read Maya Angelou's inauguration poem at the service; Linda read it in my place. Rob had wanted to fill the church with yellow roses; Linda and Randy saw to it that the church was overflowing with them.

Yet when Rob heard more about the details of the funeral he was disappointed. During the whole service, he learned, Charles's family had never once acknowledged that he had been gay or that he had died of AIDS. From what Rob had heard, he gathered that, instead of making something meaningful out of Charles's life and death, his parents had covered up the truth about who their son had been. In this regard, of course, Charles's parents weren't unusual. They were like many parents of gay people, who know but don't want to know, who love their children but are so uncomfortable with a key part of who those children are that they can't bring themselves to acknowledge it. They're psychologically incapable of bringing together the concepts of "beloved son" and "homosexual."

Rob felt that this irrational attitude on the part of Charles's parents had exerted a powerful influence on Charles's own self-image, and went a long way toward explaining why Charles had never been fully at ease with himself, had never been able to find love and make a commitment. In a way, families like Charles's had provided a model for the situation in the American military, whose leaders simply could not bring themselves to admit that plenty of men and women who were good soldiers also happened to be gay.

There was a bit of an irony, then, in the fact that the last weeks of Charles's life coincided with the climax of the fierce public controversy over gays in the military.

Back in June, Rob and I had hoped that our week at Rehoboth Beach with Linda and Ostap would provide a brief, relaxing escape from pressing issues. Instead we had found ourselves talking constantly about politics, in particular about the pending House debate on gays in the military. Rob had argued that in debating controversial matters on the floor

of the House I was always too polite and not sufficiently confrontational. He had also said that I was still too much of an
instinctive party loyalist. I had already made clear my discomfort with right-wing intolerance in the Republican party by
quitting the whip job; it was time, he said, to stand up and
speak out against that intolerance.

During the last weekend in July, then, as the long-awaited
House debate on gays in the military approached, Rob sat
down at his computer and drafted a set of remarks for me to
deliver. When I read what he had written, I was impressed: he
had managed to put into words exactly what I had been wanting to say for many months.

I knew that if I delivered these remarks in the House, the
results would be explosive, and the personal and professional
consequences for me might well be disastrous. But I also knew
that there was no question in my mind about whether I would
give this speech. I wanted to do it, I had to do it, and I *would*
do it—and damn the consequences.

This wasn't the last time that Rob would draft a speech for
me on gay issues. Though he's kept a low profile compared to
the husbands and wives of other members of Congress, he's
played a far more active role in my political career than most
Congressional spouses do. I don't know of any other spouse
writing speeches. It may happen, but I haven't heard about it.

In any event, on September 28, I stood in the well of the
House before a heated audience and began speaking.

"Imagine the reaction today," I told the House, "if I were to
come to this body today and use such ugly and demeaning
labels as nigger, kike, wop, or chinks. We reject those labels
today because we have accepted into American society the
very people they seek to demean. And yet I doubt few here are
equally offended by the word 'faggot.' "

As my remarks went on, the House grew quiet. For several
minutes, I had the members' undiluted attention. I didn't explicitly "come out" in that speech. But for Steve Gunderson,
who virtually everyone in Washington knew was homosexual, to condemn his own party's opposition to gays in the

military was an incautious thing to do. As long as Congress wasn't interested in gay issues, of course, my homosexuality didn't matter; as long as I kept my mouth shut about gay issues, it still didn't matter. But to speak up on those issues, especially in such heated circumstances and under the glare of so much publicity, was another thing entirely—it was potential political suicide.

In the written remarks on gays in the military that I filed for publication in the *Congressional Record*, I went even further than in my floor statement. (Hampered by time constraints from saying everything we want to say in our floor statements, members of Congress routinely request permission to "revise and extend" our remarks, which means that we enter in the *Congressional Record* statements that are longer and more detailed than the ones we actually made on the floor of the House.) Quoting from John Boswell's groundbreaking 1980 book, *Christianity, Social Tolerance, and Homosexuality*, I disputed the way in which fundamentalists interpreted scripture to support their antigay bias; quoting from Randy Shilts's *Conduct Unbecoming*, I noted that the same objections raised to gays in the military had been raised by Truman-era officials in regard to blacks in the military. I informed my fellow members that one of our great Revolutionary War heroes, Baron von Steuben—who today is the namesake of German-pride parades all over America—was homosexual.

"I haven't been a member of the military, and I can't speak directly from that experience," I said near the end of my written remarks. "But I have experienced what it feels like to have my life—who I am, what I am, and what I have accomplished—reduced to and judged by a single, irrelevant factor." I didn't explicitly identify that factor—but there wasn't a member of the House who didn't know what it was.

I went on to mention the Carmichael incident of two years earlier, without mentioning Carmichael by name. "Not the least of that incident for me," I said, "was that an eleven-year congressional record, and almost twenty years in public office, stood to be blown apart. My accomplishments stood to become totally irrelevant next to the single question of whether or not I was gay."

As I later explained to Patrick Jasperse of the Milwaukee *Journal*, I had referred to the Carmichael incident because I was sick of people like Dornan saying that if you weren't a military veteran, you couldn't have a legitimate position on this issue. Dornan is a veteran, I'm not. But unlike me—and unlike the fine, patriotic men and women in the armed forces who were being hunted down, tormented, humiliated, and robbed of their careers simply because they were gay—Dornan had never had his entire professional career put at risk because of an innate aspect of his identity that had no bearing on how well or badly he performed his job.

Whatever my colleagues thought about my being gay, I knew that the great majority of them respected me as a legislator and recognized that my sexual orientation was irrelevant to my job performance. The same, I wanted to make clear, should apply to people in military service. The antigay witch hunts were wrong. They had to be stopped.

That, of course, was obvious to me. But I might never have taken the dramatic political risk of saying so before Congress if it hadn't been for Rob.

Not surprisingly, my contribution to the debate on gays in the military drew a lot of press attention, especially back home in Wisconsin. The Milwaukee *Journal* published a supportive editorial, saying that "If a sequel to *Profiles in Courage* is ever written, Rep. Steve Gunderson might rate a chapter. . . . His eloquent plea for tolerance deserves a wide audience." The biggest paper in my district, the La Crosse *Tribune*, was similarly positive. And the Eau Claire *Leader-Telegram* ran a respectful editorial saying that "it is time for all Americans, including conservative Republicans, to accept homosexuals as people and respect their individual rights."

But the commentary in the "liberal press" was one thing; the feelings of my dairy farmers and their families about my stand on this issue might well be another matter entirely. I was not surprised, in the days after I delivered my remarks on gays in the military, to find my office flooded with emotional letters from furious constituents. The illogic and self-contradiction of these letters, and the riot of underlined and capitalized words and multiple exclamation points, made it clear that these people's antagonism did not derive from any calmly and carefully worked out moral, theological, or philosophical position but, rather, represented an irrational response to something they perceived as threatening without quite understanding why.

Several constituents wrote that acceptance of homosexuality had brought down the Greek city-states and the Roman empire—thereby proving that they knew absolutely nothing about ancient history except what they had "learned" from Pat Robertson's "700 Club" TV show and other fundamentalist sources. Some of the letter writers were particularly nasty: a man in Hudson, Wisconsin, suggested that my support for gays in the military was the result of "AIDS dementia." And many correspondents served up the usual stereotypes. A man in La Crosse, for example, wrote that gays depend on "recruitment, because many are dying of AIDS and they do not *naturally* reproduce themselves."

Some letters contained unintentional ironies. A retired navy lieutenant who didn't realize that I was gay argued that homosexuals had no business serving in the military, then concluded by saying that, aside from this one issue, he was proud of my record in Congress and that I "would make an outstanding submarine officer." One air force veteran (who, incidentally, lived in the town of Sparta, named for the Greek city-state famed for its invincible, openly homosexual soldiers) wrote an odd letter in which he first claimed to have been accosted by homosexuals twice in the military, then maintained that he hadn't ever been accosted. "I am writing this on a Bible, God's word, and he writes clearly that it is an abomination to him, man with man and woman with woman." (In fact there is nothing in the Bible about women being with women.) "Please don't bring up the Tailhook incident—what a lame analogy," he went on. "I'd much rather my daughter,

if it be, be fondeled [sic] by a man.'' For some of my correspondents, plainly, the issue of gays in the military tapped into
some very deep, strange, and disturbing emotions.

Most of the letters focused on religious arguments. Several
cited the handful of Bible verses which are quoted again and
again by Religious Right leaders—always out of context, of
course—when discussing homosexuality. One constituent
posed this interesting query: ''When you pass on and approach the pearly gates at the entrance to heaven and Jesus
says to you, 'What was your position on homosexual rights?'
what will your reply be?'' In his view, obviously, Jesus would
be waiting at Saint Peter's gate to punish me for supporting
equality of opportunity! So much for the God whom I worship as a God of love. It was dismaying, indeed, to be reminded
how many self-styled Christians identified Jesus not with love
but with hatred and intolerance.

Given all this, it didn't come as a total surprise when, a
month after my remarks on gays in the military, the *Leader-
Telegram* reported that a new ''Christian, pro-life, pro-family
and conservative'' group called Concerned Republicans of
Wisconsin, organized by a man named Chuck Lee, had sent
letters to dozens of Republican leaders in the state, calling on
them not to support my expected 1994 reelection bid. The letter referred to my support for ''the plan to homosexualize the
Armed Forces'' and declared that ''we as Republicans need to
stand up and defend our party against these 'Big Tent' liberals
who would destroy the party to promote their perversion.''

This was not the last I would hear of Chuck Lee.

14

The 103rd Congress, which went into session in 1993, differed dramatically from its predecessors. The Republican party was coming off its first loss of the White House in sixteen years. Antigay GOP rhetoric figured prominently in the convention, the campaign, and the transition. The Democrats, who seemed to have controlled Congress forever but had never been able to hold on to the White House, went into 1993 with a great new opportunity. Controlling both the legislative and executive branches in hand, they were in a position to do anything they wanted.

Few people looked to the Clinton administration and the Democratic Congress with the optimism and hope that the gay community did, from one end of the political spectrum to the other. Certainly Bill Clinton's courageous willingness to stand up and speak out for, to, and in defense of the gay community in the campaign caused me and Rob, in a deeply personal way, to have real hope.

Rob pushed me on the gay issue constantly. He argued that I was continuing to embrace a party that kept attacking its own—me included. Once I recognized the need to quit as deputy whip and to give up the absolute party loyalty that goes with that position, it was time for me to become the true "issues" leader I sought to be. Because we both had hope for Clinton's commitment to human rights and equal opportunity for all Americans, we both felt it was essential that Republicans like me give Clinton the support he would need on issues like gays in the military and AIDS funding.

My Democratic friends in Congress, including Dave McCurdy, Tim Penny of Minnesota, and Charlie Stenholm of Texas were very excited about Clinton's election. They believed he was their kind of centrist Democrat. Each of them talked to me about their hopes for a bipartisan, centrist coalition led by the new president. They were convinced he would change the politics of the nation and of the Democratic party. One night shortly after the 1992 election, when Dave was busy assisting the Clinton transition, he called me at home.

"So what's up with you guys?" he asked. I knew he didn't mean me and Rob; he meant me and my fellow Republicans.

"Hey, we're not the ones taking over Washington!" I replied. "Our life has got to be boring compared to yours right now!" He laughed. "So what job will you get?" I asked. "Do you want Defense, CIA, or National Security Adviser?"

"I know which ones I don't want," he said. "And I know which ones I likely won't get. So my guess is that I'll stay right where I am."

"Well, I would kind of like a friend in high places," I said. "So take whatever you can get."

He laughed again. "That's not why I called. We're trying to figure out how to get things done in the new Congress. And we need to figure out a way to bring some of you Republicans in."

"Well, it won't be easy at the top," I said. "Bob Michel feels constrained by those around him. And he was pretty loyal to Bush, so I suspect this election really hurt him. Newt and the rest are very partisan. But you know that."

"But there are a lot of people like you, Amo Houghton, and Olympia Snowe who should find ideological comfort with Clinton. How do we bring you guys into the ball game?"

"Well," I said, "we do have this group of moderates, it's very informal. But I, Fred Upton, and others could easily put together a list of people we think you could work with."

"That's exactly what we need. If you could put that together in the near future and get it to me, it would be very helpful."

"You should know, Dave, and Clinton should know that we are all committed to governing. We could all be very helpful. But none of us want to be used, taken for granted, or ignored except when there aren't enough Democrats to pass a bill."

"I hear you."

Dave was on to something. He understood how Congress worked—and how to get things accomplished in a bipartisan manner. He could have been an extraordinary asset to the Clinton administration, but the White House never listened to him as it should have, and never rewarded him properly for all he had done to help elect Clinton.

As promised, I provided Dave with a list of moderate Republicans. Not that I had to: it would have been easy enough for the White House to go through the voting records and the ratings by groups like the Americans for Democratic Action or American Conservative Union or *National Journal* and figure out who the moderate Republicans are. If they had been clever, the White House people would have invited some of us over and taken steps to put together a workable coalition of people ranging from Republican moderates to liberal Democrats.

But they never did it. It was astonishing. And this was the president who had said in November 1992 that he wanted to have a bipartisan cabinet. He *never* named a Republican to the Cabinet—and in doing so he missed a real opportunity. We have some very good, highly visible Republicans both in the Congress and elsewhere who would have made strong additions to the Clinton Cabinet. If I had been a Democratic president in his position, I would certainly have brought at least one of those Republicans on board, if only for the public relations benefit. Just appointing one Republican to the Cabinet would have sent out a message that this president was interested in working across party lines and having a broad-based team.

But he didn't do it. Clinton didn't reach out to us, not even when we reached out to him. Never once were moderate Republicans invited to the White House to meet with Clinton. The most we ever received was a meeting on Capitol Hill with his first chief of staff, Mack McLarty. That was a crucial mistake, on all their parts. It could only have been made by people who had a false sense of security as to their majority status in Congress. With the exception of a two-year Republican Senate majority in the mid-'80s, the Democrats had enjoyed control of both Houses for decades, and couldn't conceive of that changing in the near future.

Why this colossal failure? I think I know. Clinton had run against Congress in 1992, both Democrat and Republican. After the election, it was essential for him to build bridges to the Democratic majority in Congress to get legislation passed. I strongly suspect that Al Gore, who like his father was an ex-senator, advised Clinton after the election that the way to build bridges with Democrats in Congress was to pursue a totally Democratic strategy on Capitol Hill—to win over congressional Democrats, in short, by pointedly freezing out congressional Republicans.

During the transition, President-elect Clinton courted Speaker of the House Tom Foley and Senate Majority Leader George Mitchell. It soon became clear that the White House would acknowledge and approach Republicans only when there were insufficient Democratic votes to pass an important piece of legislation. One day, in exasperation, I asked a White House lobbyist why the Clinton administration never pursued building bridges with Republicans by inviting us down to the White House to meet with the president.

"To be honest," he said, "we can't invite you down. The Democratic leadership in Congress won't let us. But you can invite us to your meetings here on the Hill. And if you initiate the process, we'll respond." To say the least, we were offended.

The White House's freezing out of Republicans was a calamitously ill-conceived policy. Even before the election of 1994 gave the Republicans a majority, President Clinton wouldn't have been able to accomplish a single item on his agenda without at least some Republican votes. It wouldn't have taken a rocket scientist to figure out that the most likely place to get those votes was from moderate Republicans. If Clinton had only looked at how Reagan and Bush had managed to pass such bills as the Reagan tax cut and reduction of the capital gains tax, he would've learned an important lesson. In such cases, both Reagan and Bush had started with a Republican base and then reached out to conservative Democrats, making the necessary adjustments to bring them aboard and secure a majority vote. Clinton should have tried to do the same thing: start with a Democratic base and then reach out to Republican moderates, asking them, "What do we have to do to bring you into the fold?"

The Clinton White House's failure to court Republican votes resulted directly in the fact that not one Republican member of the House or Senate voted for Clinton's 1993 budget. That, in turn, may be the main reason why Democrats lost control of Congress. In one case after another, the lesson is clear: the support of Republicans like myself allowed Clinton to enact his National Service Program; his unwillingness to reach out sufficiently for Republican support cost him his health-care-reform package.

This failure on President Clinton's part almost guaranteed the political disaster that befell him in the November 1994 election. Yet even after the election, some people in the White House seemed not to have gotten the point. When a member of President Clinton's legislative team met with me after the election, he asked how they could build a bipartisan working relationship with Republicans in Congress.

"That's easy," I said. "Appoint a visible Republican or two to your legislative team. It will send all the right signals to the new majority. And it will allow you to build bridges to the Republicans through people they know and trust."

"I don't think we can do that," he said.

In my experience, the one person who sought Republican support for White House legislative initiatives was Hillary Clinton. While formulating the administration's health-care proposals, she met with every group on Capitol Hill that sought an audience with her. It was good public relations. But it was not meant to be much more. Democrats aggressively protected their right to design and introduce the health-care-reform agenda. That was fine, until it came time for that agenda to be introduced.

I remember one day when Hillary Clinton called my office. I was out, but Kris took the call. Dave Hobson, a moderate Republican from Ohio, got a message from Mrs. Clinton the same day. We compared notes before returning the calls. We wanted to say the same thing.

The first word I said when I was put through to her was "Hillary." I didn't call the first lady by her first name out of any lack of respect; on the contrary, she had sought a personal rapport with members of Congress, and had achieved it.

Hillary quickly made clear her reason for calling: she wanted me to cosponsor her health-care proposal. I thanked her for the offer, but explained, "You don't want to have Republicans cosponsoring your proposal when you introduce it."

"Why not?"

"If we sign up before the legislative process begins, we make ourselves irrelevant. On the other hand, if some of us work constructively with you during the process, we can achieve a bipartisan vote at the end. That's when you really want us."

Hillary seemed to understand. She thanked me graciously for my advice, and spoke enthusiastically of our working together on getting health care passed. But Republicans were never brought sufficiently into the process of policy formulation—and the rest is history. It's a tragedy, because I believe that if the White House had taken a well-conceived bipartisan approach to health care from the outset, a strong reform package would have been passed—and it would have been a feather in the administration's cap. The problem is that the reform agenda was kidnapped by big-government Democrats who sought to enact a 1990s' version of the Great Society, and who didn't want to hear what anybody else had to say.

I enjoyed working with Hillary. I think the fact that both of us had suffered unfair personal attacks created a bond between us. I remember vividly arriving at the second of two White House dinners that Rob and I attended together. I arrived late, delayed by votes in the House, and was greeted personally by Hillary. It had been a bad day for her, full of unfair press attacks on her and the president, mostly related to Whitewater.

"Can I say something to you?" I asked rather pointedly. "I want to ask you to hang tough."

"Thanks for the encouragement," she said graciously.

"No," I said, "it's much more than that. There is something going on in this town and in this country that has to stop. And it won't stop unless we fight back. It seems that when people disagree professionally these days, they fight back personally. Rather than debate the issue, they try to destroy the person. It's the politics of personal destruction. I'm going through it back home in Wisconsin, and you're going through it here. Whether it's Bill Clinton or Newt Gingrich or Steve Gunderson, these personal attacks have got to stop. I don't think democracy can survive if we abandon political debate for personal attacks. So I want you to know there is at least one Republican who wants you to stand up and fight back."

The first lady was clearly moved by my sincere empathy. And she was also clearly able to read between the lines of what I was saying. Grabbing my hand again, she confessed to being anxious. "I wasn't ready for how cruel this city can be," she said. "But I couldn't agree with you more. There has got to be a way to restore some decency to the process."

I like Hillary Clinton very much. I only wish that she and the president had recognized from the beginning that there are many people of goodwill in both parties who want to make government work, and that it's one of the main responsibilities of leaders to reach out to them and establish the personal rapport, confidence, and credibility that will be crucial in times of political crisis. I know that the Clintons are very warm people, and I know that if they had invested the time, effort, and political capital during the first two years of the administration, they could have achieved much more bipartisan cooperation than they did.

One area in which I worked a great deal with the Clinton administration was on funding for the National Endowment for the Arts, which, owing to Religious Right protests about NEA support of supposedly obscene artworks by Robert Mapplethorpe and Andres Serrano, had become the subject of huge controversy. As a member of the Higher Education Subcommittee, which has jurisdiction over the NEA, I played a key role in hearings about NEA funding. It was a challenge. The biggest difficulty you face with an issue like NEA funding is the emotionalism that surrounds it on both sides. You have to try to get people to set aside their emotions, look dispassionately at the present law, decide what the problems are with the law, and determine what needs to be done to change it constructively. That's not easy.

The process usually follows a predictable pattern. This or that group draws attention to some issue of national concern. Other groups disagree. The conflict becomes explosive. Eventually it becomes clear that committee hearings are in order. You listen to testimony from both sides. During those hearings, tentative ideas for a potential solution to the conflict begin to take shape in your mind. You start bouncing those ideas off your colleagues, and off members of these opposing groups. In the case of the NEA debacle, you ask yourself: Is this potential solution sufficient to meet the concerns of the conservative groups? Will it satisfy the arts community? Can it get passed by the Congress? If it's passed, will it work?

In the case of NEA funding, the level of emotion surrounding the issue was so great that neither side was disposed to look dispassionately at a proposed legislative solution. One side said there was no problem with the NEA as it existed, and

thus no need to talk about a solution; the other side replied
that the only satisfactory way to fix the NEA was to eliminate
it.

Now the fact is that there *was* a problem with the NEA,
though not one that necessitated its destruction. Ever since
my first term in Congress, I've been involved in the reauthori-
zations of the NEA every four years, and I've had a front-seat
view of how the process works. As a moderate Republican, I
understood the genuine need for a government-related organization that coordinates arts promotion on a national level
and that provides access to the arts for people who otherwise
wouldn't have such access. At the same time, I knew there
was a need for change—less because of Mapplethorpe and Serrano than because of various institutional corruptions. For
years, the NEA's grant-review process had been incestuous.
People who received grants in one year would be invited to
help select the grant recipients a year or two later, and often
the winners would be people who had previously been judges.
Friends took care of friends; one hand washed the other. It
was like a revolving door. It was clear to me that we had to
change that process.

We also needed to establish some way of making sure that
grants were used for what the application said they were
going to be used for. An artist would submit an application
saying that he or she wanted a grant in order to work on
such-and-such a project, but when the grant was made, the
money would be used for something completely different.
There was no established mechanism for follow-up or enforcement.

So what we did in the 1990 reauthorization was to institute
a multiple-disbursement procedure. Instead of handing over
grant money in one lump sum, the NEA would give it out in
dribs and drabs, and would have the authority, the responsibility, and the leverage to monitor how those funds were actually spent.

That was a good reform. In my view, it cleared up most of
the problems with the NEA. It was under the pre-1990 system

that the NEA awarded all the grants which would later become controversial. But that didn't protect the NEA from
coming under attack, during the last years of the Bush administration and the first years of the Clinton administration, for
having awarded those grants. The critics didn't recognize—or
didn't care—that the process had changed. Their goal was
simply to destroy the NEA; it didn't matter to them what the
facts were.

You can understand the attitudes of many middle Americans toward the NEA when you look at some of the propaganda that they've been exposed to. Not long ago I received in
my office a videotape called "What Is Sex?" that was essentially a compilation of hardcore gay porn. Distributed by the
American Family Association, and presumably sent to every
member of Congress, the videotape was accompanied by a
note claiming that the porn shown on it had been funded by
the NEA. The AFA didn't provide any evidence to support this
claim, but that hardly matters: when middle Americans go to
meetings at their churches and someone shows them excerpts
from gay-porn films and tells them they were funded with tax
dollars, they're going to believe that before they believe me or
Jane Alexander.

Can the NEA be saved? I really don't know. Since the Republicans won a majority in Congress, the situation has been
problematic. The arts community, by and large, has simply
been unable to recognize the reality of the new political environment. Early on, Newt gave the signal that he was in favor
of working out transitional programs for various agencies
whereby they might be able to survive in a new atmosphere
of severe budget austerity. What that meant, in essence, was
that agencies might have five to seven years in which they
could find a way to wean themselves off of dependence on the
goverment.

Most of those agencies, the NEA included, responded by
going into denial. They simply wouldn't accept that the political situation was suddenly very different. In an effort to save
the NEA, I developed a transition program that would have

created, over a period of seven years, a genuine and independent endowment that would provide in perpetuity an annual income as large as the current annual appropriation. I thought it was a good plan, and when the actor Christopher Reeve came into my office early in 1995 (not long before his near-fatal horse-jumping accident) to lobby for arts funding, I was eager to pitch it to him.

Reeve started by telling me that, from a Republican perspective, the arts were a great investment. For every dollar invested, he said, there were many times more dollars produced, many times more taxpayer dollars paid back into the federal government. For him, the bottom line was that the NEA was working just fine and that everything should stay just the way it was.

"Christopher," I said, "you're making a great argument. I agree with everything you're saying. But believe me, it's not going to work. Business as usual is not going to survive in any area of the federal government right now. Unless the arts community recognizes that, and takes some dramatic steps, they'll end up with nothing."

"What do you mean?" he said. "What kind of steps?"

I told him about my proposal for a seven-year process to create a true endowment. I said, "The beauty of this is that the conservatives would like it because no longer would their tax dollars be used to fund the arts, while the liberals would like it because no longer would Jesse Helms be able to define what is art. So everybody wins in the process."

Reeve was excited, and very supportive. He thought the proposal made a great deal of sense. He said, "I think we ought to be looking seriously at this." He walked out of my office pretty much sold on the plan, and started talking it up among his colleagues. But it didn't take long for the arts establishment to turn him around. "You can't be saying that!" they said to him. "You've got to oppose that!" They rejected my plan because they were convinced at the time that they could ride out two years of Republican control of Congress and restore the NEA to its proper level of funding when the

Democrats came back into power in 1996. They saw the Republican majority as a fluke—as some kind of ghastly mistake that would be corrected as soon as possible.

Unlike the NEA, the state and local arts agencies liked my proposal very much. They had been more involved in politics than the NEA people had been, and so they knew that this kind of partnership stood the best chance of giving them secure permanent support. But when you have the NEA and leading elements of the national arts community opposing you, it's very difficult to get something like this passed. I told people, "Look, I'm not going to push my plan on anybody. It's there when the arts community realizes that this is their only realistic choice." And so it stands to this day. At this writing, the NEA is operating on almost a one-third cut in funding. An agency committed to creativity, to works of the imagination, is suffering because too many of its supporters cling unimaginatively to the status quo and fail to deal creatively with the challenges facing them.

ROB

It was partly because of Steve's support for the NEA that Steve and I were invited to the White House.

It's ironic that while Steve had served in Congress throughout the Reagan and Bush administrations, it wasn't until the Clinton presidency that he and I were invited to the White House. The occasion of the first visit was a dinner and concert in honor of the NEA that took place in October 1993.

Steve and I were gratified by the invitation, but before the night of the dinner neither of us had really given much thought to the historic significance of the invitation. Frankly this represented a failure of imagination on both our parts. It's also just a function of the way we think of ourselves. On a purely intellectual level Steve and I realize that he is "the only openly gay Republican congressman" and I am his companion; but on an everyday level, we just think of ourselves as

Steve and Rob, period. We're two ordinary people, one of whom happens to be a congressman, the other of whom happens to build houses. And both of whom happen to be gay.

Certainly, for us, the chief context of our identity as a couple is not Steve's role in government but our relationships with our friends and family. That's the big picture in which we tend to think of ourselves. Besides, we're both usually so busy that we tend to view formal social occasions as commitments that we scribble into our appointment books and forget about until the time arrives for us to get dressed and go out.

So we showed up at the White House that evening in our tuxedos without really having given thought to the momentous significance of the invitation. We entered the White House on the ground level and were greeted by a staff member who was, I think, named Karen. She was well prepared and recognized us immediately, greeting us as if we were old friends. "Congressman Gunderson, I'm so glad to see you!" she gushed. "And Mr. Morris, what a treat to have you here!"

I was taken aback. My first instinct was to say, "Honey, I don't know you from Adam, but you sure do your job well!" She ushered us up the staircase, and we were greeted at the second-floor landing by Hillary Clinton.

In the White House there are two primary second-floor spaces for large gatherings, one in each wing. That evening, we ate in the west wing. There were about twelve tables, each seating about ten people. Before we went in, however, we had to be "announced." So Steve and I took our place in line behind other guests, and when we reached the threshold, someone said loudly, "Congressman Gunderson and Rob Morris."

And you know what? The ceiling didn't fall in. Nobody seemed to be scandalized. But for a split second, Steve and I looked at each other, suddenly staggered by the meaning of the moment.

I was paranoid that evening. I couldn't help feeling that everybody else there belonged and I didn't. I guess it's a natural reaction. I was absolutely terrified that someone would come up to me and start talking about foreign affairs. I said to Steve, "What if somebody asks me what I think about Bosnia?" And Steve replied to his low-key, matter-of-fact way, ''Rob, no one's going to come up to you and talk about Bosnia.''

He was right. In actuality, since it was a dinner for the NEA, there were fewer politicians in attendance than there were artists, intellectuals, and entertainers—people like Arthur Miller, Carly Simon, William Styron, Anjelica Huston, and Leontyne Price—and some of them probably felt as out of place as I did. In any event I feel much happier talking about art than about politics. As it turned out, even the politicians didn't want to talk about politics. The first guests we spoke to that evening were the secretary of education, Richard Riley, and his wife, with whom we chatted about the coastal areas, older homes, renovation, and construction. I felt at home.

When we arrived at the dinner, President Clinton was not there. But he showed up later, and made his way over to me after the meal. ''You know,'' he said, ''Hillary and I want you and Steve both to know how very glad we are that you're here and that you came together. We want you to feel comfortable here.''

I looked at him, and I almost said, ''Yeah, well, I had to check my calendar, and there was nothing else important going on, so I thought I'd drop by!'' I mean, what do you say when the president of the United States tells you how happy he is to have you in his home?

''Well,'' I said, ''we have had a wonderful time, and there's one thing you could do that would make my night just perfect. I have a younger brother who wants to be a politician, and he admires you greatly, and if you could just''—I pulled out my pen—''if you could just sign this to Dana I would appreciate it so much.''

While he was signing the menu, I noticed Hillary, some distance away, glancing in our direction. Shortly after that, I walked by her as she was talking to somebody else. I think she assumed that perhaps I was going to come her way and snag her autograph too, but I had no intention of bothering both of them. But as I passed her, she turned to look at me—she really does have a charming way about her, incidentally, in one-on-one social situations—and there was something in her eyes and in her body language that compelled me to hand her the menu and the pen. In my best impish Southern-boy manner, I said ''I know you know what I'm asking.''

''I know,'' she replied with a smile. ''I saw you with Bill.'' She looked at the menu and got a quizzical look on her face. "But you're not Dana," she said. I was astounded: she knew who I was! They meet thousands and thousands of people, mayors and governors and senators and heads of state. And yet she knew I wasn't Dana!

"No," I said. "That's my younger brother."

"Oh, it's a pleasure," she replied, and signed the menu.

The after-dinner concert took place in the East Wing and was followed by dancing. No, Steve and I didn't dance together. (I'm not sure who dances worse, Steve or Al Gore.) But Bill and Hillary did, and they were whirling around the floor together as Steve and I left at about eleven-thirty. And after a day when both of them had probably met hundreds of people, and had dined with about a hundred and fifty, Hillary glimpsed us leaving out of the corner of her eye, made a gesture to catch my attention—I was closer to her than Steve was—and said, "Rob, thanks for coming."

The second visit to the White House came some months later. It was a smaller, less formal occasion, a dinner for about forty people. The Clintons apparently have these casual dinners once a week. Perhaps because Steve had worked with Hillary on health care, and perhaps because Steve, as one of the more moderate Republicans in Congress, is someone whose tactical usefulness the Democrats value, they invited us.

Well, late that afternoon Steve called me at work and told me, "We're going to be in session late." That's not an unusual occurrence, it happens all the time. No big deal. Except this night we were going to the White House! I reminded him of that. "Well," Steve said, "it may well be nine o'clock before we get done here. You can either come here and sit in my office, or you can wait at home and meet me at the White House."

I pointed out that there was an obvious alternative. "Steve," I said, "I can just go by myself and you can show up as soon as you're able to."

Why not? It made perfect sense. I was invited, he was invited. Why not just go? Hey, it wasn't as if I'd never been to the White House before.

So that evening, when it came time to leave for my dinner date, I went out and got into my car. And suddenly I realized what I was doing. There are things about your life that you take for granted until they're put into another context. My car, for instance. Now, my 1987 black BMW was a perfectly acceptable vehicle, under ordinary circumstances. Since I drove it from construction site to construction site, however, it was filthy. The ashtray was full of cigarette butts, the floor was littered with empty Diet Coke cans, and the back seat was piled with construction supplies. Suddenly the thought of driving up to the gate of the White House in this fine but cluttered and unclean auto seemed outrageous. Did they have valet parking? As I surveyed the mess in my car, I laughed at the thought of a White House employee climbing into it and driving it away. *Oh well,* I thought, and shifted into second.

Well, the first thing I did when I got to the White House was to pull into the wrong entrance. I was given directions to the north entrance. When they let me in, I was able to verify that, yes indeed, I had by far the dirtiest car in the parking lot. Never before had such a thing bothered me. This time it did.

When I got out of the car, I looked up at that big famous edifice and my thoughts turned from the parking lot to the luminaries inside. Suddenly I realized how audacious it was for me to show up alone for dinner at the Executive Mansion. "Wait a minute, Rob Morris!" I said to myself. "This isn't the 7-Eleven! I'm not going antiquing! I'm not dropping in at Matt and John's house. This is the damn White House, and I'm going here *by myself.*"

So I hesitated before going in. All around me, people were leaving their cars in couples and walking through a checkpoint. But I held back. Finally I got a grip. "Okay," I told myself. "Don't be silly. Don't overthink it. Just go. Go! You've been here before, at least you've got that advantage. Maybe some of these other people *haven't* been here before. Just be cool. Act like you belong."

Steeling my courage, then, I went inside and walked upstairs to the second floor. I was comfortable on that floor; I had been there and knew my way around. The only problem was that, as it turned out, the dinner wasn't on the second floor; it was in the family quarters on the third floor, which is private.

My immediate impulse was to grab a scotch and go outside and smoke. But I knew that wasn't a good idea. On some days, I can drink six scotches and remain sober, but on other days two scotches knock me for a loop. I didn't want to get bombed at the White House. That was all Steve needed.

"Well, then," I told myself, "let's just go ahead. You've gone this far. You can't back out now." I went up the staircase to the third floor, all the while paying very close attention to the architectural particulars. I had never been to the third level, and doing that helped steady me a bit. Even as I ascended the stairs, in fact, I quickly became preoccupied with the details of the molding at the ceiling. At the top of the stairs, I found a woman standing in line wearing a flowered chiffon dress that looked like something my great aunt would have worn in the 1960s. She turned around and said, "Hello, I'm Sandra Day O'Connor." Squelching the impulse to say, "I'm Oliver Wendell Holmes," I introduced myself properly.

On the one hand, as I've said, I'm not overly interested in politics. On the other hand, I'm much more awed to meet people in real positions of power than I am to meet, say, movie stars. I could be introduced to Julia Roberts or Clint Eastwood and I would be able to chat pretty comfortably, I think. But Sandra Day O'Connor is another matter entirely. What do you say to Sandra Day O'Connor?

Justice O'Connor was waiting her turn to be greeted by Hillary Clinton. After her came my turn. Hillary greeted me warmly. I quickly explained that Steve was being held up by a House debate. She said, "I know, several other members of Congress are being held up too. Just come in and make yourself at home."

I circulated. Steve and the other absent members of Congress didn't show up until we were already seated for dinner. During dinner, they had to leave to cast votes. They came back for dessert. Because it was a much smaller dinner than the first one, we were able to interact with pretty much everybody there. I was gratified by the way people were relating to us. I really felt that they recognized us very easily and matter-of-factly as a couple. The atmosphere was surprisingly, wonderfully, and in fact almost suspiciously accepting. It was like, "We've heard so much about you, we want to know this, we want to know that." It was "out"—it was *very* out.

Since then we've done some other political socializing as a couple. I do hate politics, but I have learned to enjoy going to political dinners and shoving my hand at conspicuous conservatives and saying to them with a big, friendly grin, ''Hi, this is Steve, I'm Rob.'' In those settings, they're all too well behaved not to be polite—however they may really feel about me.

15

Charles's memorial service in Durham had been designed with a sensitivity to the needs and expectations of his family and their local friends and relatives. But for those of us in Washington who had known Charles, the adult gay man, that service didn't quite seem a sufficient tribute. As soon as Rob and I returned from Greece, Rob decided to plan something more fitting. On a Friday night in November, we held a memorial service in our home that also served as a fund-raiser for the Whitman Walker Clinic.

It was a beautiful evening. Rob figured that if you're going to do something, you might as well do it big. We took out the dinner table and filled the adjoining two-story living and dining rooms with forty or so small tables. The place looked like a candlelit bistro. We rented a baby grand piano. And Rob took every photograph of Charles that he could find and had it turned into a slide. Using two rented slide projectors, we showed a slide presentation in the living room that was accompanied by music from the Delibes opera *Lakmé*.

As the slide presentation ended, the lights came up on Phyllis Pastori, the singer whom we had met in Mykonos the night that we received news of Charles's death. Phyllis, who had flown down from New York to perform at a fund-raiser for my campaign the night before, sang several touching ballads. Then friends of Charles—among them Franklin, Randy, and Gabriel—got up to say a few words about him. The stories varied, but what they all had in common was the recognition that Charles had inspired kindness and laughter within all of us. What we served up, in short, was an incredible evening of Charles. We talked about his humor and his affection, his drinking and his smoking. We talked about how much we loved him. And throughout the evening we hugged, held hands, and cried.

I spoke first, saying simply that Charles had been Rob's friend before he was my friend, that he made Rob laugh, and that after he became my friend he made me laugh, too. Rob, who often can't get a word out when he's emotional, didn't speak at all.

After the tributes, Phyllis came back to the piano and sang "up tunes," songs like "I Am What I Am." For those of us who had loved Charles, it was a beautiful, purgative evening. Yes, it was a bit melodramatic—but then so was Charles.

Charles's mother attended the memorial. She had to be touched by the tone, the effort, and the words spoken by friends. But Rob felt, and still feels, that the uncensored nature of the evening unnerved her. He had warned Carol beforehand that the event would not be about protocol—that we were going to celebrate not a Charles who had never existed but the Charles we had loved. He had explained to her that this necessarily involved the presence of gay men who were saddened by their loss.

It's an odd thing to lose a friend to AIDS whose family hasn't accepted his homosexuality. The friend dies and the family moves in erasing the past, closing out the friends, and burying their child quietly. Other deaths bring families and friends together; but because of Charles's parents' attitude, his friends had been left alone to deal with his death in isolation. The memorial at our home was intended to bring us all out of isolation and to find a laugh or two amid the tragedy of it all.

Ultimately, Charles would have wanted it that way. And so people talked. They talked about his incessant chatter, his smiling face and flattering manner. They even talked about how cheap he could be with his best friends. Randy told the story of Charles and his Absolut bottle. Years earlier, when Rob and I had lived on Hitt Avenue, Randy, Charles, and a few other friends had dropped by one Friday night. Charles had brought with him a small but expensive bottle of Absolut that, he said, needed to be kept in the freezer. He made it very clear that no one but him could have any. That was okay: the cheap vodka that I kept in the pantry would be fine for us.

Randy loved to irritate Charles, so when Charles went into the living room, we watched Randy pour the entire contents of the chilled bottle into a large cup. He then filled the Absolut bottle with tap water. We observed this audacious act with amazement. As the night wore on, we kept an eye on Charles. He would go into the kitchen, fill his glass with ice, and pour "vodka" from his Absolut bottle. He would mix it with a splash of tonic and carefully squeeze in a lime. At about eleven, as we were preparing to go out, Randy asked Charles how he was set for driving. He slurred his words and hollered back, in his high-pitched Carolina accent, "I'm not getting arrested for driving while intoxicated, honey. You can drive us all in that big tank you call a car."

Randy chuckled as he walked to the freezer, opened the door, and reached for the bottle of Absolut. "Charles, you are a real dumbbell," he said, laughing. He unscrewed the bottle cap, brought the bottle to his mouth, and gulped the entire remaining contents, belching when he was done. Charles was aghast. Randy broke out laughing—and I couldn't resist the temptation to laugh as well. "Charles," Rob said, "you've had too much to drink . . . don't hit him!"

Charles replied, "I may be drunker than Cooter Brown, but I can still knock the crap out of this nitwit. Randy, why did you drink my vodka?"

Finally Randy reached for the large cup and handed it to Charles. "That's your vodka, Charles. I poured it into the cup hours ago. You've been drinking tap water and tonic all night.''

The crowd at the memorial service went wild with laughter as Randy told the story.

Every so often that evening, Rob looked at Charles's mother and tried to figure out what she was thinking about this very openly gay event. He thought a lot about her attitude toward her son's homosexuality. In many ways, Rob felt, that attitude caused Charles's death—because it made him incapable of valuing himself enough to be able to give of himself to someone else in any except the most shallow and ephemeral way.

While 1993 found me personally preoccupied with the illnesses and deaths of friends and professionally absorbed in the day-to-day issues of governing, my right-wing opponents back home were busy setting plans to destroy me politically. Had I been more consumed with local party politics, I would have noticed these developments much sooner. And once I did notice them, had I been more devoted to traditional ''power politics,'' I would have sought to organize and leverage sufficiently to halt these efforts in their tracks.

Instead I pretty much ignored these efforts and focused on my Congressional duties, convinced that my constituents would be able to separate truth from falsehood without any help from me, and that most of them would recognize and applaud my quiet efforts at honest, effective bipartisan governing. I hoped and trusted that, despite the avalanche of negative letters in response to my remarks on gays in the military, most of the people in my district would eventually recognize the issue as one of fairness and equal rights, and not as a matter of the government granting ''special rights'' or ''approving'' of a ''deviant lifestyle.''

At that point I still intended not to run for reelection in 1994. What few people outside our immediate circle understood and appreciated was that Rob and I have long desired to lead a quiet, ordinary life. My original plan—one that Rob accepted—had been to serve twelve years in Congress, which would have brought us to 1992. Rob and I had an understanding that I would get out of politics at that point. But in 1992 I found myself running again, partly because I felt challenged by the nationwide anti-incumbent sentiment and partly out of a need to vindicate myself in the wake of the House banking scandal, which had touched nearly everybody in Congress. I didn't want to think, and didn't want anyone else to think, that I had allowed myself to be run out of office.

So I had hoped to quit Congress at the end of 1994. When it first became clear that the far right would be setting its sights on me, Rob felt I should just finish my term and clear out of town. Why ask for trouble? Didn't we both deserve some peace after all these years? But as the far right increasingly made me their target, he and I both found ourselves feeling that I couldn't let them drive me out of Congress, couldn't let them think they'd beaten me. If that happened, they would use that victory as an example around the nation—and neither of us wanted that to be my legacy. Throughout the fall of 1993, and into the winter, Rob and I discussed the implications of the struggle I would be taking on if I decided to run in '94.

One indication of the kind of conflicts I would be facing if I ran again came only a week after my remarks in the House on gays in the military. Senator Nancy Kassebaum of Kansas had agreed to appear at a fund-raising dinner for me in my district. It was put together fairly late, and everything seemed to go wrong. Somehow or another the invitations got lost in the mail, so we had nobody coming and had to make some fast, frantic phone calls in order to keep the place from being totally empty. But that wasn't the only problem. I had asked Mike Huebsch, a young Republican in La Crosse, to be master of ceremonies. Huebsch is an evangelical conservative, and I had chosen him specifically in an attempt to demonstrate my commitment to a broad-based party, as well as out of a desire to help a talented young local politician. But when I made clear my position in the House gays-in-the-military debate, Huebsch decided he couldn't serve as MC—and instead of just calling me to announce his withdrawal, he talked to the local newspaper. So his withdrawal became a big local news story.

It was not a successful dinner.

Kris Deininger, who was by now my chief of staff, took the Huebsch episode as an object lesson in the perils of my tackling the gay issue. As much as she loved me and Rob, she hated the whole gay issue from the moment it first swam into our ken. She hated it because it meant nothing but pain for her—pain in dealing with the people back home, with the Wisconsin press, and with Capitol Hill. In her view, the residents of western Wisconsin were simply too devoted to "traditional values" (to borrow the Religious Right's phrase) to accept a Congressman who was publicly identified with gay issues. The more vocal I had become on these issues, the more fervently Kris had urged me to turn back, to shut up, to keep a low profile.

It wasn't that Kris didn't understand how Rob and I felt about right-wing bigotry. She felt the same way we did. But she also strongly believed that, practically speaking, as a representative of the dairy farmers of western Wisconsin, I was not in any position to speak out effectively on gay issues without utterly destroying my political career. There was a reason, after all, why the only two openly gay members of Congress were Massachusetts Democrats with large gay constituencies. In vehemently opposing my involvement in gay-rights issues, Kris was, in her view, simply doing what any responsible chief of staff would do. She was also acting out of love, for it hurt her deeply to see me attacked for being gay, whether by Bob Dornan or Chuck Lee or the constituents whose phone calls she took and whose letters she answered.

As we approached the '94 election season, there was, thanks to Kris, a new member of our circle of friends who would play a major role in my campaign. Morris Andrews was in his late fifties, had been married and divorced, and had been the executive director of the Wisconsin Education Association, where Kris had worked for a brief time early in her career. In 1992, Kris had renewed her acquaintace with Morris and, after many years as a single woman, had begun a serious romantic relationship with him. At first glance Morris seemed very different from Kris: if she was diffident and self-effacing, he was forceful, imposing, and authoritative. Always dressed casually, in slightly rumpled clothes, he came off like a hard-bitten old-time union organizer out of Central Casting.

Yet, as I would come to discover, beneath Morris's black-framed glasses, disheveled hair, and low, gravelly voice, there was a gentle, educated, and cultured man who cared deeply about basic principles of justice and honesty and who, despite our different party affiliations, shared Kris's belief in the importance of my service in Congress. In his eyes, I was a pro-education Republican, a representative with a deep moral commitment to my constituents, and one of the few people in public life who could bridge the gap between mainstream society and the gay community.

When she had first begun her relationship with Morris, Kris had worried about how I might feel about her being involved with a Democrat. I'll never forget the day in 1992 when she and I were walking down a hallway in the Cannon House Office Building and she suddenly turned and said in an anxious voice, "I need to prepare you, because I think you're going to hear some rumors about me, and I just want you to know the truth, and if you want me to quit I'll quit."

Well, I hadn't heard any rumors, and didn't know about Morris. But I had some idea of the sort of thing she might be talking about, so I looked at her and said, "Kris, I have fought and prayed for you to have the courage to like and accept yourself as who you are and to be happy with that. I don't care whom you're dating, I really don't. What's important is that you're happy with him." And that was that. Kris told me later that that brief exchange had meant more to her than I had any idea at the time.

Eventually, we found out that she was dating some older man. We still didn't know who he was. Finally, when Rob and I were planning our Thanksgiving dinner in 1993, Kris asked if she could bring him with her. We said of course. That was when she told us who it was.

Year by year our Thanksgiving dinners had become larger and more elaborate. A tradition had been established, and now friends came from all over the country for the occasion. That year, Billy came from Atlanta; Randy and his friend Bernie came from Pittsburgh; Tim, from Miami, brought his New York friend Race; Yanni, whom we had met on vacation, flew in from Greece. Several new staffers came from my Washington office, as did three from my office in Wisconsin. The local guests included Linda, Ostap, and their boys.

We made Morris feel welcome, I think, and he seemed to enjoy himself immensely. At least until Randy accosted him after the meal. Knowing Randy, I know that his question was intended in the friendliest of ways. But it struck all of us as a bit inappropriate that after we had finished eating, Randy interrupted a brief silence at the table by blurting out, ''Hey Morris, so what do you think about having dinner with a bunch of gays?''

I was annoyed by Randy's question, which was forward and challenging (but then, so is Randy). Morris had been very nice throughout the meal, and now Randy seemed to be going out of his way to make the man feel uncomfortable.

But Morris was unruffled. Looking at Randy, he said softly, ''I guess you don't know. As it happens, my daughter's gay. And she has a lover.''

In fact, as we learned later, Kris, thanks largely to her years of experience with us, had played a big role in helping Morris to accept his daughter's homosexuality. Liberal as he is, Morris had experienced some real difficulty with her homosexuality. He had had particular problems with her request that he put on a wedding for her and her lover. It was Kris, God bless her, who had said to him, ''What would you do if she was marrying a man?''

And Morris had said, ''You know what I'd do. I'd give her a wedding.''

Kris had replied, "Then what's the difference? She's a lesbian, and this is the person she's chosen to spend her life with. Why won't you do this for her?" Kris had walked him through that whole process. In the end, they did have a wedding service.

A couple of days after Thanksgiving, a realtor phoned Rob and asked to show our house. It had originally been on the market, but we had come to enjoy the place and had taken it off. Rob naturally obliged, thinking nothing would happen. To our surprise, the agent returned the day after the showing with a respectable offer. The hitch: We had to be out of the house in two weeks. So instead of unpacking Christmas boxes, we packed away the contents of our ten rooms and moved them to a pretty old house in Washington that we were able to rent.

On New Year's Day 1994, Wisconsin was scheduled to play UCLA in the Rose Bowl. Rob hates football, but he agreed to accompany me to Pasadena to witness this momentous happening. One day shortly before New Year's we were with Matt and John discussing our plans for the big event, about which I was excited and Rob entirely unenthused. "Rob," said Matt, a passionate football fan and a former college running back, "how can you not want to go?"

"Easy!" said Rob. "Football bores me to tears!"

I looked at Matt. "How much would you like to go to the Rose Bowl?" I asked.

Next thing we knew, Rob had happily bailed out of our trip and Matt had happily agreed to take his place. I managed to get another ticket for Matt's brother, and the three of us had a great time watching Wisconsin trounce UCLA, 21–16, while Rob stayed at home and made a great dinner for John (who shared Rob's sentiments about football) and Randy and eight friends whom he brought with him from Pittsburgh.

Later that month, my mother underwent a triple bypass at the Mayo Clinic. And some days afterward, Kris, Morris, Rob, and I had a foretaste of what 1994 would be like for us if I chose to run for reelection. On January 18, a letter was faxed to me from Eau Claire. Signed by Don Brill, a retired vocational education instructor, and six others, it said that until recently I had "done a good job representing the Third District." But now Republicans in the district were divided as to my position on "traditional values." The letter urged me not to run for reelection, so that I might be replaced by a less controversial Republican candidate who would unify Third District Republicans.

The letter's real meaning was clear: "You were okay before everybody knew you were a fag. Now everybody knows you're a fag. And we don't want to be represented by a fag."

That was only the first of many salvos from the Third District's far right. Three days later, Brill and several of his confreres faxed a letter to Newt Gingrich, who had agreed to come to Wisconsin in April to speak at a fund-raising dinner for me. The letter read,

Dear Mr. Gingrich,

We understand that you will be in Wisconsin on April 16 in support of Steve Gunderson's reelection campaign. This is a very great disappointment to those of us working to unify the party which he has split by his departure from Republican values. Several party leaders as well as regulars have indicated crumbling Gunderson support. Some are reconciled to the loss of his seat. We want to save it for the party. . . . Our recourse is to assure a primary race which he will lose. . . . We sincerely believe it to be in your best political interest nationally and in your own district to distance yourself from him and wait for one of the candidates in view who will unify the party and win. They are skillful and experienced winners in line with your philosophy, as we understand it. Please advise us of your judgment in this matter.

Two days later, Chuck Lee, the leader of the "Christian, pro-life, pro-family and conservative" group called Concerned Republicans of Wisconsin, weighed in with his own fax to Newt. "As a conservative Republican," Lee wrote, "I'm concerned with your decision to endorse and appear on behalf of Rep. Steve Gunderson at a fund-raiser in La Crosse, WI, April 16, 1994. . . . Recently, Gunderson has been critical of Christians and the Bible. According to David Nelson, Mr. Gunderson announced he was a homosexual before a group of 100 gay, lesbian, and bisexual activists and lobbyists at a Capitol Hill breakfast, on April 26, 1993."

This was a reference to a Human Rights Campaign Fund legislative briefing that had taken place the day after the March on Washington. The day of the march had been very sunny, and many people had gone home that evening with their faces a few shades darker than in the morning; at the HRCF briefing the next day, surrounded by suntanned people, I began my remarks by noting my own tan and saying that I had gotten it at the same place where everyone else there had gotten theirs. The room had erupted in applause.

"I can assure you," Lee's letter continued, "that your appearance will spark Christian and conservative Republican protesters, both in La Crosse and the 6th District of Georgia. Please reconsider your decision and avoid a potentially embarrassing and damaging confrontation with the very people who vote for you in Georgia and support you in Wisconsin. For your eyes only."

Lee's letter went out by fax late on the night of January 23. By one o'clock the next afternoon, Newt had forwarded it to my office along with the letter he'd received from Brill. To his credit, neither Brill's complaints about me nor Lee's brazen threat to make trouble for Newt in his own Georgia district made Newt drop his plans to campaign for me in La Crosse.

This midwinter assault from the far right had an ironic effect. Rob and I had still been on the fence about my running for reelection. The faxes from Brill and Lee were plainly meant to intimidate me into retirement and free up my House seat for a more right-wing—and presumably heterosexual—Republican. But what Brill and Lee didn't count on was that it's not in my nature to duck and run when I'm attacked. And Rob is the same way.

There is a small, wonderful Mediterranean restaurant in Washington called Beduci. While the name sounds Italian, it is in fact an abbreviated version of the words "Below Dupont Circle," which is where it's located. Though Rob and I rarely go to restaurants without taking along two or three friends, Beduci is a place where he and I tend to eat alone, usually on weekday nights. Accordingly it's become the setting of many an intense conversation. One night late in January 1994, shortly after Brill and Lee had fired their first shots across my bow, Rob and I sat down at Beduci and he, speaking slowly and carefully, summed up the events of the previous year.

In 1993, he noted, I had become increasingly recognized as a national issues leader, not a local political figure or party leader. From my House speech on gays in the military to my involvement with the AIDS Walk, I had begun to make slow, careful steps toward a more publicly gay life and toward a real integration of my congressional career with a visible commitment to gay-rights issues. The deaths of Glenn and Charles had further galvanized us to fight homophobia and AIDS.

On the other hand, Rob noted, he knew that I felt personally vulnerable. If I ran, we would both be in for the most negative and personally painful campaign we had ever been through. I did not seek public fights about my personal life, yet if I ran for reelection I would be plunged into such fights. I would be in constant danger of becoming the issue. And that's perilous, because when the politician becomes the issue, he loses.

Another consideration was that my parents were both in very bad health. (I had no idea at the time how bad.) Neither Rob nor I was eager to invite publicity that might only make matters worse for them. We were especially loath to put them through a rough year, given that they always threw themselves body and soul into my campaigns.

By the end of the dinner Rob made his conclusion clear. After listing all the reasons why it made sense for us both to pack up and leave Washington forever, he concluded: "This is a fight we cannot walk away from." As unpleasant, as grueling, and as draining as it might prove to be, I had to take up the challenge from the far right. We had no choice—we couldn't stand up and speak out as we had done, only to run away from a referendum on our platform.

I agreed.

Irony of ironies: the far right had tried to drive me away from office—but their tactics had only convinced us to run again.

16

For months there had been a great deal of speculation back home as to whether I would run for reelection in 1994. Since the far right was making an aggressive effort to try to force me into retirement, it became clear to Rob and me that we had to announce my candidacy as soon as possible. Usually I never do this until the district convention in April of the election year, because I want to remain the congressman as long as I can and not become the candidate. So when I walked into Kris Deininger's office on Thursday, February 3, and said, ''I want to schedule news conferences in Eau Claire and La Crosse next Monday regarding my future political plans,'' the very walls of the office seemed to shake. Kris and the rest of my staff could only wonder what my announcement might be. I think they rather expected me to say I was retiring. But I didn't drop any hints.

That day I typed up a draft announcement, and that night I took it home for Rob to read. He performed some light editing and gave it his seal of approval. The next afternoon, just before I left for the weekend, I pulled the staff together. Observing the tension and gloom on their faces, I could see that they expected me to call it quits. I began reading.

The statement was addressed to my constituents. "After sixteen years," I said, "I want to leave Washington and return to 'real life.' " But, I added, I wanted one more two-year opportunity to serve my district. After that, I promised, I would retire from the House. "I want to spend the next two years," I vowed, "not consumed by campaigning and reelection—but by spending my time on legislative issues important to our area." I went on to outline in detail the issues of special interest to western Wisconsin to which I planned to devote my energies, among them reform in health care, dairy policy, and education.

I didn't mention the gay issue—and thus conveyed quite clearly that I felt my sexual orientation shouldn't *be* an issue.

When I finished, the staff applauded. I don't think they had ever done that before. They were an unusually talented and loyal group, and had suffered a good deal with me over the previous two years. Most of them were seasoned enough to have a very good idea of the sort of conflicts we would all be facing over the next few months. For the moment, however, I just asked them to fax a copy of the statement to the staff in my district office—and I left for Wisconsin.

Late in 1993, Kris had walked into my office and said, "I don't know if you're going to run again or not, but if you do, you should get LaVerne Ausman to run your campaign. He would be perfect." I had realized at once that she was right. When I got home that Friday after having read the announcement to my staff, I phoned my old state legislature colleague.

He had enjoyed a busy career. After my first election to Congress, I had named him my district director. Soon afterwards, he had left to become Wisconsin's secretary of agriculture. When the Democrats had taken over the state in the mid-'80s, LaVerne had been forced from office. The Reagan administration had quickly snapped him up to head intergovernmental relations at the United States Department of Agriculture. LaVerne soon moved up to the position of Deputy Undersecretary for Rural Development. He had always wanted to become the head of Farmers Home Administration, the farm lending agency, and when George Bush became president, he appointed LaVerne to this job. LaVerne served there with distinction until the end of 1993, when the Clinton administration replaced him with its own political appointee. Thereupon LaVerne and Bev had moved back to Wisconsin.

When I heard LaVerne's deep, firm voice on the other end of the phone line, I launched right into the matter at hand. "I have good news and bad news," I told LaVerne. "The good news is that I'm going to run for reelection one more time. The bad news is that Kris and I want you to run the campaign."

"I'm honored by the request," LaVerne said. "But I'm not sure I'll be available. I'm considering going to Eastern Europe to help set up a farm credit system. Can you let me think about it?" He suggested that we get together after the Dunn County Lincoln Day Dinner, which was set to take place about ten days later, and which he knew we would both be attending.

It soon became clear that if LaVerne did take the job, he would have his hands full. When I made my announcement on Monday, February 7, it brought on a chorus of Republicans, Democrats, and local media, all saying that I had made a political error by saying that I would not run again. They argued that I would be a lame duck, and, if reelected, would be ineffective; if the Third District was going to get a new Congressman two years down the line anyway, they said, it might as well go ahead and replace me now.

I had included the promise not to run again in 1996 largely for reasons of self-discipline: I knew that if I didn't announce my retirement ahead of time, I would find some new reason to run again two years later and face Rob's glare. The other reason why I announced that this would be my last term was sheer naïveté. Somehow, I foolishly believed that such an announcement might keep the personal issues from coming up and would allow me to focus the campaign on the real issues that divided Republicans from Democrats. I proved to be very wrong about that—instead of keeping the personal issues at bay, my announcement produced just the opposite effect.

Since this was going to be the Religious Right's only chance to destroy me, they wanted to be sure and do it while they could!

In addition to LaVerne as campaign manager, I needed someone to be in charge of strategy, fund-raising, and media. It seemed to me that the perfect person for the job was right under my nose: Morris. When I approached him, he volunteered without hesitation to work full-time for the campaign, and refused to take a dime for his efforts. Both he and Kris understood the magnitude of the coming storm. Morris had enough contacts within the Democratic teachers' establishment to have heard that the opposition party, feeling I might finally be vulnerable, would be making a special effort to return my seat to their column. Kris, for her part, had heard the rumblings of my adversaries on the Republican side.

Soon I had a campaign manager, too. When I met LaVerne at the Lincoln Day dinner on February 13, he told me that he had talked the matter over with Bev and had decided to give up his Europe trip. He and Bev both felt that it was just too important for me and our party to win. He wanted to be a part of that effort. He didn't mention the word gay—and he didn't have to. We both knew that it would come up, and we both knew that in agreeing to help me, he was agreeing to do everything he could to keep me from being defeated by hate rhetoric. I rejoiced in his decision.

We had our work cut out for us. The first challenge was the caucuses, which came in February. In every election year, the party faithful in each county assemble to talk about the issues, meet potential candidates, and express their views. As I made the rounds of the district that month, putting in appearances at the caucuses, they seemed little different from the caucuses of previous years—except in Eau Claire, where the party had been taken over by Harlan Reinders and fellow Christian Coalition types. I didn't attend the actual caucus meeting that Sunday, but I arrived in time to see the three hundred or so attendees milling about the caucus room afterwards.

When I looked over the crowd, I could tell immediately that

it was composed mostly of right-wing "true believers" who had come to the caucus straight from services at their fundamentalist churches. Most were people I had never met before in politics. They were part of the "family values" army, loyal in every way to the Religious Right's high command. Not schooled or motivated in partisan politics, not educated about government or history, and not informed in any deep, objective way about many of the major issues, they were there because they had been told that the only way to save the lives of fetuses from abortion, to save their children from the influence of predatory homosexuals, and to save America from degradation was to show up at these caucuses and compel the Republican Party to do their will.

In an effort to get a bead on their attitudes, I stood at the exit of the caucus room waiting to shake the people's hands as they left. I put on a friendly, confident face, but deep down I was terrified. After nearly twenty years of service, would I be forsaken by my own party? Scanning the strangers' faces, I was filled with dread at my coming battle with the Religious Right. How had this happened? Why had God put me in this ugly, messy situation in which, after a seven-term record marked by honor and decency and genuine hard work, people in my own party were questioning my integrity, my Christianity, and my right to serve in government? I didn't want to wage a battle against elements within my own party. But I knew I couldn't be true to myself, to Rob, and to the thousands of people struggling with their own sexual identity if I didn't wage it.

Rob has always loved God and hated the organized church. For years, as someone who grew up amid the South's intense religiosity and its equally intense racial inequity, he talked bitterly of the injustices that are so often perpetrated in the name of God. Now I was seeing those injustices face to face. The most notorious and politically powerful current incarnation of the organized church had declared war on me.

And yet I held firm to the hope that all this was happening for a reason, that God had put me in this difficult position for some purpose, some greater end. After the Carmichael incident a couple of years earlier, a Baptist minister in La Crosse had told me that "God gives us mountains to climb, and then the faith to climb them." His words had rung true to me at the time, and now they came back to me with force. Subduing my fears, I gathered my courage, and stood at the door of the caucus room ready to face rejection from three hundred fundamentalist Christians.

To my surprise, with the exception of a few openly hostile individuals, the people there appeared happy to shake my hand and say hello. They were friendly. They smiled at me warmly. And then I realized that not all of these were bad people. Many of them were, to be sure, extremely naive and trusting people; many of them were hungry for clear and simple truths to cling to; and many were desperately eager to take their marching orders from any demagogue who, making the right sounds about God and country and family, claimed to be in possession of those truths.

Accordingly, these people comprised a large and potent force that was capable of being used to wicked ends by some very wicked people. If only I could figure out how to reach these people before their leaders could turn them against me inexorably. But how?

That evening I attended the Eau Claire caucus's opening dinner. Winnie Close was out sick, so Harlan Reinders served as acting chair. At such dinners, elected officials, if present, are routinely recognized by the chair and given a brief round of applause. It soon became clear that Reinders had no intention of acknowledging my presence. I was sitting with a group of my supporters; appalled by this outrageous lapse in decency and protocol, several of them urged me to stand up and make an issue of it, and said that if I did not want to do so, they would. I asked them not to. I didn't want to stoop to Reinders's level. He might not want to behave respectfully toward me, but basic political decency had always been a hallmark of my career, and I didn't want to change that now.

Shortly after the caucus, I spoke at what Bob Dornan would

later refer to on the House floor as "a homosexual dinner." In my keynote address at that dinner, a benefit for the Baltimore chapter of the Human Rights Campaign Fund, a gay-rights lobbying organization, I came even closer to "coming out" than I had in my House remarks on gays in the military. I referred more than once to "Rob and I," and though I didn't explicitly say who Rob was or give him a last name, the point was clear. All that remained was to say, in so many words, "I am gay."

If a friend of mine had asked me at the time why I didn't say that, I would have answered that it was because I felt that my sexual orientation wasn't the point. The point was to affirm my total support for equal rights regardless of sexual orientation, while challenging many of the antiestablishment ideas that had dominated gay politics for a quarter century. I realize now that for a politician to say "I'm gay," not only to his friends and family but to the general public, *does* make a positive difference, and that it was simply in the nature of the way I operate for me to come out of the closet by stages.

In any event, it was clear that the Human Rights Campaign Fund people recognized me as an emerging gay spokesman. I might not have been emerging as quickly as some people would have liked, but they recognized, I think, that I was moving in the right direction and stood to become an increasingly valuable friend and ally of theirs over the years.

Most Americans, I told the audience that evening, support the basic concept of fairness and justice, but have difficulty reconciling their traditional values with the stereotypes of the gay and lesbian community, and thus with the issue of discrimination based upon sexual orientation. Their prejudice, I went on to say, is founded not on hate but on ignorance, and if we wish to achieve equal rights for gay men and lesbians, we need to make a more serious effort to reach, talk with, and educate these people.

My message at HRCF, then, was one of conciliation, not confrontation; of education, not agitation. As I had done for years in the House, I sought at HRCF to bring together opposing factions, to move beyond a spirit of antagonism with an appeal to common humanity and shared values.

Standing there before an audience largely composed of gay men and lesbians, I talked about family, something that was a cherished value to me long before anyone coined the term "family values." "We must proclaim," I told my audience,

> that one can be pro-family without being antigay. It is not an either/or situation. The family of gay and lesbian Americans must slowly but surely help America's traditional families find comfort in this new and different American family. The AIDS crisis has created a family of primarily gay and lesbian Americans that reached out and cared for its own. It fed them and bathed them. It walked their dogs and handled their finances. And most importantly it gave them unconditional love—the foundation of the family structure. But Middle America doesn't know that. They still believe there's a war between the gay family and the traditional family—with only one survivor. We must make them understand that is not the case.

Of all the people listening to me that evening, only one person, Rob, knew how much I had grown, during our years together, in my understanding of what the word "family" could mean—and how *much* it could mean.

From family, I moved to the subject of religion. "We must," I said, "proclaim the love, the understanding, and the justice of our Judeo-Christian beliefs. This will be very difficult. For many, the Bible and their religion is a series of absolutes, rather than the living struggle of faith we understand it to be. As mainstream churches, such as my own Lutheran Church, openly struggle to reconcile these issues, we must seek not only the church's support, but offer it our support as well. Unless those who believe in the enduring love of our religious beliefs actively support and encourage these reconsiderations of theology, we will guarantee the absolutism of past religious thought."

Again, only Rob, of all the people in the audience, knew how much my religion meant to me. Only he knew how much difficulty I'd had as a young man in accepting my homosexuality because of the way I had been taught to understand my faith, and how powerfully that faith had sustained me through recent challenges.

"We must," I concluded, "reach middle America *with* middle America. I know of no group in America which is more different from its general stereotype than gay and lesbian Americans." The struggle for basic respect and equal opportunity for all Americans, I said, "cannot be won by Democrats or Republicans. It cannot be won by liberals or conservatives. It cannot be won by liberation or evangelical theology. It cannot be won by gay or straight Americans. But progress can be made, if all Americans commit to reaffirming our nation's basic commitment to liberty and justice for all."

There it was: a testament to American values, to all the things—family, God, country—that Bob Dornan claimed to stand for.

So much for the insidious "homosexual dinner."

Both Matt and John attended that dinner to offer their moral support. On a Friday night soon afterward, they went with Rob and me to a play at Ford's Theater. It was soon clear that John was not himself. On the way to the rest room, he got lost. A bit later, he said that he felt sick and was suffering sharp head pains. We thought he might merely be coming down with the flu. Afterward, over dinner at a restaurant called Georgia Brown's, he kept tripping over words and losing his train of thought.

Rob and I were bewildered and concerned. On Monday, Matt phoned to tell us that after their return home, John's condition had grown worse. By Saturday morning he had become delirious and wracked with pain. Matt had rushed him to Georgetown Hospital. After a series of tests, the doctors had diagnosed a massive cerebral hemorrhage. They had operated on Sunday. John was now unconscious and in critical condition in the intensive care unit. The doctors didn't know to what extent his motor skills would be adversely affected. Only time would tell.

That night Rob and I visited John in the hospital. The automatic doors at the entrance and the long antiseptic corridors reminded us both of the many trips we had made to be with Charles. When the nurses brought Matt out of John's room to meet us, he gave us both big hugs. "John's still unconscious," he said, looking understandably haggard after their difficult weekend. "The doctors are still unsure of the outcome of the surgery."

Days passed before John came to. When he did, he didn't know where he was or who he was. He only knew that his head hurt. In the following week, he improved considerably and was moved to a private room where we could talk. But John, while he could get words out, couldn't string them together into sentences. The doctors said that the trauma to his head had resulted in a partial paralysis of his motor skills and of the part of his brain that recalled words and assembled sentences.

During one of our visits, Linda came along. She pointed to Matt and asked John who he was, but John couldn't remember Matt's name. She asked John if Matt lived with him, but John couldn't remember. He mumbled something about Matt "not eating him good things." Then Linda asked if John loved Matt. An indignant expression came over his face. "I love him," he said fiercely, pointing to Matt. Matt came within arm's reach and John patted him on the head.

John's medical crisis preoccupied us so much that we almost forgot Rob's birthday on March 27. Though Rob, under the circumstances, felt no great urge to celebrate the occasion, a friend of his named Larry, who had recently moved to Washington from Huntsville, Alabama, insisted that we do something. Promising that it would be a low-key gathering for three or four friends, he persuaded Rob to agree to a Sunday brunch at Perry's Restaurant in the Adams-Morgan district.

Though Larry told me behind Rob's back that he planned to surprise him by inviting a dozen or so friends, it turned out that Perry's had a bigger surprise in store for all of us. What none of us knew was that on Sundays, Perry's held a "drag brunch," complete with drag queen entertainers and drag queen brunchers. As if that weren't colorful enough, on that particular Sunday the "drag brunch" was being filmed by a national network for scheduled broadcast in July. This was not exactly a campaign appearance made in heaven.

When we arrived at Perry's, Kris and Morris, who were among those invited to the brunch, took immediate note of the situation and pulled me aside in horror. Anxiously, they told me that we were being filmed; that, since we had the largest single table at the restaurant, the camera would presumably cut back to us several times during the show; and that the show would air during the campaign. Bottom line: We had to get out of there, fast!

I just shook my head and laughed. Yes, Kris was right in noting that it was not politically savvy for me to be seen on TV at a table full of gay men who were surrounded by other tables packed with flamboyant drag queens. But my years of living with Rob had taught me that you can't control everything, or try to. As I looked over at him, surrounded by his friends and flashing a smile in the midst of a time of great trouble, I said, "Kris, let's just have a good time and chalk this one up to fate."

To my knowledge, by the way, the show never aired. But perhaps it should have. The performers were good. Morris was convinced that, like Julie Andrews in *Victor*, *Victoria*, they were really women pretending to be men pretending to be women.

The next morning, March 28, exactly two months to the day after my mother's triple bypass, my father, who had suffered a heart attack while driving his truck, had his own bypass operation at the Mayo Clinic. Along with my mother, brothers, and sisters, I traveled to Rochester, Minnesota, to be at his side. Two weeks after the surgery, he still hadn't come out of the anesthesia. On Easter weekend, I sat at the clinic with my family, waiting to see what would happen. "I know you all believe in God," his doctor told us. "Well, sometimes it happens that we have done all we can, and it's up to the

Great Doctor above to determine what comes next. And that's where we are with your father. He could come out of this eventually, or he may never come out of it. We just don't know."

Had I known that all this lay ahead of us, I would never have run again for Congress.

In April came my district's congressional district convention. As the sitting member of Congress, I had a decent amount of influence over the event, which was run by our district chair, Doug Knight. A tall, lanky, unassuming man from Eau Claire, Doug had been a loyal party activist for years and was now locked in tough battle with right-wingers for control of the Eau Claire County party. This was quite ironic, for Doug could hardly be called a liberal; he's conservative to the core. But he understands the concept of the separation of church and state, and knows what role is and is not proper for a political party.

In setting the time and place for the district convention, Doug had followed my request, which was in turn based on Newt's schedule. Weeks earlier, I had asked Newt to speak at my campaign's kick-off dinner. It was a natural request for several reasons. First, Newt was the biggest draw in Republican politics. Second, I wanted to send out a signal that I was strongly supported by the voice of the conservative movement within the national party. Third, I wanted people to understand that my departure from the whip organization did not reflect a personal breach—that, despite our differences, Newt and I were still friends.

So the convention was set for Saturday, April 16, in La Crosse. Shortly after my arrival on Friday night, I picked up word that I was going to have a primary opponent. Rumors had circulated for weeks that the opposition was seeking someone to run against me. They had focused most of their energies on Jim Harsdorf, who, as my former district chair, was seen as someone whose challenge to me could dramatically symbolize what they wanted to be perceived as a growing disgust with my performance in office. Moreover, as a young farmer and a family man, Jim might be seen as someone who reflected the district's lifestyle and values more than I did. In the end, however, Jim had turned them down.

After approaching various state legislators, among others, my right-wing opponents had finally settled on Don Brill, the retired vocational education instructor who had sent Newt a fax some months earlier declaring that I didn't fairly represent the Third District and its "traditional values." A rather quiet, unassuming character, Don seemed driven by right-wing politics. From the beginning, it struck me as odd that a man who had spent his career as a public school vocational instructor should now serve as the figurehead of a movement against public education and basic decency.

Wearing a blue pinstriped suit that I and my campaign staff would see constantly during the next few months, Brill, with his white hair and mustache, projected the image of a man somewhere between a kind grandfather and Albert Einstein. But Don Brill was no gentle genius. Instead of physics equations, he produced rambling political screeds that weaved bizarre tales of government conspiracy. The focus of his campaign was to fight the immorality growing within our nation—an immorality that was, in his view, personified by me.

What was clear from the start was that for Brill, this was not a campaign about getting elected to Congress. It was about exposing and destroying Steve Gunderson. Never did Brill talk about what he wanted to do if elected. That was irrelevant. His only mission was to make sure that I was not returned to office.

What could I do but make it clear to him that I was ready to take him on? So as Brill and Harlan Reinders stood in the hallway of the Midway Motor Lodge in La Crosse, shaking hands and passing out a single-sheet critique of me that they had cooked up, I walked over to them and said in an even tone, "I can't wait for this race. Once and for all we can decide what this party and this district are all about." My confidence astounded them.

On Saturday morning, prior to the scheduled preconvention meeting with the county Republican leaders, I had planned a strategy breakfast. As I walked into the assigned room, there waiting for me were Art and Marlene Hanson, whose family had known mine for decades. Marlene had spent most of her adult life as a teacher and school administrator and was highly respected throughout the state. After her retirement, in need of a staff member with strong educational credentials, I had begged her to take a job in my district office, even though she wasn't a Republican. (We referred to her jocularly as a "Steve Gunderson Republican.") She had taken the job gladly, and for the past three years she had served as my district director.

Marlene, who had two children around my age and almost looked upon me as a third child, gave me a hug. "How are you doing?" she asked.

"Well, I got a primary opponent last night," I told her.

She nodded grimly. "We read about it in the paper this morning. Steve, I know Don Brill from way back. He's crazy." She paused for a moment's thought. "I thought these people were such devoted Republicans. Don't they know that if they destroy you, a Democrat will win your seat?"

"Marlene," I said, "they don't care who wins as long as they do me in."

Others arrived: LaVerne and Bev, Morris and Kris, Doug Knight, and my district office people, John Frank and Jennifer Schultz. Soon we were talking strategy over French toast and orange juice.

The main question at hand was how to handle the endorsement issue. Traditionally, the sitting congressman gives a sort of "state of the union" speech to the party faithful, then asks for the party endorsement. Since 1982, that endorsement had always been unanimous. This year, I had written a long and thoughtful speech that sought to put the hot-button issues in perspective. But should I ask for an endorsement? While there was little doubt that we could win a fight over endorsement, the question was whether we wanted to go through a fight.

Doug explained that under the convention rules, before the endorsement question was voted on, any and all candidates would have a chance to address the convention.

"Then let's not do it," I said. "We will have already addressed the convention. There will be nothing more for me to say. Why do I want to give Don Brill twenty minutes to demagogue me?"

"It isn't that easy, Steve," LaVerne countered. "Do you want the headlines to say tomorrow that you were not endorsed?"

"If I ask the convention today not to endorse anyone in the spirit of party openness," I said, "what's the down side? Let me work something into my speech suggesting that if people want an open, fair primary, we are happy to give them one."

So it went. I opened up the meeting later that morning with general discussions and updates, then handed it over to LaVerne, who introduced the rest of the campaign team. When he named Morris, there were murmurs: many of those in attendance were well aware of Morris's past work with the Wisconsin Educational Association—and there was no love lost between the Wisconsin Teachers' Union and the Republican party.

I noticed that sitting among our loyal supporters was Winnie Close, the Eau Claire County chair. Because we had opened this meeting to all county party leaders, we hadn't been able to keep her out. We wondered how she could look herself in the mirror and attend—but that was her problem.

Morris reported on our recent poll, taken in early March.

"Quite frankly," he said, "there is a legitimate question as to whether a Republican can win in this district. But there should be no doubt in the minds of any of you that Steve is probably the only Republican who can hold onto this seat." This was the first of many blunt assessments from Morris, who is a masterly student of numbers, votes, and surveys, and a straight shooter when it comes to reporting them. He was about to begin a process that, over the next few months, would craft a campaign focused meticulously on bringing the undecided votes our way.

"Today," Morris continued, "this district is more Democrat than Republican. Forty-five percent of the people identify as Democrats, only 36 percent as Republicans. Yet despite those numbers, there is a real testament to Steve in that 67 percent give him a favorable job approval rating, as compared to 22 percent negative. That's astounding for any incumbent anywhere.

"But liking someone does not mean voting for him. Only 44 percent of the electorate say they'll definitely vote for Steve, while 40 percent say they're willing to consider a new person. Those are good numbers. But there should be no doubt among any of you that if this party sees fit to spend the next six months beating up on Steve, the Democrats will win this seat. So if any of you are considering supporting Mr. Brill, you should know now what the implications of that action will be."

It was perfect. The expert was at work. Morris's comments were directed at people like Winnie Close, who had written a letter to the editor of the Eau Claire newspaper suggesting that I honor term limits and retire. The only question was whether she understood what Morris was trying to tell her. Evidence later suggested she didn't get it at all.

The numbers already clearly suggested what kind of challenge I would be facing in the campaign. While senior citizens and young people supported me, my problem lay with people from 45 to 65, especially men. By a whopping 18 percent margin, men over 45 wanted to replace me with a new person.

The meeting ended, and none too soon. My nerves were near the breaking point.

Later that day the convention proper began with a heady air of anticipation. A large contingent of party activists had gathered. Newt had come to give my candidacy his blessing. And the press was out in big numbers. Among the reporters present was Chandler Burr, a freelance writer who had contracted with the *New York Times Magazine* to write an article about Rob and me. The campaign staff was uneasy about the project, neither the timing nor the angle of which had yet been determined. By contrast, Rob and I, having concluded that the subject of my homosexuality could not be avoided, had decided that it would be a good thing to welcome coverage by respected national media outlets such as the *Times*.

It soon became my turn to speak. As the crowd welcomed me warmly, I approached the platform and looked over the crowd to see the familiar faces of loyal friends. They saw the battle coming, and wanted the ammunition with which to defend me. That was what I was there to give them. And then there were several members of my family, including my mother, for whom this was the first foray out of the hospital since my father's surgery. My mother has intense strength under pressure, but she was still recovering from her own surgery, and exhaustion was as clear on her face as the "Steve" and "Matt" buttons were clear on her suit jacket. She shouldn't have been there, this nonpolitical lady, but she was. For she knew that people were attacking her son, and she was determined to be there to support him.

I took a deep breath. As always before a major speech, I said a brief silent prayer. Then I scanned the crowd and began speaking.

"Thank you very much," I said. "Tonight we begin a very special campaign." I went on to talk in some detail about my record, and about the issues. "Because I am the incumbent," I stated, "my record is and ought to be the issue. And I want to be judged on how I represent the interests of this district and this nation."

Throughout the speech, the unspoken issue remained unspoken. What part it would play in the campaign, and in my constituents' judgment of me, remained to be seen.

17

That spring, as we grew more preoccupied with my father's and John's health, Rob's and my careers also became increasingly demanding. For Rob, spring meant the building season. For me, it meant the emerging tensions of the campaign.

Plainly, we had a rough few months ahead of us.

By late April the field of candidates for my congressional seat had begun to take clear shape. In previous years I had always had only one opponent; in 1994 no fewer than seven other people would end up contending for my seat: four candidates entered the Democratic primary (ours has always been considered a swing district, winnable by either party); Brill was running against me in the Republican primary, the first primary challenger I'd had since my election in 1980; and in the general election both a Perot Independent named Mark Weinhold and Chuck Lee, on the Taxpayer's Alliance Party ticket, ran third-party races. While I was busy in the House, these six men were spending all their time in the district, going from town to town telling everybody that it was time to bring me back from Washington.

Under the circumstances, Rob and I needed each other's love
and support more desperately than ever. Yet it was this mutual love and support that was quickly shaping up as the
major issue in my campaign, both externally and internally.
Donald Brill had launched his campaign against me with no
small amount of antigay innuendo and demagoguery. Morris
and LaVerne, for their part, were increasingly worried about
the issue of my homosexuality.

One subject of special concern to them was a pair of articles
about me that were in preparation for major magazines.
Chandler Burr, as I've mentioned, was profiling Rob and me
for the *New York Times Magazine*; Chris Bull, then the Washington reporter for the gay newsmagazine the *Advocate*, had
proposed doing a story about me. He sent me copies of stories
he had written about public figures who served as heroes for
the gay community. Among the people he had profiled were
Barry Goldwater and Jane Alexander, both of whom were heterosexual.

Chris had treated these subjects very fairly, and I was drawn
to the idea of a profile by him that might focus more on my
public service than my private life. Kris shared my enthusiasm. We both also felt (foolishly, in retrospect) that because
the *Advocate* was a gay publication, the story wouldn't be
picked up by the mainstream media. It seemed to both of us
that it would much better for me to be celebrated in the *Advocate* as a hero to gay Americans than for Rob and me to be
profiled in the *New York Times Magazine* as a Congressional
gay couple.

Rob disagreed strongly. Kris, as it happened, had had a hard
time with Chandler Burr, who comes on very strongly in conversation. Rob, who also comes on strongly, had hit it off with
Chandler immediately—and had recogized that if Chandler did
write an article about us, it would be a good one. Finally, Rob
pointed out that either article could be written without our
cooperation, and that the *Advocate* would certainly not run
something positive if we refused to cooperate. He insisted that
we quit dodging the truth and instead be up front and happy

about it. At his urging, then, I agreed reluctantly to cooperate with both writers.

In the face of all this, we wondered, what should our campaign strategy be? In previous election campaigns, my opponents had routinely sought to paint me as someone who had gone to Washington, lost touch with his district's rural values, and gotten wrapped up in a big-city social lifestyle. In 1984, my opponent had actually challenged me to a drug test. The day he did so, I went straight over to the House doctor's office and had a drug test, intending to bring a copy of the results to our debate and whip it out when my opponent repeated the challenge. As it turned out, I never had the chance: Dave Obey, a Democratic congressman from Wisconsin, was so appalled by my opponent's tactics that he refused to endorse him; as a result, the drug issue was dropped.

With the subject of my homosexuality now on the front burner, the question of whether I was out of touch with my district's values and way of life would obviously be hotter than ever. We decided that we had to make it clear to voters that, in fact, my record reflected those values. I believed strongly that this was so, even in the case, for example, of the inflammatory gays-in-the-military issue. I knew the people of my district well, and I considered them to be decent and fair-minded; I had no doubt that the majority of them didn't think that a member of the armed forces who had adhered to the standards of proper conduct should be kicked out just because he or she happened to be gay.

Morris and LaVerne weren't so sure. I didn't realize how deep their anxiety about this issue ran until I returned to Wisconsin on the last weekend of April. By that point, my father had come out of the anesthesia; though bedridden and mentally confused, he had improved enough to be transferred from the Mayo Clinic to the hospital in Eau Claire, which was much closer to home. That Friday, I flew out to address a civic association dinner. On Saturday, my sister Kris's third son, Bradley, who like all her children had been brought up as a Roman Catholic, was to receive his first communion. That day, before the reception that had been planned in Bradley's honor, Mom and I drove to Eau Claire to visit Dad.

We were in for a surprise. When we entered his room, we found him sitting on the bed, alert, and dressed. In a clear voice, he informed us that he had talked to his doctor and received permission to go home. We thought he was crazy. So I asked, ''Dad, where are you?''

''Eau Claire.''

''What do you want to do?'' I queried, fully believing he would not repeat his absurd statement about going home.

''I am going to go home today,'' he responded.

''Why do you want to go home today?'' I asked gently.

''Because there is going to be a party for one of Kristi's kids. And I should be there for that.''

Mom and I looked at each other in shock. He was making sense. This had not happened for over a month!

''But Dad, you're in the hospital,'' I said.

''I know,'' he replied instantly. ''But the doctor said I could go for two hours.''

My father attended the reception that afternoon, and we had more than Bradley's first communion to be thankful for.

Morris and LaVerne had insisted that I meet with them that weekend. The meeting was scheduled for the evening of Sunday, May 1, in my Osseo campaign office. I knew they had some serious things to say to me.

When I got there at eight, I could see them both through the office's big plate glass window, sitting at the big table in the front room. I joined them and exchanged some small talk. Then LaVerne cut it short. ''I guess,'' he said, ''this is about as direct and blunt a conversation with you as I will ever have.''

The tension could have been cut with a knife. I knew Morris and LaVerne, and I knew neither of them wanted to confront the subject that was staring us in the face. I didn't want to talk about it, either. But we all knew that there was no way to avoid it.

''Neither one of us is here to argue about your personal life,'' LaVerne said. ''I guess each of us has as much respect for you as anyone possibly can. That's why we are in this campaign. And nothing I say should be construed to be negative about Rob. We both know him and like him, as well. To Bev and me, you guys are like family.''

I nodded.

''But we are concerned,'' LaVerne went on, ''about the degree to which your personal lives will become the focus of this campaign. We can do a lot of things in this campaign to get you reelected. But there are some things that none of us, except you and Rob, can control. And I guess we need to know where you're coming from on all this.''

Morris broke in. ''Let me be blunt, Steve. You know I think the world of you both. And you know I am as openminded socially as anyone in this campaign. But our job is to get you reelected. And we simply can't do that if this is going to become a referendum on gay rights. People back here know about you. And they will tolerate it because you do a good job otherwise. But if you convert this election into a vote of approval on gay rights, you will lose!''

I tried to stay cool, calm, and collected. Taking a deep breath, which always helps me to keep my tension out of my voice, I cupped my hands on the back of my head and leaned back in my chair. ''There is no question,'' I said, ''about your commitment. I know that. And I certainly don't want to do anything to make this harder for any of us. The last thing my family needs right now is more personal stress.

''But,'' I continued, ''anyone who thinks this campaign can escape the subject of my sexuality isn't paying attention. The Brill parade handout is fluorescent pink, for God's sake! The only issues they mention are gay rights and the other social issues. These people are out to destroy me. Now we can let them set the agenda, and spend the entire campaign on the defensive, or we can try to control our own destiny.

''Morris, I know that you and Kris have great misgivings about this article Chandler Burr is writing. I can't speak for myself on this, but Rob has the best gut instincts about people of anyone I know. He thinks Chandler is honorable and trust-worthy. And I have to go with Rob on this.''

Two hours later, the conversation concluded with an un-easy truce. Increasingly, Morris and LaVerne had come to un-derstand—if not accept—Rob's and my conclusion that avoiding the subject of my homosexuality was not possible. We, on the other hand, had to be more sensitive to the diffi-culty of dealing with this issue in rural America. Generally speaking, rural people's images of homosexuality were founded on all the worst stereotypes. Even before Memorial Day, which traditionally marks the opening of congressional campaigns, the rumors about my sexuality and the challenge from Don Brill had drawn the attention of the national media to Wisconsin's Third District. *Newsweek*, we learned, would be doing a piece on my run for reelection and about the ''politics of smear'' as practiced by my opponents.

In western Wisconsin, each spring brings the celebration of Norwegian Independence Day on May 17. This day is always marked by the region's first parades of the season. So it was that on a rainy Saturday morning in May, we gathered in the town of Woodville for their annual Norwegian Independence Day parade. A *Newsweek* photographer met us there, and ex-plained that he wanted to show me ''working'' my district. But the rain ruined that. Not to worry, I explained: there would be another parade the next day in Westby, and I would be there. So was the *Newsweek* photographer.

It was clear to me already that our campaign would be watched by the nation. In a funny way, I relished the chal-lenge. I was convinced that if anyone could win reelection in the face of a smear campaign, it was I. And we would be doing the whole nation a favor if we could prove that negative cam-paigns don't always win.

At the same time, and for the first time since 1980, I was hesitant, reticent, and actually very scared about going back to my district to campaign. After the gays-in-the-military issue and the attacks on my sexual orientation, I didn't know what kind of response I would get from the people in my district. I expected to hear things that would hurt me deeply. But we had made a practical decision that I couldn't hide—I had to be visible. I had to be out there shaking hands and talking with people, helping them to feel personally close to me and comfortable with me, and letting them see that I was able to address the questions about my personal life without being ashamed or copping out.

Soon it was Memorial Day weekend. There were parades in the towns of Onalaska and Arcadia. The weekend also marked the beginning of the June Dairy Days breakfasts. Every June, the Dairy Promotion Committee in each western Wisconsin county hosts one such breakfast on a local dairy farm. The crowds for these events are huge—people show up by the hundreds. For politicians, these events provide great opportunities to renew contact with the local folks. It also provided me with a chance to get a sense of how my reputation was holding up among my constituents. If the warm and friendly reception at the first of these breakfasts, in La Crosse, was any indication, I would do fine. By now, I enjoyed instant recognition in my district. My interactions with voters felt natural and friendly.

But it didn't take long to discover that some things had changed in the district. Three weeks into June, I was working the crowd at the Grant County breakfast when, as I stretched out my hand to the next man lined up for breakfast, he quickly retracted his hand and grunted, "I wouldn't vote for a faggot."

All I could do was go on to the next person in line. But it hurt. It really hurt.

In our conversation on May 1, Morris, LaVerne and I had agreed to do focus groups on homosexuality. Focus groups, which are routinely used nowadays as a way of gauging audience reaction to everything from a candidate's policy positions to a TV series' story line, are small groups of presumably representative people who are brought together and asked a series of questions designed to elicit their feelings. Morris and LaVerne's purpose, in our case, was obvious: they wanted to show Rob and me how deeply my constituents were opposed to homosexuality. I agreed to their plan because I thought the focus groups might at least help us to figure out how best to discuss the issue.

We hired Frank Luntz, Ross Perot's former pollster, to set up the focus groups for us. He scheduled meetings with four groups, the first two of which were to take place at the Eau Claire Holiday Inn on the evening of Monday, June 7. I met Frank, LaVerne, and Morris at the motel at four o'clock that afternoon to look over the questions. The questions about homosexuality came at the end of the list. Some of them read as follows:

> As you may know, much has been made of Congressman Gunderson's speeches and support for the rights of homosexuals. Why has he been doing this?

> Congressman Gunderson was a leading proponent for gay rights in the military. Does this make you much more likely to vote for him, somewhat more likely, somewhat less likely, or much less likely to vote for him? Why?

> Steve Gunderson recently said that the rights for gays and lesbians do not conflict with family and religious values. He has said that people can be pro-family without being antigay. Do you agree or disagree?

> Congressman Bob Dornan, a Republican colleague of Congressman Gunderson, recently said, "He has a revolving door on his closet. He stands out there as an in-and-out homosexual lecturing our party." Dornan also said, "We have a rep on our side who's a homo." What is your reaction to this statement? Do you agree or disagree with Congressman Dornan?

> Congressman Gunderson appears to be attempting to enlarge the "big tent of the GOP." Congressman Dornan said, "What they're worried about is expanding the tent idea. What I'm worried about is the cultural destruction of the society." With whom do you agree more?

I objected to these questions, which struck me as loaded. Kris and Morris, I realized, had figured that if they could rig the questions in this way and produce strong negative numbers, they could persuade me to shut up about gay rights in order to keep Republicans in my column. Rob, by contrast, felt that if I played up my civil-rights record, which included being honest about my support for gay equal rights, we might lose many "angry white men" (as he put it), but would also persuade moderates of both parties, especially educated people, young people, women, and minorities, to vote for me.

"These are biased questions," I said. "If you want to conclude that people are not yet willing to approve of gay relationships, then let's just say so, skip the effort, and save the money. If we are sincerely interested in discovering their attitudes, let's talk."

Soon the questions were rewritten to everyone's satisfaction. Rather than asking people how they felt about my outspoken support of gay rights, the questions asked, in effect, "As long as Congressman Gunderson continues to represent the best interests of the people of western Wisconsin, do you care if he's gay?" After a productive discussion with Frank about what we wanted, he placed us in a holding room away from the focus group's meeting place. There we were able to watch the focus group on closed-circuit TV. I was nervous. It was fascinating to hear what people believed and why.

Of special interest was the fact that, until they reached the concluding questions on gay rights, I had a very high positive rating from most Republicans. The questions just prior to the gay-rights questions, which were about other civil-rights issues, drew especially high responses. "How do you feel about Steve's work on behalf of Americans with disabilities?" "On behalf of minorities?" The vast majority of Republican respondents said they were proud of that work. Yet when asked how they felt about my work on behalf of gays in the military, "given that he may be homosexual," almost 80 percent of those respondents replied that they had a negative view of that work. Interestingly, the positive scores from Democratic voters who did not respond enthusiastically to much of my record went way up when the questions turned to civil rights, and stayed pretty good through the gay-rights section as well. These results confirmed Rob's sense that I could win the election by being candid and unapologetic about my homosexuality and my belief in civil rights for all—gay men and lesbians included.

Frank's conclusions were strikingly different from Rob's, and he was direct in laying them out. First, he noted that while my constituents had a generally positive attitude toward me, they were shockingly unaware of exactly what I'd accomplished on their behalf during my years in Congress. This meant that I was extremely vulnerable to any disinformation about my record that my opponents might choose to spread. "You've got to tell the people what you've done," Frank concluded, "and you need to do it now."

Second, I had registered "strong, intense popularity among non-Republican moderate women," who could provide a margin of victory on election day. Third, while voters in their twenties—"Generation X"—were open-minded about homosexuality and liked my positions, they were "unmotivated politically and highly unlikely to vote."

Those conclusions, however, were a mere prelude to Luntz's final point. That was the clincher. "As long as your private life remains private, you should have no trouble winning reelection. If, however, your private life becomes public, you will be in real trouble. Those with a so-called Christian background are prepared to support you, even when knowing about your background. However, if you 'go public' they will abandon you.

"In short, the upcoming campaign is really yours to lose."

Kris Deininger joined Frank Luntz in urging me to downplay the gay stuff. Of course, Rob, her beloved friend and perennial nemesis, couldn't have disagreed more. She wanted to see the campaign move away from the issue, while Rob and I were trying to head it *toward* that issue, to deal with the whole business up front, to be honest. Rob kept saying, "It's better to lose with integrity than to win deceitfully."

I thought I had seen Rob and Kris fight before. But their earlier showdowns were nothing compared to the battles ahead. Rob felt that, rather than be cowed by the attacks on my homosexuality, I should use them as an opportunity to speak out forcefully about discrimination and to remind the Republican party of its historic role in fighting prejudice. Far-right people in Wisconsin were saying that I had moved to the left and no longer represented "Republican values"; on the contrary, anyone who was familiar with the history of the Republican party would understand that, like Barry Goldwater, Mr. Republican himself, I could legitimately say, "I didn't leave the party. The party left me."

Rob felt it was important for me to make this point, and make it forcefully. On the train back from New York, where we had gone with Kris and Morris for a weekend in May to celebrate my birthday, he had prepared an outline for an extensive, heavily documented background paper on the history of the party. He felt that my staff should put together such a paper for me so that I might have facts, dates, and quotations that would help me explain to the electorate what the Republican Party did and didn't stand for.

The next morning I handed Rob's outline to Kris. It was clear from her reaction that she felt Rob had stepped into an inappropriate position of authority, and that she wasn't at all happy about it.

The following week Rob asked me about the outline. I had been preoccupied with other things and had not followed up on the matter with Kris. She was out of the office when I stopped by to discuss the issue with her, and so I left her a note and headed back to Wisconsin for the weekend. When I talked to Rob that night, he said she had left a package at our front door with a note. Rob said the package contained seven or eight relevant books she had purchased; the note simply said that the staff didn't have time to take care of these kinds of things.

Rob was angry. I felt his idea had merit, but I also understood that such a project as he envisioned was outside the purview of my office staff.

The conflict between Rob and Kris came to a head later that summer over campaign literature. We had developed a process: I would write the text for a campaign brochure, and give it to Rob, who would pass it on to Dwight and Brian, who had volunteered to design my campaign literature for free. I would also hand a copy to Kris—who then, unbeknownst to me, would rewrite it to moderate my tone. Then, while I was in Wisconsin campaigning, Kris would call a last-minute meeting with Brian, at which she would replace the copy I had given him with the rewritten version that she had put together, not telling him that this was her rewrite and not mine.

So Dwight and Brian would spend all afternoon Sunday setting copy and detailing graphics based on Kris's revised language, and on Monday morning Dwight would come into Rob's office, and show him the mock-up of the brochure with the revised language. Rob would say, "Whoa, what's this?" One thing would lead to another, and Rob would call me in Wisconsin and tell me about the revised language. I would say, "Fax me a copy," and when it came in over the fax I would be livid! Who was changing my copy?

It was a difficult situation because I hate confronting people and hate interpersonal tensions—and here we were in a *constant* state of interpersonal tension. It was also difficult because we had an employee of Rob's in direct conflict with an employee of mine.

But Don Brill had unnerved Kris. At the outset of the campaign, Brill had refused to sign a "clean election" pledge—meaning no personal attacks. Later he refused to debate me. I wanted very much to debate him, because I knew that if people could see the two of us together, they would recognize that he simply wasn't capable of going to Washington and representing western Wisconsin on the diverse issues of modern-day American politics.

That was clear from his background. Brill's only elective

office had been a position on the Eau Claire school board. He wasn't educated on the issues, he wasn't able to discuss and defend his political positions intelligently; his whole campaign was premised on the idea that he stood on the side of God and tradition and that I was a symbol of everything that is destroying America. His core constituency was a small group of religious activists.

Brill's politics, to use the term loosely, were illuminated by a document that he distributed throughout the district. About 2,500 words in length, it outlined his program for building a winning Republican coalition. In the document, which made stunningly clear how extreme and bizarre his views really were, Brill declared the need to be "faithful to Republican philosophy and tradition." He described that philosophy and tradition as follows: "Belief in God, Creation, Hereafter and an ultimate accountability sets Republicans apart."

What a remarkable statement! What Brill was saying, in effect, was that Republicans are religious and Democrats aren't. But Brill wasn't through: after identifying Democrats with "gratification as the organizing principle of society" and with "the anarchy of self-interest," he went on, astonishingly, to identify the Democratic party in America with the Nazi Party in Germany and to offer a wacky potted history of the Nazis' rise to power, in which he claimed to see parallels to the rise of FDR's New Deal and LBJ's Great Society.

He went on to discuss religion. "There has been discussion that some Jews reject the concept of a Judeo-Christian ethic," he wrote. "To do this they must also reject the Abrahamic covenant and the Laws of Moses, both of which are fundamental to Christianity. If this is the case, neither is a rose a rose." Huh?

Brill took an extreme position on abortion. Addressing the question of the right to abortion in cases of rape and incest, he acknowledged, in something of an understatement, that "rape and incest are a burdensome problem." But abortion, he insisted, is not "an acceptable correction or justification for crime." (Presumably he meant to say that abortion was not justified *by* crime.) ''The remedy,'' he argued, ''is dealing with crime. Capitulating to our grievous social problems is not a winning strategy for conservatives, moral issues aside.'' In other words, the solution to conception through rape and incest isn't to abort fetuses—it's to wipe out rape and incest.

Not surprisingly, Brill's statements on gay men and lesbians were pretty chilling. Characterizing homosexuality as ''a perverse and deviant life style unworthy of recognition, ratification or support,'' he said that gays engaged in ''training and recruitment efforts.'' ''The way to expand their numbers and increase their lobby, which they are pursuing vigorously,'' he declared, ''is through promotion and indoctrination.'' Equating homosexuality with undisciplined behavior, he ominously maintained that ''as in other areas, those who do not discipline their behavior must be disciplined by others.'' The point was clear: homosexuals should be punished.

Wisconsin's Third District had not seen such a curious ''political'' document in living memory. It made three things clear: one, that Brill wanted to be taken seriously as a political thinker; two, that he was, in fact, an extremist crank of the first water; and three, that, however hard it was to take him seriously as a political thinker, Brill had to be taken seriously as a political threat, as he had a solid base of support in the district's religious Right community. Though relatively small in number, the folks on the Religious Right could be counted on to make up a huge percentage of the voters in the Republican primary, which was not expected to draw a very large turnout.

It was clear that the Christian Coalition was strongly behind Brill. The primary ''voter guide'' that they distributed throughout the district was a masterpiece of dishonesty, designed to make Brill look attractive and to make me look like someone who didn't share their views. The ''guide,'' which consisted of a single sheet the size of a large postcard, contained a chart purporting to compare Brill's positions on ten issues with mine. The chart didn't go into any detail: it took a ''thumbs-up or thumbs-down'' view of issues, reducing each to something that a candidate could either "support" or "oppose."

The guide's only thoroughly honest representation of my position was on the first of the ten issues, "Increased Federal Income Taxes." The guide admitted that both Brill and I were "opposed."

Then the lying began. Under "Balanced Budget Amendment," the guide indicated that Brill supported it and that I opposed it. The reality was that I had voted for virtually all of the balanced budget amendments that had ever come before the House, and had cosponsored the majority of them. In fact the first bill I had cosponsored as a member of Congress, way back in 1981, had been a balanced budget bill. But the Christian Coalition had managed to find one such bill that I had opposed, because it had required a three-quarters vote to raise taxes. For this reason, apparently, they declared me "opposed."

They also said that I supported "Abortion as a Health Care Benefit." I wouldn't put it that way. In my view, people ought to be able to buy the kind of coverage they want with their own dollars; that's not saying that taxpayers are going to fund it.

Under "Voluntary Prayer in Public Schools," the guide listed me as having "no response." That's interesting. The truth is that I didn't respond to their questionnaire, period. This was patently dishonest on their part, because they knew very well that I support voluntary prayer in schools. But they didn't want to acknowledge that, so they wrote "no response." They did the same thing with "Banning Ownership of Legal Firearms" and "Capital Punishment for Murder." Again, because I shared their positions on those issues, they listed me as having "no response."

They said that I support "Taxpayer Funding of Obscene Art." Yet I was the one who had written the reforms for the NEA's grant-review process, which were designed, in part, to *prevent* funding of obscene art. From the Christian Coalition's point of view, however, my vote against Bill Dannemayer's proposed 50 percent cut in NEA funding made me a supporter of funding for obscene art.

They also listed me as a supporter of "Federal Government Control of Health Care." Nothing could be further from the truth. That's an absolute lie.

I was infuriated by the dishonesty of that voter guide. Here I was, a Republican who voted with them on many issues, but they were knowingly misrepresenting my positions in order to lend support to their man Brill. I was so angry that I went to Newt and Bob Walker and told them to speak to their friends in the Christian Coalition and get them to lay off me. And they did: in the general election, the Christian Coalition distributed no voter guides in the Third District of Wisconsin.

I've said that I can understand the extremism of the Religious Right. Any time you see a country undergoing as much change as America is undergoing today—economically, professionally, and socially—a lot of people are going to be looking desperately for a clear, firm foundation. That's a big reason for the success of the fundamentalist and evangelical churches, which offer simple, black-and-white answers to life's complex questions.

Those churches are not all bad. There are good, well-meaning people in virtually every one of them. One of the tragedies in American politics is that elected officials have assumed constituencies, and by having assumed constituencies, we have certain assumed *non*-constituencies. I would have loved to sit through the Christian Coalition's Washington workshop in the summer of 1995, and I'm sure would have heard much that I agreed with and much else that I found very interesting. But the great tragedy is that if I had gone to that convention, I would have been a lightning rod. People would have assumed that I was there with bad intentions, a hidden agenda.

And that brings me to a larger point, which is that the most painful and vicious aspect of everything I've been through is the implication that if you're gay—or moderate—you can't believe in God. When others take it upon themselves to define for me who is and is not a Christian, I not only find that offensive personally, I consider it a threat to civil society, and a contravention of what faith is supposed to be all about.

During the spring, while Kris and Morris were working with LaVerne on my campaign, Rob spent a good deal of his time working on Kris's and Morris's wedding. Kris, who was fixated on my reelection effort and who, in any case, isn't the type of woman who gets caught up in the details of wedding preparations, didn't care if she was married at the National Cathedral or in a room at the Holiday Inn. Rob, however, wanted to see the thing done right. So it was that, on June 25, about 150 of Kris's and Morris's friends and relatives arrived at a banquet room in the Hotel Washington to find it elegantly decorated with white bows and candles and bundles of fresh magnolia branches and blossoms, many of them from our backyard. Despite his preoccupation with his expanding business, with my campaign, and with John (whose health was improving slowly), Rob had somehow found time to plan the wedding down to a T. It all came off beautifully, and made for a few hours' joyful respite from the constant anxiety of the campaign.

Meanwhile John McCormick of *Newsweek* had finished writing his story about my campaign. On July 1 he called me to say that because the material was so personal, he considered it delicate enough to merit reading me the story prior to publication. In twenty-two years of reporting, he said, he had never before read a story to its subject. He wasn't offering me a chance to change his interpretation—only to correct any inadvertent errors of fact that might have found their way into his copy.

As McCormick read the story to me, my heart sank and my stomach knotted. *Newsweek* wasn't just telling my district I was gay—it was telling the world. And I had been in politics long enough to know that whenever a campaign gets focused on a candidate's personal life, it's a minus—because the electorate always assumes such a focus means scandal.

McCormick's piece, which under the general heading "The Year of the Smear" was coupled with a story by Eleanor Clift about attacks on women officeholders by antifeminists, took its title, ''Poster Boy,'' from a remark by Chuck Lee, who had said that I was ''rapidly becoming the poster boy for the homosexual movement.'' As the title suggests, the piece was focused entirely on my homosexuality. And while McCormick was not sympathetic to the antigay bigots, neither did he seem to approve of my handling of the issue. ''Gunderson,'' McCormick wrote, ''argues that his sexual orientation is not anybody's business—which would work better, politically, if he were not so conspicuously trying to have it both ways. Rumors about his private life have surfaced in past campaigns. But Wisconsin is a civilized place, and Gunderson has benefited from a tacit 'don't ask, don't tell' arrangement with the voters and the news media.''

He noted that the situation had changed after the strident antigay rhetoric of the 1992 GOP convention. ''Appalled that his party had been 'kidnapped by the hard right,' Gunderson began speaking out for tolerance. He also resigned as deputy to Newt Gingrich, the Republican House whip, to distance himself from what he saw as the party's narrow-minded positions.''

McCormick went on to say that my ''claim to privacy'' was ''wearing thin''; apparently because I had mentioned Rob at HRCF, I was no longer entitled to keep silent about my private life in other venues. When McCormick had finished reading the story to me, I challenged him on this and on his statement that I was ''trying to have it both ways.'' He said he had known I would object to that.

''Having it both ways,'' I insisted, ''means living as a gay man while voting against gay rights.'' I said that I knew secretly gay members of Congress who did do that. I had consistently voted against any bill that discriminated against gays. After all, that was why I was getting attacked by the right!

Second, I told McCormick that he was taking my fight against antigay discrimination out of context. My entire public career, I explained to him, had embodied a commitment to justice and equality, from my support for the Equal Rights

Amendment in the Wisconsin state legislature and my co-sponsorship of the Americans with Disabilities Act to my work on behalf of education for the deaf and my work on the Civil Rights Restoration Act. McCormick did revise his story to include a line taking this objection into account: "He doesn't 'advocate gay rights,' " McCormick wrote. "He is, he says, 'a fierce opponent of blatant discrimination' against any group, including women and the disabled."

Third, I told McCormick that if his article was really supposed to be about "The Year of the Smear," then he should talk about the tactics of the smearers. I told him about a Brill campaign handout that was still being distributed, even though it retailed untrue charges that we had corrected way back in April.

McCormick's article concluded with a statement that I couldn't help agreeing with. Though I would "probably survive the primary," he said, my Democratic opponents in the general election would be likely to employ the same "coded" antigay attacks against me that Brill was using in the primary. The penultimate paragraph of his piece ended as follows: "Steve Gunderson is 'out of touch with his district,' a leading Democrat says, particularly on gays in the military. Translation: tolerance has its limits, even in Wisconsin."

Usually I spend the Fourth of July weekend shuttling between the many parades in the district and my hometown's Lions Club celebration. But this year I had been asked by Pastor Robert Duff of Eau Claire's First Congregational United Church of Christ to speak at his church's Sunday morning service. As the day approached, I discovered that the invitation had attracted some controversy. Brill's people had kicked up a fuss, and now the Eau Claire *Leader-Telegram* was making an issue out of the fact that I, a political candidate, would be speaking in a church. When I arrived at the church that Sunday morning, TV cameras were whirring.

Pastor Duff greeted me warmly, and I apologized for the controversy my presence had caused. He protested that he was delighted and honored to have me there.

The church was crowded and beautifully decorated with red, white, and blue bunting. The singing was full of enthusiasm and good will. I was very moved by the service. My old friend and supporter Dave Duax, who was a member of the church, gave me a warm introduction. Then I stepped up to the lectern, taking my usual deep breath, saying my usual quick prayer, and looking out over the congregation full of people I knew: my cousin Kara; her husband, Ralph; her grandmother Ethel; my longtime campaign treasurers, Dick and Kathy Dean; and Doug and Karen Knight.

Also present, to my surprise, was Winnie Close. She belonged to First Congregational, and she behaved graciously toward me. I should have been glad of this, but I couldn't help wondering how she could be nice to me on a Sunday and then spend the rest of the week contributing to the anti-Gunderson smear campaign.

I spoke in the sermon about the fact that patriotism is easy when you're fighting a war—whether a hot war or a cold war—with another country. But today, I said, we're not at war with another country—we're at war with ourselves. We're becoming a polarized nation. And because of this, patriotism in the post–Cold War era is going to present us with some very serious challenges.

After my sermon, Pastor Duff commended me in front of the congregation for my courage on behalf of justice. I appreciated his words more than he could ever know.

The next day, I was campaigning in Platteville when I found the issue of *Newsweek* containing McCormick's article in a local drugstore. I read it shortly thereafter while Neil drove me to our next stop, Casseville. That night, back in La Crosse, I called Rob in Washington to discuss the article, which he had read and discussed with Morris and Kris. They were, he told me, totally unnerved and unhappy. Morris had insisted that Rob come to watch videotapes of a focus group. Rob had declined. He knew that Morris's intent had been to demonstrate to him how incendiary the fact of my homosexuality was, and to persuade him to shift gears.

After I hung up, I showed the article to my mother. She read it at her dining room table while I went through the next day's schedule. "What do you think?" I asked.

She paused and said simply, "I don't know."

When my sister Kris phoned that evening, she said that she thought the article was good. I didn't know what to think. This was all virgin territory for me.

As the campaign progressed, two things became clear. First, we had to get out our message during the primary. Brill didn't have much money to spend on his campaign, but he had the fundamentalists. And they were rabid. Second, we had to counter the attacks. All seven of the men running for my seat were crisscrossing the district, telling anyone who would listen how bad I was. We couldn't let them erode our support.

Besides, with the *Newsweek* story now out, and at least two more major magazine pieces focusing on my sexual orientation in the pipeline, it was clear that our campaign had to focus on my record. And that was something we had apparently not done adequately in recent years.

But all this takes money. And it soon developed that we were not going to raise as much as we had hoped. Our county fund-raising effort was not getting off the ground. Clearly, my speaking out on gay issues, and my increasing openness about my own personal life, had created serious fund-raising problems. We had no doubt that if we could communicate our message, we would win. But would we be able to afford to get that message out?

Money wan't the only problem. Many people who in the past had been willing to give me vocal, visible support were now hesitant to do so. They felt that the fact of my homosexuality was a time bomb waiting to explode, and they didn't want it to explode in their faces. LaVerne and my campaign staff spent a lot of time listening to these people's concerns, talking to them, pleading with them, trying to get phone calls returned and to get people to take an active part in the campaign.

In the midst of all this, Rob intervened with a suggestion

that seemed truly out of character for him. Why, he asked, didn't we hold a fund-raiser in D.C.? He had concluded, he explained, that it was time to ask our friends for contributions. We had resisted tapping into our friends, as this seemed an obnoxious imposition. More important, Rob had made every effort to keep politics out of the house. Most of our friends were apolitical, as were our conversations with them, and Rob wanted to keep it that way. But this time around, such a fund-raiser seemed to be necessary.

ROB

Our friends *were* apolitical. Yet it occurred to me that it was getting far too late in the day for them to continue to be apolitical. The Religious Right was making every effort to misrepresent gay Americans, and the more I listened the more angry I grew. Franklin and I had started listening to the religious radio station at our offices, just as a way of monitoring these people, and we would compare notes when we met for dinner or drinks.

At dinner one night, I asked Franklin if he thought it would be inappropriate to have a fund-raiser in Washington and to ask our friends to contribute. I was aware that many gay people consider Steve part of the problem, since he's a Republican and they still see Republicans en masse as a problem. Franklin was enthusistic about the idea. With his encouragement, I decided to move ahead with plans for the event.

By the time I had decided to hold the fund-raiser, most of Steve's summer weekends were already taken up with meetings, parades, and fund-raisers back in his district. We managed to find a Sunday afternoon in July when he could return to Washington for the day to attend the event. That settled, I set my thoughts on a location. Kris and Morris volunteered their house, but I decided it was too small for our purposes. For the same reason, I didn't want to have it at the house Steve and I were renting. Then it occurred to me that our ex-neighbors in McLean, Tom and Lynn Friel, had offered to help the campaign in any way they could. Their house was large and had a great backyard with a magnificent shade tree. I knew the house well, since I had designed and built it in 1989.

I called the Friels. As I had hoped, they were genuinely glad to offer their house as a party venue. The next step was to design the invitations—Dwight and Brian took care of that—and send them out. We sent them to over three hundred people. Some were clients of mine; some were married couples in McLean who considered themselves "progressive Republicans" (which is a Washington euphemism for conservatives who "tolerate" gays); some were lesbians; and some were gay men, mostly young professionals, businesspeople, and government officials. My small staff spent the next three weeks setting up the affair. I learned from the experience that people who do this sort of thing for a living work hard for their money! The tent and tables and chairs had to be ordered. Alcohol had to be donated. Food came from wholesalers. My brother Dana barbecued. The cash bar was staffed by friends.

Early on the afternoon of the fund-raiser, Morris and Kris came to collect the donations. As the afternoon progressed, the yard filled—and it filled not with my clients, not with the "progressive Republicans" of McLean, and not with lesbians, but with gay men. I had sent invitations to a wide variety of people, but a casual observer that afternoon would have concluded that the event was McLean's first gay tea dance. This turnout underlined something Steve and I already knew—that while Steve had his enemies among radical gay activists, his message resonated with the mainstream gay community, not only in Washington but around the country.

Not everyone there, of course, was a gay man. Linda, for example, valiantly tended bar most of the afternoon, though she barely knew the difference between soda and tonic. And Phyllis, as her contribution to the campaign, came down from New York to entertain.

The climax came when Steve got up to explain what his campaign was all about. What was at issue, he said, was something much bigger than him, or me and him; at issue was what America would be like over the next generation. Would it be a society of openness and acceptance, he asked, or one of hate?

18

The campaign for visibility and money—and votes!—drove on throughout the summer. A week after Rob's fund-raiser, we held a high-dollar function in Eau Claire with my friend and former congressional colleague and ex-Secretary of Labor Lynn Martin. Smart and good-humored, Lynn had been my classmate in Congress and has always been a friend. Her district had been adjacent to mine, and her famous line to all her dairy farmers was, "I represent you well. I do whatever Steve tells me to do!" Having read that my seat was targeted by the Democrats, Lynn called and offered to help. She was the first of many high-profile figures to campaign for me that summer and fall.

The weekends in late July and August were crowded with county fairs back in the district. These provided us with our first chance to distribute campaign literature. We had put together a brochure outlining my accomplishments, something that—to my detriment, according to Frank Luntz—I had never bragged about. Throughout August, with Congress out of session, I traveled from town to town, working my way up and down the main streets. The priority stops were the cafés, in which I shook the hands of every patron. My goal was visibility and personal contact, and I did everything possible to achieve it. And as I moved through the rigorous days, I pushed myself to the point of exhaustion. At the end of every day Neil Gawinski, the Osseo college student who served as my driver and traveling secretary, was wrung out—and he's a lot younger than I am.

That summer, every day seemed to bring another unexpected development. When I called Rob from Wisconsin late one night, he told me of a gay publication he had just run across called *DCQ Fag Boy News.* "You're going to love this," he said, and read to me from a full-page story headlined "Steve Gunderson: Gay in Washington DC, Straight in Wisconsin." "Gunderson," Rob read, "screws us by day and goes out and finds one of us to fuck at night. *DCQ* will be running a poster of Gunderson in an upcoming issue, calling on Gay men to boycott the Dairy Queen's dick and butt." Such was the tenor of radical gay political discourse. I found it appalling; Rob thought it kind of funny. "It doesn't hurt you," he maintained. "It just establishes what jerks *they* are."

The end of August brought increased media attention to the primary campaign. Every morning found me doing radio or newspaper interviews. One morning, for example, I went to Saint Paul for an interview with the *Pioneer Press*, which is the daily paper for my district's northern half. Its liberal-to-moderate readers would, we hoped, form a counterweight to their far-right neighbors. In days to come, I traveled to other cities outside the district—Milwaukee, Madison, Dubuque—for interviews with other newspapers that are widely read in different parts of my district. It was a logistical nightmare that often involved spending ten or twelve hours a day on the road. But that's the way you wage a campaign when you represent a large rural district whose major media are based elsewhere.

Though some longtime supporters had turned their backs on me, I was gratified by the loyalty of others. The retired chancellor of the University of Wisconsin at Eau Claire came with his wife to one of my campaign appearances, declared their respect for my efforts, and offered any help I might need. In Augusta, a former head of the Wisconsin Vietnam Veterans grabbed my arm affectionately and said, ''Don't back down an inch. Let me know how I can help.'' And a man from the Homebuilders Association told me that his organization had raised $4,000 for my campaign, the maximum legal contribution. As I wrote later in a set of notes to myself about the campaign, ''Some people do make all this worthwhile.''

On the weekend of August 16 I wasn't supposed to be in Wisconsin campaigning, but I went anyway. I *wanted* to be there. I wanted to go to the Clark and Pierce county fairs. As I wrote at the time, ''I feel this urge to touch the district.'' And I was glad I did. Days earlier, a Minnesota man had walked into my Osseo campaign office and asked, ''What's the maximum contribution I can give Steve?'' Told that it was $1,000, the man wrote out a check on the spot. At the Clark County Fair, this man came up and introduced himself. He explained that he had read in *Newsweek* about my commitment to social justice and wanted to help. I was stunned and touched: people in western Wisconsin do not throw around thousand-dollar sums recklessly.

The next morning I gave a long interview to Eric Lindquist of the Eau Claire *Leader-Telegram* who said he wanted to do a feature on Steve the person. I was impressed by his sincerity— and by the article, too, when it came out. As I told Lindquist, it was important to understand that Brill and Lee had no political program and no desire to serve in Congress. Their solitary goal was to destroy me. I added that while I had never known a Democratic opponent to misrepresent my record intentionally, Brill knowingly, and routinely, lied about my record— and this was a man who set himself up as a symbol of Christian morals and family values. His wholesale cynicism was appalling.

Lindquist's article didn't mention Rob, or my homosexuality, at all.

After the interview I attended a brunch at the home of my Saint Croix County coordinator, Betty Smith, who had invited potential supporters over to hear me speak. The brunch gave me a good opportunity to put everything in perspective. I talked about the politics of polarization. I explained my commitment to governing, as opposed to gridlock. And I discussed the effects of the politics of polarization on my own race: with the Democrats on one side and Brill on the other, I was in the middle, getting beat up from both sides. The brunch was a success: everyone there wanted to help, wanted to write personal letters in my support, wanted ammunition to fight back against the Brill handout.

From Betty Smith's, Neil and I went directly to the Pierce County fair, where I got a very good reception. When I went to the Republican booth, I saw Brill standing there off to the side. It was an awkward situation, but I wasn't about to let him control it. So I stood front and center, along the path where everyone walks past, and shook hands. People recognized me. I thought, "Thank God they know who I am."

Meanwhile Brill was standing a few feet away, watching me and trying to interact with passersby. Every now and then I glanced over at him. He was a terrible campaigner who seemed uncomfortable in public. If I say so myself, the contrast between us was dramatic. If he hadn't been such a mean, dishonest customer, I would have felt sorry for him.

While I was eating dinner that night at the fair, Mike Ellis, a party activist and evangelical Christian who was running for state legislator, came over to chat. He told me he had the impression that Brill's support network was based in the Baptist Church; Brill, he told me, had appeared recently at the Baptist churches in Menomonie and River Falls. "I'd be glad to do a commercial endorsing you as an evangelical Christian," Mike said. I thanked him for the offer, though we ended up not making such commercials.

As we were leaving the fair, we ran into Harvey Stower, one of the four candidates in the Democratic primary. He was getting beat up by his opponents at the time, and said to me in a friendly way, "I'm not sure I want your job!"

A week later I was back in the district. On August 24, after a full day of campaigning and a long ride back to my mother's house in Pleasantville from the Grant County fair, I was both exhausted and scared. The *Advocate* and *New York Times Magazine* pieces would be out soon. It was now clear that Chris Bull of the *Advocate*, rather than writing about me as a hero of the gay community like Jane Alexander and others, was doing a piece on Steve Gunderson, gay congressman. This bothered me. While many of my constituents were apparently willing to harbor suspicions about my personal life, I was increasingly worried that Morris and LaVerne were right in arguing that voters would turn against me if they saw their suspicions confirmed in black-and-white.

Another concern was our campaign organization. It was late August, and the organization wasn't as well developed as it should have been. Fund-raising was a disaster. In previous years we had always organized our fund-raising county by county. I had decided that that didn't make much sense. Why didn't we organize by profession or interest? Why not ask two or three bankers, say, to send a letter to all the bankers in the district or state explaining that I'd been supportive of their issues, that it was important to them professionally that I be reelected, and that they should give me their support? This was my idea, but no one had followed through on it. This consideration was all the more important because if the *Advocate* and *Times* profiles caused a new round of sensational articles in local press when they appeared in September, donations to the campaign might never materialize.

When I got back to my parents' house that evening, I called Rob. He had talked again with Morris and Chris Bull. Morris said he was growing irate and was convinced that the article would destroy the campaign. Though Chris had originally represented himself as intending to do a strictly professional profile that would not involve dealing with my personal life, he had now confirmed to Rob that his article would be a personal profile, focusing on Rob's and my relationship and not on my political accomplishments. Neither Rob nor I was thrilled at the prospect of becoming gay Republican poster boys. As I ranted about being labeled a gay Republican, Rob interrupted me and agreed dryly.

"Gay Republican," he said. "I'll never live the Republican part down. What will my friends think?"

After the joke, however, he grew serious. "One," he said, "don't be consumed with trying to stop something you can't stop." The *Advocate* profile was a fait accompli.

"Two," he went on, "we have to sit down and agree upon a common strategy to deal with the gay issue. Morris, Kris, Keven, and us must talk." "Keven" was Keven Kennedy, my press secretary. "And if it takes a yelling match to get everyone in sync—then so be it. But get it over with.

"Three, if you're embarrassed about being gay, or come off as being timid about it, you're dead! People don't trust wimps. So you've *got* to figure out exactly what you're going to say when somebody asks you about it."

I began August 26 with a conference call to LaVerne and Morris in which I raised my concerns about organization and money. Unless something took hold, I suggested, we wouldn't have enough money to last till November. They listened. And then Morris asked me to call him privately about "the other matter." I didn't have to ask what "the other matter" was.

Later that day I did an interview with Mary Jo Wagner at Wisconsin public radio in Eau Claire. After we were off the air, she asked about the forthcoming story in the *New York Times Magazine.* I said that the *Times* writer had talked to Rob and me back in April, but that I wasn't sure now when, or even if, the story would appear. "You have to know," Mary Jo said, "that while I've respected your personal privacy, I don't want to be scooped by the *Times.* In outing you, that is."

I was indignant. "Oh, please!" I said. "I was outed four years ago! How many times can you people run the same story?"

That afternoon, Neil and I found ourselves ahead of schedule, so we pulled into a wayside rest area near the town of Alma. It was a very hot, sunny day. I called Morris from a pay phone.

Morris said he had talked with Chris Bull of the *Advocate* the night before. He had asked Chris, ''How would you feel if Steve loses the election because of your article?''

''I'm a writer, not a politician,'' Chris had replied. ''I don't think about such things.''

Morris expressed to me his deep empathy for what I was going through. ''No one,'' he said, ''should have to bear a burden like this while simply trying to do his job.'' I'll never forget the paternal tone of his voice. Morris can come off as a very rough man, but during that phone call he was anything but rough.

''The only way to stop the *Advocate* article at this point,'' Morris said, ''would be to go above Chris Bull's head, directly to his editor. The problem isn't the story itself—it's the stories that will be written about the story.''

''I agree.''

I didn't think we could stop the *Advocate* article, and that was deeply frustrating. When I spoke with Rob by phone later that night, it was clear that he didn't think the article could be stopped, either. Nor did he think it *should* be stopped. Rob wasn't as interested in political strategies as he was in telling the truth. Out of frustration he finally said, ''Steve, I've seen the opposition. If your constituents would rather have an idiot as a representative than you simply because you are gay, then why would you want to represent them anyway? Just tell the truth—and if you lose, you can find a real job with some real privacy.''

I laughed when I hung up from that call, because I knew that he was ultimately right—and that, of all the things that had come to me during my time in office, Rob was the most valuable one, and the one that would remain with me if I lost.

Congress reconvened for the fall session after Labor Day and I returned from Wisconsin. The primary was only a week away.

On the day before the primary, there were no votes to show up for on the House floor. I took the morning off and tried to relax. I did my usual morning run, played with the dogs, and went shopping. The next day, Tuesday, would be Rob's and my eleventh anniversary. We had never missed it before, but this year I would be in Wisconsin.

I wanted to buy Rob something special. I had seen a wonderful book about beach cottages in a Wisconsin Avenue bookstore, but when I went back to the store I wasn't able to find it. But I did find an even more appropriate volume: *The Foods of Greece*. The book was perfect: it was in Greece that Rob and I had spent our happiest moments together; Greece symbolized our yearning for peace and tranquillity; and cooking was one of our great joys.

So I bought the book and a card, and stopped by a florist to pick up a bundle of cut flowers. At home I wrapped the present and wrote a note on the card apologizing to Rob for the way in which my work always got in the way of our relationship and thanking him for his constant love and support. After hiding the gift and flowers in the basement, I went into the office at noon to catch up on some of the work that had accumulated during my absence on the campaign trail.

The next day I awoke at 6:40. Rob was still asleep. Rex and Della followed me downstairs. I went to the basement, brought up the gift and flowers, and set them on the table in the study, where Rob drinks his coffee each morning while watching Katie Couric on the *Today* show. I was deboning the chicken we had cooked the night before when Rob came down, innocently walked into the den, and said, *"What is this?"*

"It's our anniversary, isn't it?" I said.

He laughed and said, "If you think you can get off the hook with a present and a bunch of flowers, you are crazy. Win the primary and we'll celebrate over dinner when you return."

He showered and went to his office. I went to mine and caught the 2:20 flight to Minneapolis–Saint Paul. Rain delayed the takeoff, and when we reached our destination the plane pulled up to the gate only fifteen minutes before my connecting flight to Eau Claire was scheduled to leave. I ran the entire length of the airport terminal, reaching the departure gate with five minutes to spare. But when I presented myself at the desk, wringing wet from the run, the man said, ''Sorry, it's already loaded.'' I couldn't believe it—I was five minutes early and he wouldn't let me board the plane.

Furious, I made a few choice remarks and took the man's name down for a letter to Northwest Airlines. Then I walked back to the airport's main entrance and took a shuttle to the rental car center, only to find that all the cars in the airport were gone. What could I do? How could I get home? It was like a bad dream. Finally I had the idea to take a shuttle to the Mall of America, where I found a Thrifty Rent-a-Car office. They had one Camaro left. I took it and raced home, already late for my election-night dinner.

Since I desperately needed to change my shirt, I drove straight to my parents' house in Pleasantville—only to find every door locked. (My parents *never* lock their doors.) So I drove on to Osseo, where Matt and I were holding our joint election-night get-together at the country club.

Far from being the elegant, elitist place that the name suggests, the Osseo Country Club is a white cinderblock building with a small U-shaped bar, a pool table, a TV, a cabinet with golf clubs and other greens materials, and a large simple gathering room with a flat ceiling about twelve feet high. It's a community meeting place that doesn't require membership; anybody can go there on Friday night for the fish special or have their wedding rehearsal dinners there. It's where my grandfather held his retirement party.

When I walked in, I found the place crowded with my relatives, members of my office and campaign staffs and Matt's campaign staff, and friends of Matt's and mine. Also present was a La Crosse *Tribune* reporter who was waiting to take a picture of Matt and me. At that moment all I wanted was a beer—or two, or three.

My sister Kris, seeing that I was wringing wet, insisted on going home to get me another shirt. While I waited for the shirt, I had a late supper there with my nephew Aaron and his wife, Jeni.

And then it was primary election night.

Matt and I awaited our returns together. It was really his night. This was his first run for public office, and he had surprised almost all the cynics. Of the four Republican candidates who were vying to run against Herb Kohl in November, he had gradually established himself as the best informed, most thoughtful, and most courageous.

A self-proclaimed centrist, Matt had taken on the extremism that was destroying both political parties—a politically reasonable enough position in a general election, but one fraught with perils in a 1990s primary. He appealed to the Republican party to nominate someone committed to the principles of Lincoln who could win in November. He was the only pro-choice Republican in the race. And perhaps largely out of love and respect for me, he made a point of declaring his opposition to discrimination based on sexual orientation. Neither of these positions is a promising one for a Republican primary candidate, and unfortunately pro-choice and gay-rights groups don't contribute heavily to GOP candidates, even those who support their positions.

Despite these obstacles, surveys showed that if the turnout reached 20 percent, Matt would run a dead heat with the leading candidate, Bob Welch, the darling of the state's conservatives.

Matt's numbers came in early. By ten o'clock Welch had been declared the winner. Only 12 percent of the eligible voters had participated in the Republican primary, and the exit polls showed that they were, as expected, largely fundamentalists. They had all consolidated behind Welch as the only way of stopping Matt. (The last thing they wanted was another ''liberal'' Gunderson in Washington.) Matt handled the loss as well as anyone could.

We later learned from a Kohl campaign source that, according to Kohl's surveys, Matt would probably have won the general election if he had been nominated. In the end, unsurprisingly, the moderate Kohl beat the extreme right-wing Welch in a landslide. Matt was, in short, exactly the kind of Republican candidate who could win a senatorial election in

Wisconsin. The lessons here for the Republican party are obvious.

Matt's quick loss didn't bode well for me and everybody knew it. The first returns from Barron County indicated that Brill had the lead over me. As the night progressed, the lead shifted back and forth. In the end, I received 67 percent of the vote to Brill's 33. Considering the low turnout and the fact that pro-lifers, Christian Coalition members, and NRA members made up 80 percent of the Republican vote, it was astonishing that I won. I was blunt with the press. "The people saw through Brill's lies and distortions," I told every reporter who asked. "They rejected the politics of hate and reaffirmed the politics of governing."

Brill was one of the few opponents in my congressional career who didn't call me on election night to concede. He finally phoned the next day, and left a goofy message about both of us having "learned a lot" as a result of the race.

His attempt to destroy me had failed. But the anti-Gunderson effort by people on the Religious Right wasn't finished. Now their hopes turned to Chuck Lee, an even more unpalatable candidate than Don Brill. A former drug dealer with a criminal record who was running on the U.S. Taxpayers line, Lee manifested, if such a thing is possible, even less sense of decency in his campaign than Brill.

When I woke up the next day, I learned that my Democratic opponent would be Harvey Stower. After some early morning telephone interviews and coffee with friends, I held a strategy meeting with my campaign staff in a private room of the local hotel, the Alan House. While the younger members of the staff wanted to celebrate, the older members weren't in a good mood. We felt the organization had not done all that it could have done for the primary. Morris felt that we had big money problems. LaVerne wondered how many disgruntled Republicans we could win back. Marlene, my district director, was concerned that Stower's ties to the Democratic party establishment would bring him a lot of endorsements and money.

But there were some positives. First, I got my family back.

During the primary season I had insisted that my family expend its energies on Matt's campaign rather than mine. I'd had them for twenty-two years; this time it was Matt's turn. Now that Matt had lost the senatorial primary, however, my family was ready to throw itself fully into my reelection campaign.

Never has there been a more loyal political family than the Gundersons of Wisconsin. Over the years my parents have traveled throughout the district on my behalf. My sisters, along with their husbands and children, have given generously of their time. My brother Scott has often raised money for me; Matt ran two of my campaigns and has worked on all the others. My brothers Nels and Kirk helped with the annual Brat party and other fund-raising events. For us political campaigns were like family reunions.

Second, with Harvey Stower, a Methodist minister and a truly decent person, this would be an issues campaign—not a war of mud and personal attacks. He was vulnerable on the fiscal front. Also, the Democratic party was obviously divided, for there had been no love lost during the Democratic primary between the Bear and Stower camps, especially over the abortion issue.

Suddenly, indeed, there was a new social issue in this campaign, and it was not my sexual orientation. For years I had been endorsed by the Wisconsin Right to Life Committee for my opposition to abortion on demand, supporting it only in cases of rape and incest and when necessary to save the life of the mother. Over recent years, the pro-life movement had increasingly rejected those three exceptions, and as a result had given me less and less support.

In 1992, they had promised me an endorsement, only to turn around and try to exert pressure on me. As someone who had consistently maintained that military families deserve the same protections under the law given to the civilians they defend, I had supported efforts to allow abortions in cases of rape and incest and to save the life of the mother at military hospitals in foreign countries. When the Congress overrode

President Bush's veto of such provisions in 1992, the Wisconsin Right to Life Committee informed me that they would send out a mailing in support of my candidacy only if I voted to sustain Bush's veto.

Having already been promised their endorsement, I was furious. I placed a call to Sue Armacost, the Wisconsin lobbyist for the group. "I'm so glad you called," she said. "We wanted to talk to you."

I quickly interrupted. "This is *not* a conversation," I said. "This is a message. You promised me your endorsement based upon my voting record, and my opponent's stated pro-choice position. Now you have chosen to renege on that commitment unless I change my position on the military hospital issue. You knew my position on that issue long ago, and it hasn't changed. I have never before in my Congressional career had a political group attempt to blackmail me, deciding to hold their endorsement pending a certain vote after it had already been promised.

"Well, I have a message for you. I will win this election without your endorsement. And when I do, I don't ever want to see you or any other lobbyists from your organization bothering me or my staff!"

With that, I hung up the phone. And I haven't talked to her since.

Now it was 1994, and Harvey Stower had already wrapped up the Wisconsin Pro-Life Organization's endorsement by being as anti-choice as was humanly possible. This gave LaVerne an idea. Shortly after the primary, he called the Wisconsin Pro-Life Organization, identified himself as a member of my campaign staff, and asked them whom they were endorsing in the Third Congressional district. Barbara Lyons told him they were supporting Stower. LaVerne replied, "I'm curious as to why you've endorsed him despite Steve's voting record."

"Well," Barbara said, "Steve has had a decent record. But we support Stower because he's entirely pro-life, without any exceptions for rape and incest. With someone as pure as Harvey, there really is no choice."

LaVerne copied this down, then immediately sent the organization a letter asking for a verification of the statement. Once they wrote back verifying it, LaVerne used it prominently to make it clear that, on the abortion issue anyway, Stower was a radical reactionary.

As that incident demonstrated, our campaign didn't have the kind of money or organization that we wanted—but we had the expertise of LaVerne and Morris, and that made up for a lot of shortcomings.

Even Mark Halverson of WWIB Radio, when he interviewed me on the day after the primary, pointed out that Stower's abortion position was to the right of Billy Graham's. Already I was getting the idea that abortion rights might figure almost as prominently in the campaign as my sexual orientation.

By 11:45 that morning, I was free to head back to Washington. I was overjoyed at the thought that Rob and I might actuallly be able to have dinner together.

The next day, Thursday, started out as a relaxing one. It was a Jewish holiday and was supposed to be my day off before the campaign resumed on Friday. Exhausted, I slept till nine—which, for me, was like sleeping till noon. I went running, got my hair cut, and took the dogs for a walk. But the blissful interlude didn't last long. Before lunch, the phone rang and it was John Frank. "It's an emergency," he said. "Political disaster."

"What?" I asked.

He explained. The *Advocate* article was out. The phones at my office were ringing off the hook. Members of the press wanted me to comment. "Simple," I said. "Tell them I haven't read it, so I have no comment."

Later John Frank brought by a photocopy of the *Advocate* article. I read the article, "Outward Bound," with real despair. As expected, this wasn't about "heroes of the gay cause"; it was another outing. And what an outing! Chris Bull went on for several pages about Rob's and my eleven years together. This wasn't a political profile, it was celebrity gossip.

When Rob returned home, he read the article, but not without first taking a deep breath. When he saw the full-page photograph of him and me that illustrated the piece, he screamed an obscenity in a long, drawn-out Southern accent. "How on earth," he asked, "did they get this picture so big?"

A week or so earlier, he explained, he had received an urgent call from Chris Bull. "We've been trying and trying to schedule a time to shoot photos of you and Steve together," Chris had said, "but you never seem to be together these days—he's up in Wisconsin campaigning, and you're in Washington. And now we've got to go to press. So could I borrow some pictures?"

"Of course," Rob had said. We had both been so anxious lately, emotionally overwrought about the campaign and the attendant publicity, that we weren't particularly photogenic, to say the least. Rob was pleased by the chance to give Chris Bull pictures of us looking happy and relatively carefree.

The one they had chosen had been taken at a Human Rights Campaign Fund dinner. The original picture couldn't have measured more than two and a half inches by three and a half inches. It was of me and Rob and Randy and Bernie. Two couples. We were crowded together in the photo, clean and scrubbed and wearing tuxedos. Very happy. What Rob didn't expect was that they'd crop out Randy and Bernie and blow the rest of it up into a full-page, eight-by-ten portrait. Everybody at my office was furious. Here was their congressman in a full-page picture that focused on his identity as half of a tuxedoed couple who looked like two grooms on a gay wedding cake. They didn't hesistate to make it clear that they were furious not at the *Advocate* but at Rob—because, after all, he was the traitor who had supplied the magazine with the photograph.

The next day Morris phoned. He had seen the *Advocate* article and thought we had to talk before I flew off to Wisconsin that afternoon. I told him to come by at three. He arrived at four, plainly distressed. Kris was not with him—for reasons that were beyond me, she was furious at us about the article.

"We'll have to scrap the commercials," Morris said. We had

been planning to shoot some campaign ads on Saturday—the usual kind of positive-image ads that you see on local TV during congressional campaigns. Now Morris was canceling the taping because, he said, "You can't use those kind of ads anymore. Not now." In his view, the *Advocate* article had turned the world upside down. He didn't yet know what to do about it, didn't know how to "package" me in the wake of this latest outing. I think the decision was made in a state of panic.

ROB

My parents, who were coming for a visit that weekend, had known for some time that the *Advocate* article was in preparation. When I brought them back from the airport, the first thing my mother noticed was the magazine sitting on the coffee table. "Is this it?" she asked, her eyebrow raised and an enormous hesitation in her voice. She obviously hoped that this wasn't it.

"Yes," I said with mock cheer. "That's it!"

My mother, generally a vivacious, voluble woman, opened the magazine to the photograph and sat down immediately. "We really can't talk about this," she said. Like many Southerners, my parents think *any* publicity about a person's private life is irredeemably vulgar. "We understand what you and Steve are doing," she went on in an uncharacteristically sharp tone, "but do you have to take on the banner of the entire gay community? Do you have to do it so publicly? *I don't understand this.*"

We heard my father coming downstairs. She stood and slipped the magazine down behind the sofa.

All this fuss over a magazine profile seemed silly to me. But everybody took it very seriously. And Chandler's *Times* piece was still to come. My parents actually distanced themselves from us for a short spell as that piece approached. In an attempt at humor, my mother said one night over the phone, "Rob, we're glad you and Steve are out. But your father and I like the closet. At least for now."

19

The *Advocate* article generated a lot of press coverage in Wisconsin. After it came out, LaVerne and Morris decided to do an ad in the form of a half-hour TV show reacquainting people with "the real Steve Gunderson." It had a sort of "town meeting" format, and LaVerne and Morris deliberately included people in the audience who would ask antigay questions. The show came off well because it gave me an opportunity, which we were unable to get in the press, to discuss the actual issues in some detail.

Though Stower was presenting himself to the voters as a liberal, the truth was more complicated than that. What he was trying to do was to combine Democratic voters who shared his economic liberalism with social conservatives who would support him because of my homosexuality and his abortion position. It was clear that he hoped the combination would be enough to win the election for him.

Stower was very careful not to mention my homosexuality himself. But he didn't have to; it was out there, and he automatically received the support of those who were turned off by my sexual orientation. For those people, issues and competence were irrelevant.

The campaign suffered another setback in September when Dave Obey signed a widely circulated letter soliciting financial support for Harvey Stower. Obey is the senior Democratic congressman from Wisconsin, and his letter was significant because members of Congress have long honored an unwritten "gentlemen's agreement" never to campaign against sitting members from their own state. Yet because the Democratic party considered me vulnerable, they had prevailed upon Obey to circulate this letter. I prevailed upon the other Republicans in the state delegation to ask Obey, "What is this? Why have you broken the rules?" Obey claimed that signing a fund-raising letter was different from actually campaigning for a candidate.

The Wisconsin press remained a problem. By this point they had written dozens of stories about my being gay and very little about the real issues. I kept asking the Wisconsin reporters, "How many times can you 'out' me? I thought a guy could be outed only once." But no—every time there was some new story in some national publication about my being gay, the local papers all felt obliged to write a story about the story. Meanwhile, I couldn't get the local press to cover the health-care and education and agricultural issues on which I was spending the bulk of my time.

I was so exasperated that I sent a memo in September to Milwaukee *Journal* reporter Patrick Jasperse summing up my professional activities during the preceding week. As I informed him, I had been involved in the reauthorization of the Elementary-Secondary Education Act; I had offered a motion on school prayer that had passed in the House by a vote of 369 to 55; I had seen the full House approve funding for my plan for 21st Century Learning Centers, which would convert schools into community learning centers with interactive technology; I had seen almost all of my Dairy Export Enhancement Act included in the Congressional Document on GATT that was sent to the White House; and I had spoken to the La Crosse Medical Society, declaring health-care reform dead for the year and explaining why.

None of these events, I noted, was covered in the Milwaukee *Journal*. "But, then," I wrote sardonically, "I guess I should have expected it—none of this is real news! And you wonder why I get frustrated with a paper carrying the same story about my personal life for the fifth time."

It *was* frustrating to me to observe the media's preoccupation with my personal life at the expense of issues. Things like Learning Centers and health care might be less immediately titillating than gossip about a public figure's sex life, but these were things that would directly affect the lives of every *Journal* reader, while my private life had no bearing on them whatsoever. It seemed to me that however curious people might be about my life, a responsible press should focus on things that really mattered to its readers, not on irrelevant things that they might happen to find diverting.

Even *Time* got into the act. One of their reporters spent a week covering my race, and one of their photographers was with me for two days. They were planning to run a pre-election piece on Newt—a piece that turned out to be destructive—and they wanted to run a story about me in the same issue. The point of the story would be that not only was Newt Gingrich bad, but the Republican party was destroying one of its most talented people simply because of homophobia.

The reporter assigned to me was very unhappy. "I don't know what I did," she complained, "that got me assigned to this story in rural western Wisconsin." But she did her job. She attended a debate between me and Stower, and she clearly thought that I had won it. She witnessed a series of my appearances in college classes, at which I was very well received. Where was her story? She was miserable. I remember leaving one of those college classrooms with her and saying, "You know what? Here's your story. In Wisconsin's Third District, it's performance that counts."

Needless to say, the story never appeared in *Time*. Since their reporter found that people respected me for my professional competence, she couldn't write the piece her editors wanted. I told Newt about this afterwards. I said, "Use me as an example. When people say, 'How can you say the press is a liberal cynical bunch?' well, here's an example that doesn't affect you."

I didn't realize during the campaign how much flak LaVerne was taking for my homosexuality. "You know," he said to me after the election, "I can't tell you how many people brought the issue up to me. And I would reply, 'Look, I know Steve like a son. I know Rob. I've been to their house. I know their friends. They've been to our house for dinner. And they are just wonderful people, and you cannot judge them simply by their sexual status.' "

It's heartbreaking to imagine LaVerne speaking these words over and over during the campaign. I realize that no sum of money could've induced him and Bev to go through what they they suffered on our behalf. Those two deeply good, religious people did what they did entirely out of love for us.

I did witness one encounter between LaVerne and a disgruntled member of the electorate. One evening late in the campaign, an evangelical Christian woman from my hometown walked into our campaign office, where many of us were stuffing envelopes, and started railing at me for being gay. I said nothing. What could I have said without appearing to be self-serving? But LaVerne didn't hesitate in his reply. "You know," he said, gently but forcefully, "in church last Sunday we were discussing this text. . . ." And he talked to the woman about how we have to appreciate different people with different attributes and different gifts. He didn't directly address the subject of homosexuality, but he defended Rob and me eloquently.

October brought with it the biggest celebration in my district, the Oktoberfest parade in La Crosse. All the public officials and political candidates in the area show up for that parade, as do some one hundred thousand spectators. All the Republicans are on one float, and all the Democrats on another. That morning, before the parade began, I worried about how the people would respond to me. I had the distinct impression that some of the other Republicans were worried about this question too.

But we needn't have worried. To my surprise and delight, I got a tremendous reception. People applauded, cheered me, called out my name. That was my first real indication that a lot of folks in western Wisconsin had been paying serious attention to my campaign, that they recognized I was standing up for basic principles of fairness and justice, and that they were on my side. One of the other Republicans on the float with me, Sheriff "Butch" Halverson of La Crosse County, said, "Steve, this crowd really likes you."

"I know," I said, with some wonderment.

"Sometimes," I continued, "if you're in the trenches fighting long enough, people will respect you for your endurance."

October also brought the biggest single media event of the campaign—and, in fact, of our lives: Chandler Burr's article in the *New York Times Magazine.* Published on October 16, it opened with a full-page portrait of me, and facing that a large headline: "Congressman (R), Wisconsin. Fiscal conservative. Social moderate. Gay." Under that, in slightly smaller type, it read: "Steve Gunderson is a problem for the Republican Party, and his homosexuality is the least of it. The big question: is there room for a centrist in the new G.O.P.?"

Chandler's piece wasn't another outing—it was a coming out. In this article, at last, I declared explicitly that I was gay. Together, Rob and I had decided that it was about time I did so, and we felt that the best place to do it was in a reputable national journal.

We were both very pleased with Chandler's article. It was intelligent, balanced, and fair. As Rob had suspected from the start, Chandler understood what we were about and respected us for it. He placed my support for gay rights in the context of my long-established support for civil rights for all Americans. And, as the subhead indicated, he focused less on my homosexuality than on the issue of whether or not my party was inclusive enough to continue to accept me, not only as a homosexual but as a moderate. Chandler did a good job of summing up my ideological independence:

> His voting record after seven terms is as personal as a thumbprint. He favors a balanced-budget amendment and supported the contras and the Reagan military buildup. He advocates a capital-gains tax cut, voted for the Gulf War and NAFTA and has an endorsement from the National Rifle Association. At the same time, he favored sanctions in South Africa, was an Equal Rights Amendment supporter since the start of his political career, has supported the National Endowment for the Arts and helped develop the Americans with Disability Act. And, while Gunderson is generally anti-abortion, he has voted for limited use of fetal tissue in medical research.

Chandler quoted my colleague Fred Grandy: "Gunderson is first and foremost a capable and effective member of Congress. . . . If Steve is a bad role model, then the G.O.P. has already become a crumbling cult." Also included in the piece were some interesting quotations from Newt, in which he tried to support me while not appearing, as they say, to "endorse homosexuality." "You know," Newt told Chandler, "in a sense the definition of Gunderson's courage personally is that he has not allowed any of the normative patterns to coerce him. He's not liberal enough for the gay community to be totally comfortable and he's not straight enough for the conservative community to be totally comfortable. He is who Steve Gunderson is. It's a unique testimony to inner strength. I really admire him a lot. And people like him, people with a sense of integrity and commitment who do what they believe in."

Morris and Kris, of course, were horrified by Chandler's piece. There, in the Sunday supplement of the nation's newspaper of record, three weeks before the election, was their candidate, big as life, cheerfully attaching the word "gay" to himself. As far as they were concerned, the *Newsweek* and *Advocate* pieces had rocked the boat of our campaign badly enough, but Chandler's piece was a tidal wave that would sink us for sure. They thought I was mad to have done it.

Rob and I hoped, naturally, that they were wrong. We hoped that western Wisconsin voters would prove less judgmental and more discerning than Kris and Morris expected. But frankly we weren't sure what would happen. We didn't fool ourselves about rural Midwesterners' attitudes about homosexuality. What we did know was that we had been honest—and we were glad of that. We also knew as we read Chandler's piece that, win or lose, one chapter of our life together had ended forever and another had begun.

At last, we were unquestionably *out*. Henceforth there would be no more finessing of questions about my personal life, either by me or by my staff. I was now unequivocally one of three openly gay members of Congress; I was the only openly gay member of the Republican caucus; I was the highest-ranking openly gay Republican official in the history of the United States of America; and I was the first Republican congressman ever to seek reelection as an openly gay man.

Exactly twenty years earlier, in his sister's house in Saint Paul, Minnesota, a shy, baby-faced country boy, torn between sportscasting and politics, had decided to pursue a life in public service. Could he ever have conceived, as he opened a copy of *Sports Illustrated* and happened upon a quotation from the book of Joshua, that this was where that decision would lead?

"Be strong and of good courage," the quotation had read, "fear not nor be afraid: for the Lord thy God will not fail thee nor forsake thee." I had pursued my dream, and though I had not always been as strong or courageous as I wished I had been, my God had never failed or forsaken me. Indeed, as I looked back at those twenty years, which in the living had often seemed so chaotic and confusing, they seemed to lead quite clearly to this moment, when Rob and I stood before the world as a proud, loving couple whose lives gave the lie to every stereotype about homosexuals. I saw now that God had been preparing me all along for his service, and had led me to a time and a place where I might best serve him, frail and flawed though I was, with what gifts I had.

In late October, I returned to Washington from Wisconsin

for a meeting of the board of trustees of Gallaudet University. Rob and I were driving together when I turned to him and said, "I really think we're going to pull it off."

Rob smiled back at me with feigned indifference and said, "Hey, wouldn't that be cool?" We both laughed. It was the understatement of the year.

In the days before the election, there were further positive signs. A remarkably encouraging article in the Milwaukee *Journal* reported that most voters appeared to agree with me that my personal life should not be an issue in the race. "Not one of two dozen voters interviewed at random throughout the district," noted the article, "said that Gunderson's personal life was a factor."

" 'If somebody had asked me about that 10 years ago, I wouldn't have voted for him,' said Keith Noll, 46, a Gunderson supporter who lives in Colfax. 'But my mind's changed about that. It doesn't affect what he does in the Congress.' "

My coming out didn't lose me the editorial support of the regional newspapers. The Milwaukee *Journal* endorsed my candidacy, as did the Saint Paul *Pioneer Press*, the *Wisconsin State Journal*, the Eau Claire *Leader-Telegram*, and the La Crosse *Tribune*. "The national spotlight has been shining on this race," noted the Milwaukee paper's editorial,

> but not because of the plight of the region's dairy farmers or the tough economic conditions that many families face. No, Gunderson has been spotlighted because of his recent acknowledgment that he has been in an 11-year relationship with a man.
>
> Gunderson has handled this publicity over his homosexuality with grace. . . . We believe that Gunderson has to be returned to Congress to continue the fight for fairer dairy programs, better access to affordable health care for rural residents, curbing the budget deficit, and bringing good-paying jobs to the Chippewa Valley.

A few days before Election Day, Rob flew to Wisconsin. Gloria, Dwight, and Brian, who had worked hard for the campaign and wanted to be with us on election night, flew out the following day.

On Tuesday morning, I cast my vote in Pleasantville. Then Rob and I drove into Osseo to meet the others.

We had done everything we could. I had received the endorsement of every daily paper. Despite the problems with money and field organization, we had ended up putting together a strategically brilliant election campaign, thanks to LaVerne and Morris. And we had the feeling that people in the district had gradually come around.

Increasingly, Rob and I had both felt good about the campaign. But we couldn't be sure we would win. The electorate could go either way. Every pollster knows that voters, especially when they feel they might be perceived as intolerant if they tell the truth about their voting preference, often tell pollsters that they'll vote one way and then vote the other. Nobody at my campaign headquarters that night was suffering from an excessive sense of security about the outcome of the race.

Everyone was there that night: my Washington and Wisconsin staffs, the key party campaign people, all the county coordinators, the young people from the college campaign, and my extended family and friends. This was the last hurrah—our last election night. We all felt a wonderful closeness to one another, a let-bygones-be-bygones feeling after the tensions of the campaign. There was also a sort of melancholy fatalism in the air, a recognition that the election was out of our hands and that all we could do was wait. I think most of the people there had a pretty good idea of how much Rob and I had endured during the campaign. So even those who couldn't fully accept our relationship respected us.

While I talked to reporters and friends, Rob and Dwight sat glued to TV screens. I suspect Rob was more nervous than I, though he kidded as always and hid his real feelings. I know this much, however: from the outset of the campaign, Rob had boldly defied conventional wisdom and encouraged me to stand firm. If I lost, he worried that my local supporters would hold my homosexuality up as the reason and him as the culprit.

When the first returns came in early, they showed me enjoying a slight lead. That was reassuring. However, we both knew that the counties reporting tended to be the more liberal to moderate counties—those that might be expected to vote for me over Stower.

Shortly after ten, Rob ran over to me excitedly. The network news, he said, was reporting that Oliver North, the extreme right-wing Republican candidate for Virginia's senate seat, had lost to the Democratic incumbent, Chuck Robb. Few people in the room recognized the implications of this loss, but Rob and Dwight, who worked in Virginia, and Gloria, who lived there, were elated. Rob said, "If the voters of rural Virginia can reject North, the voters of rural Wisconsin will see through your opponent." (Not, mind you, that Harvey Stower should be compared to Oliver North.)

By eleven o'clock the more conservative counties had reported in. With over 80 percent of the precincts counted, I was still ahead by a narrow margin. At midnight it became clear that I had won. We were overwhelmed—and relieved that the experience was over.

Everyone was greatly moved by the victory, me included. Yet in my usual way, I refused to display my emotions. Even Rob cautioned me against it. As I walked to the podium to give my victory speech, he pulled me aside. He knew what I was feeling and, referring to a respected colleague of mine from Colorado who has become known for her occasional displays of emotion, he said firmly, "Don't pull a Pat Schroeder and stand up there and boo-hoo."

So when I stood up to address my supporters, I kept my feelings in check. The people of western Wisconsin, I told them, had spoken—and they had decided which issues were important and which issues weren't. I thanked my supporters. I thanked my family generally, then I mentioned my mom and dad, Rob, my brothers and sisters, my nieces and nephews. I also recognized LaVerne, Morris, and all the campaign staff; Kris Deininger and the Washington staff; and Marlene Hanson and the district staff.

I ran into Kris later at the bar, off to the side of the main room. She was remarkably calm. She hugged me and said "Congratulations" and took a sip of her drink. She had already had a couple. We talked casually for a while about the election, then she paused. "You know," she said gravely, "all I ever wanted to do was to protect you guys." Her eyes welled with tears. *"I didn't want to see you hurt."*

Kris left Washington at the end of February 1995 and moved back to Wisconsin with Morris. She took a job as chief of staff in Congressman Scott Klug's district office; Morris resumed working on education issues. Before they left, Rob and I suggested that the four of us plan a vacation together. On her last Friday at work, Rob and I threw a farewell party for her and Morris. A few days later, on her last day in the office, she said it was much harder to leave Washington than it ever had been to leave Wisconsin.

That afternoon, when the hour arrived for her to go home, I was in a meeting with Newt and some other Members that I couldn't leave. I was worried that Kris would leave without my having a chance to saying good-bye—and that would've been the rudest possible thing I could do. Fortunately we had to break for a vote, and I was able to catch Kris by phone. We exchanged a few parting words. When I returned to the office later that night, I found a note:

> It's 6:00 and the end of a weary, teary day. I'm glad you're not here because leaving is difficult as it is. I have found that it has been much more difficult to leave Washington than it ever was Madison. Perhaps that's because the friendships I have made here are more than just the friendships of high school pals. They are friendships based on joys, sorrows and challenges. That dawned on me as I looked around the room of your house on Friday evening. Whether it was your and Rob's struggle for acceptance . . . Gloria's struggle with her divorce, Matt and John's struggle with AIDS, my struggle with marrying Morris

. . . certainly we have shared the ups and downs of life. But, as Morris says, that *is* life's travel.

Well, thanks for the call. Now I can end this morbid good-bye. I do hope we'll plan those vacations. And you know that I will always be there for you both if you ever need me. You have certainly been good to me.

With love and respect to you and Rob . . .

Kris

That letter summed up something important. It summed up the fact that Kris's life with us had been a genuine growing experience for all of us. Since moving to Washington, she had become a part of something I don't think she would ever have imagined—she had come to be a part of our family. A family with two gay men at its center.

When Rob and I returned to Washington after election day, we plunged into preparations for Thanksgiving. Friends began to trickle into town. Randy, who had been transferred from Pittsburgh to a Boston suburb, arrived first. Then came friends we had made in the previous year or so: Tim from Florida, Scott from South Carolina.

On Tuesday I shopped for food. Tuesday night we baked corn bread and a German chocolate cake. On Wednesday morning Rob hit the flower store, I shopped some more, and we both did a thorough house cleaning. By noon, eggs were being cooked, onions chopped, and celery sliced for the stuffing. I made a pan of brownies, a fresh salad, and a casserole. That evening, Franklin, Brad, and Gabriel helped set up. On Thanksgiving we got up early, popped the turkeys into the oven, showered, and watched the Macy's parade while peeling potatoes and carrots, slicing lefse (Norwegian potato bread), and wiping paw marks off the windows.

By three o'clock, guests began to arrive—twenty-eight in all. Dwight and Brian brought thirty small carved pumpkins filled with butternut squash. Brad and Gabriel brought desserts. Gloria brought vegetables. Kris and Morris brought two large bowls of ambrosia. Linda came alone: she and Ostap had separated, and he had taken the boys to visit his family in New York.

As the tall white candles were lit, the room took on a festive and elegant amber glow. We had drinks. When the guests heard Kate Smith's version of "God Bless America" blasting through the speakers, they knew dinner was ready

We took our assigned places. I clicked my water glass with my knife for silence. Then, as I do every year, I stood, looked over the faces of our family, and fixed my gaze on Rob, handsome as ever. His eyes were focused on me as I spoke.

"Rob and I welcome you to our table. This is the tenth year we have celebrated Thanksgiving with each other and with our friends. As most of you know, this time with you is very special for us. It's our opportunity every year to thank you for your love and friendship. We want to pay special tribute to John Frank, who has joined us for every Thanksgiving dinner and has watched this family grow and evolve. We want to remember Glenn and Charles for the joy they brought to our earlier Thanksgiving dinners. They are gone now, but never forgotten. We also want to welcome those of you who have never been here before. We hope you will continue to be part of our lives and will join us in years to come."

I paused and looked again at Rob. As always, we had talked earlier, while dressing for dinner, about what I should say in my toast. As always, Rob had had his own ideas and had offered suggestions. This time around, however, there was no question in either of our minds, and no disagreement at all between us, about what the thrust of my remarks should be.

"There has been a lot of debate this year," I went on, "about family and family values. Some people in our country would look at the people around this table and say that this is not a family. But if family can be defined as people who give of their time, their talents, and their hearts to those they love, then certainly this *is* our family.

"I don't need to tell anyone here that, for this family at least, this has been a difficult and challenging year. But it's also been, in the end, a very positive one. Look around the table: these are people who care deeply about you. They have certainly demonstrated in the past year how profoundly they care about us. As we reflect on this year, Rob and I feel truly and deeply blessed to have had the love and support of all of you through all the difficulties and challenges. God willing, we will all be together again like this next year.

"So as we celebrate Thanksgiving 1994, we raise our glasses in thanksgiving to God for family. Our family. All families."

With those words, I lifted my wineglass. And twenty-seven other glasses, sparkling with reflected candlelight, rose triumphantly into the air.

AFTERWORD

After Thanksgiving, Rob and I moved once again, this time to a house in Washington that Rob had renovated. We sold it in June 1995 and moved again to a new home he'd built in McLean. Over the course of 1995, we attended family weddings in Georgia and Colorado, a wedding and an anniversary in Iowa, and a funeral in Alabama. I traveled to over fourteen cities and gave more than a hundred speeches on various topics. Throughout the year, in Washington, New York, and Savannah, we worked with Bruce on this book. We also endured a six-month ordeal with Rob's back. A disc had ruptured, and following months of consultations with neurosurgeons and negotiations with his health-care provider, he underwent lumbar surgery in June. It galled us that although we have been together for twelve years, our relationship is not recognized legally and so Rob is not able to share in my medical benefits, as any heterosexual congressional spouse would. Rob scheduled the surgery just before our planned trip to Greece in August, and so was able to recuperate in Mykonos. We rented the same house we had stayed in several years earlier, this time with Brad, Gabriel, and Randy. As before, we spent nights at the Piano Bar, listening to Phyllis sing. On Thanksgiving 1995 we had an even bigger dinner than ever, with over thirty familiar faces and three tables overflowing with food and laughter.

Our families remain disappointed that we cannot seem to find enough time to spend with them. Some things never change.

Politically, 1995 was a remarkable year for me. On the day of my reelection, the Republicans won control of both houses of Congress for the first time in decades. This made my life more hectic than ever. As a perceived leader of moderate House Republicans, who can side with Newt and deliver a victorious party-line vote or side with President Clinton and create a bipartisan majority, I was seen as having considerable power; my own closeness to Newt further enhanced my access and influence.

Though I remained high-profile because of my homosexuality and my devotion to gay rights and AIDS issues, I spent most of my time, as always, working on education and agriculture. As chairman of the Livestock, Dairy, and Poultry Subcommittee, I was uniquely positioned to affect dairy policy, which needed reform more desperately than any other area of American agriculture; my seniority on the Education Committee (now called Economic and Educational Opportunities) and my friendship with the new chairman, Bill Goodling, also provided new opportunities.

Early in the session, Newt put me in charge of a task force to reform Washington, D.C.'s schools. The appointment abounded in ironies: the most conservative speaker in our time had designated an openly gay Congressman to lead educational reform efforts for the children of our nation's capital; a rural Republican congressman whose district has the smallest percentage of non-whites in the U.S. was charged with making decisions for an overwhelmingly black and Democratic city.

Newt's naming of me made it clear that my homosexuality was not an issue—which is exactly the way it should be. But there was plenty of controversy as it was. School reform was a hot-button issue; conservatives and liberals were deeply divided over methods, and blacks in D.C. resented the very idea of being dictated to by a GOP Congress, whose motives they distrusted. I attempted to defuse these tensions by meeting with virtually everyone who had something to say about the issue, and put together a plan that seemed to me a model of conciliation. Partisan bickering continued, but friends on both sides of the aisle thanked me for the sincerity of my efforts and the soundness of the results.

I spent much of the year preaching to dairy farmers about market reforms. We simply had to wean farmers from counterproductive subsidies. As the balanced budget bill came to the floor for a vote, it became increasingly clear that powerful Republican representatives of other dairy districts, who were not on the Dairy Subcommittee and had not been involved in any of our hearings on the issue, were nonetheless fiercely lobbying Newt to maintain the former, expensive policies. I was appalled and felt confident that Newt would ignore them. For weeks we had arduous debates in which Newt essentially functioned as a referee.

I was on the House floor when Pat Roberts, chairman of the Ag Committee, told me that Newt had decided that for the sake of passing the budget, he would pull the committee's dairy recommendations from the bill and let the old policies stand. The big guys had won! Newt had buckled under their pressure. I was shocked. I had preached the party line to my constituents and the dairy industry, only to be sold out by my own leadership.

Had Rob been right about Newt all along? Could it be that I didn't really know Newt? Humiliated and infuriated, I called Rob at work. "I got rolled by Newt," I told him. There were other votes to be taken that afternoon, I said, but I was heading straight home. Perceiving that I was crushed, Rob was already home when I arrived. Newt tried to call me at home that night and the following day; I didn't take his calls. The next day, without my knowledge, Rob sent Newt a letter.

Dear Mr. Speaker:

I spent the better portion of the evening last night consoling Steve Gunderson. He is unaware of this letter. I would just as soon it remain confidential but I wanted to share our conversation with you. Clearly, he is disillusioned with the leadership's current position on a few dairy-related issues, but I suspect his real disappointment and the source of his most profound sadness is with your lack of support for him.

As you must be aware, the leadership has assumed certain positions regarding dairy policy which will jeopardize Steve's relationship with his constituents. The same policies compromise his credibility among his colleagues within the dairy industry. He'll deal with this as he's dealt with other unfortunate incidents in the past. You know he's a trouper.

We didn't discuss politics last night. Rather, we went directly to the issue of trust and loyalty. I do not have to tell you that Steve has considered you a source of great inspiration over the past five years. He has said repeatedly to an often hostile press that he considered you a ''big brother.'' Steve's faith in you has always been profound if not bordering on naive and, sadly, his current disillusionment is equally intense. Political battles come and go and Steve has always been fortified by them. This incident however has only served to undermine his faith in you and his place amidst Republicans in general.

I have known Steve for thirteen years and have cautiously watched his faith in you and his commitment to your cause grow. His hurt today reminds me of a man without a country. He is frankly lost and there isn't a great deal I can do to help.

You must face political casualties every day. I know you recognize the difference between the loss of a political ally and the loss of a trusted friend. With all due respect, I think you may lose both. In the event you ever doubted it, you should know that in Steve Gunderson you had a loyal friend and a trusted ally. I would suggest that in an arena of demanding egos, a selfless fighter would be a handy thing to have in the back pocket and hope you will talk to him directly.

Rob later changed his mind, obviously, about his desire to keep this letter confidential. Newt, in any case, never wrote back and never mentioned Rob's letter to me.

Though education and dairy remained the focus of my legislative efforts in 1995, as the only openly gay member of the Republican caucus, I also became the key contact on everything related to gay rights or AIDS funding. Looking back at my experiences along these lines, I see that they spell out some key lessons that many Americans, both gay and straight, may profitably ponder as they attempt to deal fairly and effectively with these issues—and with the human experiences and problems that underlie them.

First, the lesson of radicalism. I had come out—and in a big way. But some radical gays, breaking the promises made on those 1991 Valentine's Day cards, still didn't love me. One night in December 1994, in what felt like "déjà vu all over again," Peter Carmichael and some friends of his surrounded Rob and me in a Washington bar and screamed at us: "You are killing us! Silence equals death!" Carmichael poured a beer over my head. Rob, who was fed up with such encounters, retaliated in kind, and for good measure bonked Carmichael over the head with his beer mug. "Let's get out of here," Rob said. Carmichael and his friends followed us out to our car, where one of them called out: "Rob, you better find a new boyfriend—this one isn't going to be around very long!"

Driving away, Rob and I looked at each other in open-mouthed astonishment. How long would these self-proclaimed activists continue to throw tantrums? How long would the gay community be held hostage by their self-serving antics? The world was changing—and I was determined to help change it. A month earlier, rural western Wisconsin had reelected a Congressman who had appeared with his male partner in the pages of the *Advocate*. I had made clear my dedication to gay-rights and AIDS-funding legislation, which I was uniquely situated to guide through a Republican-controlled Congress. Yet Carmichael and his ilk continued to portray me as the enemy.

That has to change. Gay activists have to accept that gays aren't automatically Democrats, that Republicans aren't automatically enemies, and that it is vital to have friends in the majority party. More specifically, it is crucial to have openly gay Republicans who are willing to do the sometimes tough and thankless work of sensitizing the party to gay issues, gay rights, and gay humanity.

The urgent need for gay people to make their presence felt in both parties was dramatically underlined several times in 1995. In the summer, Mike Bilerakis of Florida, chairman of the Health Subcommittee, called a hearing on reauthorization of the AIDS-funding bill, the Ryan White CARE Act, and asked me to be the lead witness. Rob and I both thought that if Matt Fletcher was up to it, he should attend and speak, so that he might put a face on AIDS for the newly Republican-controlled committee. As a Republican who had worked on Capitol Hill, he was the perfect person for the job. Matt agreed to do so. "While most of us were enjoying the ascendancy to majority status last fall," I told the committee by way of introduction, "Matt Fletcher retired. It was not by choice, but due to AIDS. He and his partner of fourteen years are both suffering from AIDS." Matt spoke eloquently, and the committee was deeply moved. He made an enormous difference.

Worried that the Ryan White bill would either be held up or modified by amendments from hostile elements within my party, I went to Dick Armey, the House majority leader, and pleaded with him to suspend the usual process and send the bill through without procedural interruptions. Months earlier, Dick had created a publicity firestorm when he referred to openly gay Congressman Barney Frank as "Barney Fag." Dick said it was a slip of the tongue, and I rushed to his defense, noting that in all the years I had sat beside him on the Education Committee, he had never uttered a bigoted statement about anyone. When I went to him about the Ryan White bill, he remembered my support. In an action that was unprecedented for a bill of such financial magnitude, he put the reauthorization on the Suspension Calendar, meaning that no amendments could be offered. Committee leaders from both sides of the aisle were shocked and delighted. The bill breezed through the House without hateful, homophobic amendments and was sent to conference with the Senate.

That experience underscored what should be an obvious lesson: that politicians who are willing to burn bridges by fulminating self-righteously over a slip of the tongue might win applause from the likes of Peter Carmichael, but they don't achieve anything of substance in the long run. Those of us who want to effect real change for gay people and people with AIDS need urgently to put slights, slips, and conflicting egos into perspective and recognize how politics really works.

The most visible example in 1995 of making politics work for gay people in the Republican party came in late summer. Boarding the plane in Washington for the first leg of our trip to Mykonos, we ran into a friend who said he'd just heard that Bob Dole had returned a campaign donation from the Log Cabin Republicans, a national gay and lesbian organization. I knew immediately that this would be big news—and that I, as a strong Dole supporter and an openly gay Republican, would be more ''in the middle'' on it than anyone in America.

Returning to Washington after our vacation, Rob and I reviewed the press reports. Incensed by Dole's action, Rob said I had to do something. I agreed. So I drafted a letter. Rob revised it; I toned down his revisions. But the letter remained a strong challenge to Dole, pointedly asking whether his return of Log Cabin's donation meant that he also rejected the support of others, such as myself and members of his staff, who were gay.

That night, Dole called me at home. ''Steve,'' he said, ''some things are more important than politics. You have always been a friend. If there was anything in our actions that hurt you or others, I am truly sorry.'' He explained that the Log Cabin donation had drawn immediate inquiries from reporters who saw a story in his acceptance of gay money, and that his staff, acting without his knowledge, had returned the check in an effort to defuse the issue.

"Frankly," he said, "they made a mistake. They should have simply said the donation was an appreciation for my work on behalf of Ryan White and left it at that. It would never have been an issue." Bob reiterated his commitment to fighting discrimination. I thanked him for this, and for his call. The next morning, my letter made the front page of the *New York Times.* When reporters called, I kept the specifics of my talk with Bob private, saying only that he had reiterated his commitment to fighting discrimination and that I still supported him. Five months later, Bob said publicly what he had told me that night—that his staff had made a mistake in returning the donation.

Even more than my resignation from the whip job, my letter to Bob Dole put Republicans on notice about antigay prejudice; combined with the general outcry over the return of the check, the letter made it seem less likely that the 1996 campaign would be a rerun of '92. Some Republicans plainly learned the lesson of the incident. In the fall, the Human Rights Campaign (which had dropped the word "Fund" from its title) donated $5,000 to the National Republican Congressional Campaign. Bob Dornan wanted to return the money; Newt and others in the leadership disagreed, and publicly and graciously accepted the donation. Yet as the election season progressed, the antigay rhetoric of several candidates, notably Pat Buchanan, made it clear that not every Republican politician had put homophobic rhetoric behind him—and that there remains a considerable minority of Americans who respond enthusiastically to it.

In 1995 I was honored to spend time with two AIDS community heroines. I shared a Human Rights Campaign Seminar platform with Mary Fisher. And Rob and I had supper with Dr. Mathilde Krim, the pioneer researcher, activist, and founder of the American Foundation for AIDS Research, who said that in five or ten years researchers would perfect the ability to design individual protocols that would give HIV patients, like diabetes patients, a normal lifespan. This was the best news Rob and I had ever heard; it was also important for a Congress debating budget priorities. So I offered to set up meetings for Dr. Krim with other members. By late November, she was giving my colleagues in both parties the same hope she had given Rob and me. This was the kind of bridge-building I believed in. There was every reason to hope that these meetings would help pave the way for increased AIDS funding.

In the summer, something wonderful took place. Raised in the Roman Catholic Church but aware that it had little compassion for them, Matt and John had fallen away from the Church. Now, however, they expressed a desire for pastoral care. I asked my pastor, George Evans at the Church of the Redeemer in McLean, if he would minister to non-Lutherans. "Of course," said Evans, a bluff, stocky former Marine chaplain who looks like George C. Scott in *Patton* and whose erudite sermons are studded with quotations from theologians like Dietrich Bonhoeffer and poets like W. H. Auden.

I introduced Evans to Matt and John over lunch one day in July, and soon they were both spending Sunday mornings in the pew with me and our friend Mary Jones. These developments disturbed Rob. John had facial lesions and carried an IV pack on his back; it was obvious he had AIDS. Recently, a House colleague had reprimanded me for bringing them to dinner at the Members Dining Room and thus "exposing innocent people"; Rob worried that the congregation at Redeemer would react in similar fashion. His fears proved groundless: my fellow parishioners opened their arms to Matt and John, truly living God's word.

In October, John took a major turn for the worse. On Wednesday, the first of November, Matt called and said that he wanted us to come over and say good-bye to John. He was degenerating so quickly that the doctors didn't know how long he would remain conscious. Standing beside John's bed that night, I said, "John, this is Rob and Steve. And we're here because we love you."

In the last few words he would ever say, John emerged from

his partially comatose state and raised his hand. "I love you, too," he said.

John lingered for days as Matt held vigil. Rob and I spent Thursday night at their house. Each breath had the potential to be his last. Before the sun rose on Sunday morning, November 5, 1995, John died in Matt's arms.

With Matt, Pastor Evans and I planned John's memorial communion service at the Church of the Redeemer; Dwight, Brian, and Rob designed the printed program. On December 9, the pews at the Church of the Redeemer overflowed with friends and members of the congregation who had loved John or who had come to respect his bravery. Matt and John's family filled the front rows on one side of the church. In one of the most moving moments, John's sister Mary Kay rose to read the epistle, then spoke to the congregation as she fought back tears. "John's death," she said, "has been very difficult for all of us. Knowing he was loved and supported by so many of you here today makes it easier. On behalf of all the Dents, my parents, my sisters and their families, I want to thank all of you." She paused and turned to Matt, who was sitting in the front row. "And I want especially to thank you, Matt Fletcher, for loving my brother. Matt, you made John so happy. We will always love you for that. You have become our brother and you will always be a part of our family."

Pastor Evans gave a powerful sermon, the opening line of which caused audible intakes of breath throughout the church. "I'm a fundamentalist," he told us in his booming baritone. Then he added: "And fundamentally, there's not enough talk in the church these days about love. God must be increasingly annoyed with those who continue to give him a new personality. The fundamentals of Christianity are summed up by Jesus: 'Love the Lord God with all your mind, and with all your heart, and with all your strength. And love your neighbor as yourself.' "

That afternoon, God and family and gays came together. None of the two hundred people at that service could have left the church without a deepened understanding of Matt and

John's love. That evening, when the reception, held at our house, was over, Rob said to me, "If every AIDS-related death could end, as this one did, in an opportunity to share with straight Americans the truth about gays and lesbians, the hostility would stop. This may have been just a small step, but I wish John could know what he accomplished today."

One of the implicit lessons of that day, then, was the power of integration: Matt and John had belonged to that church only briefly, but they had affected it—and it had affected them—in a truly Christian way. I'm thankful that Matt and John found an accepting home at the Church of the Redeemer, and I regret bitterly that many gay people never find such a place, and die in a state not only of physical debility but of deep spiritual hunger. Just as the Republican party needs to recognize and respect the humanity and diversity of gay men and lesbians, so many churches must wake up to their cruelty toward the gay community.

During the course of 1995 and early 1996, as Rob and I worked with Bruce on this book, we reflected on the mystery of our life together. Set down on this earth at a certain time and in certain places, tied irrevocably to our families and homes and traditions but oriented from infancy in a way that at first alienated and confused us, and that we had felt compelled to come to understand, we had found our way through fear and loneliness to each other, to love, and to integrity and wholeness. We had met strangers who over the years had become cherished friends, and whose suffering had challenged our courage and conscience. For those friends' sake, we had struggled—and continue to struggle—to make a difference. In our houses, Rob's made of wood, mine made of laws, we seek to build better homes—not only for ourselves but for our friends, families, and nation. We may not succeed on any or all counts. But our parents taught us to try; our devotion to our friends will not allow us to cease; and our love for each other sustains, inspires, and motivates us every step along the way.

ACKNOWLEDGMENTS

This story finds its origins in the hundreds of photographs either framed and hanging throughout our house or clipped and arranged in numerous albums. It is not a political story; nor is it a story about designing and building homes. This is a story about a relationship between two men and the family we have created.

To Bev and LaVerne Ausman, Bill Becker, Clay Bedford, Tim Crutchfield, John Frank, Sue Kaestner, and Matt Fletcher, who knew and shaped us long before the two of us knew each other and who have grown with us over the past thirteen years, we will be eternally grateful.

To Brad Davis and Gabriel Nossovych, Kris Deininger and Morris Andrews, Pastor George Evans, Gloria Freund, Mary Hayter, Linda Kosovych, Mary Jones, Randy Latimer, Franklin Maphis, Dwight McNeill and Brian Noyes, and Larry Wilson, who experience our highs and lows week by week, year after year, thank you from the bottom of our hearts.

To our angel, Mary Fisher . . . thanks.

To our agent, Kris Dahl; Bruce's agent, Eric Simonoff; our editor, Peter Borland, and his assistant, Kari Paschall; and everyone at Dutton, thanks for believing in this project from the beginning. Your persistence has made it all happen.